Secrets of the Sorcery War

Elise Carlson

Faraway Fiction Press

Secrets of the Sorcery War is a work of fiction. Names, characters, locales and events are either products of the author's imagination or used in a fictitious manner. Any resemblance to actual persons, living or dead, or actual events is purely coincidental.

First published in Australia by Faraway Fiction Press

Text © Elise Carlson, 2022

Cover illustration and interior art © Elise Carlson, 2022

Moral rights of the illustrator Judah Lamey (glintofmischief@gmail.com) have been asserted.

Cover Design, map and illustrations by Judah Lamey

The font used for chapter headings is called Unzilash and was designed by Manfred Klein.

ISBN 978-0-6454633-4-7 Ebook

ISBN 978-0-6454633-7-8 Paperback

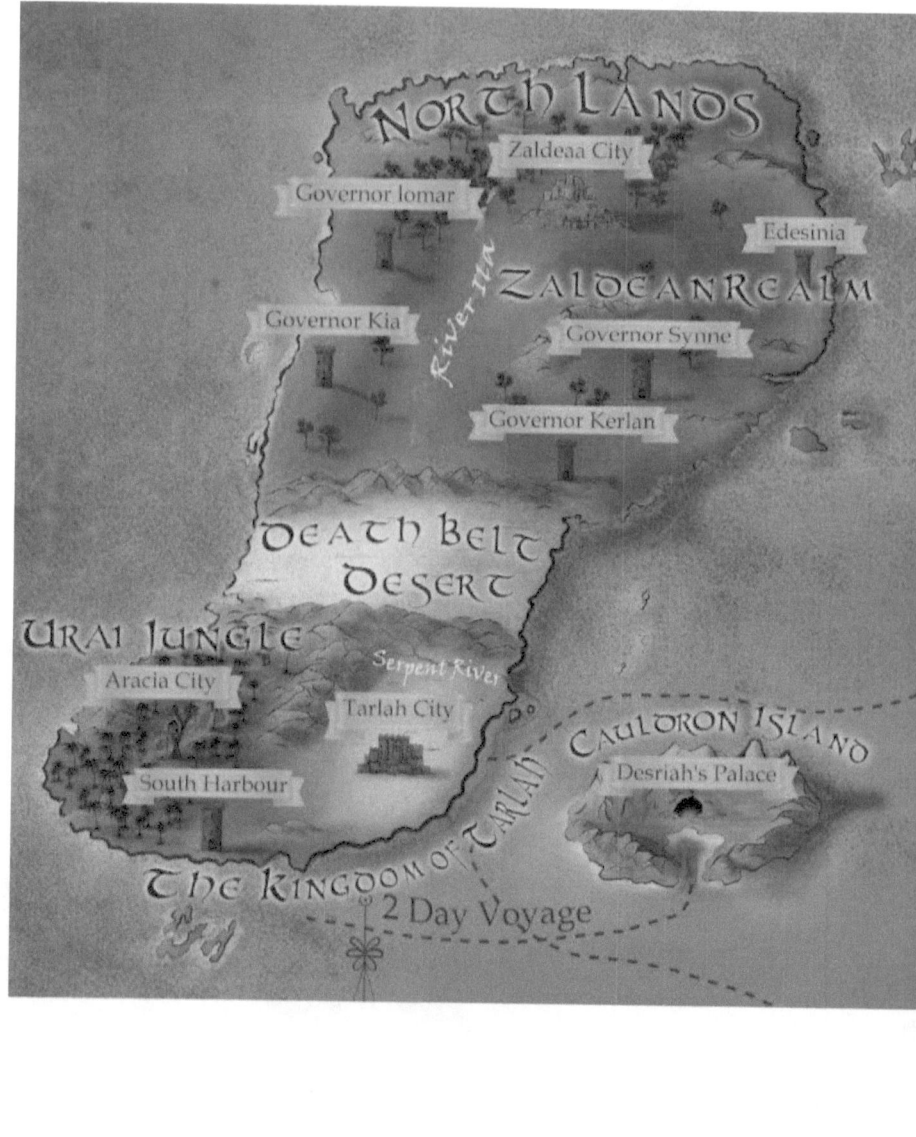

UMARINARIS

Five Weeks Voyage

MYLETH ISLAND

Desriah's Castle

THE ISLAND OF THE GUARDIANS

City of Peaks

Mijora's Dwelling

Dramatis Personae

Tarlahns

Heir Ruarnon (they/them)

King Urmillian (Ruarnon's father)

Queen Corina (Ruarnon's mother)

Prince Omah ((Ruarnon's uncle)

Princess Telena (Ruarnon's aunt)

Lenaris, Ruarnon's best friend (she/her)

Companion Pamoran (Lenaris' father)

Companion Tor, Ruarnon's tutor (he/him)

Advisor Monin (Pamoran's father)

Captain Arleath, of Ruarnon's bodyguard (he/him)

Aza, First General (he/him)

Takanis, Second General (she/her)

Zaldeaans

King Kyura (deceased)

Companion Karmarn (Ruarnon's Uncle)

Governor Armar (he/him)

Governor Syenne (Kyura's sister)

Governor Iomar (he/him)

Governor Iagl, Iomar's twin, (he/him)

Governor Derlan, the twins' father, deceased traitor.

AUSTRALIANS

Linh, Year 10 student, (she/her)
Fiona, Linh's best friend, (she/her)
Troy, becoming Linh's friend, (he/him)
Michael, new friend, (he/him)

URAI ·

Mocco, apprentice elder, (he/him)
Mawana, Mocco's cousin, (he/him)
Kahorn, elected Urai King, (he/him)
Mirata (Mocco's mother)
Tither (Mawana's father)

TIMBALENS

Nuard, scholar, (he/him)
Familon, archer (Nuard's daughter)
Commander Imphin (he/him)
Captain Doorna (he/him)
Boormar, soldier, (he/him)
Emperor Yarath, (he/ him)

CREATOR GODS

(Absent since creation.)
Mijora (earth goddess)
Esla (sea goddess)
Esira (sun god)
Erhmun (wind god)
Chaos (god of sorcerers)

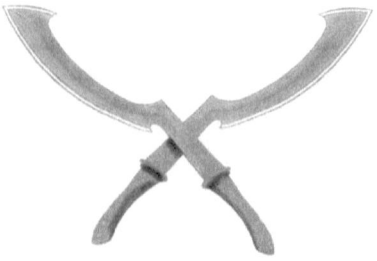

Chapter 1

The Urai -Ruarnon

Regent Ruarnon strode down a red carpet lined with bronze armoured guards, who bowed helmed heads as they moved towards the dais. Sculpted bronze imitated sun rays emanated from the empty thrones of their absent Father and Mother. Ruarnon sighed at the elaborately carved travel throne before therm. It was time to sit where late Uncle Omah had sat. To make new memories of the throne they associated with their late mentor, uncle and friend, as they welcomed the first Urai ambassador Tarlah had received in living memory.

Ruarnon turned, placing the past behind them, and sat, following Omah's parting advice to act decisively, by facing whatever the future brought. They inclined their head to their aunt and two advisors as the three entered the throne room, bowing their heads in return and taking their places at Ruarnon's right hand.

"Mocco, son of the Urai King Kahorn and Ambassador of the Urai," a crier announced from the entrance.

Mocco entered, his deep brown eyes fixed on Ruarnon. He was tall, his ebony skin multiple shades darker than Ruarnon's, his eyes the same warm brown and almond shape, his lips similarly full. Only his black, finely braided hair and kilt woven from leaves differed. Every feature they had in common set Ruarnon apart from many Tarlahns, and it was a breath of fresh air.

Ruarnon smiled as they rose and said, "Welcome to Tarlah, Ambassador Mocco."

Ambassador Mocco bowed his head.

"Come."

Ruarnon led Mocco to a sitting room right of the dais. They sat in a gold gilt chair, gesturing Mocco into a bronze gilt chair.

Mocco frowned, then sat.

"The Council of Elders approve of your Benevolence' Peace with the Zaldeaan Realm," Mocco said in flawless Timbalen. "They have observed your legal reforms in the Realm and Tarlahn labour compensating for shortages in the absence of the Zaldeaan Army."

Ruarnon tried not to grimace. The Zaldeaan army's absence made it possible to occupy the Zaldeaan Realm. And Ruarnon's army dispatching the damars overrunning the Realm made many Zaldeaans grateful to be occupied. But the missing army, its commander Ruarnon's uncle, Ruarnon's parents and Companion Pamoran all appeared to lie in the hands of the damars' creator,

Narz. And Companion Noma's western expedition had just reported an eyewitness account of men casting magical fires on the shores of Narz's lands, obliterating an entire forest. It was the second claim that Narz's people could wield magic. If so, Ruarnon had no idea how to counter Narz to recover their captured family members and Lenaris' father.

"I am sorry," they replied. "My parents are also missing and your mention of the army reminded me of an additional obstacle to their recovery."

Mocco fidgeted with a ring on his thumb. "I am not sure I would be here today were it your father sitting on the throne. We know of his involvement in the rebellion that gained Tarlah's independence and in the Sea Wars. To you he may be the warrior Tarlah needed to defend itself, but our Council of Elders didn't trust his reliance on might. They suspect he would have executed the Zaldeaan governors.

"But you let them live. You let them keep their positions. You have taken risks with your safety to ensure the Zaldeaans work with you in maintaining Peace between Tarlah and the Zaldeaan Realm."

"Only while their army is still missing," Ruarnon replied. "Governor Syenne herself told me all bets would be off then. But I was pleasantly surprised to secure the Zaldeaan Realm for so long."

"The Council of Elders believe you have done so in a way that parallels how our Urai tribes and Elders work together for the good of all Urai. You have earned my father's respect and caught the Council's attention. That is why Father has sent me, with the

Council's blessing, to invite you to Aracia, our capital in the heart of the jungle."

Ruarnon's mouth dropped open. *Their* own actions had prompted the Council of Elders to end the Unspoken Agreement by sending an Urai ambassador to Tarlah City? How many times had they listened to Mother play her Urai flute and dreamed of meeting the people her side of the family were descended from? People rumoured to have the greatest knowledge of this continent's plants and native animals and to have medicinal knowledge well beyond Tarlah's.

This wasn't just a childhood dream; it was a chance to advance Tarlahn knowledge of healing and secure access to Urai remedies. It could even create a new alliance, one that may aid Tarlah's defence in future... If Ruarnon presented to and negotiated well enough with the Council of Elders.

Ruarnon's lips split in a broad smile. "I would be honoured to accept their invitation."

They hesitated. Before they visited the Zaldeaan Palace for the first time, Companion Tor, their former tutor and father's best friend had schooled them in Zaldeaan etiquette. But when it came to the Urai, they were ignorant of far more than etiquette, ignorant enough to cause a diplomatic incident. They suspected the Urai knew exactly why the Unspoken Agreement had come about, making it taboo for Tarlahns to enter the jungle, whereas Tarlahn history Ruarnon had studied always danced around it. But they knew the Urai hadn't fought in The Wars between Tarlah and the Zaldeaan Realm. They suspected that would be part of the answer.

"Your people never fought in the Wars?" Ruarnon asked.

"Under our laws, disputes unresolved by other means can be resolved by duelling, but duelling to the death is forbidden and killing is reserved for slaughtering animals for food."

Ruarnon frowned. "The Zaldeaans keep invading us and North Landers pay them tribute. Surely the Zaldeaans attacked your people too? How did you defend yourselves?"

Mocco's eyes widened. "You don't know?"

"Our records include fanciful tales of travel through the jungle and imply that the Unspoken Agreement involved our ancestors committing some great wrong and that your people have an aversion to fighting. That is all."

Mocco rubbed his clean-shaven chin. "Perhaps shame stilled the historian's hand. There was a great wrong and the Wars were the ultimate cause. With the end of the Wars and the arrival of the damars, my father believes it is time to end our seclusion, but the Council of Elders are not so sure. That is why he has invited you to stay with us at your earliest convenience."

At the edge of Ruarnon's gaze, Advisor Monin's silver brows furrowed at the implication he would have little time to prepare Ruarnon for this visit. But Companion Tor and Aunt Telena's eyes shone with anticipation.

"We would be delighted to visit you next week," Ruarnon told Mocco.

A week later, Ruarnon's best friend Lenaris approached them in Tarlah Castle's main courtyard. She wore an embroidered, sleeveless travel tunic and sandals, and stood tall and stately, with neatly braided Tarlahn blonde hair, blue eyes and lightly tanned skin.

She smiled at Ruarnon. "What did my grandfather make of the Urai contacting us again?"

Ruarnon smiled. "It was a shock to Monin. I'm not sure he thinks there's much value in restoring relations with them, but Tor assures me he's bitter they never supported us in the wars against the Zaldeaans. And the generals say the Urai are excellent trackers. They can help us track down escaped damars in the wilderness and I know how much their remedies and alliance would help us."

"Your mother would be delighted to hear we are returning to the jungle," Companion Tor called from beside the carriage waiting in the courtyard. He stood tall and proud, fully recovered from the wound he had taken in the battle on Death Belt Desert, though his braided light brown hair glistened with more silver now. Tor's blue-eyed gaze was steady, his voice calm, as it had been when he was Ruarnon's tutor, and continued to be now he was Ruarnon's Companion and Advisor.

"Corina might not have shown it to you," Tor continued, "but her family have always regretted and missed the relatives they left behind in the jungle when the Unspoken Agreement began. She still knows some Urai but has precious few Tarlahns to speak it too."

Ruarnon bit their lip. Mother treasured her Urai flute, now safely stored in the chambers she should be living in. She had played it often and always believed the Urai still thrived. There was no telling when they could visit the Urai together, but they could create a Tarlah in which friendship with the people their mother and they were descended from was restored.

"I'll do my best," they said.

Tor smiled, inclining his head, and stepped up onto the platform of one of three waiting chariots.

"And your best to prove to my grandfather that you can handle diplomacy as well as war," Lenaris added with a wink.

Ruarnon fought back a laugh. Advisor Monin was their eldest and hardest to please advisor and Lenaris seemed to delight in supporting Ruarnon in exceeding her grandfather's high expectations. Ruarnon suspected her father, Companion Pamoran, might have encouraged them similarly, if more subtly, had he not also been abducted by Narz.

Lenaris stepped onto the chariot ahead of Tor's, but Ruarnon paused.

Their four Australian friends stood with Aunt Telena, on the left side of the courtyard. The Australians had grown restless since agreeing it was too dangerous to accompany Companion Noma west. Now they, like Ruarnon, were waiting to learn more about Narz's homelands from Companion Noma's expedition.

Ruarnon hoped to learn enough to inform a recovery expedition likely to succeed in freeing their family, Pamoran and the Zaldeaan soldiers. The Australians hoped to learn if western magic wielders could operate the archways that had brought them to Umarinaris and were willing to send them home to Australia. Only armed with that information could Ruarnon reasonably launch a recovery expedition and the Australians actively pursue their way home in a state that resembled safety.

Ruarnon said their goodbyes, grimacing with guilt. A visit to the Urai would be a great distraction for the four Australians, but Advisor Monin was adamant that a diplomatic mission to restore a bond that had been broken generations ago was not appropriate for foreigners from another world, who spoke their minds too freely. Ruarnon privately agreed, but they would miss their friends.

They stepped onto their chariot beside their driver, nodding to Captain Arleath in the lead chariot to depart. The chariots rolled through the castle gates, into the usual bustle and hum of conversation in Tarlah City. Golden or dark haired Tarlahns on foot stepped aside, children saluted and Ruarnon returned the double-armed salute: *Tarlah stands* and *the Zaldeaan Realm stands*.

The chariots took them along stone paved streets reflecting hot sunlight, past mud-brick apartments, beyond the clink of tools, chattering schoolchildren carrying satchels and bronze armoured guards, through the open city gates. Green fields and dusty cart tracks in which children played drifted by. East of Tarlah City, the fields gave way to ferns, bright flowers, trees rising to great heights, and a shady canopy under which insects roared.

The horses and chariot wheels trampled ferns along an overgrown track winding around tree trunks into the Urai jungle. Small stumps suggested seedlings had been cut and the track cleared periodically. But most signs of the Urai were above, where a maze of wooden ramps and plank bridges linked buildings constructed on branches. One ramp spiralled down a nearby forest giant, circling under itself until it reached ground level and a walled stone enclosure.

It had been generations since Tarlahn eyes had gazed at this city. Since their mother's ancestors had left it. She would have loved to be here. Perhaps one day, having safely recovered her from the west, Ruarnon could bring her.

Mocco stepped out of the walled enclosure. The carriages halted before him and Ruarnon climbed out first.

"Welcome to Aracia, home of the Council of Elders and the Craft Tribes. Come," Mocco added, turning to a wooden ramp up a nearby forest giant. Ruarnon followed, keeping a cautious hand on the rope railing as they spiralled higher and higher above the leafy forest floor.

At the end of the ramp, a plank and rope bridge spanned between trees. Bridges and ramps spread in all directions, linking small wooden buildings built against the trunks of forest giants. Urai moved along the ramps, most with dark skin, but the shade varied, as did their hair and eye colour. Ruarnon blinked. By the time of the Unspoken Agreement, Ruarnon's mother's descendants had married Tarlahns, so they remained in Tarlah. Apparently some Tarlahns had married Urai and remained in the jungle, severing ties with their people. What had divided families so?

Ruarnon stepped onto the bridge. Air shifted around them as it swayed in the breeze and their heart missed a beat. Mocco strode across confidently and Lenaris followed him with a contented smile, so Ruarnon tried to keep pace with her, keeping one hand on the rope railing on their left. People on bridges nearby eyed them curiously, a group of children pointing and waving. Ruarnon inclined their head at the children, who smiled and waved more enthusiastically.

A man waited at the far end. He wore a fine gold circlet of floral cut gemstones atop his black braided hair and a linen kilt brightly dyed with swirling oranges and yellows contrasted against his dark skin. Mocco introduced him as Kahorn.

"Welcome to our home," Kahorn said in confident Timbalen. "Please, come inside."

He led them into a small sitting room with large cushions around its walls and two small tables in the middle, with bronze cups of purple juice on them. They settled onto well-stuffed cushions and Ruarnon noted that everything was made of rich brown timber. It was smaller than expected, with only the silk cushions hinting at rank.

"I hear your castle is different," Kahorn said to Ruarnon.

"Your people seem to have little need of defence," Ruarnon replied.

"There have been serious conflicts between tribes," said Kahorn. "That is why the Council of Elders came to be and why this city became our only permanent dwelling, at the centre of all tribal lands. It is a neutral territory where the Council resolves disputes and presides over the Institute of Learning and the trade of master crafts people's goods with the North Lands. Their central governance of some things has reduced and ended conflicts between tribes."

"You trade with the North Landers?" Ruarnon asked, intrigued that the two reclusive peoples were in contact and remembering that fear of sorcery had deterred the Zaldeaans from attempting to take the North Lands by force.

"Yes."

"I know of their abilities," Ruarnon continued.

Companion Tor shot them a warning look, while Lenaris frowned. It might be too soon to ask but Ruarnon was immensely curious.

"I was wounded in Zaldeaa City and healed by a North Lander Healer. I know why they keep to themselves, and the Zaldeaans did not conquer them by force. Is the same true of your people?"

Kahorn's eyes widened and Mocco's jaw dropped.

"We have not their power," Kahorn replied. "Do you know how the bond between our peoples was broken?"

Ruarnon shook their head.

"During the Wars, the Zaldeaans expected us to fight alongside you. They attacked us first. But when their arrows and spears fell to the ground and an invisible barrier stopped them from entering the jungle or attacking us, they fled, fearing sorcery. They have feared us and respected our sovereignty ever since."

Ruarnon stared. The war between Tarlah and the Zaldeaan Realm had raged south and north across Death Belt Desert for decades. And all that time, reclusive neighbours of both had kept their distance, secretly wielding magic...

"Consider how the Wars would have looked if we shielded Tarlah City in the first siege," said Kahorn.

"You could have done that?"

"Only crucial areas. A breached wall, for example."

In the first siege, Zaldeaans had forced entry to Tarlah City by ramming the northern walls and Tarlah had fallen because of it. Ruarnon began to see the problem.

"So there was conflict," Tor said quietly, his gaze distant. "I assumed as much, but the reasons were unclear to me until now."

"The North Landers paid tribute to the Zaldeaan Realm and had acknowledged the Zaldeaan king as their Prime Ruler by then," Kahorn continued, "but Zaldeaans had not yet dared recruit them into military service. If we aided you with magic, and the Zaldeaans feared our sorcery enough to press the North Landers to fight, Prophetess Lylah feared magic would be wielded on both sides. She feared another Sorcery War."

Lenaris gasped, while Ruarnon's mind grappled with the idea, though its logical implications were clear. "And your people understood Lylah's concerns, whereas mine did not?" they asked.

"The Sorcery War was not such a distant legend in those days. Your people viewed conflict involving magic with fear, but many were more frightened of the Zaldeaans. A few days before the northern walls of Tarlah City were breached, a band of Tarlahns escaped to the jungle to demand aid and were so aggressive that a frightened ambassador blocked them with shield magic. They attacked his shield in desperation, until the strain of maintaining it killed him.

"We refused to aid your people. Tarlah city fell to Zaldeaans ruling by the sword. They executed many Tarlahns and Tarlahns entered the jungle demanding to know why we had abandoned them. Fights broke out and people were killed on both sides. Then a Tarlahn woman's last surviving child was killed by the careless blow of a Zaldeaan soldier. She blamed my ancestors for letting the city fall to Zaldeaans and poisoned one of our streams, killing an entire tribe. Guilt and shame became stronger than grief and the

Council of Elders and the Tarlahn king closed the borders. Entering the jungle became taboo for your people, in what you call the Unspoken Agreement."

Ruarnon shivered. They understood their Ancestor's desperation during the siege, having lived through a siege themself. But blaming the Urai for the city's fall and the executions afterwards had merely killed Urai. It was as wasteful and cruel as the succession war Ruarnon had cut short in the Zaldeaan Realm. And their Ancestors had been responsible.

It made Ruarnon's stomach lurch. The Ancestors had been a source of hope and inspiration throughout the Wars. That must be why memory of the murders wasn't preserved in Tarlah.

Tor shook his head, his features a mask of solemnity, confirming to Ruarnon that their former tutor had known little more.

"I am sorry," they said softly.

"It is in the distant past," Kahorn replied, making a dismissive gesture with his hand. "We will judge you by your actions. I tell you because as long as some of our people could wield shield magic, and that ability was desired in The Wars, the Council of Elders decided it best for our people to remain in the jungle and for ties with Tarlah to remain severed."

Ruarnon nodded. "Now, we have power slings and power bows that your shields may not withstand for long. And against damars, traditional shields are defence enough."

Kahorn nodded solemnly.

"The Zaldeaans did not realise that," Mocco said bitterly, shoving his cushion into shape. "We sent scouts, but their panic was so widespread that they would have assumed *we* sent the damars had they seen us. We could hardly aid them when they were likely to fight us, so we left."

"You tried to help them?" Ruarnon asked.

"I was elected King during the damarian invasion," Kahorn replied. "The creatures posed a threat to all peoples on this continent and the circumstances called for a single leader with the authority to make swift decisions. The Council of Elders were highly reluctant to risk pitting our shield magic against damars, but I insisted on investigating the possibility."

His gaze narrowed. "It was not only conquest that brought you to the Zaldeaan Realm; was it Ruarnon?"

"I wanted the damars destroyed," Ruarnon replied. "They attacked Timraith Island and wiped out some of my subjects before I knew of the monsters' existence. I was determined to save what could be saved."

"Your love of people is stronger than hatred of your enemies?"

Ruarnon blinked. "Tarlahns and Zaldeaans are all my concern now, as my subjects."

Kahorn smiled. "I believe the Council of Elders will see in you what I see, given the opportunity. Relations with our Urai Tribes will be their decision. But I should like to see us think beyond our borders again. And my sister, her brother and my nephew would also be happy to see that."

"Mawana will join the first Urai delegation to Tarlah if he can," Mocco added.

Ruarnon detected disapproval in the set of his jaw.

"He takes after his father," Kahorn replied. "Not all of us can be kings or Elders."

Mocco smiled.

"You want to be an elder?" Ruarnon asked.

"I am an apprentice elder," said Mocco. "Becoming an Elder takes many years of supervised experience. I hope it may one day bring me back to Tarlah. It is so different and I have seen too little of it."

Ruarnon smiled at their Urai acquaintances being as curious about Tarlah as Ruarnon was about the Urai.

"Maybe the rumours in the castle will prove true," said Lenaris. "And this will be a new age."

And the bulk of the weight to achieve that age would be carried on Ruarnon's shoulders, again.

"If you meet the full Council, there will be seven of them," Mocco explained, while Kahorn departed to arrange an audience for Ruarnon with the Council of Elders. "One elected by each tribe. They are… less receptive to change than Father."

Ruarnon bowed their head, appreciating the warning. Hopefully all seven didn't resemble Monin too much.

"Is it true some of the Council Members are women?" Lenaris asked.

"Yes," said Mocco.

"Then it is better than Tarlah," she replied.

Ruarnon's brows rose, but Mocco slowly smiled.

"We may benefit as much from conversation and exposure to Urai attitudes as the Zaldeaan Realm does from your Benevolence's legal reforms," said Tor.

"It may not be easy," Mocco cautioned. "Here, any decision that could change the fate of the Urai must be approved of by all seven Elders."

Fireflies fluttered in Ruarnon's stomach, and they were reminded of their first Royal Council Meeting during Uncle Omah's regency, in which they had been painfully aware of being a child at the table. The Council of Elders were even more likely to see Ruarnon as such, especially if they were as wizened as their name suggested.

"They will be ready for you when we reach them, if we leave soon," said Kahorn as he re-entered the room.

"Fortune be with you!" said Mocco.

Ruarnon wondered how the man knew the Tarlahn expression for wishing people well. They suspected the Urai remembered more of Tarlah than Tarlah did of them, which did not position Ruarnon well with the Elders. But Advisor Monin, Aunt Telena and Companion Tor had spent a week preparing them for today and it was time to seize their chance to restore relations.

Ruarnon followed Kahorn over several wooden plank bridges, around small wooden buildings, to a quiet corner containing a single building. It was slightly larger and distinguished by an archway elaborately carved to resemble intertwined branches. Inside the archway, a pair of doors were carved with Urai jewellery, weapons, plants or creatures: seven objects, presumably representing each tribe.

The fireflies stirred again in Ruarnon's stomach as they stepped through the arch. They resisted the urge to clutch the hilt of the short sword they always carried for reassurance, in case it

23

looked hostile and tried to smooth their expression into an open and pleasant one. The Elders were grey or silver-haired, their skin lined, yet each sat on silk cushions on the floor with cross-legged dexterity that surprised Ruarnon.

"Welcome Ruarnon, Regent of Tarlah," the woman on the far left intoned. "We are well aware of Kahorn's intentions, but we are not so certain of his ideas."

The fireflies in Ruarnon's stomach fluttered in a frenzy. Ruarnon took a deep breath, followed their instincts and Advisors' guidance and said, "I assume you want what's best for your people. Perhaps you believe that is what has served you well in recent decades."

One of the men before them shifted, while a woman leaned forwards with interest. The Elders seemed surprised at where Ruarnon was taking what they assumed was the woman's invitation to speak, but Ruarnon embraced their instincts and continued.

"But the world is changing. The Zaldeaan army is missing, murderous creatures have been shipped to our continent from the far side of the world, and I am sorry to inform you that the Zaldeaans have designed power bows and power slings that can likely penetrate even your shield magic. I wonder if anyone can shut out the world in this age.

"The Zaldeaans were arrogant and complacent in their military might because they have always been the dominant power over Tarlah. But the damars and the Zaldeaan army's disappearance laid them low. If we have more contact with Narz, if he is still a threat to our lands, I would have everyone on this continent stand united against him. Your people have the skills to track damars. Mine have effective tactics to fight them. Together we stand stronger than apart."

"The damars' arrival was a shock to our continent, yes," said a wizened man on Ruarnon's right. "But there is no evidence to suggest they will return and that our people are in any way disadvantaged by our continued seclusion."

"There was no evidence the Zaldeaan army could be swiftly bested and made to disappear, or that Tarlah would suddenly gain the ability to rule the Realm," Ruarnon countered. "Yet both happened and no one saw them coming. I would rather act to prevent foreseeable threats, then drown when the river floods."

The woman on the left's eyes lit up at Ruarnon's inclusion of an Urai saying in their argument.

"The damars who tried to reach our people died crossing the desert," the same man asserted. "They are yet to be a threat to us."

"No one knows why they landed on Zaldeaan shores," Ruarnon countered. "Nor do we know where Narz may strike next, or why. What I do know is that your people lack fortifications to defend against the damars. Should they land on your shores, you would need our tactics to rally and destroy them before they overrun your tribes."

The woman on the left nodded. "I think we can agree that in the event of the damars returning, an alliance with Tarlah would be wise. We know your campaign against them in the Zaldeaan Realm was highly successful and that your tactics against them achieved what the Zaldeaans could not. But what of our relations in ordinary times?"

Ruarnon swallowed nervously. They wanted to recover Uncle Karmarn and the lost Zaldeaan army. But they couldn't lie about what that would mean. And Zaldeaans in one of Governor Syenne's provinces, the one formerly governed by the warmongering, traitorous Governor Derlan, already chaffed at Tarlahn rule of the Realm.

"Tarlahn military supremacy is not sustainable," Ruarnon replied. "Even if I fail to recover my uncle and the Zaldeaan army from the west, all it would take is for the current and next generation of Zaldeaan boys to grow into men and become soldiers for my army to be dangerously outnumbered. And you must know that while the Timbalens are currently keen to maintain a presence in these seas and to expand Timbalen sea trade, their aid is not to be taken for granted. A generation from now, there are no guarantees that Tarlah and the Zaldeaan Realm will not be at war again. I will do everything in my power to prevent it. But as ruler of Tarlah, I must be prepared to defend my people in all circumstances."

Ruarnon sighed, discomforted by the other thing they had to say.

"I know shield magic has kept you safe, but if it is the only magic you wield, and if physically pushing magic shields can break them... I fear Zaldeaan power bows and power slings could pierce your magic. If the Zaldeaans realise that, you may be vulnerable to invasion after all. And I doubt the Zaldeaans would trade medicinal plants with you if they can take them by force."

Several Elders shifted. They had sat steadfastly so far, but these ugly ideas had penetrated their masks of wise, calm, unshakable rulers.

"Unless you possess magic I'm unaware of, I fear your people are at least as vulnerable to Zaldeaan mistreatment as mine."

"You are sincere in wishing to safeguard both peoples against the worst we know this world can throw at them," said the woman.

"Have we heard enough?" She asked her companions.

Several eyed Ruarnon, some sternly, others sadly. One by one, they nodded.

"Thank you for telling us your intentions," she said to Ruarnon. "We will take some time to consider, but we will likely wish to speak to you again this afternoon."

Ruarnon inclined their head and the eyes of the man opposite them widened.

Kahorn opened the door for Ruarnon and they took several deep breaths as the door closed behind them. Then Kahorn led them towards a nearby balcony on which Mocco waited with Tor and Lenaris.

"They liked Ruarnon," Kahorn reported.

"How could you tell?" Ruarnon asked. "I found them unreadable."

"I suspect they wondered if you would possess the arrogance of the first Timbalen settlers our people encountered. I wondered as well. But you showed them respect as our governing body. If anything, you bowed to their positions."

Ruarnon's brows furrowed. "Is that not right? In their meeting chambers, in the Urai Capital?"

Tor's eyes shone with pride. "I doubt any Timbalen Emperor would defer to any governing body or individual, be it at the seat of their power or not. They may appreciate the respect, and I hope they admired how you countered their doubts rationally and calmly, taking nothing personally."

Ruarnon heard what Tor wasn't saying in the presence of the Urai, "As I as your tutor and others have taught you."

Kahorn smiled. "I suspect they did."

Mocco raised a tray, offering everyone goblets of fruit juice. The drinks were a brief respite, and then Kahorn and Ruarnon were called back into the chamber.

"You possess the foresight we prize on our Council," said the woman on their left.

Ruarnon flushed at her praise.

"I wondered, when I heard of your youth, if we would hear words your advisors had put into your mouth when you spoke. But your conviction and sincerity suggest that much of what you said came from you. That what matters most to you may not be your advisors' highest priorities. You have a genuine regard for your own and our people. And possess none of the arrogance of your forebears, as we had hoped from the first Tarlahn ruler with Urai heritage.

"We would like to invite you, Kahorn and two advisors of your choice to join us in negotiating the resumption of relations between our two peoples."

Ruarnon's smile split into a broad grin.

Negotiating trade and travel agreements took several days. Ruarnon learnt more about Mocco's training as apprentice Elder and met his cousin Mawana, who captured animals for the Institute of Learning to study. Mawana took them on several jungle expeditions, grinning at leopards in a way that made Ruarnon twinge with guilt at leaving their Australian friends at home. Then the agreements were signed, and it was time to return to Tarlah. Ruarnon, Tor and Lenaris shared a last morning meal with Kahorn and Mocco, at which they were interrupted.

"A coastal messenger wishes to speak to you, your Majesty," a young woman said to Kahorn. "He says there are dangerous creatures on ships sailing nearby."

Ruarnon tensed and their heart skipped a beat.

"Damars?" Kahorn asked.

"I do not know what else it could be."

"What would they be doing south of the jungle?" Lenaris asked.

"Your Australian friends encountered damars on Timraith Island," Tor replied. "Perhaps these damars have the same purpose as the ones the Timbalens cut down."

Ruarnon shivered. No one knew why those damars had been shipped east of the mainland when all others had landed on the west coast.

"They must have stayed beyond sight of the Zaldeaan west coast," Companion Tor added. "Otherwise the Zaldeaan governors would have warned us."

"And they have left our western coast untouched," Kahorn added.

"Leaving Tarlah as a possible target, if it *is* damars," said Ruarnon.

"Then you had best come with us to investigate," Kahorn invited.

Ruarnon nodded, following Kahorn and Mocco back down the ramp to the jungle floor, where they mounted borrowed horses. Ruarnon rode in tense silence, gazing ahead as Mocco led them through the trees, until the trail ended among sandhills. Then everyone followed Mocco on foot, along a rocky point stretching across the water, towards a broad-shouldered man.

"We have seen ships approaching from the West, your Majesty," the man reported without preamble. "They are south of here and their current course will take them just within sight of our southern coast as they sail east. Some creatures broke out of a damaged cage and dove overboard. They attacked a passing shoal of fish, but were unable to swim and drowned."

Ruarnon closed their eyes and asked, "Were they short, grey-skinned, with pointy teeth and yellow eyes?"

"You have seen them," the man replied.

"How long will it take them to pass our coast, or reach it, if that is what they intend?" Kahorn asked.

"Two or three days before they reach the south-easternmost point."

"Then I shall station lookouts on land."

"We will keep a lookout at sea. The coastal Elders have agreed to suspend sea trade until the creatures move on or are dealt with."

Kahorn nodded his approval. Ruarnon shivered. Narz had an unknown interest in Tarlah, but he had only used Zaldeaans to capture Ruarnon's parents and Companion Pamoran. Was he moving directly against Tarlah now?

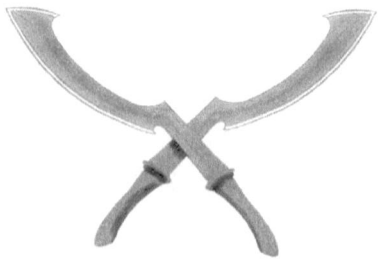

Chapter 2

A New Threat ~Ruarnon

Ruarnon sat at the head of the table in the Golden Meeting Hall, surveying the Royal Council's reactions to their report on damars being sighted in nearby seas again.

"What do you think?" Ruarnon asked.

"Narz is no longer interested in the Zaldeaan Realm," replied scarred, silver-haired Advisor Monin, sitting alert and upright, as he must have been when he defended Tarlah as its leading general. "The Zaldeaan army was what he sought there."

"The fleet points towards Cauldron Island," said Companion Tor. "But Timbalen expedition records say that island is ringed by steep cliffs and consists mostly of barren, uninhabitable plains and I can think of nothing that may interest Narz there."

"I wonder if Narz is pursuing whatever he sought in Tarlah," said Lenaris, "his reason for having their Benevolences and my father abducted."

"Sending damarian ships against us would be foolish," said General Aza, sitting on the edge of his seat, his posture suggesting he may leap to his feet at any moment. "The damars' greatest strength was the shock of their existence and their savagery, which are no longer a surprise to us."

Ruarnon frowned. General Aza was right. But if damars were the only force Narz could spare for invasions across the sea, would he pursue his interest in Tarlah with them regardless?

"We assumed Narz had sound reasons for having our King and Queen and Companion Pamoran abducted and for invading the Zaldeaan Realm with damars, and that ignorance was our greatest barrier to understanding his motivations," said Companion Tor, his voice calm, belying the circles under his eyes. "But as he is still a threat, I think it is time to acknowledge we might have been mistaken.

"Narz's use of damars in the Zaldeaan Realm was ruthless cruelty, more mass murder than invasion. All it achieved was death —not conquest. And sailing halfway across the known world to abduct an army from a foreign land, risking that army mutinying, killing his soldiers and stealing his ships? To me, that policy suggests he is not rational."

Postures stiffened around the table and Ruarnon bit their lip.

"Abducting an army and transporting them halfway across the known world involves an terrible level of risk," General Aza agreed. "I half expected Companion Karmarn to break free, defeat his captors and sail his fleet home by now. The fact he hasn't makes me wary of the ruthlessness I suspect keeps that army captive, and wary of Narz's ships sailing near our waters once more."

"We must assume the fleet is aimed against Tarlah to ensure that we are properly defended against it, but it may strike anywhere," said Advisor Monin, sitting in his usual upright position of authority.

"Ensuring the defence of Tarlah against damars means killing all and any damars that enter our waters," Ruarnon asserted. "On land, they spread too swiftly. But we know they cannot swim, so engaging those ships in deep water is the best way to protect our coast."

"That is aggressive policy," Monin cautioned. "If we are not Narz's target, it may make us his target."

"Confronting them with anything less may end in disaster," said General Aza, "as it did for the Zaldeaans. The only way to protect yourself against damars is to destroy them at the first opportunity, not give those ships time to manoeuvre near our shores. But what made the Zaldeaan army surrender? And in countering the damars, do we leave ourselves vulnerable to a threat even the Zaldeaans could not vanquish?"

Ruarnon's chest tightened. They couldn't risk anything like what happened on the Zaldeaan western coast occurring on Tarlahn shores. But what chance did Tarlah stand against whatever convinced the mighty Zaldeaan army to sail off, letting damars ravage the Zaldeaan Realm in its absence?

"There is more to consider," said Advisor Monin. "Narz has only targeted islands inhabited by humans and has left the west jungle coast untouched, so if Tarlah is not his target, the next most likely target is the Timbalen Empire. We are yet to sign a renewed treaty with them. We are not bound to defend them. If the Timbalen Empire is the damars' target, I propose allowing the damarian fleet to sail by."

Ruarnon's mouth dropped open. At first they saw disloyalty in Monin's words. But Companion Tor didn't seem surprised.

"General Takanis notes that our soldiers are still recovering from seeing bodies of people of all ages scattered in the damar-ravaged parts of the Zaldeaan Realm," General Aza reported on behalf of the Second General, whom Ruarnon had sent to South Harbour with reinforcements.

General Takanis tended to notice and boldly state different things to the men in the room and Ruarnon regretted her absence, but rank and tradition said if both generals couldn't attend the Council, the senior should attend.

"Takanis says letting the fleet sail on would give the soldiers more time to heal," General Aza continued. "If this fleet sails beyond our waters, she is confident that a bird carrying our warning and knowledge of effective tactics to our allies will enable them to defend themselves."

Ruarnon slumped. She was right. The Timbalen army was a far greater force. With advance warning and tactical advice, it should crush shiploads of damars. But letting those ships sail near Tarlahn waters, unaware of the fleets' destination and thought of those creatures roaming Tarlahn coastal villages made Ruarnon's skin crawl.

"Can I remind the Council that Companion Noma's report confirms Governor Armar's report about sorcery coercing the Zaldeaan fleet to sail west, and that we have no other logical explanation for it sailing away?" Lenaris asked. She was a little paler than usual, probably at thought of challenging the Council not long after joining it in her new role as Ruarnon's first Companion of roughly their age.

"I know it sounds like preparing to confront villains from a child's tale," Lenaris continued, "but I feel we should discuss the possibility that whoever is transporting damars may be able to wield magic."

Monin gaped at his granddaughter speaking boldly about something he still held reservations about the existence of.

"General Takanis and I have considered it," General Aza replied.

Ruarnon's eyes widened. Experiences in the Zaldeaan Realm had changed those two. They were more open-minded and seemed to be working more closely together in their roles as First and Second General now.

"We see no need for anyone who can wield magic to accompany the creatures to these seas. If they are transported in cages, as the Urai eyewitness report suggests, we think it likely the cages are designed and transported in a way that ordinary humans can unleash damars from their ships, without endangering themselves. We suspect that if anyone in this day and age can wield magic, they will be highly valued. And with Narz's previous expedition having ended in disaster for him, and this entire continent on high alert against his ships' return, we feel it is unlikely Narz will risk his sorcerers to achieve means he has sent few ordinary humans to pursue."

"Precisely," said Monin, recovering from his shock at a speed that reminded Ruarnon of his extensive experience. "It is merely a question of whether Narz's damars target Tarlah or not."

"The failure of his previous mission and his clear intent to pursue its goal now may also be reason for Narz to send greater force against us this time, to ensure his success, if there is something here he desperately wants," Tor asserted. "And if Narz's methods are not entirely rational, that becomes more likely."

Silence met his assertions. Ruarnon was quite certain that both their generals and Monin were deeply reluctant to consider how Narz may achieve his goals if he wasn't limited by rational thought. Ruarnon suspected that scared their advisors more than the possibility of magic wielders being on those ships. But whether Narz was in his right mind or not, whether sorcerers stood on the decks of his approaching ships or not, it all boiled down to did Ruarnon engage those ships?

"What does the Council think of our ships being loaded with soldiers, fitted with arms and stationed ready to defend our waters?" Ruarnon asked. "Of them keeping their distance and not engaging unless it becomes crystal clear we are Narz's target?"

Tor inclined his head. "I think that is the only practical course."

General Aza his inclined head, followed by Lenaris.

"I won't argue to leave our waters undefended," said Monin. "But I should like to discuss clear terms in which we shall consider those ships to be aimed against us, to avoid unnecessary injuries and loss of life."

Ruarnon supressed a smile. Monin was always last to agree and strongest in his opinions. But this was agreement enough. And waiting and watching to see whether damars would hunt Ruarnon's subjects would be as tense as confronting damars in the Zaldeaan Realm. But they would have to put the possibility of confronting whatever abducted the Zaldeaan army out of their head, because it was unlikely they could do anything about it.

The discussion turned to preparing soldiers and the distance the damarian fleet could be from Tarlahn shores for Ruarnon to have time to reposition their ships to defend Tarlah. But Ruarnon's shoulders tightened with tension as the discussion went on. General Takanis' observations made them realise they hadn't spent enough time with their soldiers since securing the Zaldeaan Realm. They should have guessed that if they woke in a sweat in the middle of the night, the screech of dead damars still ringing in their ears, so would some of their soldiers.

Many soldiers were battle weary and many Tarlahns wanted to believe these were the days of Peace. That the days of fear, insecurity and sacrifice were over. They may not respond well to potential battle so soon, especially against the damars. And Ruarnon feared Tor may be right. Narz's goals may not be rational. His methods may not be rational. And what if he *had* stationed a magic wielder on one of his ships?

Uncle Omah's most important lesson had been to act decisively in dangerous times, but whether Ruarnon's decision was to attack or ignore the damarian fleet, they feared their decisive action could go terribly wrong.

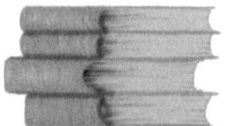

CHAPTER 3

LOOK AND LEAP ~LINH

Linh stood on a grassy terrace in Tarlah Castle's gardens, oblivious to orange, pink and yellow flowers bobbing in the gentle breeze rustling branches around her, as Ruarnon updated her, and her lost Australian friends, Fiona, Troy and Michael.

"The damars are back," Ruarnon said. "The Urai are tracking them at sea, and we don't know what their target is. I'm preparing ships to defend Tarlah, and the Urai are readying ships in case Cauldron Island, off our east coast and where some of their people are camping, is attacked.

"The Urai have confirmed that human handlers are on board the ships to release the damars from their cages. And the Urai will help defend Tarlah if we are attacked, or else sail on to defend Cauldron Island. They are your best chance to ask westerners to confirm if archways leading to your homeland, and sorcerers capable of operating them *are* in the west. Mocco has offered to let you sail with him."

Linh's jaw dropped, as she gazed unseeing across terraces of flowering trees. After months of dead ends and Tarlahns,

Zaldeaans and North Landers being unable to help them, they could finally access confirmation of how to get home. The problem was, at Timraith Island humans had unleashed damars from their cages at sea and hadn't gone ashore. That suggested the best way to speak to westerners now was to set sail. But at sea, the westerners would be battling Tarlahan and or Urai ships. Yet if Linh and her friends waited safely on shore, they had no way of knowing whether the Urai or Tarlahns would successfully capture live westerners for questioning.

"I should warn you," Ruarnon added, "Lenaris is concerned that magic wielders may be present on the western ships, to control the damars. We have no way of confirming that."

Linh clutched the nearest tree branch. Six months after obliviously stumbling through an archway and finding themselves stuck on Umarnaris, how were they back to the same decision they'd made on Myleth Island: travel into certain danger, or remain ignorant of how to get home?

Linh didn't notice Ruarnon leave. Or hear Michael speak, until Fiona nudged her and nodded at Michael.

"Let me get this straight," said Troy, as he paced across a grassy terrace on Linh's right, his chaotic brown curls flapping about his flushed bronze face, his usually warm brown eyes alight with anxiety. "We didn't sail west with Companion Noma because the Tarlahns have no idea where anything is in the Far West, and for all we know, it's overrun with Narz's sorcerers and damars. But now we're considering sailing with Mocco's ships, when we haven't even *met* Mocco yet, *and* we could end up fighting damars and possibly magic wielders?"

He turned and continued pacing across the terrace. His green Tarlahn tunic was short enough to show his stocky calves and arms. He was still round in the middle, but travel, weapons training and pursuit of distractions from being stranded in another world had slimmed his limbs and hardened his muscles. Knowing what had caused the weight loss, Linh missed the rounder Troy, who was more prone to laugh, smile and yes, drive her up the wall with his antics. That had been a happier Troy. And she'd tolerate a reasonable amount of cheek from him to have that Troy back. It used to be her who worried most, but Troy's anxiety was eclipsing hers.

She suspected Michael would have a good reason for boarding Mocco's ship —he usually had very good reasons. Michael stood aloof too, gazing between the trees and their bunches of leaves and flowers. He was nearly Troy's height, with black hair, hazel eyes, a broad nose and a dark brown face. But the features Fiona said were attractive were taut today. And those hazel eyes burned with passion.

"The only reason we think the Far West is our way home is that Timbalen and Tarlahn myths say there are archways there," said Michael, "and sorcerers who can hypothetically operate them. The people sailing those ships should be able to confirm whether sorcerers —aside from Narz and his mates— *are* wandering around in it or not."

"Why not ask Mocco to ask them for us?" Fiona offered.

She still wore her golden-brown hair in a pigtail, despite Lenaris' offers to braid it in Tarlahn style. Like Linh's black ponytail, it was a connection to home. And as always, Fiona's blue eyes shone with hope, while Tarlah's harsh sun had added freckles to her pale nose and cheeks.

"Because when we agreed not to sail on Companion Noma's western scouting expedition," Michael answered, "I forgot that *both* the Timbalen and Migryan languages, like the Timbalens and Zaldeaans themselves, originated in the west. Yet they're completely different languages now. So even if Companion Noma's expedition overcomes its fear of encountering sorcerers who can apparently incinerate them, and the expedition proceeds, it will be carried out in Timbalen. If the westerners speak Migryan, they *won't* understand. For all we know, the westerners could speak another language entirely, or multiple other languages. Companion Noma's expedition might not give us any information at all."

Linh's stomach dropped. Lenaris had argued passionately that it was pointless risking their lives sailing west with an expedition ship that could be sunk. Tor had admitted he feared for his sister, Companion Noma's life. And Ruarnon had said they fully anticipated mounting a larger expedition, based on the knowledge the first uncovered, to sail west. That was the western expedition Ruarnon, Lenaris and Tor all thought Linh and her friends should sail with. And she and the others had been persuaded.

Neither Michael, nor Linh, Fiona or Troy had realised the likelihood that the westerners didn't speak Timbalen. Perhaps the only people the westerners would understand was Linh and her friends, because of their strange ability to understand and be understood by speakers of multiple of Umarinaris' languages, as their time in the Zaldeaan Realm had proven.

"Whatever language the westerners speak," said Michael, "I'm betting *we* understand it too and they can understand us. Worst case scenario, I shout a question at them from a rowboat, in the event they don't attack Tarlah *or* Cauldron Island."

Linh grit her teeth, then tugged her ponytail, because the teeth-gritting wasn't enough. One word had plagued them since they first arrived in Umarinaris; *if*. When nothing was certain, you didn't peg your hopes on *if*. You seized any evidence of certainty that came within your reach. That was why they had come to Tarlah and the same logic would take them onboard Mocco's ships to confront the damars. Especially when the *if* of Companion Noma's expedition being helpful was fifty-fifty at best. When the ifs were that big, you bet on the ones that didn't leave you stranded in another world and dying of old age without ever seeing your mum, dad or Ba again.

Enough time had passed that Linh could admit to herself that her mother and Ba, who'd escaped a warzone in Vietnam when they were young, may prefer that she stayed safe in Tarlah and build herself a life here, instead of risking her life to get home. But Linh wasn't ready to let them go and not just because she didn't know how to reach them. If they were dead, ancestors forbid, that would be different.

And she'd been *so* looking forward to starting V.C.E. To turning eighteen, getting to vote for people who gave a shit about people and to have so many more subjects to choose from at University. She'd turned seventeen since she arrived here. She should be halfway through V.C.E. by now and celebrating her eighteenth with her family, at home, in the coming months.

But Linh and her three friends had done little to get home since helping persuade Ruarnon to occupy the Zaldeaan Realm weeks ago. And speaking to a North Lander in the Realm had been a dead end. It was over six months since they'd first decided to sail to Tarlah, after learning that no one in the Timbalen Empire could help. Six months chasing myths and they had no more reason to hope they could get home and were no closer to doing so now than they'd been on day one.

For all Linh knew, Red Cloak, after fleeing the archway she and her friends had stepped onto Umarinaris via, had no purpose for them and or had died since bringing them here. Linh didn't want to take more risks, but her hope was fading and this was her only option to keep it alive.

"I could go by myself," said Michael. "We don't all need to put ourselves in danger."

Linh's breath caught at the idea.

"Can you give us a moment?" Fiona asked.

Troy's brows rose in surprise as Fiona turned towards Linh. She'd never asked for a private word before. Michael nodded and Linh walked with Fiona down a green terrace, then along the next. They stopped in the shade of a leafy flowering tree.

"I think Michael is fed up with chasing myths," said Fiona. "He's logical and he wants facts. I'm worried his quest for that is driving him hard enough to put himself in unnecessary danger. And that scares me because it's not like him."

"He's right though," said Linh.

"But I'm worried it's his anger at himself for not seeing the hole in our decision not to sail with Companion Noma that's driving him to offer to go by himself. Like he's punishing himself.

I don't like it and I'm worried his anger at himself will blind him to the dangers he wants to put himself in."

Linh shook her head. "How can you read people so well? He's being logical and rational as always, but you're right, something's off. But why would he blame himself? I didn't notice the possibility the westerners won't understand the Tarlahns either, and we're the ones who've studied ancient history where loads of small kingdoms speak different languages side by side. *We* should have seen it too."

Fiona's shoulders sagged. "We should have. But are either of us insisting we can face danger alone, while everyone else stays safely on shore?"

Linh shook her head. "He may think he's smarter than me and it's possible he's right, but that doesn't make him responsible for all of us. How could anyone be responsible for *me*? I'd tear them limb from limb for trying!"

Fiona's eyes shone and Linh smiled as her friend burst out laughing.

"If he can't see that about you, then he's not as clever as he thinks," Fiona replied. "But do you remember him saying his parents were often drunk and he practically raised his younger sister, until the three of them died in that crash? What if that made him feel like he was the adult in the room? If it makes him feel he *has* to look after us, when Tor or Lenaris don't do it for him?"

Linh frowned. "He hasn't exactly bossed us around. He's always explained why he thinks we should do something."

"Exactly. He's tried to think everything through for everyone else. He's tried to puzzle out and solve everything on his own. It's only because he shares those thoughts that any of us have had a chance to weigh in on them. Maybe he's felt kind of responsible for us all along, but it's only obvious now he thinks he's let us down and is angry with himself for it."

Linh shook her head. "What did I do to deserve a friend who's so thoughtful about and who gets other people so well as you do?"

Fiona smiled. "Well, you do share my love of the ancient world and you shut down that bully pretty well when he mocked me for being a nerd on our first day at Kinnara High. You've looked out for me too."

Linh considered it and decided their differing strengths complemented each other nicely. But they needed to make a decision. "I think you're right," she said. "Whatever the reason, Michael seems upset and or angry at himself and it does look like he's trying to put himself in danger... like he's trying to make it up to us. That's messed up! I'm *not* letting him go by himself!"

Fiona smiled and cocked an eyebrow. "So you're going to accompany him because you're angry at him being so reckless with his safety, when he's being reckless because he's angry at himself?"

"I'm perfectly calm on the matter, just forceful in my will," Linh managed to get out with a straight face, crossing her arms, before cracking a grin. "Seriously though, he's not going on his own. And the idea has Troy on edge. Even I can see Troy seems worn down, as well as anxious. I know he still cracks jokes and tries to annoy me now and then, but he's not himself either. I don't think he's in a good state to manage Michael, though he may not agree to stay here."

It suddenly occurred to Linh that Fiona hadn't said a thing about what she wanted. Linh assumed they were having this conversation so Linh could back Fiona up with Michael. But what did Fiona plan to tell Michael?

"What do you want Fi?" Linh asked.

"You know how many siblings I have," Fiona told the ground. "I won't give up on trying to get back to them. And I don't want to risk those westerners dumping damars at sea then sailing off before we speak to them, when we could yell our questions at them from Mocco's ship's deck if need be. I think Michael's right. This is a risk we need to take. I just don't like the idea of him taking it alone, in the state he's in."

"Are you coming with me?" Linh asked.

Fiona smiled. "I'd follow you to most places."

"Only most?"

"Well, I do like boys," Fiona replied, her cheeks flushing slightly.

Linh grinned. "I can't say I understand why, but then I don't truly understand anyone being romantically or sexually attracted to anyone, yet most people seem to insist on it, so I can hardly hold that against you."

She gave her friend a smile and Fiona hugged her. Linh hugged her back.

"We could tell Michael we're going, and he and Troy can stay here," Linh said as they stepped apart.

Fiona grimaced. "I worry that might hurt his feelings. And Troy will probably be happier with us than... Lenaris for company."

Linh smiled. Lenaris reminded her of a strict schoolteacher sometimes. Troy needed that to keep him in line, but in the absence of Linh to tease and Fiona being nice to him, it was likely to get Troy down.

"You, Fiona Dolberry, the most considerate and careful person I've ever known, think the four of us should set sail on ships likely to battle damars at sea? What has Umarinaris done to you?" Linh asked, hands on her hips.

"Well I mean, if you don't like it..." Fiona began, misunderstanding.

Linh cut her off. "I think you're probably righter than I know," she said, placing an arm around her friend. "I was just commenting on how our time here has turned everyone upside-down."

"*You* haven't changed a lot," Fiona replied.

"How many times have I killed Troy since we got here?" Linh asked.

Fiona beamed. "I guess we've all changed. But I think Michael and Troy might need our help for theirs to be a change for the better."

Linh nodded and they walked back to the boys.

"If Troy wants to come," Linh declared, "then we're all going. Michael, I like you and I'd rather not fight you over it, so it would be great if you could accept that we're all going."

"That's high praise from Linh," Troy whispered behind his hand to Michael, loud enough that everyone could hear him. "And you *don't* want to fight her. She'll take your head off. Just smile and nod."

Fiona beamed at him. Linh was trying to glare at his cheek, but she was fighting a huge smile because that was the ghost of happy, mischief-loving old Troy speaking and it was good to see him again.

"I…" said Michael.

Were those tears in his eyes? Linh sighed and cut him off. "Fiona and I should have realised the westerners could speak other and any number of languages. That wasn't your oversight, it was all three of our oversight."

"Excuse *me*," said Troy, "but even us lay people know our neighbours in South-East Asia speak multiple different languages, so we *all* screwed up."

He crossed his arms stubbornly at Linh, failing to not smile, then turned to Michael, his smile softening. "And just because you're a bloody genius doesn't mean we can expect you to get everything right. *I* make mistakes all the time."

"You don't exactly try to avoid them much, do you?" Linh asked.

Troy grinned. "Where's the fun in life if you never do anything silly?"

"So you have a lot of fun then?" Linh teased.

Troy shook his head. "My learned colleagues, I apologise for my failure to adequately demonstrate the fun that can be had when you cease being so clever and serious all the time and do silly things like me. I solemnly swear to do better in future."

Fiona giggled.

"I just…" a tear trickled down Michael's face.

"Mate," Troy said, placing a hand on Michael's shoulder, "If you want to argue with us on this one, you're going to have to take on me as well as Linh. And if Fi decides to jump in, you'll be totally and utterly, royally screwed. So really, we should just hug it out."

More tears ran down Michael's face, but he was smiling now. Troy gave him a bear hug.

"Is it just me, or did Troy just rally because Michael needed him?" Linh asked Fiona quietly.

"He did," Fiona replied, beaming. "But it isn't over yet, because I don't think Lenaris or Tor know Mocco offered to take us on board. I suspect they'll have reservations when we tell them."

Fiona hugged Michael too and they gave him time for the truth of their words to sink in. Then Linh led the way to the Royal Training Courtyard, where she suspected she would find Lenaris. Ruarnon and Companion Tor were there too.

"We'd like to accept Mocco's offer to sail with him," Linh told Ruarnon without preamble, causing Lenaris to pause in returning her weapons to their holders and halting Ruarnon and Tor in their tracks.

"Why would that be necessary?" Tor asked.

"Because we can't be sure the westerners speak Timbalen," Linh replied. "They might speak Migryan or for all we know, some other language. The only way we can be sure they understand our questions about getting back to Australia is if we ask them ourselves."

"I should have realised that," said Ruarnon and Linh caught Troy eyeing Michael meaningfully. Michael's spread in a small smile.

"You realise you could get yourselves killed seeking information on how to get home?" Lenaris asked coldly.

Linh almost flinched at her tone.

"We didn't die the last time we fought damars," Troy replied. "Or on Timraith Island before that."

"There will be no cavalry to aid your escape or give you an advantage this time," Tor cautioned.

"They don't have to be above deck during any fighting," said Ruarnon. "From the way damars were bashing their sticks against doors and walls in Zaldea City, they don't have the first idea how to open doors. And if our friends barricade themselves in, the damars won't stand a chance at reaching them."

Lenaris frowned and Linh saw concern in Tor's eyes, but it seemed Ruarnon's Tarlahn logic had saved the day, again. Both Ruarnon's Companions bowed their heads.

"Who will you send as observers?" Michael asked.

"Me," Lenaris replied. "So no sneaking on deck during the fighting," she added, her gaze firmly on Troy, whose eyes widened in false innocence.

"Tor will remain with me onshore, where we can give orders for the defence of our whole coast, if needed," Ruarnon added.

"I hope you don't need to," Fiona replied so sincerely that all three Tarlahns bowed their heads.

It was settled then. Linh and her friends would pack, then head to Tarlah Harbour to set sail in hopes of learning how to get home, at the risk of being caught in battle on the high seas, a second time.

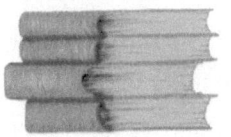

Chapter 4

Surprises at Sea: Linh

Two days later, Linh stood beside her Aussie and Tarlahn friends on Tarlah City's harbour, watching rows of paddles extending from a dark timbered Urai ship's lower deck and manoeuvring the ship into port.

"Isn't wearing armour tempting fate?" Troy asked.

"We cannot know if Narz has sent human soldiers as well as damars," Ruarnon replied.

Linh fought back a grimace. Tarlahns were cautious. She sincerely hoped they were being overcautious this time. But she had to admit, the extra weight of bronze encasing her chest and back, and the helmet around her head was reassuring, as was the short sword at her hip. Having fought damars before, she didn't want to be going anywhere near them with anything less, even if decks or doors stood between her and them.

Ruarnon stood rigid with tension. Linh followed their gaze. Her heart rate increased as the damarian ships sailed into view on the far right, southeast of the Tarlahn coast. Their present course would take them north-east of Tarlah City, and east of the Zaldeaan Realm's east coast, but there was still time and space for the fleet to turn west to attack. And nothing to distract anyone from that possibility, as they stood in tense silence while Mocco's anchor was lowered.

It was a relief when the gangplank extended and Mocco walked down it, his dark features set in a serious expression. He wore full bronze Tarlahn armour, though Linh suspected an Urai craftsperson had etched the twinning vines around the chest plate.

Ruarnon greeted him and introduced everyone.

"I have cabins ready, but you may like to join me on the foredeck as we set out," Mocco offered Linh, her friends and Lenaris.

Lenaris accepted and Linh said goodbye to Ruarnon, then she followed Lenaris up the plank, across a crowded middeck bustling with crew members, then up the steep forecastle stairs. As she crossed the foredeck, a salty breeze blew in Linh's face and rippled her Tarlahn tunic, which flapped beneath her armour, a reminder that she was moving again. After so long on Ruarnon's continent, the knowledge she was actively seeking her way home loosened the tension in her shoulders slightly. She relaxed, leaning on the railing and gazing out to sea.

"This is my cousin, Mawana," said Mocco, nodding to a young man approaching them across the deck. "He catches wild animals for the Institute of Learning to study."

Mawana was taller than Mocco, and broader. Linh caught Lenaris appraising the fitted bronze armour he wore, which, being Tarlahn in style, left little about his six-pack to the imagination and exposed his ebony biceps. But it was the way his almond brown eyes shone and the smile on those broad lips that caught Linh's attention, because it reminded her very much of Troy, despite the differences in colouring and ethnicity.

"It's a shame you missed our adventures in the jungle," Mawana told Linh and her friends, as he leant on the railing beside them, "but as I cannot introduce you to my interesting neighbours, perhaps you can tell me about yours? Ruarnon says Australia is full of poisonous creatures."

Linh frowned at the enthusiasm shining in his eyes, but Troy was happy to oblige. He described everything from redback spiders and tiger snakes to blue-ringed octopi, not quite distracting Linh from her surroundings, as a steady drumbeat sounded below deck.

Rows of oars protruded from the lower bulwarks, splashing into the deep water and rowing in time, shifting the ship until its prow pointed east. More crew scurried about setting sails and they departed Tarlah Harbour with the wind in their ears and sails flapping overhead.

Incoming waves began to break against the ship's stern, foaming alongside its bulwarks, while more waves stretched out to sea on Linh's right. On her left, sandy coast and the odd fishing village stretched beyond the shallows, while dry grassland and fields stretched inland. There was no sign of any Tarlahns swimming, wandering the beaches or tending fields. Ruarnon had ordered everyone near the coast to stay inside as a precaution. But only occasional Tarlahn farmhouses had wooden fences, which seemed more for demarking whose vegetable garden was whose than keeping anything out.

Linh shivered. "They're going to have to bar their doors and windows if the damars make it to land," she said.

"Our archers learn their craft from hunting," said Mawana, "If the Tarlahns can't halt the damars in their tracks, we will."

"Who's captaining the other Urai ships?" Michael asked, pointing to two ships emerging from the horizon behind the damarian vessels, whose course was still east of Tarlah. Linh crossed her fingers it stayed that way.

"My father and my Aunt Tarata, Mocco's mother," Mawana replied. "They normally captain trade ships sailing the western coast to the North Lands, but they were as eager to set out on this voyage as I was."

As they sailed on, the Tarlahn coastline fell slowly behind. Fishing villages retreated into dry yellow grass and fields around them. Sandy shores blended back into the mainland. Then the continent itself began to retreat. Linh heaved a sigh and exchanged a smile with Fiona.

"Surely those ships aren't headed for Tarlah?" Troy asked.

"We are headed directly towards Cauldron Island," Mocco replied, not taking his gaze off the sails of damarian ships piercing the horizon ahead. "I think mother is right and those ships are bound there."

"But Timbalen records say it is uninhabited," said Lenaris. "What could Narz want with it?"

Mawana eyed Mocco, who sighed, then replied, "Some of our people live in a settlement that serves Lylah's sister Flariah. She has asked our ships to block the damarian vessels' retreat, should they attack her coast."

Lylah had a sister? What mystical powers did Flariah have? But that was a question Lenaris would probably argue would step on Urai toes, so Linh asked her next question. "Doesn't she have ships of her own?"

"The settlement is not very big," Mawana replied. "And Flariah's people haven't been interested in sailing for years. It makes the faeron sick and gorans are more interested in rock carving than carpentry."

"What would Narz want with any of those people?" Linh asked.

Mawana shrugged. "I doubt he came for the reptiles. Unless he's after the dragons."

Linh's insides turned cold.

"*Dragons*?" Michael asked.

"You know huge winged, reptilian things. They like to fly around at dusk, hunting their dinner."

Linh shook her head. He *had* to be joking! Surely Tarlahns would know if there were dragons on Cauldron Island? But Lenaris was gaping at Mawana. Apparently they didn't know. Mawana seemed to know an awful lot about dragons, enough to make Mocco frown critically as he continued to talk and they sailed on, until Fiona interrupted.

"Is that Cauldron Island?"

A pair of tall stones was emerging from the horizon ahead. Each grew gradually larger, as the damarian and Urai ships sailed closer. Rocky, wall-like hills slowly emerged alongside them, and the towering rocks gave way to opposite facing, sheer cliffs, creating a narrow passage between them. The damarian ships were on a course to sail into that passage. But what on earth would Narz seek on Cauldron Island?

"That's Tava's Gap," said Mawana. "Leading to Blue Bay. It's a narrow passage, so we should be able to contain the damarian ships."

"Then what?" Troy asked.

"They'll try to fight their way out when they realise they are trapped," Mocco answered.

Fiona gasped.

"Do not worry," said Mawana. "The gorans and faeron will attack them from land. We will most likely be stopping sailors trying to flee when they see us manoeuvring to block Tava's Gap."

"So you're confident of taking captives?" Michael asked.

"The geography lends itself to that," Mocco replied.

Linh turned to Fiona, her shoulders slumping.

"So we didn't need to endanger ourselves to question the westerners?" she asked.

"I am sorry," said Mocco. "The Council of Elders were happy to send ships to secure our coast and honour our mutual defence treaty with Tarlah, but only mother seemed to think Cauldron Island could be a target. I wouldn't have offered you the chance to come on board if I hadn't thought it may be your only chance."

Linh frowned. "If Tarlahn's didn't know the island was inhabited, and presumably the Zaldeaans don't either, and your people are the only ones, how does Narz know it's inhabited?"

Mawana shrugged. "Our people didn't tell him."

"My father and Ruarnon's parents could have told him Cauldron Island exits," said Lenaris, "And that it is uninhabited, has no food or water and contains extreme geographic dangers to human life. Perhaps he knows enough about what he seeks to ask questions that revealed to him whether it was there or not."

"There's another possibility," said Michael. "Narz acted like he knew the Zaldeaan army existed, and he might have aimed to capture them all along. Now, he seems to know more about

Cauldron Island than most. *Is* he mad, or does he have access to better knowledge than communication technology makes possible here?"

Linh shivered at the word 'technology' and what it reminded her of. "We saw an archway near Lylah's home in the jungle. And there *is* an archway in the North Lands —the North Landers just don't know how to use it. What if Narz knows? If he's sent spies through the archways and that's how he gathers information?"

"Meaning the only person we'd have reason to believe *might* be able to send *us* home through an archway —aside from Red Cloak— is the damars' creator?" Troy asked, his brows climbing up under his fringe. "*That's* reassuring!"

"It makes sense though," said Michael. "We're missing something about Narz, maybe many things."

"Now may not be the best time to discuss this," said Fiona. "We can't be more than an hour out from Tava's Gap."

Mocco studied Fiona for a moment, apparently recognising the tension in her eyes and the fear in her pale face, which was making her freckles stand out.

"If it comes to fighting," he said, "Ruarnon says you are not very experienced and are to stay below deck."

Lenaris eyed them carefully, but Linh would like to never meet, see or hear a damar again. She doubted her friends' feelings on the subject differed.

"I'll keep you company," Mawana added with a grin.

Before them, Tither and Tarata's ships sailed into the shadow of Tava's Gap. The Gap ran deep, its sheer cliffs dotted with a few trees, their growth stunted by rocks. Gulls cried out and circled above them. Closer by echoed the footsteps of Urai archers gathering on the foredeck.

The Gap was too narrow for captains to risk sailing side by side, so Tither's ship sailed in first, then Tarata's, Mocco's following. The mountains ringing Cauldron Island and the Gap were the perfect natural defence, limiting where ships could approach and how many approached at once. All Flariah needed to have done was station archers with fire arrows on the edge of the cliffs rising on Linh's left and right, and they could have fired the damarian ships before any of them made landfall. But that would have made taking captives difficult. Did Flariah have questions for the westerners too?

The Gap spanned only a few ship lengths. Tither's ship was already turning left out of it, Tarata's angling right. Mocco's ship's captain yelled, and sailors reefed the sails high overhead, prompting the ship to drift to a halt at the end of Tava's Gap.

The bay opened before them, stretching to a low shoreline on its far side, along which four dark vessels were anchored, their sails reefed. One damarian ship was approaching. It was made of dark timbers, but a grey line rippled around its deck: damars, probably hundreds, armed with pale spears rising high above their short figures.

"Time to go below deck," Mocco told Linh and her Aussie friends. "That fight may reach us."

"LOOSE!" Tarata cried in the distance.

A glowing arc sailed through the air, towards the damarian vessel. A few feet from the damarian bulwarks, the entire arc plummeted. Fire arrows hissed as they fell into the sea, and their flames were snuffed out.

Linh gaped.

"LOOSE!" Tither's voice bellowed.

Glowing arrows arced towards damarian sails from the opposite side. They too fell short, plunging into the water beside their target. That *had* to be shield magic.

"They've got *sorcerers onboard*," Linh whispered.

Fiona shivered violently.

"I won't be able to defend you four," said Mawana. "You're going to need me, cousin."

Mocco stared with his mouth open. Then he turned to Mawana. "Go with them! Stay out of sight, keep watch through the spyhole and help me when you can. Lenaris, stay close to me."

Mawana frowned, while Lenaris peered dazedly across the bay.

Linh hesitated. A man in the damarian fighting top opposite raised his arm. Flame glowed above his hand. He dashed his arm forwards and a thin line of flame streaked across the air towards Tarata's ship. Linh stared at fire burning through the sky. Her eyes told her it was magic. Her mind resisted the possibility.

White flashed above Tarata's deck. Flames burst alongside it, flaring to great heights. A semi-opaque dome expanded outwards from Tarata and fire flared across its outside. Then the shield curved towards the fire, engulfing it. The shield faded and where it had burned, only smoke drifted.

Linh's heartbeat thrice. A second line of fire streaked through the air. Tarata's shield caught half of it, but fire danced around its side. The aft mast caught alight. The magical fire blew away as smoke, but the mast continued to burn. Urai rushed towards it, pulling off their shirts to smother the flames, while more raced to lower buckets over the bulwarks to bring up sea water.

"*Your* family can wield *magic*?" Lenaris asked Mocco, her face pale.

Mocco blinked, seeing Mawana and the others still on deck. "*Go!*" he urged.

"Follow me!" Mawana called, rushing towards the foredeck stairs.

Linh struggled to pull her gaze away from the mesmerising sights ahead, but Fiona yanked her arm and pulled her through archers she hadn't noticed gathering on the foredeck behind them. Michael was dragging Troy.

"Sorcerers!" Troy cried as they ran. "We're about to be attacked by a bloody *sorcerer*?"

Linh shivered and gripped the railing with unnecessary force as they hurried down the foredeck stairs. Damars were bad enough.

Her heart thudded against her chest as she followed Mawana between heavily armed Urai soldiers assembling on the main deck. Then Mawana flung open a door into a cabin below the rear deck, gesturing them inside. Linh waited for the others to pass her, then slammed it shut. Barricading themselves ought to shut damars out, but what defence was that against a sorcerer?

Mawana seized a trunk beside one of the two beds built into the cabin walls and dragged it towards the cabin door.

"Damars aren't intelligent enough to open doors," said Troy, eyeing Mawana with one eyebrow raised.

"I prefer to be prepared for everything," Mawana replied. "Especially when I know almost nothing of these creatures."

"You don't seem like a preparation kind of guy," said Troy.

Mawana smiled. "Do not tell my cousin, but not getting killed working with the animals I study requires forethought. I try not to show it the rest of the time, in case Uncle Kahorn ropes me into becoming an apprentice Elder."

"You don't want a position of leadership?" Linh asked.

"I cannot think of anything worse. Give me interesting creatures to work with and the jungle to roam and I will be happy. Tie me to responsibility and sitting through tedious discussions and I will climb the trees to escape."

Troy grinned and Linh rolled her eyes. She, Troy and Michael helped Mawana stack the second chest on top of the first. Linh stepped back. Sweat dripped beneath her bronze armour and the linen shirt she wore underneath it and her arms ached from lifting the chest.

"Why does Mocco want you out of sight?" Michael asked.

Mawana eyed the cabin wall and shook his head, pacing the room. "He's scared. He's never tested his magic against a hostile force before. He knows I've used mine against predators and probably fears I'll take dangerous risks. He might be trying to protect me from myself."

Mawana stood to his total, considerable height, leaning against the trunks to peer through a small glass window above the door, keeping watch on the main deck. Fiona looked through a small cabin window opposite the door. Tava's Gap was falling behind them.

They were sailing towards a ship with a sorcerer on board. Linh's heart hammered against her chest. She gripped her sword hilt, trying to get her rapidly increasing breathing under control.

A roar of creaking timbers broke the silence. Linh was flung forwards as the floor shifted violently.

"We just rammed the enemy ship," said Mawana. "My cousin must be engaging them. Keeping the sorcerer busy by defending his ship against three others ought to weaken him."

Linh leaned against the wall, dizziness overwhelming her at the idea. Troy stood stock still and only Michael and Fiona seemed to be hanging on Mawana's every word. Michael was watching the door and walls like a hawk. Fiona was breathing heavily and drawing her sword, despite that no one appeared to be attacking them… yet. Linh was fingering her sword hilt and gripped it firmly.

Footsteps thumped somewhere on deck, accompanied by the faint hissing of damars and muffled yelling. Linh's muscles tensed as adrenaline flooded her veins. Damars *couldn't* be on board. They'd have to climb the railing *and* fight through soldiers. What the hell was going on out there?

Shouts, shrieks and the beginnings of a melee began outside.

"Linh, your nails," said Fiona.

Linh was gripping her hilt so tightly that her fingernails were digging into the palm of her hand. One was drawing blood. She adjusted her grip, but didn't loosen it.

Troy had begun pacing the room, while Mawana stared through the spy hole.

"Stop!" Michael commanded.

Troy turned, looking wrong-footed.

"I think I hear footsteps. They're getting closer."

Mawana stepped back from the trunks, bending his knees, so he didn't have to duck his head below the ceiling. "I hear them. Sounds like a whole pack approaching."

Mawana pulled a metal-plated club from his waistband, as a hiss echoed beyond their cabin door.

"How can they have got around the Urai soldiers?" Linh asked.

Michael drew his sword. Troy swallowed nervously and did the same. Linh bit down nerves and drew her sword, Fiona moving beside her. Linh took a deep breath and remembered that fighting involved aggression. She was good at that.

A damar screeched outside and the patter of footsteps followed. Crash! The door rattled and Linh tensed. There was another crash and another. Linh shut her eyes.

"They *don't* know how to use axes!" Troy protested.

"They're cleverer," said Michael, his gaze distant.

"The chests are heavy," Linh pointed out. "It would take a whole pack to push through and they're *hopeless* at teamwork."

But the ability to use an axe and keep striking the door, not just any bit of wall at random, suggested these damars *were* smarter. How much of a threat did that make them?

The crash of axe blows continued.

"He must know I'm in here," Mawana said, shaking his head. "Why else would he have creatures target this cabin instead of soldiers they can see on deck?"

"I don't know if anyone *can* command damars," Troy replied. "They tend to just run amok."

"This is not amok," Mawana asserted. "It is a concerted attack."

Linh tried to shake away her dizziness as that truth sunk in. The door rattled and cracks climbed into view above the chests. Thuds sounded, as timber panels fell to the ground. The door stopped rattling. Damars hissed, one shrieked and the chest wobbled. Then it began to inch unevenly forwards.

"Definitely smarter," said Michael, sweat trickling down his forehead.

Linh's insides turned to ice. She doubted the ability to use tools or work in teams had made the damars less savage or strong. New-found intelligence would make them deadlier. Her heart hammered against her chest. How did you fight *intelligent* damars?

The chests stopped moving. The first damar emerged. It was barely up to Linh's shoulder, its hide pale grey, its yellow eyes glinting while its fanged mouth opened in a snarl. Mawana's club struck its head with a crack, sending the creature sprawling. Mawana stepped full circle, knocking the second damar to the ground. The third damar thrust its spear towards him. Troy seized the spear with his left hand and ran the creature through with his sword.

"Don't grab their weapons," he yelled. "It's bloody strong as I am!"

Mawana's club knocked a fourth damar's spear aside. He leapt sideways as it thrust at him. Two more damars emerged. Michael rushed forwards, knocking one spearhead aside. The second spearhead created sparks as it ground against Michael's armour. Michael cried out as the blade bit into his upper arm.

Linh ducked the blade and thrust her own sword into the creature's middle, grimacing as her blade ground against bone.

Fiona groaned, her blade resisting a spearhead swinging at Linh's head.

Linh withdrew her weapon and tried to back up. There wasn't enough room. She knocked Fiona, who screamed. Linh ducked the spearhead stabbing towards her as she stumbled back. She gasped, as an unseen force pressed her, and her body fought the pressure. A spearhead was grinding against the side of her armour.

She cut upwards, her blade angling the spear away, but the damar pushed back. She kicked desperately at its shins and it fell. Mawana's club thudded against its head and it lay silent.

Mawana danced around Linh, steering her aside with his free hand. He knocked out the damar Fiona was fending off with her sword. Troy moaned ahead of them. He was clutching his exposed armpit, which was bleeding heavily.

Damars lay unconscious or bleeding around him. Michael lay on the floor, looking dazed. He sat slowly, seeming to have no new wounds other than the bloody gash on his arm.

Linh ran to Troy, tore a handful of linen off the bottom of her tunic and stuffed it under his arm. He cried out again.

"I'm sorry," she said, her fingers trembling as blood seeped through the cloth. "But we have to stop the bleeding. It looks bad."

Linh jumped at a loud groan. It was Mawana shoving a chest back against the cabin door, beyond which shouts and the clash of weapons and armour had got louder.

"I don't see any more coming towards us. My kin are keeping them busy on deck," Mawana reported, surveying the main deck through the top of the hacked-apart cabin door. "Get him on the bed. Michael put a hand on that wound and keep it there till I tend it."

Linh tried to keep pressure on Troy's wound, as Troy slowly sat on the other bed. His face was ashen and sweaty. His eyes were still wide with fear or shock.

"He can still sit upright," said Mawana, moving Linh's blood-soaked handful of tunic and replacing it with a wad of linen. "The wound can't be too deep. Best he sleeps it off."

"What?" Troy asked.

"Hold this," Mawana told Linh, who bit her lip and forced her trembling hands to reapply pressure to the wad of fabric Mawana held over Troy's wound. Fiona stepped beside her, holding Troy's hand, her eyes wide with worry.

"Lie down," Mawana told Troy, who shifted and lay on the bed.

Mawana opened one of the trunks and fumbled for a moment, then returned to Troy's side. "Drink this," he said, offering Troy a wooden cup.

Troy took it and grimaced as he drank. Then Mawana took the cup back and Troy rested his head on the pillow.

"What was that?" Michael asked, as Troy's eyes drooped.

"Sleeping drought," Mawana replied. "I use it on wounded animals sometimes."

Mawana shifted, then moved back into Linh's view with bandages.

"Ease your pressure off, slowly," he told Linh.

She obeyed, flinching at how much blood Troy had lost. Mawana partially lifted and hastily set about bandaging Troy's wound.

"You don't just catch animals?" Michael asked him.

Mawana smiled, still intent on his work. "I've kept all sorts of animals as pets. But treating them isn't as scary as treating a wounded human."

Faster than Linh anticipated, Mawana tied off the bandages. "That's the best I can do till our surgeon sees him. I'm not sure how best to treat anything deeper than a cut. Show me your wound," he added, turning to Michael.

Michael lowered the hem of his linen tunic.

"You'll need stitches."

"Can you knock me out first?" Michael replied. "I'm guessing painkillers here aren't great."

"They aren't. But a blow from my fist will put you out more surely than the sleeping draught."

Linh's mouth dropped open. Michael nodded.

Mawana moved so fast that Linh flinched in surprise at the crack of his fist striking Michael's head. Michael fell back on the bed.

"Keep pressure on his wound," Mawana ordered Fiona, while he rummaged in the top trunk. Then he approached with a needle and thread.

"You're doing it yourself?" Linh asked, gaping.

Mawana grinned. "I make all sorts of specialist clothing for my job. I'm handy with a needle and thread. I'll take care not to mar your friend's good looks with an ugly scar."

Linh frowned but Fiona giggled.

"What's happening outside?" Mawana asked.

Linh wasn't sure if he wanted to know or was just encouraging them to look away while he stitched Michael up or both. She was happy not to watch the grisly work, so she stood and peered over the trunks. It was quieter beyond the cabin door now. She could see why.

"The main deck is starting to clear. I see a few soldiers fighting before the foredeck. It looks like they've pushed the damars back."

A loud splash punctuated her comment. "Or thrown them overboard," she added, grimacing.

That was death by drowning for damars. Why would anyone pit the creatures against soldiers, knowing they'd be killed off like that?

"Good. Any sign of smoke?"

Linh tensed, remembering the sorcerer's fire magic. She scanned the deck and shook her head. Though there *was* smoke in the air.

"It doesn't seem to be on our ship. But something is burning."

Mawana exhaled deeply and Linh turned, bracing herself for an ugly sight. It wasn't too bad. Michael's arm was stitched and Mawana was wiping away the blood. He was calm and knew what to do. He seemed experienced at this kind of thing.

Linh shoved the image of a spearhead moving towards her and the other stabbing for Fiona away. There hadn't been much room, but she'd panicked, been clumsy and endangered her best friend. Guilt made her stomach roil. At least Fiona seemed unharmed. Linh's armour was scratched, but she was pretty sure the blood on her hands and clothes was mostly Troy's. The sight still made her lightheaded. They'd have to try harder not to panic next time.

Mawana finished his work and stood, surveying the bodies of creatures across the cabin floor, which he had probably slain, his mouth a grim line.

"I have seen strange creatures on Cauldron Island, but we have never anything like *them*. They are almost as strong as Troy but no brawnier than Fiona. Their strength is entirely unnatural. I have never seen anything so vicious. An animal that attacks people who do not threaten it and whom it does not intend to eat… with weapons… They are an abomination.

"I will send guards to stand with your friends while they rest. I need to check on my cousin, father and aunt."

He stepped swiftly over the bodies, vaulted the trunks and disappeared up the foredeck stairs. A pair of Urai soon approached, nodding to Fiona as they climbed the trunks. One smiled at Michael's arm. "That boy is good. He'd make a fine healer."

"What's happening outside?" Linh asked and the mirth faded from both soldiers' faces.

"Tarata and Tither are fighting their way towards the sorcerer. He is trying to kill them. Mocco is trying to defend them and no doubt his cousin will help."

"Have your people ever fought sorcerers before?" Fiona asked.

The man's firm grip on his sword hilt and the muscles around his bare shoulders tensed. "Never."

Linh's breath caught. But keeping an unconscious Michael and a drugged, sleeping Troy company while Ruarnon's new allies fought for their lives made her limbs rigid with tension.

"Is the deck of this ship clear of damars?" she asked.

The soldiers nodded. "We are to stay with these two. We can't follow if you leave this room. And it's not a good idea."

But she wouldn't have to. The top trunk didn't fully cover the bottom one at Linh's end. There was just enough room for her small foot to step on, as she climbed onto the second trunk, to sit with her head bent under the ceiling. She turned to cries, hisses and clashing weapons on her left.

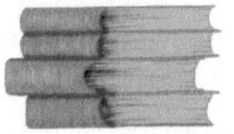

CHAPTER 5

SORCERERS -LINH

L inh stared at a glowing object in the sky ahead. Fire burned through the air towards the ship's deck on her left. Her heart thundered against her chest. Someone groaned. The fire began to flare sideways. The flames flickered, a warm breeze blew across the deck, then the fire faded to smoke, which was blown away by the wind.

She clutched her chest, grappling with the fact that in a split second the whole deck and every Urai soldier standing on it had been spared being set alight.

"By the sky gods!" one of the soldiers murmured behind Linh. "They *can* wield shield magic!"

"You didn't know?" Linh asked shakily, unsure whether the idea of being attacked or defended by magic made her giddier.

"The prophetess has always chosen families to stay with her in the jungle, just as her sister chooses others to stay on Cauldron Island. But we never knew why. There were only stories and it appears the wildest ones are true," the woman replied.

Linh shivered. The Tarlahns had seemed to think magic and the Sorcery War were a myth. Even the existence of damars hadn't fully convinced Monin. But the North Landers *and* Urai could wield magic. And Narz employed at least one magic wielder. The world was a more dangerous place than it had been when she arrived.

Linh blinked dazedly at her surroundings. Mocco's ship lay sideways across Tava's Gap. It felt stationary. On her left, damarian screeches rose. Tarata's and Tither's ships were anchored flanking the damarian ship. Damars shrieked on the foredeck left and above. Crudely cut damarian spears clashed with Urai animal hide shields. Urai advanced, their shields pressing damars back as they stabbed round them with spears. Fire burnt down to the damarian main deck, obscured by its foredeck.

"Chaos take them!" Mocco cried on Linh's right. "She is going after him herself!"

Linh's jaw dropped. A lone woman was climbing the rigging above the damarian foredeck, towards the fighting top. Linh's fists clenched as fire flared towards Tarata. White flashed above the Urai woman, flames glancing off it. The sorcerer was trying to kill Tarata and Tarata *could* wield shield magic. Linh's head spun.

Tarata wasn't alone. Her guards climbed below her, fighting off damars pursuing her up the rigging. More Urai climbed the rigging on the left, led by the biggest man Linh had ever seen. Was that Mawana's father, Tither?

Bare-chested and leather clad Urai fought their way onto the damarian foredeck. Linh frowned at those fighting closest. They stabbed at damars which ducked or sidestepped their spear points. She gaped as a damar stabbed at an Urai neck instead of the woman's bronze-armoured chest. The woman deflected the blow, so it stabbed at her exposed thigh. The wounded woman backed up. The creature sidestepped a spear thrust from another Urai and jabbed at the man's exposed upper arm.

Linh's insides turned cold. These creatures had a sense of self-preservation. They knew that striking bronze armour or shields did no damage. And how to survive fighting and attack to wound. She stared, as damar after damar tried to deflect Urai spear thrusts. This wasn't a collection of brutal hunters. It was a damarian army.

Linh frowned. The damars on the damarian foredeck seemed to be getting more numerous as she watched, despite Urai cutting enough down to make her grimace. One point was thick with damars. Were they climbing up from below deck?

"Infantry, target damars on the rigging!" Mocco ordered on the foredeck. "Guard the rigging for Tarata and Tither!"

Above the damarian decks, Tither swung his feet up, as rigging halfway to the fighting top smoked. Linh cringed at further evidence of fire magic trying to burn people, while she watched helplessly. One of Tither's guards swatted his burning shirt with the flat of his sword. Surely Tither had shield magic too. Was it weakening?

The sorcerer's hands flashed with fire. Linh tensed. An arrow struck him in the shoulder. The fire vanished and more arrows fell harmlessly as the sorcerer drew his sword. Linh sighed.

Shouts rose closer by. Urai had raised a gangplank from Mocco's foredeck to his mother's. Mocco's soldiers clambered across, disappearing down Tarata's foredeck stairs. Linh couldn't see where they were boarding, but after a while, Urai were advancing up the damarian foredeck.

Linh's breath caught. Tarata hunched below the small dome of her magical white shield just below the fighting top. She'd reached it! But fire flared against her shield continually. Like an unceasing flame thrower. Linh gaped. It froze her to her seat.

More and more fire flared out, onto the shield. Powerful. Unstoppable. Even if Tarata could shield herself from it, what if she passed out from the exertion? What if that raw heated magic rained down on the damarian decks? Or on the deck Linh sat on?

Linh began shivering uncontrollably, gripping her sword hilt for dear life. But what good was a sword against the inexorable fire pouring down in waves on Tarata, atop the damarian main mast?

A large figure moved nimbly on the fighting top, the shadow breaking her transfixed gaze on fire flowing from the sorcerer's hands. Tither's sword blade flashed in the sunlight, as he thrust it forwards. Sparks flew, as his blade ground against the sorcerer's shield. The sorcerer trembled as they faced off against each other.

Tither's sword pierced the shield and sorcerer. The sorcerer screamed, dropping his sword, which tumbled to the deck below. Tither struck him in the face and he crumpled at the big man's feet.

Linh shuddered. Then she gasped for air and tried to relax her tense body, which appeared to have stopped breathing. The sorcerer lay on the base of the fighting top. He wasn't moving. The threat was neutralised.

Neutralised. Why were her shoulders so tight? Why was it still hard to breathe?

Tarata's guards felled the last damars on the rigging. Urai stood lower down, fighting off damars attacking from the dark decks.

"It's like he summoned them." One of the two guards in the cabin behind her leaned over the trunk beside Linh, shaking her head in wonder.

Linh frowned.

"More attacked the rigging when Tarata neared the sorcerer," the woman added, her voice dull, but sounding oddly normal, given the sight that was burned into Linh's retinas.

Linh shivered. "Mawana thought the damars who attacked us were sent after him. Maybe the sorcerer can control the damars, somehow."

It was a terrifying thought. Surely only a psychopath could, or would choose to control creatures like that, let alone wield them against humans?

"You can come out now!" Mawana was waving from the foredeck. His features softened as they met her gaze. "It's safe, I swear on my life!" he added.

Linh managed a weak smile in reply, then climbed down from the trunks. She planted both feet firmly on the ground and took a deep breath, trying to pull herself together. Two beds caught her eye, and the unconscious forms of Michael and Troy lying on them.

"They won't be moving for a while," said the other soldier. "We'll stay with them till the fighting's over."

"Can you tell them we're with Mocco?" Fiona asked from the edge of Troy's bed.

The man nodded. His companion shoved both trunks aside, letting Linh and Fiona out of the cabin. Linh felt her shoulders tensing and exhaled deeply, willing them to relax. The main deck was almost empty. There were few traces of blood, which she wrenched her gaze away from. Most fighting seemed to have happened on the damarian ship and maybe Tarata and Tither's ships.

"Mawana wouldn't have called us out if it wasn't safe," Fiona said quietly. "What did you see?" she added.

"Fire pouring from a sorcerers' hands, halting centimetres from Tarata's face." To Linh's surprise, it helped to say it. It made breathing a little easier. "They're like gods," she added. "The sorcerers with their fire magic and the Urai with their shield magic. The damars were like ants clambering futilely for attention below as those two fought. I never had any illusions of grandeur, but that display of raw power, I've never felt so small. Not in the face of anything else."

"What happened to the sorcerer?" Fiona asked, her face pale.

"Tither knocked him out, but he stabbed him first. I hope it was fatal. We're all much safer if it was."

Fiona's mouth dropped open at Linh sincerely wishing someone dead. But it didn't alter Linh's feelings, other than adding a pang of guilt to them. She grit her teeth, fought down the apprehension building in her chest and led the way across the main deck. Her shoulders were still incredibly tense but walking and trying to breathe normally helped.

The shouts, screeches of damars and hisses were louder from the main deck. But the sound distracted her from the flow of fire and her helplessness atop and surrounded by flammable wood.

She took another deep breath and climbed the foredeck stairs. Fresh air blowing across the foredeck prompted Linh to breathe more deeply, and her shoulders to relax, as she filled her lungs with clean air.

Tither still stood atop the fighting top, supervising his soldiers as they passed the limp sorcerer to each other, down the rigging. The threat was still neutralised. She could watch the battle in relative safety.

"Ware!" cried a man on another Urai ship. Linh frowned, as she stepped beside Mocco and Mawana at the railing, where Lenaris stood frozen, her mouth wide with awe.

"We can wield shield magic," Mawana said softly, holding Linh's gaze, probably suspecting how stressed she was.

"I suppose you can knock out sorcerers in one punch too?" she asked, attempting humour, eyeing Mawana's considerable biceps.

Mawana's face split in a grin. Then he grimaced at the sorcerer. "I'd rather not get so close to the bastard."

"Your father is handling it well," said Mocco, his gaze also fixed on the unconscious sorcerer. "The fruit does not fall far from the tree," he added, in what Linh initially thought was a question but must be a statement, to make Mawana smile that way. Mocco returned his cousin's smile.

They could both wield shield magic. The idea would have been discomforting, had she not seen the sorcerer wield fire magic first. But Mawana's easy manner and the usually stiff upper-lipped Mocco bantering with his cousin put her more at ease.

She scanned the sea beyond, wondering what the cry had warned against. Two dark timbered ships advanced towards the stationary ship Tarata and Tither's ships were anchored beside. Both damarian decks were bare.

Fire arced above one approaching ship, burning towards Tither's. Linh's shoulders tightened. She flinched, as flames lashed

Tither's portside bulwarks, which caught alight. Fiona shivered beside her, as soldiers on-board shouted.

Mocco raised his hands, pointing beyond Tither's ship.

Was he going to wield magic? When they were standing right beside him?

"Cast it around the sorcerer cousin," Mawana said quietly. "He is a smaller space to shield."

Linh relaxed slightly. Keep the magic away. She didn't want it anywhere near her.

To the left, shouts rose from Tarata's ship, where more flames flared.

A pale white shield formed around the sorcerer Mocco faced. Sweat beaded down Mocco's forehead.

Linh scanned the damarian ship directly ahead. Tarata faced the sorcerer Mocco was shielding and appeared to be helping Mocco. But Tither was still supervising his guards as they lifted the wounded sorcerer below sight onto the main deck, leaving Mawana to contain the second sorcerer by himself. How strong was the cousins' magic?

Mocco groaned. The sorcerer on the approaching ship punched Mocco's shield. Linh flinched. He struck again and Mocco paled as he strained to reinforce the shield. Linh wanted him to bolster his shield. To keep everyone safe. But it was sapping all his energy…

"Don't push yourself too hard," Mawana cautioned, not taking his eyes off the other sorcerer further left. "Let go for a moment and let him fall over."

"I didn't invite Ruarnon's friends onboard to get them killed," Mocco replied softly, his voice strained.

Linh stared. Sorcery terrified her, but was a man she had just met risking his life to save her and Fiona? They could swim. Jumping overboard from this height was unthinkably frightening, but Mawana would probably throw her overboard if she asked. And fire wouldn't do much harm if they all dived underwater...

The two damarian ships advanced within arrow shot of Tither's. Half the sorcerer's fist poked through Mocco's shield. Fiona gasped. How much energy was maintaining a shield against that level of force draining from Mocco? How many punches of the shield would kill him? Sorcery sent shivers down Linh's spine, but Mocco looked prepared to kill himself stopping it, and she wouldn't allow that.

"Mocco, you have to let go!" Linh urged, reaching to hold his shoulder, until he turned a tense glance to her.

The fist withdrew and the sorcerer pushed the shield with both hands. Mocco's shoulder was sliding from Linh's fingers. She gaped, as he fainted. On the edge of her vision, his shield collapsed. Lenaris caught Mocco and lowered him to the deck. His chest rose slightly, then fell. Linh gasped. He was just unconscious. Thank the Ancestors!

Further left, the sorcerer staggered forwards. He raised his arms. Fire flared above and burned away from him. Arrows from Tither's deck struck him and the fire was extinguished as he fell.

Linh's shoulders sagged and she breathed freely again.

With their protector defeated, the paddles of that damarian ship extended, as sailors tried to retreat. Tither and his soldiers boarded his ship and its sails were set in pursuit.

Mawana groaned. His shield also contained a sorcerer, who was pushing against the shield with both hands.

"Don't keep doing that!" Linh warned. "Try something different," she clutched at straws. "Something he won't expect!"

Mawana smiled wickedly. His shield vanished. Another formed in the air between Mocco's ship and the approaching vessel, moving swiftly. The second sorcerer cried out and turned to flee. The shield struck him and sent him flying. He landed heavily on the far side of his foredeck. Mawana leaned heavily on the railing with both arms, gasping for breath, sweat dripping down his forehead.

"Are you ok?" Linh asked.

Mawana nodded. "I know my limits."

How on earth could he know his limits? When Mocco clearly didn't. Had he used his magic in battle before? But the Urai hadn't fought in his lifetime...

Fiona shuffled beside her. She was positioning Mocco in the recovery position, with Lenaris' help. Mocco's face was frighteningly pale.

"Is he all right?" Linh asked.

Mawana's brow creased as he knelt beside his cousin. "He has never exerted himself like this before."

"That looks like surrender," said an Urai soldier nearby, pointing across Blue Bay at two damarian ships anchored before Rueman's Plains. A dozen men stood on both aft decks, none wearing armour. A man on each deck held a spear aloft, with a white tunic tied to it.

"It may be genuine surrender," said Lenaris. "They think we have four sorcerers walking our decks."

She said it almost happily. Standing on a deck with two men who could wield magic, even if one was unconscious, didn't seem to worry her at all.

Linh strained her ears. "One of those westerners is trying to talk to us," she said. "But I can't make out his words."

Mawana called to the captain to take them closer. Sailors scurried overhead, lowering sails. Then Mocco's ship turned, sailing around Tarata's, towards the far side of Blue Bay, where two damarian ships were still anchored. The remaining two damarian ships were trying to sail for Tava's Gap around Tither's ship, which gave chase, Tarata's turning to help.

A man on one of the two anchored ships shouted and Linh frowned. She had no way of knowing whether the man was speaking Timbalen, Migryan or another language. To her ears it sounded like English. "I think I understand him," she said.

Mawana's eyes widened. "Surely the distant land you come from isn't in the Far West?"

"He says there's been a misunderstanding," Linh pressed on. "That he means no harm to his kin."

Mawana's eyes widened, but thankfully he didn't comment on Linh not answering his question. She exchanged a relieved look with Fiona.

Mawana shook his head. "My people are not descended from the Far West. We have lived in our jungle since the beginning of the world. How can *we* be his kin?"

Linh bit her lip. If she yelled for clarification, experience in the Zaldeaan Realm told her Mawana and the Urai would hear her in Timbalen while the westerner would hear her in whatever language they spoke. And the soldier who had witnessed her speaking two languages simultaneously in the Zaldeaan Realm had been freaked out by it.

She was saved the risk by the man speaking again. She shivered at his words, then translated for Mawana. "He considers your family to be kin. He thinks you're sorcerers and he doesn't want to fight his own kind. He's a sorcerer, but he's surrendering."

"Only until he sees which side wins the battle on the island, I expect," a soldier on Mawana's other side commented.

"The man on the other ship's a sorcerer too," said Fiona. "He says he doesn't wish to fight his kind either and that he surrenders."

The revelation two more sorcerers stood within arrow shot had Linh clutching the railing tightly. Even if they claimed they weren't going to fight, they could overpower Mawana, if they changed their minds.

"We will deal with them, son," Tither's voice called nearby.

Mawana shook his head and smiled. The damarian ships which had attempted to flee were turning towards the coastline, as was Tarata's ship. Tither's ship was sailing back to shore, angling for the two anchored ships.

"How will he deal with them?" Linh asked Mawana.

"There's two of them, one of him and their friends both tried to kill us with fire magic we're barely strong enough to withstand," Mawana replied. "And they could be lying. Father won't take risks."

Linh reminded herself to breathe, as Tither's soldiers approached the sorcerers. She stared, as the Urai stepped right beside the sorcerers. Fists swung as fast as Mawana's had to knock Michael out, bringing both sorcerers rapidly to their decks. Linh sighed. The Battle of Blue Bay was over. But it looked like four of the five damarian ships had unloaded their savage cargo. What were the damars and possibly more sorcerers fighting on Cauldron Island?

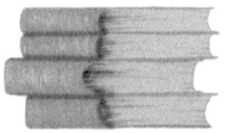

CHAPTER 6

CAULDRON ISLAND'S SECRETS ~ LINH

Father is signalling us closer," Mawana told Linh, Lenaris and Fiona, as a pair of Urai carried Mocco off to join Troy and Michael in the cabin and the ship sailed nearer the mainland.

"We won't be involved in any more fighting?" Linh asked.

Mawana shook his head. "Flariah gave strict orders that none of our ships is to make landfall. We are simply to guard the western ships until the end of the battle, so no one on land can swim out to them and sail away."

"She wants to capture all the humans Narz sent?" Lenaris asked.

"It sounds like she wants to capture everything," Mawana replied. "Though I cannot imagine how she plans to contain the damars. I have only once encountered creatures so savage."

"Where?" Lenaris asked.

Mawana nodded to Cauldron Island. "If the other reptiles on that island are like the one I once fled, the fighting between reptiles and damars will be vicious."

His lips twisted in distaste.

"You… pity the damars?" Linh asked.

"No creature should die the way I suspect many will on that island," Mawana replied.

Linh frowned and decided she didn't want to know what he meant. She suspected Fiona didn't either.

"I won't let the ship get too close," Mawana added. "I don't presume to speak for the three of you, but I have no desire to watch slaughter."

Why was Lenaris gazing dreamy eyed at him? Why was it making Fiona smile?

Linh shook her head and surveyed the approaching coastline with her heart beating too fast, and adrenaline building inside her, not that she had any intention of fighting, and not that fleeing was an option. Inland from the rocky shore ahead, a mass of grey-skinned creatures tried to fight its way in all directions on land.

On the far side of the battlefield was the bright glow of many figures standing side by side. They appeared to be people, humanoid in shape but too tall. Either side stood broader, equally tall figures, towering over the damars. Linh squinted. The broad figures were swinging clubs, knocking down damars advancing towards them.

"Gorans," said Mawana. "Normally, they carve stone and some like to read. They are only bad-tempered if you offend them. I expect they find damars offensive."

"Are they *giants*?" Fiona whispered.

"They are at least a head taller than me and some are taller," Mawana replied.

Linh exchanged a wide-eyed look with Fiona. Mawana was over six feet tall. How tall were gorans? Seven feet? Eight?

The glow across the rear of the battlefield was moving—the writhing grey mass of damars before it slowing and standing still. There was a gap between the glowing people and the damars. And it was widening, the edge of the damarian lines rippling as if their front lines were falling, for no apparent reason…

"What are the bright things?" Linh asked.

"The faeron," Mawana replied. "They are another ancient people. And from the way damars are collapsing before them, it appears they can wield sleep magic." Mawana's face went slack. "I didn't know that was possible."

Linh stared at the glowing faeron. At tens of people hidden away on a desert island, whom not even the neighbouring Tarlahns knew existed. Had Narz known they were here? But why attack them? Why antagonise an entire magic wielding race who had done nothing to him?

Linh shook her head. The more she learned of the Narz, the more questions she had and the less sense he seemed to make.

"He sent enough damars to fight everyone," Fiona said softly. "Even with those lizards fighting at the edges. The faeron, gorans and lizards are outnumbered. Maybe three times over. It's as if he sent damars here hoping they'd kill every living thing."

Fiona shuddered and Linh squeezed her shoulder, her own shoulders tightening with tension.

No one thought Narz had sent damars to the Zaldeaan Realm to massacre Zaldeaans. But given the numbers and the damarian instinct to kill any other living thing that came near them, what else could they achieve here?

"What's that?" Fiona asked.

Linh followed her gaze to a chasm across the plains, with a strange red glow emanating from it.

"The banks of Lava River," Mawana replied, "a subterranean stream of liquid fire flowing through the base of a deep chasm in the rock."

Linh stared at the glowing crack. No wonder the Timbalens never settled here. With its inhabitants and geography, it must be the most dangerous place this side of Umarinaris.

She turned back to the battle. Gorans started to encircle damars on the nearest side. There was still room to flee, but the remaining damars faced the battle, the odd creature falling or stumbling forwards, pushing each other to get to the fighting.

She shook her head. Damars the Tarlahns had fought in the Zaldeaan Realm had hunted in packs. At most, two packs would attack the same group of soldiers. But there must be several hundred packs in front of her, shoulder to shoulder, all fighting the same enemy side by side, faeron, goran or lizard.

"Why are they fighting together?" she asked.

Mawana shivered. "They press towards Flariah's people with the same focus and determination as the ones who attacked us in Mocco's cabin. In stark contrast to everything Ruarnon told my family about damars. As if something drives them forwards. I suspect there are sorcerers on the battlefield, controlling them, somehow."

"Look!" Fiona cried.

A thrashing human rose above the damars, kicking and twisting as his body floated in mid-air over the writhing grey mass. Fire flared before him, streaking through the air in multiple lines and Linh stopped breathing. The fire halted beside the gorans on

Linh's right, before a figure in shining bronze armour, whose long red hair blew in the wind. A human. Their arms were outstretched, a white shield emanating from them. When the flames neared, white mist engulfed them and smoke puffed up through it, clearing to nothing. A human sorcerer fighting *for* Cauldron Island?

The figure hanging in the air seized something that glinted in the sunlight –a blade– and slashed at the air beside them. They tilted, hanging diagonally. They cut an arc around themself, slashed under their feet and dropped halfway back down to the damars.

Linh frowned, but Mawana's mouth was opening in wonder. "His blade can cut magic..."

"He's the one controlling the damar packs," Lenaris added, pointing at damars on the right side of the battle. They were shoving each other in all directions, some skirting the nearest lizards and running away across the plains.

Iron specs glinted over the battlefield. Gorans were shooting arrows at the sorcerer suspended above the damarian mass. Their arrows glanced off a meter short, raining among the damars. Fire flashed around the gorans beside the red-haired figure, but faeron were moving towards them, a yellow shield forming before the faeron, engulfing the flames and reducing them to smoke.

A few bowshots away sorcerers were loose on the island, and being contained by faeron, who appeared to be a race of sorcerers. The hair on the back of Linh's neck and all down her arms stood on end as she gaped.

The floating sorcerer jerked, spasmed, then hung limply. He floated towards the red-haired human and a goran slung him over its shoulder and disappeared behind other gorans. Damars screeched and began to flee from the near side of the battlefield, where neither faeron, gorans, nor lizards had encircled them. Glowing faeron sprinted around the battlefield towards the fleeing damars.

The redhead turned to the fleeing creatures. The damars slowed, then halted. Others were turning from foes surrounding them on three sides and fleeing towards the gap their companions had made. They too slowed.

Linh gaped as the damars formed lines and marched towards barren hills behind the battlefield.

Mawana shivered. "I had no idea Flariah had that kind of power," he said.

"That's Flariah? She's as powerful as the sorcerer she just defeated," said Lenaris.

"More so I suspect," Mawana replied. He hesitated, then added, "I know Lylah and Flariah look human, but I've never really been convinced."

There was a thump on the deck. An Urai sailor had fainted. Another had his hands raised beseechingly and was whispering, "Protect us from them! Let no one suffer again the horrors we have heard of the Sorcery War!"

"It might be good Ruarnon isn't here and they left their army at home," Mawana said quietly. "The sight of that much magic being wielded…" he shook his head. "It makes *me* dizzy, and I have been forming shield magic since I was four years old. It is a shock to my people, but I suspect seeing people shape magic will be a worse shock to the Tarlahns. Though you seem to be handling it well," he added to Lenaris.

Lenaris shook her head wordlessly. She stood still, though Linh noticed her tan knuckles turning white as she gripped the spear she held.

"It is the myths brought to life," she said. "I see it, I have seen it, but part of me still does not believe."

Mawana smiled. "I felt the same way about learning magic. I'd promise that seeing and wielding it gets easier, but my first sight of magic being shaped was Lylah demonstrating it in a safe environment, not on a battlefield." He paused, then his eyes lit up as he added, "but perhaps you are made of stronger stuff than I."

Fiona had a hand over her mouth and was trying not to laugh. Sorcerers were fighting each other for the first time since a war most people on board this ship viewed as a myth, and he was *flirting* with her?

"Then again," Mawana added turning to Linh and Fiona, "if Fiona can smile at a time like this, clearly her spirit is strongest of all."

Fiona did laugh out loud then.

"You're worse than Troy," Linh said, shaking her head.

For a moment Mawana looked worried, but then Lenaris shocked her by saying, "More mature though. And neither is a bad thing."

Mawana's lips split into a smile and Linh shook her head. When Troy woke up and realised just how much he had in common with Mawana, the two of them were going to be insufferable. In the meantime, there was a war on.

Gradually, hundreds of damars on the nearest side of the battlefield formed lines and marched into the hills, following Flariah, like a twisted retelling of the Pied Piper. Faeron were beginning to march either side of the damarian lines, making Linh wonder if their magic was helping control the creatures.

"It's silent out there," said Fiona.

She was right. The hissing and screeching had stopped. The damars were barefooted and Linh stood too far away to hear the soft pad of their footsteps as they marched. But the creatures made no verbal sounds, no hisses or screeches, as if Flariah and her faeron had absolute control of them.

The question Troy would have asked leapt to mind. "Please tell me Flariah has never wanted to wage war against anyone?"

Mawana's eyes widened and his brows furrowed. "I believe she has trained some North Lander sorcerers, possibly their most powerful ones. But the North Landers are sworn never to use their powers aggressively. I think Flariah taught them to master their powers, so they were not a danger to themselves or others."

Linh shivered again. "She and the faeron are controlling the damars like they've done this before."

Fiona gasped. "The lizards are scurrying away. *All* of them. Why did *they* help the gorans and faeron contain the damars? Gorans and faeron are intelligent, but reptiles?"

Linh bit her lip and shook her head. "Can Flariah control *them* too? Is that why she and the faeron seem so practised at herding damars?"

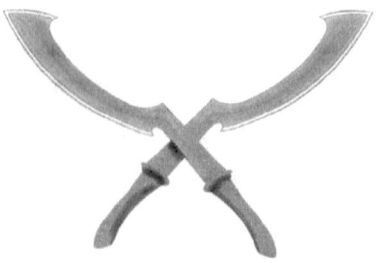

Chapter 7

In Flarian's Palace –Ruarnon

Ruarnon sat at the table in their ship's cabin, with their head in their hands. The report they'd received from the battle at Cauldron Island had come from Lenaris and Linh, with Mawana weighing in. Lenaris' handwriting was neat and recognisable, but simply ceased mid-sentence several times, while Linh's handwriting was erratic, several half-sentences heavily crossed out. Linh's shock and confusion were clear from the writing alone, but her words…

They confirmed the man who held Ruarnon's parents' prisoner had sorcerers at his command, at least one of whose powers was comparable to the very worst sorcerers of the not-so-mythical Sorcery War. Ruarnon's stomach roiled at someone they trusted confirming in absolute terms that they were poorly equipped to recover their parents and Pamoran, let alone their uncle or any Zaldeaan soldiers from the Far West.

Monin had always thought the latter a foolish dream and even Tor had reservations about it. But Ruarnon could hardly mount an expedition to recover most of their living family members, after months of uncertainty, and not attempt the same for Zaldeaan subjects missing brothers, fathers and uncles. Now, it seemed a moot point.

They jumped at a knock on the door.

"Ruarnon, it is Tor."

The Royal Council already knew the contents of Linh's letter. Monin had had visible reservations about a report partly written by a seventeen-year-old girl and an outsider at that. Still, Lenaris and Mawana's comments had given even Monin pause and Ruarnon had granted their advisors the voyage to Cauldron Island to process the report, before they discussed its contents. But delaying that conversation only added tension to Ruarnon's posture.

"Come in," Ruarnon replied.

"Do not worry about it all now," said Tor, the moment he had closed the cabin door. "The sorcerers and sailors the Urai captured will provide information and there is no point considering the danger until then."

Ruarnon tried to ignore the tension that made their shoulders ache. Only the Urai had any means of resisting sorcerers and there were only four Urai Ruarnon knew of who could wield magic, none of whom had any reason to join Companion Noma's western expedition to gather information, let alone help Ruarnon recover their loved ones from the Far West.

"Worrying about it now," said Tor, "is like worrying about how the construction of a new road will work before you map it out on the terrain, and decide whether you will dig tunnels through hillsides or build bridges. I know the odds do not favour us, but we are yet to consider how to counter them or to question westerners who can provide information."

Ruarnon nodded. But all this sitting around and waiting for news and information, which continued to be bad news, was becoming frustrating. It made their limbs itch to get up and move. Yet all that lay before them was more information gathering, more endless debating and planning. Of course it was necessary, but it was getting harder to bear.

As days and whole seasons had slipped by, the sight of their parents in memories faded, the sound of their voices became fainter and began to blur with those of men and women Ruarnon heard more often and more recently.

"Let's go on deck," Ruarnon suggested. "I want a good view of Cauldron Island. To see the place Narz attacked for reasons we once again cannot identify."

Tor inclined his head and followed them to the foredeck. The rocky mountains Linh had described as ringing the island weren't visible on the horizon yet. It sounded like Mocco and Mawana had done what they could to protect Ruarnon's friends, but they had struggled to meet damars on foot in an enclosed space.

"I'm worried about Troy," Ruarnon said.

"I suspect Lenaris will continue training your foreign friends in hand-to-hand combat. The boy has something of Arlian in him. If I know her, she will do anything to ensure she does not lose another protégé."

Ruarnon sighed. Tor was right, on both counts. Lenaris seemed stricter with Troy, harder on him, but perhaps she was more protective of him and feared the qualities he had in common with Arliarn could get him killed too.

Hypothetically, Ruarnon's Australian friends wouldn't need to face danger again until they sailed with the recovery expedition Ruarnon desperately hoped they could still send west. But this was their friend's second unintended encounter with damars and their third encounter with the creatures overall. Their Australian friends tended to end up in danger and the more time they spent training with Lenaris the better.

Without the company of friends as a distraction, it seemed to take a long time before two towers of natural-looking rock rose like gateways on either side of a blue stream of water to Blue Bay. The entrance was narrow enough and the mountains surrounding the island ragged enough, that you'd have to approach from the right angle to stumble across it, if your captain wasn't navigating using Mawana's directions.

The Timbalens who first settled Tarlah hadn't found Tava's Gap. The report Companion Tor had dug out of the castle archives spoke of scaling the mountains, of barren soil, frightful temperatures and deep pools emitting dense clouds of steam, in which the Timbalens suspected dinner could be cooked instantaneously, but probably not eaten, as the utensils holding the dinner in the pools would probably melt.

The Timbalens had named it Death Island and few Tarlahns had sailed there. Two who reached it reported dangerous reptiles and hadn't climbed down the mountains into the island's interior. But that was where someone Ruarnon had only just learnt of the existence of, named Flariah, had invited Ruarnon and their friends to visit, to question western captives with her.

"I should mention," said Tor, "I suspect Monin is conferring with your other officials and the generals in our absence."

Ruarnon bowed their head. Whatever the Council learned from the westerners, Monin was unlikely to respond well to it. Ruarnon wasn't sure if the man's caution would go as far as abandoning the king and queen of Tarlah in the Far West, but given the dangers, expense and time it would take... He may be taking advantage of his position as acting regent in Ruarnon's absence to see who would support him in denying the Zaldeaans aid in the Far West.

"He wants me to stay by your side for the duration of our stay," Tor added.

"And does not trust Flariah as far as anyone can throw her?" Ruarnon replied.

"We have always heard rumour of there being a prophetess in the jungle," Tor added. "But we knew nothing of Flariah and according to Mawana, few Urai know of her. It appears a great secret has been kept from us concerning neighbours closer than the Zaldeaan Realm. That makes even me uneasy."

Ruarnon inclined their head. "What bothers me more is that Narz seems to have known this secret and how Flariah may respond to his attack. And he's gained nothing on Cauldron Island. If he attacks it again, we'll have another war on our doorstep."

"There must be limits to his resources," Tor insisted.

"I fear we're yet to see them," Ruarnon replied.

The mountains before them became larger, as Ruarnon's ship, the Iylena neared Tava's Gap. It was all dry rock, with only the smallest shrubs clinging to its inside slopes. It was the most impressive natural structure Ruarnon had ever seen, a perfect height to conceal some form of magic Linh had been vague about, and Flariah's people, whoever they were.

Gulls cried out, as the Iylena entered the Gap and the wind became gentler. The ship slowed as the captain navigated the gentle bends of the cliff-lined channel. The rock reflected sunlight and the air grew stuffy as the Gap narrowed. Then it opened out again to a bright jewel of glistening water, Blue Bay.

Raised in a small kingdom facing the perpetual threat of invasion, Ruarnon had spent much of their childhood imagining the world beyond Tarlah's walls. They never imagined they would one day venture to a place like this. If they were honest, it made them want to see more, despite how dangerous this island was.

Five ships were anchored to the right side of Blue Bay, their timbers even darker than the three Urai vessels anchored on the left. The Urai would have spent the night on board, tending their wounded from the battle. Today was a day of rest and tonight was a celebration, though Ruarnon was unclear on who was celebrating, other than the Urai.

"Let's get ready to go ashore," Ruarnon told Tor.

They had donned their gold regent's circlet and the usual gold ornaments in their braid. Mawana had told Lenaris the protocols for a visit in the letter, which permitted Ruarnon, Tor and Ruarnon's bodyguards to carry swords at their waists on the island, but as it was a peaceful visit, the three of them wore only silk tunics, leaving most of their arms and their legs bare up to the knee. Which suited Ruarnon perfectly, as descending the foredeck stairs into the heat, to wait while the boat was raised from below deck, was enough to make them break out in a sweat.

They nodded to Captain Arleath, who led Ruarnon's usual ten bodyguards towards the boat, each of them wearing bronze armour, minus their helmets and spears. Flariah wished to escort

Ruarnon's party onto the island herself and apparently they would be safe. Still, Linh had seemed uncomfortable about the island's inhabitants, whom she'd written about only vaguely. None of it made Ruarnon comfortable about leaving their armour on board, but if people could wield magic on this island, bronze armour was unlikely to be useful.

Ruarnon boarded their boat with their guards and Tor. As the boat was lowered over the side, Fiona waved from on shore. She stood with Michael, Linh, Mawana, Lenaris and...

"How is Troy standing?" Tor asked. "I thought he was stabbed?"

"I do not see any sign of bandages on Michael's arms either," Ruarnon added.

They'd woken up in the Zaldeaan Palace to find a North Lander had healed the power bow bolt wound in their shoulder last year, but they had heard of no one with healing powers since. The Urai only claimed to know shield magic. Had someone from Cauldron Island healed Ruarnon's friends?

Paddles splashed in the calm waters on either side of the boat, as Ruarnon's bodyguards rowed them to shore. Mawana raised a hand in greeting.

"How fairs Mocco?" Ruarnon called, as their guards secured their boat to a pole rising from the rocky, low shoreline, which seemed to descend steeply down to the depths of Blue Bay.

"He and Aunt Tarata are still resting," Mawana replied. "A night and a day were enough for Michael to be well rested from magical healing and possibly Troy, but magical overexertion can only be cured by rest."

"I will be watching you," Lenaris said to Troy, who still looked a bit pale but smiled. Tor was probably right about the dynamics between those two. And while Troy certainly had a mischievous side, he didn't seem to mind being bossed around.

Ruarnon followed Captain Arleath and their bodyguards, balancing carefully on the boat's bench, then stepped ashore. A barren, rocky expanse of plains stretched before them. Tarlah was dry, but this place had no trees at all. Only small shrubs grew from cracks in rocks on the hills ahead, the plains lying bare and dusty.

A woman moved towards them, accompanied by... Ruarnon gaped. The people walking with her stood a head taller than her considerable height, but they were not human. Their skin was bluey-grey in colour and as they drew nearer, it appeared as thick as hide. They were bald, with broad jaws and noses, broad torsos and muscled bare arms. They wore linen vests and shorts and looked large and robust enough to scoop Fiona up and throw her with one arm. They also bore some resemblance to damars, which sent shivers down Ruarnon's spine.

The woman walking between them seemed utterly unphased by the strange people's builds. She was also very tall, yet elegantly proportioned. Her sleeveless dress of bronze discs flashed in the sunlight as she walked, and a sword rocked against her hip. Her fiery red hair was braided back, and she had freckled skin and an intense, green-eyed gaze, which lingered on Ruarnon and Tor.

"Welcome to Cauldron Island," she said. "Follow me."

Ruarnon had never met the Timbalen emperor, but they suspected that if they did, the man would struggle to present as calmly and as in command as this woman. She struck them as someone who had never doubted her position. It was intimidating and they were glad to see it gave Tor pause too.

Linh was unusually quiet, avoiding looking at Flariah and Fiona seemed more hesitant than usual. Flariah unnerved them, and Lenaris gazed upon her with awe. Ruarnon looked forward to discussing openly, and without fear of letters being intercepted, their accounts of the battle of Blue Bay.

For now, they led their companions after Flariah, shaking their head that she gave them no more information than that. Monin would have a fit if they just walked wherever she led without asking questions.

"Where would you like to speak to us?" they asked.

"In my palace," she replied. "The prisoners are all locked away and the faeron and gorans are more than a match for the sorcerers."

Ruarnon's heart skipped a beat. Surely that meant Flariah was holding the sorcerers' prisoner too? That she had people powerful and adept enough at magic to do so? Who on Mijora's earth was this woman and who were her people?

Flariah led everyone towards the rocky hills lining the plains. Ruarnon's friends stared at three unnaturally steep mountains in the distance.

"Are those volcanoes?" Troy whispered. "You don't think they're active, do you?"

"I think that's steam rising beyond the hills," Michael replied. "Maybe from hot springs or mud pools, like they have in New Zealand."

Ruarnon shook their head. No wonder the Timbalens had left this place well alone. So why had Flariah chosen to live here?

Flariah led them through a cave entrance in the hills, down stone steps to a rock-walled passageway lined with paintings of strange figures and symbols, bordered in wavy line patterns. Ruarnon stared at the rock art. It didn't resemble Tarlahn, Timbalen, Urai or Zaldeaan styles. Who had done these paintings?

They followed Flariah into a vast chamber. Daylight passed through skylights onto bright flowers, creepers and small trees carpeting the hilly floor before them. Small waterfalls trickled down the back wall and the sound of running water echoed. Sunlight reflected off streams, swirling on the high ceiling overhead.

Ruarnon stared, as they crossed a small bridge over a stream reflecting swirls of light, and followed Flariah down a path through the greenery. The water, leaves and flowers extending in all directions were more abundant, lusher than any oasis Ruarnon had seen in Death Belt Desert. Were they natural?

They followed Flariah down another stone path past a waterfall, then through an archway into a dark, torch-lit room. Shelves lined its walls, holding slates of metal inscribed with strange symbols.

"Metal *pages*?" Linh asked.

"Of the same alloy as faeron spears and chain mail," Flariah replied.

"*Alloy*? The faeron have science?" Michael asked.

Ruarnon frowned at 'alloy' and 'science'.

"Once," Flariah replied. "But much of their knowledge is now lost."

Ruarnon followed Flariah into a smaller torch-lit room, its walls covered from floor to ceiling with frescoes of Cauldron

Island, fish and a pale blonde girl standing on the deck of an Urai ship. Her colouring looked Tarlahn. Why was she on an Urai ship?

They entered a rock cut dining hall. Simple, serviceable wooden tables filled it, enough to seat forty or so people at once. Flariah stopped at the head of a long table and gestured everyone to sit. Mawana sat on her left, welcoming Ruarnon beside them. Lenaris and Tor sat on their right, leaving Ruarnon's Australian friends to sit opposite.

Urai approached with drinks and platters of roasted meats and salads. Plates were passed down the table, and everyone served themselves using large wooden fork-like utensils and following Mawana's lead in eating with their fingers.

"What do you know of Narz and damars?" Flariah asked Ruarnon as they ate.

Was that the reason she allowed Ruarnon to visit this island and learn its secrets? So they could trade information?

Ruarnon and Tor gave her a lengthy description. Flariah studied them, rarely blinking, drinking everything in and giving away none of what she thought. She acted like a ruler from myths of the Sorcery War before the arrival of magic shattered the absolute confidence the kings of the west had had in their power. Who was this woman?

"It would appear you have reason to be as curious about Narz as I," Flariah concluded when they finished. "I shall question the crew and sorcerers now. You may join me."

Ruarnon's eyebrows rose, before they could stop them. None of the history they had read of Tarlahn kings mentioned any ruler who could put others in their place as effortlessly as Flariah. They had a feeling their stay with her may be uncomfortable. But it was worth it for access to more detailed information about their parents' captor than Companion Noma seemed able to get her hands on in the west.

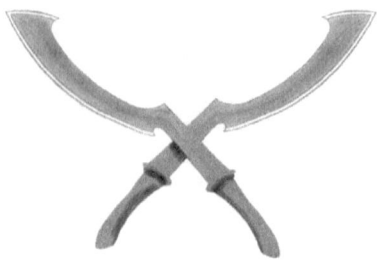

Chapter 8

The Prisoners —Ruarnon

I better check on my cousin, but I hope you obtain the information you seek," said Mawana, rising from the table.

"Why don't you take Troy and Michael with you?" Lenaris suggested pleasantly.

Mawana frowned politely, while Troy's brows rose high enough to disappear under his curly hair.

"Come on," said Fiona, standing, and shooting Lenaris a small smile while the boys stood.

"They need more rest," Lenaris whispered in Ruarnon's ear. "Linh can translate for us, if we need a translator."

She'd spoken with a smile, but that hadn't been a suggestion. And at Ruarnon's frown, Tor nodded his approval. Of course. Admitting them to the room to question the sorcerers would be like taking them to a Royal Council Meeting. They weren't members of the Royal Council. Tor didn't think it was appropriate.

Technically, it wasn't. Ruarnon was reluctant to part with them so soon, especially when they weren't sure what exactly had happened in Blue Bay. But Michael was pale, Troy looked tired and Ruarnon was sure Lenaris' was sincerely concerned for their well-being.

"I think that's a good idea," Ruarnon added. "There may be time to explore this island later, but I don't want Troy falling into a pool of boiling water or mud because you were too tired to judge your footing safely."

They smiled and Troy grinned, his frown fading as he stood with Fiona. Mawana engaged Troy and Fiona in conversation, flashing Lenaris a smile. Michael followed them, his limbs hanging more heavily than usual as they left.

"Are you all right Linh?" Tor asked quietly.

Linh's face was very pale.

"You're certain they can't wield even the least of their powers?" Linh asked Flariah.

Lenaris' eyes widened, but she didn't admonish Linh for questioning Flariah's assurance or being rude to their host. What had they witnessed in Blue Bay?

"None of their powers," Flariah confirmed, her gaze softening a little at Linh's fear. "Only one sorcerer the Urai fought yesterday survived. The other two are the ones who surrendered to you without fighting."

Linh shivered. "Which one lived?"

"The sorcerer Mawana disabled."

Ruarnon saw her shoulders relax. "Do you feel comfortable translating for us, if needed?" they asked her. "Would it help if we call Fiona back?"

"I wouldn't mind you calling Mawana and his shield magic back," she replied, "but I suppose you have faeron and their magic in the questioning room?" she asked Flariah, who nodded.

Linh shivered, then raised her chin. "Then let's go."

She was still frightened. Ruarnon could see it in her eyes. But they also saw determination in the stubborn set of her jaw. Tor stuck by her side, as everyone followed Flariah out of the room. Ruarnon trusted him to keep an eye on her. But why did they get the impression the faeron also made Linh nervous?

Flariah led the party to a small room with a table and chairs running along it. Three pale-skinned, light-haired men sat opposite her, all wearing full-length sleeve silk tunics, leggings and boots. The sailors standing behind them wore plain smocks and trousers and eyed their robust goran guards nervously.

The gorans stood with feet spread and arms crossed, wearing leather kilts but carrying no weapons. They gazed sternly at their captives while a bright person in a chain mail tunic stood between each sorcerer.

Ruarnon stopped in their tracks, as did everyone else. While the gorans appeared to have hide rather than skin, the faeron had fine scales. Their faces were ovoid, with human, sharply intelligent eyes. Seeing both species of giant in an enclosed space took Ruarnon's breath away.

Tor cleared his throat. "You wish to question them all together?"

"How they react to each other may tell us as much as what they later divulge when interviewed separately," she replied.

Tor frowned. "They do not understand us?"

"No," Flariah replied, "but my sister informs me that the younger members of our party can translate. Though it will likely shock our prisoners."

Ruarnon surveyed the prisoners. The youngest man in silks eyed the faeron curiously, as did the middle-aged man next to him. Ruarnon suspected they were the two 'powerful servants of Narz' Linh had mentioned surrendering. Sorcerers. The man next to them smiled insolently and had bruising and swelling down one side of his face while his right arm, hand and fingers were bandaged. Ruarnon assumed that was the sorcerer Mawana had somehow knocked down.

Ruarnon hesitantly sat beside Flariah and Tor. Lenaris and Linh followed.

"Your powers will be of no use to you here," Flariah told the sorcerers once everyone had sat. "The faeron maintain an enchantment as old as time, which occupies every magic particle in this room. Would you care to translate for me?" She added, turning to Linh.

Linh repeated her words, gazing in the sorcerers' general direction, instead of looking at their faces. The sorcerers' frowns smoothed, the two on the left sitting up straighter as they eyed Linh.

"What do you know of your purpose on this island?" Flariah asked and Linh repeated.

"We know that legends of the Sorcery War and Creation are lies, fabricated by priests and kings of the ancient past to hide their corruption and shame," the sorcerer with the bandaged shoulder replied smugly, with the air of someone about to give a lecture, Linh repeating his words when he paused. There was something odd about him. The grey streaked through his hair suggested he was around his middle years, but his eyes burned with an intensity Ruarnon disliked and distrusted.

The sailors' faces paled and the other two sorcerers frowned as they realised Ruarnon and their companions could understand Linh too.

"What proof do you have of that?" Flariah asked.

"The truth!" the man declared, too caught up in the conversation to notice anything amiss. "The senior gods would have allowed us to suffer in ignorance, fall victim to circumstance and blunder through the dark, until after thousands of years, some humans miraculously became wise enough for them to teach us their Ways. The Mountain God was not so cruel. He granted sorcery powers to the wisest mountain leaders to heal the sick, protect themselves from invasion and ease the hardships which plagued humanity in the Age of Ignorance.

"Earth Goddess Mijora's people came to those mountain leaders for healing and advice and their kings grew jealous. They sent spies to learn to confiscate sorcery power and had scholars produce devices for stealing it. With sorcery at their fingertips, each king thought to conquer his rivals. Their greed, selfishness and ambition plunged the world into the Sorcery War.

"Only when the most powerful mountain leaders took back what was rightfully theirs did the wars end. By that time, princes and priests spoke of wisdom and discipline and were so ashamed of their ancestors that they spread lies. The people so feared sorcerers that they believed. Sorcerers hid their powers, living in shame and anonymity.

"But it shall be no longer! His Worthiness Narz is descended from those blessed leaders and he will spread the truth. Under his rule, we can be proud and learn to use our powers as they were intended!"

Ruarnon gaped. The myths they knew of the Sorcery War contradicted each other. Some mentioned magical weapons to fight sorcerers with and others didn't. Companion Tor said no respectable scholar would stake their career on the accuracy of any myth, given no written records survived from that era. Yet it seemed Narz had told this man a version of the Sorcery War he liked, and the man had embraced it whole-heartedly, unquestioningly, with no reason to do so other than personal bias. It was utterly irrational.

Its irrationality distracted Ruarnon until they realised the man said the mountain god granted sorcery powers for healing, defence and to ease the burden of human life. The damars nature defied every one of those purposes.

"If that is why you believe you wield magic," Ruarnon asked, "By what right did Narz attack the Zaldeaan Realm?"

"The highest, self-defence," the other middle-aged sorcerer, a milder sounding man, replied. "The Zaldeaan army had already hunted and slain any sorcerers who dared oppose the expansion of their Realm. Once your kingdom fell, future Zaldeaan kings would take their eternal desire for glory and bloodshed across the ocean.

"Our continent is made of small kingdoms, who would have allied too slowly against them. We would have fallen swiftly. And when the Zaldeaan king realised sorcerers would be the greatest defenders of our continent, he would have hunted us down too."

Ruarnon's jaw dropped. King Kyura hadn't even wanted to invade Tarlah. And to Zaldeaans and Tarlahns alike, the Far West was the mythical land the Sorcery War was fought in. No one had had contact with it or the wealth to invest in a many-week voyage without maps, charts, or any idea what they would find. True, the Zaldeaans were the best army on the continent and a formidable force, but to claim they had been a threat to Narz...

"Do the rest of you believe this?" Ruarnon asked.

The young sorcerer's eyes widened. The one who was convinced by Narz's Sorcery War myth crossed his arms and kept his expression completely neutral.

"If Narz was so afraid of the Zaldeaans, why provoke them by attacking them with damars?" Tor asked.

"We needed a force to lure their army to their shores, from whence we could capture and take control of it," the milder middle-aged man replied. "Now, the very force that would have conquered our smaller kingdoms and hunted our sorcerers protects them."

Ruarnon shook their head. Two of Narz's sorcerers sounded delusional. What in Chaos was going on?

"Why would you be pleased about an invasion that saw women and children murdered?" Ruarnon demanded.

"There was no murder! It was war!" the man intent on Narz's version of the Sorcery War objected.

"Are you aware of how damars fight?" Ruarnon asked. "They hunt in packs. If one damar finds prey, the others move on. The Zaldeaans did not know this. They failed to contain them."

The man seemed unmoved, but the milder sorcerer frowned and the young sorcerer fidgeted with his sleeve, looking pale. How much, or how little did they know about the creatures they had transported yesterday?

"Those creatures ran wild and my army had to hunt them across the width and length of the entire Zaldeaan Realm!" Ruarnon continued, driving their point home. "The Zaldeaans can only estimate how many women, children and elderly were killed before Zaldeaan commanders realised they needed to take their army home."

"Then they valued the glory of conquering Tarlah over the lives of their people," replied the wounded, deluded sorcerer. "They failed their people. We protected ours."

"Why didn't you wait for their army to return?" Linh demanded. "*Hundreds* of civilians were killed. Those deaths are on *your* heads!"

The young sorcerer shivered. Tor frowned and Lenaris' eyes widened at Linh joining the conversation, instead of merely translating, but Ruarnon wasn't surprised she couldn't help herself.

"We waited for the army to return," the deluded sorcerer replied. "Lord Vye unleashed one ship a day. And waited the whole day. They preferred attacking Tarlah to defending their people."

"You despise them?" Ruarnon asked.

"Quite," the man replied. "It astounds me their enemies do not. How you have found it in your hearts to pity *them* is beyond my understanding."

Ruarnon shook their head. How could anyone murder hundreds of innocents and blame it entirely on the people who failed to protect them, ignoring the blood soaking their own hands?

The man had no humanity. But the young man was trembling and the milder man was turning paler.

"Do you think Narz could persuade ordinary men to be this callous?" Ruarnon asked their companions. "Or are these men bewitched?"

"Zaldeaan commanders have persuaded their soldiers to behave like this in the past," Tor replied. "You are fortunate not to have witnessed the crimes committed during The Wars."

Ruarnon felt cold inside. Uncle Omah had alluded to such things.

"Is this what Narz brought you into the open to achieve?" Ruarnon asked the sorcerers, disillusioned. "Massacring people halfway across the world in case one day, after they conquered Tarlah, they decided to come after you?"

"He wants us to *protect* our people," the milder man insisted. "He is training sorcerers to detect and prevent crime and sorcerer healers to cure injuries and illnesses physicians cannot. His vision will create safer, healthier lives for all his subjects, sorcerers and non-magic wielders alike."

"And a safer world for *us* Poran, don't forget the important part," the deluded sorcerer added.

So Narz was a monster abroad, but everyone loved him at home, because he somehow managed to pretend to be nice when dealing with his own people? It made Ruarnon sick to their stomach.

Poran was studying Ruarnon, blinking rapidly. He believed everything he was saying and saw no contradiction between his apparent goodwill and Narz's evil intent in the Zaldeaan Realm.

"This duty of protecting your people is what brought you to my shores?" Flariah asked.

"Yes," Poran replied. "Armies like yours have not been unleashed since the Sorcery War and if we have our way, they never shall. Those creatures should have been destroyed long ago."

"Come off it!" Linh retorted. "Narz created damars and they're ten times worse!"

"You do not understand the nature of the creatures on this island," Poran replied patiently. "They were bred as armies. Their scales and, in some cases, enchantments within their very skin make them extremely difficult for conventional soldiers to kill. Armies like this once slaughtered one of the greatest armies of men in my homeland and were used to begin a conquest of the world. Did you think we would let them do so again? This army is worse than the Zaldeaans. It is a tool that will do the bidding of whoever wields it."

Ruarnon shivered. Narz *did* know things they didn't. No one in Tarlah had any idea creatures like that existed, let alone could be found on this island. Even Tor was staring at the sorcerers. Only Flariah seemed unmoved by words that were a revelation to everyone else.

"You came here to avenge deaths from the Sorcery War?" Flariah asked, her gaze sceptical.

"No, we came to prevent their repetition," Poran asserted.

"Why would they be repeated?" Flariah asked.

"Because they are a perfect tool in the hands of our greatest opponents in the Far South."

"Surely you understand that an enchantment binds my army and only a sorcerer of great power could control the enchantment?"

"So I was led to believe. And to answer your next question, yes, there are sorcerers in the Far South who would oppose us, who can control that enchantment and who are evil enough to wield your army."

"And you believe they could overpower me?"

He looked her in the eye and replied softly, "Yes. I fear they could."

"Who are these sorcerers?" Tor asked.

"Do not speak of them!" the deluded sorcerer replied. "They disgrace the name! They are the only ones worthy of the slaughter the Guardians carried out against us during the Sorcery War!"

Ruarnon frowned. This man saw Narz as a kind of sorcerer saviour, but there was a whole category of sorcerers he wanted dead?

"Have you nothing to say?" Tor asked the young sorcerer.

The young man shook his head mutely.

"About any of this?" Tor added.

"You do not have to answer Dargus," Poran said gently.

"I did not wish to harm the Zaldeaans," Dargus said to the table. "I wanted to protect my people. I thought the damars were fighting an army. I did not know damars had run free."

Dargus shuddered.

"There were too few soldiers to contain them. What did you expect?" Ruarnon asked.

"The way they… hunt …I didn't know," Dargus replied.

Poran sighed. "They were never intended to be used against humans. Only our shortage of manpower and the Zaldeaan thirst for blood let me consider helping transport them. They are the kind of force only to be unleashed against those who truly deserved it. The Zaldeaan army did. But what you have said of damars crossing the Realm, I do not understand how that was possible."

"Lord Vye unleashed most of the damars," said the deluded sorcerer. "It took that many to get that selfish army to abandon their conquest and save their own families."

Poran's face went slack. "They were for *show*. His Worthiness said!"

"Even sight of more damars offshore wasn't enough to get them to put to sea," the deluded sorcerer continued.

Ruarnon's heart skipped a beat. "What made them sail to Narz's lands?"

"The Zaldeaan army didn't believe in magic. So Lord Vye gave them a demonstration. One bolt of lightning into their army made them believe."

Ruarnon's jaw dropped. Governor Armar had received a report of lightening striking from a clear sky, but even he hadn't tested Tarlahn trust by claiming tens of soldiers had been murdered by sorcery. No one would have believed that. But that was likely what had coerced Ruarnon's Uncle Karmarn to direct the Zaldeaan ships to sail west, leaving damars to ravage the Realm in their wake. Ordinary Zaldeaans had barred their doors and were safe from immediate threat of damars by then, but neither Ruarnon nor the Zaldeaans had any defence against magical attacks.

Poran's face turned stark white at the deluded sorcerers' words and the young sorcerer stared at him in stunned silence. They seemed entirely ignorant of the cruel capacity of sorcerers they served Narz with.

"Vye couldn't," Dargus said softly. "Only the kings of the Far South would... Oh, Luvaras help us –he's one of *them*, isn't he? Doesn't he know this expedition was to protect us from *his* kind?"

Poran's face went into his hands. "It cannot be," he said softly. "His Worthiness would have known."

"I don't see why it should be," said the third sorcerer, crossing his arms. "Vye understands a price must be paid for change against the tide and he made the Zaldeaans pay."

Poran's pale face took on a shade of grey at those words and Dargus shifted his chair sideways, away from the deluded sorcerer. Both men looked like they might be sick.

"We will take a break," Flariah declared calmly. "It seems we all have much to process."

She stood and Ruarnon followed Flariah out, back through the palace corridors and beams of light shining through skylights to light the earthen floor beneath their feet.

"What did they tell you?" Michael asked from the dining room table, as they neared the end of the corridor.

Troy lifted his head off the table beside Michael, looking sleepy.

Mawana shrugged at Lenaris' inquiring gaze and Fiona reported, "Troy had a nap, but Michael couldn't switch his brain off, so we came to hear what you learned."

Tor frowned, and Lenaris eyed Ruarnon questioningly. Telling them everything was like debriefing them on a meeting of the

Royal Council. Ruarnon would happily have Michael and Linh's insights on the Council but adding Lenaris to it was enough of a change for Monin, and making all four Australians Companions would rouse even Tor and the generals' eyebrows. The fact all four of them were foreign went against long-standing Tarlahn tradition. But Monin and the generals weren't here. And Ruarnon and their companions were pausing before the table, where Michael, Troy and Fiona sat expectantly.

"Two of the sorcerers delivering damars here also delivered them to the Zaldeaan Realm," Ruarnon replied, "because Narz somehow convinced them the Zaldeaans are out to conquer the known world and kill every sorcerer who could stand in their path. They say Narz's main goal in his homeland is to end fear against sorcerers, let them out of hiding, and have them use sorcery for healing and the greater good.

"The third sorcerer blames the release of the damars in the Realm on an underling called Lord Vye. What he said of Vye's actions made the first two sorcerers think Vye is related to sorcerer rulers in the south, who are supposedly descended from sorcerers of the Sorcery War. The first two sorcerers believe Narz failed to notice Vye's identity and believed they merely meant to intimidate the Zaldeaan army to surrender by displaying damars to them."

"So all the sorcerers are completely delusional?" Troy asked.

"It sounds to me like two of them meant well," Ruarnon replied. "Like Narz twisted their thinking."

"He demonised the Zaldeaans," said Linh. "Made them out to be bloodthirsty, conquering savages who had it coming."

"We're a long way from anywhere twenty-first-century concepts like 'emotive language' and 'demonising people' mean anything to the locals," Troy objected.

"The idea of demonising people is ancient," Linh replied. "The Romans demonised Carthage to justify destroying it and seizing its trading ports nearly two thousand years ago."

"I do not recognise either word," said Ruarnon. "But why on Mijora's Earth were those sorcerers willing to believe so much on Narz's say so, with no evidence, when common sense says otherwise?"

"Like every gullible fool on social media?" Troy asked.

Linh nodded, her face going slack. "It's like the sorcerers have been brainwashed."

"But that's impossible," Troy replied. "This world has no concept of science, let alone psychology. How can Narz understand how the mind works well enough to brainwash people?"

"When our Tarlahn friends have no idea what we're talking about," Michael added.

Ruarnon bowed their head, conceding the point.

"It explains why they failed to realise the insanity of launching a pre-emptive strike against an enemy they had no proof would attack them," Linh replied.

"That much I understand," Tor said softly. "The sorcerer's reasons for invading are well-reasoned nonsense."

"Are you telling me Narz can manipulate people into committing atrocities?" Troy asked, his eyes wide.

"No," Michael replied slowly. "We're afraid he already has."

"I don't see how he could understand enough to do that either," said Fiona. "It's not like he used everyone's religious or political beliefs."

"He's clever," Michael replied. "If he bred damars, a new species of creature and tampered with their instincts to make them what they are, he's a genius."

"Narz an *evil genius*?" Troy asked sceptically.

"It's *not* going to be that simple," Linh replied. "And I don't think the reason he's done terrible things will be any less complex."

"Well, the sorcerers sound mad to me," said Lenaris. "What else can they be, when they are full of conviction about a Zaldeaan invasion, yet have no evidence to support their conviction?"

"They're not mad," Linh insisted.

"It sounds to me like they could be too rational," Michael replied. "Like they have an answer for everything and have been brain washed."

"Do you mean he has somehow washed their minds?" Ruarnon asked, grappling with the foreign concept.

"Yes," Linh replied. "Washing them clean of everything that would object to what Narz wants them to think and do. That's how they sounded to me."

Ruarnon's mouth fell open. That was the opposite of everything their Royal Council valued. If Narz had a means for doing that, he could turn Umarinaris upside-down.

"Surely such a thing cannot be done!" Lenaris objected.

"Multiple dictators in our world have used religion, politics or ethnicity to demonise one group of people and persuade or bully ordinary people into killing them," Linh replied. "Witch burnings,

Hitler, the Khmer Rouge: they killed millions of innocent people between them."

"You are saying they are bewitched?" Tor asked.

"That might be how you can understand," Linh replied, "but bewitched without magic. Using similar logic and reasoning to what the Royal Council uses, to manipulate the sorcerer's emotions and control their point of view."

Ruarnon shivered. They had always seen Zaldeaan attitudes to war and conquest as inherently cruel, but Zaldeaan warrior culture and the belief Zaldeaans were superior to Tarlahns had developed over several centuries. Narz had made these men believe what he wanted seemingly overnight. Was his power over people's minds as great as the sorcery power Ruarnon was beginning to fear he wielded?

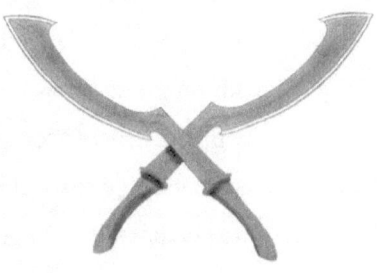

CHAPTER 9

SELENIA ~RUARNON

H eat warmed Ruarnon's shoulders as they stepped
out into the sunlight, crossing the dry plains
between Flariah's palace and Blue Bay with their
companions.

"Benevolence," said Tor, "Give yourself time to absorb what
we have just learned and suspect. My knowledge of the
manipulations of warlords is greater than yours, yet even I am
deeply troubled."

Ruarnon nodded but didn't meet Tor's gaze. They changed
their clothes for the night's celebrations in complete distraction.
Narz made Zaldeaan attempts to manipulate King Kuyra look like
child's play. A few Zaldeaans had bullied Kuyra to do something
he hated, but Narz had convinced decent men that his acts of evil
were justified and made men *want* to commit them. He was
infinitely more dangerous. And far from equipping Ruarnon to free
their parents, the discussion so far had only made them more

nervous of the many forms of power Narz seemed to wield and feel more overwhelmed about countering them.

A short time later, Ruarnon followed their captain and bodyguards to one of the Iylena's boats, wearing their red and gold silk regent's tunic and the regent's gold circlet at their brow. Moonlight shone off polished bronze armour as four soldiers rowed them to the edge of the plains, where Mocco and Mawana waited bare-chested. Mawana's dark blue silk kilt had silver embroidery, while Mocco's was cream silk with gold embroidery. The skin around Mocco's eyes was dark.

"You are well enough to join us?" Ruarnon asked, as they and their guards disembarked and the sailors rowed their boat back.

"Uncle Tither says Mother and I must have an early night," Mocco replied with a smile, "but sleeping all afternoon has given us strength enough to sit through a meal."

"There is no...." Ruarnon took a deep breath and forced out the words, "permanent damage?"

"No. However, I could not shield myself tonight to save my life. Flariah recommends we avoid using shield magic for a week. Mawana tells me I missed much, that you questioned the sorcerers?"

Ruarnon nodded. "I am deeply troubled by what we learnt."

"Then perhaps we can sit in companionable silence over dinner," Mocco replied. "I will not have the energy to listen to long conversations, let alone speak during them."

Ruarnon smiled. Spending a night in the company of friends would be pleasant, before they considered how everything they had learned impacted recovering their missing family members and Lenaris' father.

Lenaris and their Australian friends greeted them, all wearing short sleeved silk Tarlahn tunics. Troy and Michael wore borrowed tunics of red and brown, while Linh and Fiona wore blue and purple. Lenaris eyed them with satisfaction and Ruarnon guessed that weapons training may not be all they received from her.

Everyone set off across the plains.

"What's with the uh… skirts?" Troy asked Mocco and Mawana.

"The correct term is 'kilt'," Michael replied. "They're only skirts if you wear something under them. That's how it works in Scotland."

"Michael!" Lenaris admonished.

Mawana shrugged. "There is nothing rude about traditions."

Mocco stared awkwardly ahead and Lenaris flushed. Ruarnon struggled not to laugh, as their Australian friends looked away to hide their amusement. Mawana seemed to share their lack of impropriety. No wonder they appeared to get along.

"It is not uncommon to discard small clothes on hot days in Tarlah," Ruarnon added diplomatically.

"Yes, but it is hardly polite to discuss it!" Lenaris objected and Troy and Linh's eyes widened, while Michael chuckled.

"How is talking about what you're doing ruder than doing it?" Troy asked.

"They're as bad as the British," said Michael, shaking his head.

Ruarnon refocused on their surroundings in the pause that followed. They were approaching a cave lit by burning torches suspended from its walls and a passageway extending back through the rock. They followed the passage to a vast underground cavern, crowded with faeron, gorans and Urai. A balcony rose behind the crowd and Tarata waved from a table atop it. Mocco led them to the table while Flariah moved towards a stage opposite, leaving a fair-skinned girl with long blonde hair and several faeron at her table.

"Flariah's ward, Selenia," Mawana told Ruarnon quietly, following their gaze as the others climbed the balcony steps after Mocco. "I met her when I accompanied my father in delivering new servants and bringing those whose service had ended home."

"She grew up here?" Ruarnon asked.

"Yes," Mawana replied, "but Flariah is very protective."

"What of her family? And why is her colouring Tarlahn?" Ruarnon asked, as they sat beside each other at Tarata and Tither's table.

"I do not know," Mawana replied. "But she is in some kind of danger."

"Welcome," Flariah announced, her powerful voice carrying over the crowd, leaving silence in its wake. "We are here to celebrate the defeat of the only army ever to invade this island!"

She paused for roars from gorans, which startled Ruarnon and made Troy spill his drink.

"Tonight, my jungle servants and the faeron will entertain you with music and dances. But first, a toast to allies and victory!"

Ruarnon picked up the silver goblet before them and drank with the crowd. Then faeron began to play a strange song with metal flutes, while jungle servants brought platters of roast meats, fruits, salads, goblets of juices, and desserts swimming in sweet sauces, and the feast began, soldiers serving themselves from tables below the balcony.

Mawana entertained them with tales of wanderings on Cauldron Island. When the music changed to Urai drumming, he led their Australian friends to the dance floor. The Australians tried to copy his rapid, rhythmic movements, which matched the beat flawlessly, but struggled to position their limbs correctly, and couldn't keep up. Lenaris joined them. Ruarnon carried a chair for Mocco and placed it beside the dance floor, then stood beside him, content to watch. Urai joined the dance, and Tarlahn soldiers formed a ring, clapping the rhythm, while Selenia watched on Ruarnon's left.

"You have not seen the Megrasa before?" she asked, her eyes on the dancers. Ruarnon took a moment to realise she was speaking to them.

"I have not seen any Urai dances," they replied. "My people have only just resumed relations with them."

"Do your people really know little of magic?" she asked.

"I have not seen anyone wield it. I was unconscious when a North Lander healed me in the Zaldeaan Realm."

"So you are Regent Ruarnon? I am Selenia."

Ruarnon bowed their head in acknowledgement. "Mawana said you grew up here. It does not seem a safe place for children."

"It is safer than my homeland. My whole family is under an enchantment. Our maid fled with me when it was cast, and we escaped. I was very young at the time."

Ruarnon's eyes widened. "You are from the West?"

She nodded.

"And your maid came all the way here? I thought there had been no contact with the West for centuries?"

"That was probably true, until we came. I remember the maid singing to me of Safe Haven, the old song from the Sorcery War. I think the idea of such a place lived on, and my family's maid sought it. Lylah Saw us coming and had the Urai bring us here."

"Can you return home?"

"I am still in danger in Tira and Flariah says my training is incomplete, so I am not yet ready to help break the enchantment to free my family. There is little point in returning until then."

"Do you know who enchanted your family?"

"Narz. My family opposed his reign, and he will expect me to oppose him too and perhaps lead a rebellion against him if I return."

Ruarnon sighed.

"Flariah says people can do terrible things out of fear," Selenia continued. "She said crimes committed against sorcerers after the Sorcery War drove surviving sorcerers into hiding. She worries Narz's desire to bring sorcerers into the open may result in similar fears and crimes, that it may cause chaos. That is why Lylah is watching Tira, my home city, and my continent closely."

"But breaking the enchantment could place you in the middle of that chaos?"

She met their eyes. "After a lifetime of wondering what my family are like and wanting to meet them, I will prepare, and hopefully find the courage to face whatever I must face in the West. Narz's power and damars frighten me, but I will have to confront his power to see my family."

Ruarnon tensed. "So will my people. Narz holds my parents, my friend Lenaris' father Companion Pamoran and my Aunt Merlah, Uncle Karmarn and cousin Coroth prisoner."

Selenia's eyes widened. "I thought I was alone. What did Narz want with them?"

Ruarnon sighed. "I do not know. My family were ignorant of Narz's existence and know nothing about magic. They are no threat nor of use to him."

"I used to imagine what it would be like to be a ruler, to have the power to make decisions and protect people. I wondered if I could fight Narz if I had my own army. Then I grew up and realised the world is not so simple. You have an army, but you are nervous about confronting Narz?"

Ruarnon shivered. "Nervous barely describes my feelings. My powers are nothing compared to his."

"Can the Urai help?"

"I do not think so. Few of them know shield magic, and I cannot imagine the Council of Elders permitting those who can risk their lives helping me."

"You should ask anyway. The Urai are an adventurous people with a love of knowledge. Some serve Flariah in exchange for reading her libraries, which preserve ancient histories of my homeland, the Sorcery War, and the rise of the Timbalen Empire. Sending envoys to my homeland would greatly extend their knowledge of the world and its history. It may appeal to them."

That surprised Ruarnon, but it explained why Flariah had Urai servants. And they couldn't definitively rule out Urai support unless they asked and were denied, but it was too soon for that.

"Tonight is not supposed to be for dark conversations," Selenia added with a smile. "It is supposed to be a celebration. Shall we dance?"

Ruarnon smiled and offered her their arm, and they joined Ruarnon's friends on the dance floor, across which a lively and familiar flute tune began to play. Ruarnon led the dance, and Selenia mirrored their graceful arm movements as they swayed, spinning on the spot, then they twirled each other to the tune of the lead flute.

Selenia caught on swiftly, laughing when Troy twirled clumsily past. She watched with her mouth open as several Urai raised Mocco's chair between them and twisted and turned Mocco in time to the music while he smiled. Then the tune slowed, and Mocco's chair was turned more slowly, then circled the dance floor, sweeping him away, and Lenaris and Mawana danced beside Ruarnon and Selenia. Troy whistled, making Mawana flush, but Lenaris didn't notice.

Everyone struggled to match Mawana's moves to the fast-paced drumbeat which followed and stared as Mocco and his chair were thrown into the air and caught, to spectators' cheers. By the time the final strings were plucked, and everyone smiled and applauded, Ruarnon conceded that despite everything, they had enjoyed themself.

Flariah announced a spectacle outside, and Ruarnon, Selenia and their friends followed the crowd through the passage to the plains. They gathered beneath a bright half and a quarter moon and twinkling stars, and Mawana pointed out a bright blue and a yellow constellation, explaining that some tribes worshipped them as sky gods. A murmur rose through the crowd, and a shining star streaked through the darkness, arching across the sky, disappearing below the horizon. Ruarnon wondered how Flariah had known. Perhaps Lylah had told her.

The crowd dispersed, and Selenia turned to Ruarnon. "I am glad we met," she said.

"So am I," they replied, smiling and bowing their head in goodbye.

Selenia returned to Flariah, waving when she reached the palace entrance. Ruarnon waved back. They liked her, but they wondered what had prompted her maid to flee across an ocean no one had traversed for centuries just to protect her.

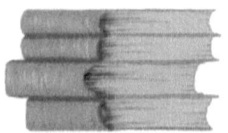

Cḧapter 10

Exploration -Linḧ

Under a bright morning sun, Linh and Fiona thanked Mawana and Mocco properly for keeping them safe in Blue Bay, and everyone said goodbye to the cousins, then watched the Urai ships preparing to sail from the deck of Ruarnon's ship. Mocco waved to Tarata as each boarded their own ship, and Tither clapped his arm around Mawana with a force that would probably knock anyone else down, as father and son boarded Tither's ship together.

Linh sighed. She was still a bit on edge, struggling to relax the tension in her shoulders. She had to remind herself how effectively Flariah had the sorcerers detained, though sitting opposite them and translating for them had been unnerving. It was lucky the conversation had been so engrossing and swept aside her recent memories of fire and sorcerers punching through the cousins' shield magic.

Now, so soon after battle, everything seemed deceptively calm. Everyone was happy and the Urai were sailing home victorious, Mawana with his father to his mother and Mocco with his mother to his father. It was hard not to think of her family. Of her mother's strict yet reassuring admonitions and her father's kind smile. Powerless to return to them for months on end, Linh found it less painful not to think of them, to live her life here as it was.

Ruarnon gripped the Iylena's railing as they gazed at the departures. Linh supposed sorcerers needed adding to the list of damars, great power and distance standing between them and their family. She missed hers, but at least she could be sure hers were safe.

"Am I right in thinking it's not just family you miss?" Troy asked Michael quietly. "Or is Andy family?"

To Linh's surprise, Michael smiled down at the sea. "When did you realise we were together?"

Troy grinned. "Most people probably think you're just best mates, but maybe one time I had my eye on him, and I saw how he looked at you."

Linh's mouth opened slowly. Troy was keeping an eye on… *oh*. Troy did love people. Was he bisexual? Fiona didn't seem surprised. She was better at noticing these things.

Michael smiled again. "He's always had so many girls after him. And the other guys were busy talking about that and girls in general. They probably assumed I was ace, and maybe aromantic. Then I was in a car accident on the holidays. He knows that's what killed my family. He was more upset about it than I was. That's when he realised how he felt about me, and that he's bi."

"But you knew you were queer all along?" Troy asked and Michael nodded. "And it was always Andy?"

Michael smiled faintly and nodded again.

"That's the other reason you were so keen to question sorcerers," Fiona added. "You want to get back to him."

Michael sighed, his gaze still on the ocean. "I didn't want to rush him. And I didn't want to make things weird between us. I wanted to support him as he figured it out himself, in his own time. Then I got stuck here, after only three precious months since we became boyfriends."

Troy shook his head. "You should have told me. We all noticed you were distant those first few months. I thought I might know why, but …you're not the easiest person to talk to about personal stuff."

Michael turned to Troy. "Not everyone's as good at talking as you are."

Troy's brows raised.

"I know," said Michael. "People called you a loudmouth at school, and sometimes they'd tell you to keep it to yourself. But it's healthier talking about shit. I learnt that the hard way. Andy's the only one I ever talked to about stuff."

"I know I'm not your six-foot tall, gorgeous, blond surfer boyfriend," Troy said, "And I'm clumsy as compared to Andy's easy way of talking to anyone and everyone, but I'm here for you mate."

"We are too," Fiona added.

There was a pause, then Linh realised Fiona was eyeing her pointedly. "I'm just struggling a bit with the idea that you actually need people at times," Linh blurted.

Michael sighed. "Everyone does. Some people just suck at it. But you're better at being there for people than you think," he added to Troy. "You even make Ruarnon smile, and that doesn't look easy."

Troy smiled.

Michael quirked an eyebrow at him and Troy's smile became a grin. "I don't reckon they'd date a kid like me," Troy whispered.

Michael's smile broadened and Troy grinned. Of course Troy was pan. Though Linh found it interesting Troy could be attracted to the quiet, reserved, brilliant mind of the Regent. She hadn't thought they would be his type.

"There are some things Selenia and I think you Australians may like to see here," Lenaris said, startling Linh, who had forgotten Lenaris and Ruarnon stood not far to her right. "I don't think it will help you get home, but it may add to your knowledge of that."

Linh frowned. What *things* might those be?

"How do you know?" Michael asked.

"Selenia told Mawana, Ruarnon and I last night. It isn't safe to roam this island alone, and Flariah seemed reluctant about the idea, but Selenia knows it well enough to guide us safely around. And it will be another day before my grandfather can join us in questioning the westerners."

"*You* are suggesting roaming the most dangerous island in these waters?" Ruarnon asked, one of their eyebrows raised.

"When was the last time you had a day off?" Fiona asked them.

Ruarnon's face fell. "I do not recall. There is always so much work to be done."

"It will give you a well-earned break," said Lenaris, though Linh wondered if Lenaris had an ulterior motive.

Half an hour later, Linh followed Selenia, Ruarnon and her friends across Rueman's Plains, with a pack strapped to her back, suspecting this was not the best of ideas, but Troy was incorrigible. The plains were bathed in dry heat as the sun climbed higher in the sky, reminding her of home. Selenia led them on a winding course through rocky hills beyond Flariah's palace entrance, past lizards' sun baking on nearby rocks and the occasional snake.

"It's so barren," said Fiona. "All plains and slabs of rock."

"It is volcanic," Selenia replied. "Do you see that crack in the rock that is yellow on the sides? It is leaking sulphur."

They wove through barren rocks, pausing for a lunch stop in the cool shade of a large cave. Lenaris and Ruarnon finished eating first and duelled with grace, speed, and smooth footwork Linh suspected she could never match, no matter how long they stayed in Tarlah, while the others finished their meal.

"Can you fight?" Selenia asked her friends.

"Not like that," Troy replied.

"We didn't learn how to till we came here," Fiona added.

Selenia's eyes widened. "Are there not wars in your homeland?"

"Not in our country," Troy replied.

"All my life, there has been war in my homeland, in the west," Selenia replied, explaining her journey to Cauldron Island.

"Does Narz know you're here?" Michael asked.

Selenia sighed. "The enchantment that binds my family once bound me too, but it broke, freeing me. We think Narz knows and that he is looking for me."

Ruarnon approached, sheathing their sword.

"And he would expect Tarlahns to know if a Western Ship sailed into their waters," said Michael. "I wonder if he abducted Ruarnon's parents and Pamoran because he thought they could tell him where you were."

"A western ship was sighted near here during the damarian invasion of the Zaldeaan Realm," Selenia replied. "If a powerful sorcerer on-board detected Flariah's army, and if Narz thinks I have the power to control her soldiers, he may expect me to invade him with it."

"How would *you* control Flariah's army?" Lenaris asked.

"I can craft magic. I have done it several times, though the faeron discourage me. I wonder if my family are sorcerers, and Narz assumes I am too."

"I wonder why Lylah didn't mention you," said Michael. "She said us four and Ruarnon are catalysts for peace in Narz's war."

"I think she knows more than she is telling," said Selenia. "The time has come for me to find out, especially if I am the reason half of your family has been abducted," she added apologetically to Ruarnon.

"I imagine my family are safer in Narz's hands than you would be," Ruarnon replied, looking torn.

They crossed more dry and barren plains after that, with crusty, cracked soil stretching before them and a mountain looming ahead. Linh didn't think much of the menacing, ape-like reptiles which snarled at them from a mountain ledge, but she was interested in the cave paintings in the hills opposite. The first cave had daylight slanting at odd angles through cracks in its ceiling, which lit a long stretch of earthy coloured paintings.

"This is what I wanted to show you," Selenia told the Australians. "Does any of it look familiar?"

Linh frowned and examined the walls. Opposite the entrance, glowing painted figures of faeron touched symbols and danced, underlined by a cursive, curly script with many dots, which remained unintelligible. Linh frowned. She had been able to read any script in Nuard's library or Ruarnon's, or in the Zaldeaan Palace. Why not this one?

"It's the script from the archway on Oval Island!" said Fiona. "From all the archways we travelled through to get here. The faeron must be the giants who built the castle —the climate refugees."

Linh's mouth opened in surprise. She scanned the cave wall. The paintings were of square architecture, glass roofs reflecting sunlight, and vast, elegant gardens. Sailing ships rose majestically from the sea beneath an airship suspended by a giant balloon. A colossal bridge spanned across another sea to a forest, where a giant gateway rose, through which turquoise water lapped at a sandy beach.

"That is a faeron Gateway of Umarinaris," said Selenia. "There were many gateways once, and they led to the castle from which the faeron could travel to anywhere in Umarinaris. It was their greatest achievement.

"If they are how you arrived here, then you were lucky. Sorcerers died trying to operate the gateways during the Sorcery War. I expect very few are still safe to use."

"A castle that takes you anywhere in this world," said Michael, "is how we came to be in the Timbalen Empire. We got there via a gateway inside a castle."

Selenia's eyes shone. "I always hoped it still existed. I used to dream of wandering through that castle as a child, roaming through its gateways to every island and continent."

"Is there a gateway here?" Linh asked, fighting hope. "Can the faeron still operate them?"

Selenia's face fell. "Flariah says it no longer works. And the faeron have forgotten. But there are many Gateways in the West. It was home to faeron cities, with gateways linking the important ones. The faeron would not teach humans magic because of the propensity for war they witnessed in your world, but I suspect the faeron's last great act was to teach the Guardians magic to help them win the war. Perhaps the Guardians still know how to operate the gateways."

Linh slumped. It was good to have confirmation gateways existed in the West, perhaps enough that at least one of them still worked and was safe to use. But reason to believe the long-vanished, mythical Guardians could operate the gateways offered no comfort.

Though Linh's love of ancient civilisations wouldn't let her brood. The elaborate artwork beckoned.

"Look at the engineering," she said, studying paintings of bridges spanning valleys to link mountains. "These paintings look ancient, but the engineering in them is modern. Those airships look like zeppelins, but we didn't invent those till the 21st century."

"Then what happened to faeron tech?" Troy asked.

"Lands the faeron settled grew too cold, and they became sick and began to die," Selenia told him. "So they moved on, and the cities they abandoned fell into ruin. As the world cooled, they used the gateways to relocate here and to an uninhabited desert island far away, the only places still warm enough. The knowledge of how to make airships fly was lost, and cooling seas and storms made the faeron ill, so they abandoned their bridges and sailing and have remained on this and the other island ever since."

"They just accepted?" Ruarnon asked.

"No, they didn't. Their sorcerers built the most powerful gateway yet, hoping to travel to a distant place with a warmer climate that could sustain them. It took a unit of time that does not exist in any human language I know, and faeron died trying, but they succeeded. They travelled to a hot, dry country like this one, but humans already lived there. So they brought a ship through the gateway and sailed for uninhabited lands. Snow and ice covered the south, and lands north of it were too wet. Northwest, they found a warm continent, but it was inhabited by humans who looked to them as gods, while the warm continent around the inland sea was ravaged by war.

"After many months searching, the faeron decided there was no place for them. They returned here, bringing with them refugees seeking safe haven. They brought my ancestors to the Far West and sent humans from hotter, humid climates to the jungle and the East Islands via gateways. Then they retreated here and to the desert island and accepted their decline."

"The inscriptions in the castle on Oval Island refer to that," said Linh. "*We have failed.*"

"*All* the humans here are descended from our world," Troy added, shaking his head.

Linh's mind teemed. "That could give light skinned, blond Tarlahns Celtic heritage. Darker haired people could be eastern

European or Central Asian. The Urai could have African heritage, but they seem to have Polynesian features too."

"They resemble my mob in some ways too," said Michael. "I wonder if the East Islanders are of Asian descent. We've seen few people with those features here. And it sounds like the faeron sailed a good way around our world, if the hot land was Australia, the snowy south was Antarctica and the inland sea was the Mediterranean."

"Did a dragon fly through the faeron gateway to the other world?" Fiona asked.

"It did. It took the faeron some time to hunt it down," Selenia replied with a smile.

"Dragon myths in our world are based on a *real* dragon from here?" Troy asked, his features wide with disbelief.

"Dragon myths are prevalent in Asia, which we're south of," said Linh. "I bet that dragon flew north."

It was mind-blowing, confirmation that every person and every aspect of human culture they had seen in this world had its origins in her's. All because the faeron gave their world over to human refugees, when her country insisted on locking up refugees for the 'crime' of arriving 'illegally' by boat. The contrast made Linh think of the faeron as elderly, wise and kind, and Australia as a selfish brat refusing to share its toys.

"Ruarnon told you we came from far away and you guessed this was how we came here?" Fiona asked Selenia, who nodded. "Who do you think could have brought us?"

Selenia hesitated. "Opening the gateway to your world would take incredible power and risk the lives of multiple people shaping magic to do it. Whoever opened the gateway to your world must have very powerful motivations for doing so. The faeron only attempted it to save their entire race.

"If the Sorcery War had just ended, I would suspect the Guardians opened it. They seem to have disappeared after the Sorcery War, and I have often wondered if they crossed this world and perhaps entered yours by gateway. But I can think of no one else who would have reason to take the risks the faeron took operating the gateway that brought you here. What was happening over six months ago that anyone from Umarinaris would be so desperate to leave it?"

"Kyura had barely begun his struggle to stay in power and it wasn't yet clear that war threatened Tarlah," said Ruarnon. "And Mocco said all was well in the jungle then."

"And the Timbalen Empire was hunky dory," said Troy.

Selenia's mouth dropped open. "We think Narz learned that the enchantment no longer bound me around six months ago."

"I wonder if he's been using the gateways to spy," said Michael. "First on the Zaldeaan Realm, then maybe from the jungle, to prepare his attacks."

"Would he use gateways to try to recover you?" Ruarnon asked Selenia.

Selenia answered to the wall paintings, "Narz could be looking for me via gateway. The Guardians are rumoured to have settled in the eastern seas and the Timbalen Empire is there. Narz may think either one was a likely refuge for me. You could have arrived here by accident, when one of Narz's sorcerer spies was exploring the gateway to your world."

Linh gripped the cave wall, as vertigo made her feel like she was falling. Was that why their arrival in Umarinaris made so little sense? Had it been coincidence that she and her friends stepped through a gateway just as a sorcerer was opening it, to see where it went?

"We went to the Timbalen Empire because we wondered if that was where Red Cloak had gone," said Michael. "But we ended up on a tiny island with no one on it, and the only other people around were local."

Ruarnon's brows furrowed. "Sending you to the eastern end of Umarinaris, where no one knows anything about Narz's plans, would be a good way for Narz's spy to hide what they were doing from you. It gave you no chance to ask questions, nor the opportunity to warn the Zaldeaans or Tarlah that the Urai gateway was being used to spy on us. It gave you no chance to give up his secrets to the wrong people, and it let you live."

Linh felt hollow. Could Red Cloak have led them to Oval Island's Castle and left the gateway to Myleth Island invitingly open, instead of killing them, to keep the fact he could open gateways secret? He had acknowledged them, but rushed ahead, refusing to speak to them, making limited eye contact, as you might, if you didn't want to get attached to someone you were planning to kill, or banish to the ends of the earth?

Michael sat on the cave floor. "That actually makes sense. For the first time since we arrived here, Red Cloak's actions make sense."

"Don't forget," said Fiona. "The gateway opened twice. Once when we were a good distance from it, and again as we were walking through it."

Ruarnon sighed. "To our knowledge, no one has been through the gateway to your world since the faeron, centuries, perhaps several thousand years ago. What if this Red Cloak opened the gateway a second time to let you through, to test if you survived the journey?"

Michael groaned. "That's exactly what I said when we got here. I wondered if Red Cloak was rushing off to tell someone higher up that their experiment had worked: they'd opened the gateway and we'd come through it alive and in perfect health."

"But, if Narz was opening gateways and sending spies through them to find you," Troy said to Selenia, "Why didn't Red Cloak ask us about you?"

"And if he was testing the gateway, why not send us home again?" said Michael. "Because the only way anyone in this world can travel through that gateway is out of Umarinaris to our world, so it isn't much use to Narz without proof people can survive doing that."

"Which goes back to why leave the gateway open to Oval Island, on Nuard's doorstep?" said Troy. "Why make it easy for us to wander to a remote corner of the Timbalen Empire and hang out with a friendly old scholar who was delighted to have visitors?"

"I still wonder if that was a merciful way to silence test subjects after opening the gateway to your world," said Ruarnon. "But I would like to know what purpose Narz, Red Cloak, or anyone else intended to use that gateway for, if their test succeeded."

That was the ultimate question. Linh had a bad feeling Poran may not know the answer.

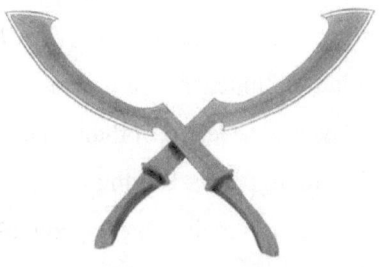

CHAPTER 11

INTELLIGENCE FROM THE WEST -RUARNON

R uarnon sat at the head of a rectangular table in Flariah's dining hall, with their friends and advisors.

"The sorcerers' unleashed creatures which murdered innocents," said Monin said to Ruarnon. "There is no question as to their guilt."

"If two of these men would not have harmed anyone without Narz's influence," said Companion Tor, "to what extent are they accountable for unleashing damars, and to what extent does the king who corrupted them, ordered the invasion, and created damars bear responsibility?"

That was the part Ruarnon didn't like. Tarlahn law did not answer those questions. The law said all three sorcerers were murderers and that their lives were forfeit. Yet the wills of Poran and Dargus were not their own. They were as much Narz's tools as damars.

"Innocents have died," said Monin, "these men volunteered for this mission, and they unleashed the creatures that killed those innocents. Surely their sentence will be death?"

Ruarnon leant heavily on the head of the table. Questioning the sorcerers had stirred up their anger about the devastation damars had caused in the Zaldeaan Realm. But King Kyomi's Peace Speech asked people to let go of their anger and said forgiveness was the path to peace. Having presented Kyomi's speech as the way forward to their subjects, could Ruarnon abandon it themself?

"What good will killing them do?" Linh asked.

Monin glared at her, likely perplexed she was offering her opinion to the Council when she was officially here to translate when they questioned the sorcerers. She flinched when she noticed, then surprised Ruarnon by looking Monin right in the eye, her jaw stubbornly set, as if demanding not only that he let her talk at a council meeting, but demanded he *answer* her questions at it.

Lenaris' features tensed at the sight. But instead of losing his temper and throwing Linh out, as Ruarnon half anticipated, Monin's frown smoothed. He turned calmly to Tor, who spoke next.

"If these men can be made to see Narz for the villain he is," said Tor, "might they unmask him to his sorcerer followers and dissuade sorcerers from serving him? Good may come of mercy. It would extend the logic of allowing a thief to repay the value of what he stole through labour."

"But is a life saved equal to a life taken?" Lenaris countered. "And can they save as many people as they allowed to die?"

Executing them was vengeance. Tarlahn misplaced attempts at vengeance on the Urai had culminated in the murder of an entire tribe. Vengeance was a path to destruction. Ruarnon did not want to pursue it, but the law proscribed it.

Yet, Linh and Tor were right; having Poran denounce Narz to sorcerers was the only thing Ruarnon could do to counter Narz's ruthlessness, the only good that could come of this situation. If they could find the source of the sorcerer's conviction and break Narz's hold, they could turn Narz's weapons against him and give both men the chance to atone for their crimes.

But the third sorcerer was ruthless and dangerous. He needed to be contained by faeron, or executed, to ensure he did not re-offend.

Ruarnon led their council into the questioning room reluctantly. Everyone took their seats opposite the three sorcerers, who sat with silent faeron between them. Flariah was absent; Ruarnon would report to her later.

"Why did you agree to work for Narz?" Ruarnon asked Poran and Dargus. Linh repeated their words in what sounded like Timbalen, which the sorcerers somehow understood.

Ruarnon waited for Dargus to finish speaking, then listened to Linh's repetition in Timbalen. "Ever since the Sorcery War, many people have been too afraid of magic and too mistrustful of sorcerers to let us heal them. His Worthiness would change that. My sisters are birthers, who moved to Azula to work at the Temple of Healing, where they could use magic openly. They have saved more babies, and mothers lives from complications during childbirth than any non-magic wielder can. I am not so skilled with healing nor of the right disposition for a Keeper of the Peace, but I wish to protect people who are. That is why I volunteered for these eastern expeditions."

Ruarnon frowned. The deluded sorcerer's claims about Narz wanting sorcerers to use magic for the 'betterment of humankind' sounded like outright lies, but if magic *was* being used for healing in the Far West...

"Why do you serve Narz, Poran?" Ruarnon asked.

"One of my earliest memories is of a shepherd boy being chased out of town because the sheep he tended magically recovered from foot rot. My parents and I spent my childhood living in fear, hiding my powers. My wife used hers to heal in secret, but when a deadly fever swept the city, she offered magical healing publicly, with our king's approval. Because of her fame, our neighbours knew our children were sorcerers and feared the havoc they may cause learning to control their powers. We were shunned and feared. We moved to Azula so our children could receive a magical education, my wife could heal, and we could live without fear."

Linh frowned. "Is that how Narz gets them in? By creating a safe haven for sorcerers, so they flock to him?"

Monin's jaw dropped. He seemed too surprised by her logic to protest at her speaking up again.

"You truly believe he would change Umarinaris just to win followers?" Poran asked. "How is a girl so young as you so sceptical?"

"When he commits mass murder on one continent," said Linh, "then poses as a saviour on another, he seems two-faced. I think one face is a lie and I think it's the one he wears at home."

"Jandar told you the damar murders were *Vye's* fault," Poran protested. "Daxius, my king and His Worthiness' right-hand man, asked me to watch Vye, and I suspect Vye knows it. He sent Dargus and I home so we would not witness his crimes."

Linh bit her lip. "Or so your image of Narz wasn't cracked, when you saw too much to doubt that Vye was acting on Narz's orders."

Monin shook his head at Linh's grasp of the situation and Ruarnon almost smiled. Perhaps it was time to make Linh their official Companion.

Poran's mouth dropped open. "You sound like a Galvation. Determined to believe sorcerers are evil. They have thought us so since their home city was destroyed during the Sorcery War and have ignored all good any sorcerer has done since."

Linh shook her head. "I saw a sorcerer heal Ruarnon's wound in Zaldea City. And Mocco and Mawana's magic saved us all in the Battle of Blue Bay. Magic *can* be used for good. But all I've seen Narz use it for, here and in the Zaldeaan Realm, is evil. Had Ruarnon not looked after the Zaldeaans, they would have spent Autumn or Winter starving. How do you justify that?"

"If Ruarnon is King of Tarlah, then of course his Greatness was going to conquer them," Poran replied.

Ruarnon blinked, then realised 'his' referred to them.

"Their Benevolence uses 'they'," Tor corrected.

Poran's eyes widened silently, and Jandar snickered. Tor glared at the man, but Ruarnon rolled their eyes the man's immaturity.

"My apologies," said Poran, inclining his head. "I meant no offence. But the Zaldeaans were leaderless, and their Greatness conquering them would secure peace with Tarlah."

Ruarnon's chest tightened. Poran took for granted that Ruarnon was a good Zaldeaan King. Just as he took for granted that Narz was good. He failed to see any difference between the two rulers.

"Even if what you believe is true," said Monin, "If Vye murdered Zaldeaan soldiers to bully them into obedience, surely there were signs *that* was his nature. How did Narz overlook them?"

Poran paled. "Narz gave him a command where he could not be supervised by sorcerers powerful enough to control him. His Greatness must know something went wrong because he has kept Vye by his side ever since. He chose Tyrook to lead this expedition, despite doubts Tyrook was powerful enough to keep the damars functioning as an army."

"Why did Narz put Vye in charge?" Tor asked.

"He was the only one fearless and powerful enough to control multiple damar packs back then. He was the protection measure, if the rest of us lost our grip on the enchantment binding our pack."

"Narz intended Vye to ensure packs *didn't* break away from the battle?" Linh asked sharply.

Poran's brows rose. "He was to ensure none of them ran off and attacked *anyone*. Vye appeared the best leader to counter that."

Ruarnon shook their head. It was obvious to them that Vye had made no attempt to wield magic to contain damars in the Zaldeaan Realm. The man was a monster, yet Poran couldn't see it. And Narz had employed that monster, despite being suspicious of his true nature, and had given Vye a command that let him kill hundreds of innocents. Ruarnon sighed, suspecting they would never dissuade Poran from his determination to see good in Narz.

"If sorcerers live in hiding and fear in the west, why would Vye so blatantly abuse the command Narz gave him?" Monin asked.

"There are… others. How Vye behaved in the Zaldeaan Realm reflects their views and values. They think they are above non-magic wielders and ordinary sorcerers. And they are exceptionally powerful."

"That sounds like sorcerers who fought the Sorcery War," Lenaris commented with a frown.

"These are their descendants."

Ruarnon gaped.

"If Vye thinks so highly of himself, why did he leave his homeland to serve Narz?" Monin asked.

"I assume his rank is not as high as he wanted, and he believed His Worthiness could offer power. Those are the two things dearest to their kind, rank and power."

If Narz was a ruthless, bloody tyrant, surely he too was a descendant of sorcerers who fought the war? But in luring sorcerers to become magic-wielding healers, Narz was giving people time to overcome their fear and insecurity to serve him. He was being patient.

Whereas the impatience and cruelty of what Poran claimed Vye had done befitted evil sorcerers who fought the war. If their descendants were recruiting followers, surely they would enslave sorcerers? Vye may be the monster Poran thought he was, but perhaps Narz *was* different, in some ways.

"How do you explain Narz creating such evil creatures in the first place?" Lenaris asked.

"They were a failed experiment, but his Worthiness told me there are some things no man can face —things he created damars to counter. I believe the creature armies we attacked here are what His Worthiness was referring to."

"Did Narz not tell you?" Ruarnon asked.

"He does not like to speak of damars. Nor do I. They are dangerous and vicious; I do not deny this, but I much prefer having brought damars here to fight this island's creatures than men."

"You see damars as tools?" Ruarnon asked.

"That is what they are, a fighting force of killing tools. I do not deny it."

How could he admit that, yet not see their creator as evil?

"And you Dargus?" Ruarnon asked. "What do you think?"

"I think what happened in the Zaldeaan Realm was wrong. It sounds like hundreds of innocents are dead. His Worthiness should have prevented that! But, if the damars I unleashed went running wild across the Realm," he gripped the edge of the table, and his knuckles went white, "then you should execute me. If they fought anyone… I only meant them to fight soldiers, but if they killed innocent people, I deserve to die."

Ruarnon blanched. How could Dargus see damar attacks as evil and think *he* should be executed, yet see Narz guilty only of negligence?

Poran was turning grey. "I do not want to imagine what those things I delivered to the Realm did, but some of them must have killed ordinary people because I let them out of cages. We should be executed."

"You fought a war. You were winning. They fought poorly. They were losing," Jandar objected. "That is hardly *our* fault."

"We are accountable for our actions Jandar," Poran said sadly.

Jandar shook his head.

"What is to be our fate?" Poran asked, looking Ruarnon in the eye.

"I was going to ask you to dissuade sorcerers from assisting Narz's invasions of people who mean him no harm and to do everything you can to prevent him from committing future atrocities."

Both men's features widened.

"But we are murderers!" Dargus objected, teary-eyed. "You cannot release us after what we did!"

"I am Prime Ruler of the Zaldeaan Realm. If releasing you gives you the chance to prevent anything remotely like that atrocity from happening again, I will do so."

Their eyes widened further.

"Your Benevolence would have us save others?" Poran said slowly. "I can denounce Vye to His Worthiness, if Vye does not kill me first."

"Send me to the Realm," Dargus said emotionlessly. "I will be useless in the west, and I owe the Zaldeaans my life."

"No," Ruarnon replied. "Despair will not atone for what you have done, and executing you does no one any good."

"Then how do I atone?" Dargus asked, his voice cracked, tears spilling down his face.

Ruarnon wondered how such a man had volunteered for *two* damarian invasions.

"If you want to help Zaldeaans," Linh said, "tell Ruarnon anything that could help them return the Zaldeaan army to their people."

Monin cleared his throat loudly and glared at Linh. The anger burning in his eyes said he was outraged that Linh dares speak on Ruarnon's behalf. Lenaris tensed at the sight. But Linh was following the conversation too passionately to notice, as were the sorcerers.

"I will tell you anything you wish to know, as the Zaldeaan king," Poran added, his face haggard and eyes dark.

This was not the way Ruarnon wanted to get information. Vye's true nature and what they had done in delivering damars to the Zaldeaan Realm had broken them. Ruarnon needed time to think, before asking the long list of questions they had about Narz.

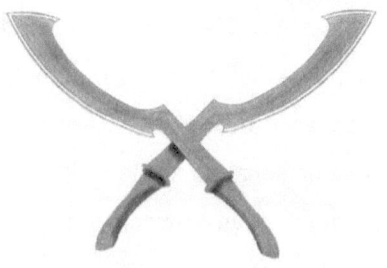

CHAPTER 12

KNOW YOUR ENEMY ~RUARNON

After a midday meal in Flariah's dining hall, Ruarnon asked Poran and Dargus, via Linh, "How much do you know of Narz? I assume you have met him?"

Both men still looked pale. Had Poran's eyes been that dark before? Dargus fidgeted, glancing around the table as if unsure what to say. There could be no doubt that answering this question would involve saying things they should not be telling Narz's enemy. They couldn't stay loyal to Narz and answer Ruarnon. But was Dargus fidgeting, or squirming with guilt? Desperation to atone battled loyalty to Narz in both men's eyes.

Poran let out a deep sigh and Ruarnon wondered which driving force had won out.

"I have met His Greatness twice," Poran replied. "He presents as a grave leader, focused, determined and more in tune to the needs of his people than any king I have met."

Even as Poran potentially betrayed his king, his admiration for Narz was clear. It made Ruarnon suspect he was answering sincerely.

"He is an intelligent man with a sharp mind, though he can be blind-sighted by his passion. They say in elite circles His Worthiness has been the king of Azula for a hundred and fifty years. The elderly swear he does not age. And he is extremely wealthy, owning vast personal estates."

Ruarnon's mouth fell open. How could anyone have ruled anywhere for that long?

"He purchased Arveta's crown from its ruler," Poran continued, seeming to find it easier to disclose information now that he had started. "He negotiated to rule Tiama and its former king Daxius became governor under His Worthiness. He is the only man to take other kingdoms without the bloody conquests common in our homeland. Only with our eastern neighbours is there open conflict, but the Galvations hate sorcerers."

"You all heard the same version of how Narz gained these kingdoms?" Tor asked.

Jandar nodded. "He sets an example to our continent of what great rule looks like. One day he shall rule the whole continent. And while Vye had notions of expanding faster with sorcery, Narz will not let him. He insists on just rule."

Ruarnon resisted the compulsion to argue that point. Poran and Dargus still seemed willing to atone, while Jandar may give away valuable information because he seemed to enjoy blowing Narz's trumpet. But Poran's admiration for how Narz was expanding in the west was clear. Other details he gave at random, but his focus was details that made Narz the ruler he admired, the ruler Ruarnon suspected Poran still wanted Ruarnon to see.

"As I have told you," Poran finished, "the King Narz I know is a good king. All his policies in Azula reflect this."

It seemed Linh was right; Narz presented an entirely different face at home.

"The Zaldeaan army fought against the Galvations," Poran added, cutting into Ruarnon's thoughts. "The Galvations were prepared to fight to the last man, and His Worthiness hoped extra soldiers would persuade them to surrender."

"Did it?" Ruarnon asked.

"They fled or tried too. Most of their people were captured and are now His Worthiness' subjects, but some fled to the woods to resist."

"And what of the Zaldeaan army?"

"They occupy and patrol Galvatia in search of rebels. His Worthiness recalled his army to the capital because the southern kings fear he is uniting kingdoms against them, and he suspects they will in turn ally against him."

"Would the Keepers and Healers fight? Ruarnon asked.

Poran's mouth dropped open. "They are not trained to fight. Keeper's training focuses on using magic to investigate crimes. They specialise in accurately identifying criminals, especially powerful people who abuse their positions and use murder and bribes to conceal it. Spy magic has been invaluable for that. Healers are devoted to repairing the body and eradicating illness. Both are gaining the people's trust with their actions. If they were to fight, it would make the people fear Narz's rule and perhaps prompt rebellion."

"He actually cares about justice?" Linh asked, open-mouthed.

Monin opened his mouth, probably to tell Linh to close hers. But Ruarnon wanted the answer to that too. And Ruarnon was in charge, not Tarlahn traditions about who could be on the Royal Council and who could speak at its meetings. They caught Monin's gaze and shook their head. Monin's face smoothed over again. How did he do that, become suddenly so calm when he looked about to lose his temper?

"Or pretends to care about justice," said Tor. "That may win him many supporters."

"It is the main thing inspiring sorcerers to serve His Worthiness, but strange to hear you speak of what he does at home as a lie. Many in our homeland would not believe the wars we wage on his behalf."

If Narz presented as just, how did he justify taking Ruarnon's parents and Companion Pamoran captive? And who had shipped them to Narz?

"Did any Zaldeaans sail back with you when you left the Realm after releasing damars?"

"Yes. Three Zaldeaan generals captured early in the fighting."

Ruarnon's heart skipped a beat. "What did they look like?"

"Unwell. One was a woman with dark hair and skin, and one of the men had dark hair, but the other was blonde, and they were all in their middle years."

Which matched the state and general appearance of the three people Iagl's harbour officials reported being shipped out of Edesinia and round the North Lander coast.

"What happened to them?" Lenaris asked eagerly.

"They remained unwell during the voyage, so the scout who captured them took them to Narz's castle instead of the prison where Galvation leaders are detained. He said the healers should be able to treat them."

"Then what?" Lenaris asked.

"I enquired about them when we left for this voyage, and Narz became uncomfortable and said the healers were having difficulty."

"They were still in his castle?" Ruarnon asked.

"I believe so."

"What illness did they have?" Lenaris asked.

"They were still being drugged," said Tor. "The 'scout' who helped capture them drugged them during the voyage, so they couldn't tell Poran or Dargus who they were. Narz didn't want to admit they were wrongfully imprisoned, so he lied."

Tension that had been part of Ruarnon's body for months seeped out of them. They relaxed into their seat, assured at last that their parents were alive in their new location, and exchanged a relieved smile with Lenaris.

"Who were these people?" Poran asked. "How do you know them?"

"They are my parents and Lenaris' father, both abducted, then smuggled out of the Zaldeaan palace before the damars attacked."

Poran frowned. "That does not make any sense."

"How many Zaldeaan commanders were shipped with them?" Monin asked.

"None."

"Then why did they get special treatment?" Lenaris asked.

Poran sighed. "I assumed Narz's discomfort was because his healers had come up against an illness they could not cure. It is more likely that he was lying, but what threat did Tarlahns pose?"

Ruarnon shrugged. "None. We thought Narz might want information from them."

"Then why not send an envoy? Why smuggle them west?"

"Perhaps he wanted to speak to them in person," Tor deduced.

"But our greatest threat, our greatest danger is in the south, not the east. How could anything they know possibly serve his Greatness?"

Ruarnon shook their head, disappointed to find Poran as lost as they were.

"I can draw you a map showing Narz's Castle and what I know of Galvatia to help you plan to free them."

One of Ruarnon's scribes leant him a scroll, ink and a stylus, and he sketched out a map of Narz's territories. It faded into obscurity in the east after the city of Galvatia and showed many small kingdoms south of Azula. Poran gave it to Ruarnon, who smiled, glad to see where their parents were.

Their advisors asked more questions. Scribes Tor sent for made extensive notes.

"Do you know anything about Narz sending spies through magic archways?" Linh finally asked.

Poran frowned.

"What children's tale is this?" Jandar asked.

"There are some archways in ruins from before the Sorcery War," Dargus replied. "With a strange spiral script no one can read carved into them. I sensed magic in one once."

Linh smiled at confirmation the archways still existed in the west, and that one contained magic, which presumably meant it was operational.

But Poran's brows raised at the idea. "I thought tales of adventures through archways were as credible as tales of slaves from the Sorcery War haunting the dungeons, or warnings to never sleep in the ruins, lest tormented spirits push loose bits of rubble down onto your head that you may join them in the afterlife."

"Don't forget how the Guardians fled through them, after wiping out half of our ancestors and winning the Sorcery War," Jandar added.

So westerners *had* heard the same tales as Selenia.

Everyone ran out of questions after that. "Thank you," Ruarnon said to Poran and Dargus. "What you have provided will help us a great deal."

"What will you do with the information?" Poran asked, and Ruarnon saw guilt in his eyes and his knuckles turning white as his fists clenched.

"I shall use it to free the Zaldeaan army, my family and Lenaris' father and bring them home."

Poran's hands relaxed.

"Is that all?" Dargus asked. "With everything you suspect His Worthiness of?"

"I do not have the resources for anything more, and vengeance has no place in either of my kingdoms, so I will not seek it. Besides, his wars are beyond my responsibility, which is to my subjects under his power, and my subjects at home."

"I believe your parents' abductions are a mistake," Poran said woodenly. "I will ask His Worthiness to release them. And do my best to expose Vye. Will you help me, Dargus?"

Dargus paled and shivered at the idea, but he nodded. "Vye must be stopped before he hurts anyone else."

CHAPTER 13

PREPARATION: RUARNON

Ruarnon stood by the rocky shore of Blue Bay with their companions, watching a North Lander ship carrying Jandar set sail, while rowboats ferried western sailors to their ships. The North Lander rulers had acknowledged Ruarnon as Prime Ruler and assured them that North Lander Law Keepers could secure Jandar, while he served a life sentence of forced labour.

Ruarnon turned to Dargus and Poran.

Dargus met their eyes. "Thank you for the chance to help Poran counter Vye and prevent atrocities. I feel it is more than I deserve."

"I disagree," said Ruarnon. "May fortune go with you."

Dargus smiled sadly and bowed, but Poran merely nodded, slumped under the weight of Zaldeaan deaths. Ruarnon hoped they forgave themselves one day. Western sailors rowed them to their ship, and Dargus raised his hand in goodbye, as his ship sailed across Blue Bay. Ruarnon returned the gesture.

Then it was Ruarnon's turn to say goodbye. They turned to Flariah. "Thank you for letting me speak freely to the sorcerers. Do you believe Lylah's prophecy fulfilled?"

Flariah shook her head. "If Narz intended to destroy my creatures, he has failed, and there is another island like this that he may know of."

Ruarnon wondered if Narz still feared Selenia or southern sorcerers commanding creature armies, and if more western ships were on their way. But armed with Poran's information, it was time to call Companion Noma home and plan a recovery expedition. And with Tarlah and the Zaldeaan Realm secure, Ruarnon ought to formally renew Tarlah's alliance with the Timbalen Empire. Duty beckoned.

They turned to Selenia. "Will we see you again?"

She smiled and replied, "I think I will manage that."

"You are welcome to stay with us in Tarlah City if you can visit my continent."

"We shall see."

She embraced them. Troy gave Ruarnon a strange gesture, raising a single thumb. Selenia laughed. "I think Troy may be under the wrong impression," she whispered.

"It would appear so," Ruarnon replied. "I understand the way Mawana and Lenaris feel about each other on an intellectual level, but not on a personal one."

Selenia smiled. "I seem to only feel that way about girls. But I should like to be friends."

"So would I," said Ruarnon.

Ruarnon led their friends to the boats and the Iylena's foredeck, from which they waved to Selenia, who waved back, as the Iylena's sails were set. The Iylena's prow pointed towards the cliffs of Tava's Gap, and Blue Bay retreated beyond sheer cliff edges. Ruarnon enjoyed the view until the Iylena sailed into the open sea, then entered their cabin, where they found Tor, Monin and Lenaris seated at their table and joined them.

"It would be prudent to inform our allies of your intentions," Monin advised. "The skills of their Elite Guard are legend, and their assistance could be invaluable."

Ruarnon had vague hopes of the Timbalens lending them soldiers, but they had not considered the Elite Guard because they rarely, if ever, left the empire.

"I advise making that request in person," Monin added.

Did he worry Ruarnon would go haring off to the West just because they could see where their parents were on a map? Lenaris' sigh suggested so. But Monin was right; the treaty with the empire needed renewal, and it was an excellent opportunity to discuss Timbalen assistance with the emperor in person. Knowing Narz's power, if the Elite Guard had any magical abilities, their help could be invaluable.

"Tor, could you send instructions to begin preparations for our voyage to the empire to Tarlah. I would appreciate Monin reviewing the former alliance papers and suggesting any required changes. I should like to set sail by the end of the week and visit the Realm first, to update the Governors in Edesinia."

Both men and Lenaris bowed their heads in acknowledgement, and Ruarnon dismissed them.

The return voyage to Tarlah was smooth and brought welcome news. It appeared Selenia had been right about Urai curiosity, as a letter from Tarata said Mocco was to act as Urai ambassador and negotiate a trade agreement with the Timbalens. Mawana was to keep him company, and probably hoped to lend Mocco his adventurous spirit. And Lylah wanted to meet Ruarnon and their Australian friends.

A day later, Ruarnon gazed out a carriage window as golden grain fields, and paddocks of grazing Tarlahn sheep and mature lambs gave way to the dense green foliage of the jungle. Their carriage slowed and halted. Ruarnon, Michael, Troy, Linh and Fiona climbed out and met Lylah at the jungle's edge, while their guards waited on horseback beside the road.

Lylah's almond-shaped eyes were piercing. They appeared to have seen far more than her middle-aged, dark features suggested was possible. She gave their friends the hint of a smile, then turned to Ruarnon. "I am beginning to see many futures. After your last conversation with Poran, I *Saw* you in the West. Many people have many decisions to make, but as Narz's war unfolds, the common thread in the futures is that you five, in the right places, at the right times, make all futures brighter. You are all catalysts for peace."

Ruarnon's mouth opened slowly. "If we are unable to recover my parents, aunt and cousin, I must be crowned as ruler. I should marry and have children to be my heirs. I cannot fulfil that duty if I get killed in the West. Sailing there goes against everything my father and uncle taught me."

They felt no enthusiasm for marriage. The only good thing to come from their parents' abduction was that their mother's courting and eventual marriage plans for them had been put on hold indefinitely, and Ruarnon hadn't been required to give a single thought to them. It could be delayed, but not avoided.

"Your heart lags behind your mind in this, but it will catch up," Lylah replied.

Ruarnon inhaled slowly, fighting their heart's attempt to beat faster. They could not walk away from the duty their uncle gave his life to fulfil.

"If you don't go," Troy said uncertainly, "are we going on our own?"

Ruarnon stared.

"Sailing with your expedition is our best chance of finding a way home," Linh reminded. "Selenia and Dargus have confirmed gateways exist there, and it sounds like the one Dargus visited still works. And if we get the chance to do some good in the Far West, we'll probably end up trying."

"If I stay," Ruarnon replied softly, "I abandon you to this duty of brighter futures and your fate in our world." The weight of decision and responsibility settled on their shoulders.

"You've got the whole voyage to the empire and back to decide," said Fiona. "It's not something to rush."

The Royal Council had yet to identify and weigh all relevant factors. Ruarnon would wait until they had considered everything, prolonging the final decision until they had dismissed all counterarguments and chose what their duty demanded. They nodded, slumping under the weight of a decision that may prove harder than deciding to occupy the Zaldeaan Realm.

"Ruarnon might be able to persuade kings to change the future, and so can Mic and Linh and maybe Fiona," said Troy, "but what am *I* supposed to do in the West, or Narz's war?"

"You are all greatly needed," said Lylah. "I see that now. At first, I assumed Ruarnon needed you. They have, and your presence benefits more than they know, but there is another. There is a terrible struggle unfolding. I cannot *See* it properly, and I do not understand it, but someone involved in that struggle thinks of you four. To them, you are the balance between order and chaos. I believe I am starting to *See* Red Cloak, though he tries to hide. I believe he brought you into this world."

"What does that mean?" Linh asked.

"It means his magical defences are weakening."

"What's Red Cloak's role in Narz's war?" Michael asked.

"He lies at the heart of it. I *See* only glimpses of the futures of Red Cloak, Narz, Lord Tarz, Lord Vye, and a girl called Teliph, but only when their defences weaken, because they can shield themselves from my *Sight*. They stand at the heart of the struggle, but most of what they do and the struggle itself is hidden to me."

"And I?" Ruarnon asked.

"Your influence is linked to your friends'. You amplify their influence, and they yours. Calamity may be avoided by them alone, but the best future I foresee, and all better futures contain the five of you in the West."

"But I have no duty or responsibility towards those lands."

"You will seek an alliance with Narz's enemies, the Galvations. You will assist one another, this I *See*. That is how, where and when you become catalysts for the continent. You will be unable to play only the part you intend, Ruarnon. You will find it impossible, while your friends will embrace their destiny as it unfolds. Whoever brought you four knew their choice and its implications for the future when they chose you."

Ruarnon's friends stood stock still, with open mouths. They doubted what they could do in the West. Ruarnon understood that, having been plagued with doubts about recovering their parents ever since they learned Narz had them.

"Those you send west must accompany you on your eastern voyage. My sisters are undecided now, but they will teach you things you need to know to equip you for the West. They live on what you call the 'Island of the Guardians', at which you can stop on your way to Timbala City. Your western expedition will fail if you do not obtain what they offer you."

"How can they help us?" Ruarnon asked.

"Flariah's creature army is not the only secret we have kept. There is another, but I cannot reveal it because the others do not yet agree. They will, after you set sail."

"My advisors will say this is needlessly rash," Ruarnon replied. "Setting off to visit people we did not know existed, to accept an unknown form of aid."

"I will not break my oath to my sisters because of the stubborn and misguided suspicions of old men."

Troy grinned, and Ruarnon bowed their head. "I do not expect you to."

But they weren't looking forward to explaining to their advisors. Monin would wonder if the sisters could be trusted, question their interest in the West, even think Ruarnon was chasing myths in pursuing the legendary Island of the Guardians.

Even Tor may suspect that. Both generals would be wary. Even Lenaris may doubt.

But Lylah had been concerned about the Zaldeaans too. She had written in the World Book to persuade the four Australians to go to Tarlah, and they had helped Ruarnon decide to occupy the Realm and end the War of King Kuyra's Succession. Ruarnon trusted her. And Flariah's army had lived since before Tarlah was founded, yet never harmed anyone on Ruarnon's continent. Ruarnon trusted Flariah too and was inclined to trust whoever guarded the army on the Island of the Guardians.

"We shall visit your sisters. But I cannot make any promises about going West."

"That is enough for now, and it will be enough for my sisters. I will send you a map and a star chart identifying the constellations your navigator will need to find their island. And in that case, I have a request for you. Can you take Selenia with you?"

Ruarnon's brows rose.

"She would benefit from visiting what you call The Island of the Guardians as much as your people will."

"She is welcome to sail with us," Ruarnon replied.

"Thank you. And take care. You are yet to see the worst of Narz's power or the last of magic, and his war is not yet finished in the east. Be on your guard."

They thanked Lylah, and Ruarnon spent the return journey to Tarlah considering how best to explain what she had said to the Royal Council. They met Tor, Monin, General Aza, General Takanis and Lenaris in the Golden Meeting Hall soon after they arrived. Fireflies danced in their stomach as they took their seat at the head of the table, with rows of previous rulers busts overlooking them from one side, as they announced that they wanted all soldiers who would sail west to accompany them east.

As they expected, even Lenaris' eyes widened.

"Your Benevolence wishes to take three shiploads of soldiers east?" Monin asked. "That is a good deal of expense."

"I wish them to train under my leadership before I send them West," Ruarnon replied, meeting Monin's gaze. "Lylah wishes us to meet her sister, who lives on an island concealing secrets, one of which she believes will aid our western expedition."

"Your report says magic was involved in the fighting at Cauldron Island," said General Takanis, the tendons standing out in her forearms showing her tension as she leant on the table, her voice steady and calm. "And that suggests magic was indeed involved in capturing the Zaldeaan army. How can we be sure you would not be sailing into a similar trap?"

General Aza eyed Ruarnon keenly beside her. For the first time, Ruarnon wasn't just going to have win over Monin, they'd have to persuade both the generals and from his silence, perhaps even Tor. Lenaris was frowning, but she gave them the subtlest of encouraging nods.

Why must Tarlahn tradition insist the Council's decisions be unanimous? True, it would check hot-headed kings, but tradition didn't seem to account for experienced advisors caught up in the past, unwilling to move in new ways necessitated by an ever-changing present.

"Our King and Queen are the captives of a sorcerer-king," said Ruarnon. "If we are not willing to face magic, we must abandon them."

Lenaris tensed. That would condemn her father to the same fate. Monin grimaced at giving up on his son, while both generals solemnly bowed their heads, conceding the point. Tor's eyes were a pool of worry, in concern for his two closest friends. No one on the Council wanted to abandon the King, Queen or Companion Pamoran.

"If Lylah's sisters know anything of magic," Ruarnon continued, "or how to fight it with conventional weapons, that is knowledge I cannot pass up, as Heir and my parent's child. And Flariah appears to have lived alongside us, with an army of dangerous creatures she can control by magic, her entire life. Yet she has never harmed us. We did not even know she or her creatures existed. If any of the Sisters meant us harm, would they not have hurt us already?"

"A few of our ships across the ocean are more vulnerable than our entire army stationed in our home city," General Takanis countered. "I want to know the geography of the island the fleet would visit. And our fleet could not be anchored in a natural harbour like the Urai fleet was on Cauldron Island. It would need to behave with caution around strangers and strange islands.

"You are right that these sisters do not seem to mean us harm, but clearly Narz is at war with them, and we know he is willing to wage that war across the ocean. It is only a matter of whether he has more ships to send, and whether in sailing to visit Lylah's sisters our ships are caught in the crossfire."

"Lylah warned me of this," said Ruarnon. "I have already contacted King Kahorn, the North Landers and Governor Armar by messenger bird. No other western ships have been sighted sailing in any of this continent's waters. I would send the Iylena's birds to all three locations, and leave some here, so that any of you could send word of the approach of western ships to me at sea, should western ships depart after me."

That was the threat they expected most of the Council to object to, the possibility of encountering more of Narz's ships at sea, or getting caught up in fighting when Narz attacked Lylah's sisters' island. But by the time Ruarnon sailed to the Timbalen Empire to ask for aid, their advisors should be ready for final discussions and to prepare the western recovery expedition to set sail. They did not want to delay their eastern and western voyages, or meeting Lyah's sisters or the Timbalen Emperor, unless they had confirmation Narz *did* threaten either voyage.

"Our ships would need to be ready to flee and whoever goes ashore ready to return to the ship as swiftly as possible, should western ships be sighted on the horizon," said General Aza.

Ruarnon bowed their head. There was no question of avoiding Narz's sorcerers on an eastern warpath. Ruarnon's ships would be outmatched by fire-wielding sorcerers, and getting caught between the sisters' creature armies, damars and sorcerers on land could be catastrophic. If Narz's ships appeared when Ruarnon's were near the sister's island, they'd have to retreat to sea until the fighting was over.

Lenaris sat up straighter. "I know it is not appropriate for our young Australian guests to contribute to this council."

Monin's face clouded over and he glared at his granddaughter.

Lenaris avoided looking at him, gazing across the table at the generals and to Ruarnon as its head. "But Linh and Michael asked me to remind this council that damars attacked the Zaldeaan Realm and Cauldron Island. That Narz has twice had the opportunity to attack us and proven his military interest lies in other targets."

"And his ships ignored ours on their way to Cauldron Island," General Takanis added, "despite that I had our ships lined along our southern coast, their decks packed with armed soldiers and our preparedness to fight them was made clear. Do you and the Australians doubt Narz would waste his resources fighting us, when he seems bent on destroying these creature armies?"

Lenaris inclined her head.

Monin shook his. "It is highly inappropriate for foreigners of no special status to weigh in on council matters."

But Ruarnon wanted them to, whether Monin liked it or not. "Perhaps it is time I gave them status," Ruarnon countered, meeting Monin's gaze and clamping down on their nerves about challenging the man directly, for the first time. "One companion is hardly enough."

Monin eyed them stonily. Fireflies danced in their stomach, but they would not be swayed. And it wouldn't do for Linh to have stared down their most senior advisor, if they as regent could not...

"Then perhaps it is time they were adopted," Monin replied.

Ruarnon's eyes widened. They weren't sure of Monin's intent, but if Linh thought Tor, or anyone else had been formally appointed as her guardian, or boss, as she would see it, Ruarnon suspected even Fiona couldn't contain her protest.

A wicked smile spread across Monin's war-hardened face.

"Generals, what do you do when you come across uppity soldiers who dare to analyse or second guess their superiors — correctly?"

"Promote them," General Aza replied. "Some minds are better suited to strategizing than fighting, and if they do so in a manner that respects our command structure, we are happy to assign them a role to which they are fitting."

"Hence our Heirs must be most capable of all," Monin added, and a hush fell over the Council, as Monin turned to Ruarnon. Monin smiled. "Your father gave myself, the leaders of my generation, and your quick-witted uncle and highly capable soldier of an aunt a merry chase as king. He didn't have half your discipline.

"Whereas you were so quiet that at first I doubted your mettle. But since marching an army into the Zaldeaan Realm you have done nothing less than quietly and discreetly set about moving mountains. You have the bravery of soldier, without their swagger and the mind of a general. You refuse to accept any tradition you do not find practical; you insist on befriending foreigners who, despite their total lack of manners, can argue and reason as well as if they had a royal education. And you Lenaris, were prepared to defy tradition to support them in this. Colleagues, I believe it is time we welcome the youngest two members of this council to a status of full adult membership."

Lenaris blushed. Ruarnon's eyes widened. Then they shook their head, as Tor smiled proudly, both generals grinned and Monin raised a goblet and nodded for servants at the side of the room to deliver more, so everyone could drink to Ruarnon and Lenaris. Monin's objections had always had an edge to them…

"You're as bad as father, always testing me," Ruarnon said, meeting Monin's gaze as they set down their goblets.

"How long have you suspected I *was* testing you?" Monin asked.

Ruarnon sighed. "A while. You *do* disagree with me on much, don't you?"

Monin nodded. "I was concerned your open mindedness would get you into trouble. But your foray into the Realm and association with Linh suggests you have a talent for seeing potential in unlikely places and you seem determined to do so in the east as well. So perhaps Tor, you and Derire would consider adopting more children?"

Ruarnon frowned.

Tor smiled. "Drake is not my natural born son. He was born into a poor family, sent to the army because he lacked skills and needed to earn his own living. General Takanis spotted his potential and recognised he could serve Tarlah better as a high official, but that required an education only a family such as mine could provide. So my wife and I adopted him.

"Should I adopt the Australians, and you appoint them as your official Companions, their status as my adopted children would be the one we would make public. That would be perfectly acceptable to Tarlahn sensibilities."

Ruarnon's face went slack. Did *Monin* see Linh's potential as Companion? Was he *suggesting* Ruarnon make arrangements so all Tarlah would happily accept her as such?

Monin shook his head. "Linh is a girl after General Takanis and your father's own hearts. Fiona is too flighty for my liking, yet what Lenaris says of her makes me think she is stronger than she looks and her value lies in how she helps others. And while Troy is more of a scoundrel than even your father, it seems he is as loyal a companion as you could seek. While in your generation, I suspect only Michael and Linh can match your mind.

"You make other young people look like children and while the Australians act their age at times, Linh showed me on Cauldron Island that her reasoning, though different, is as sound as anyone's on this council. And rarely are rulers gifted with Companions so stubborn in their support as I suspect she will be. I suppose it is those differences that make you wish to have them on this council?"

Ruarnon inclined their head.

"There is much in the Old Ways that keep us going," said Monin. "But clearly you realise I use them as much as a test of character as for their value. And while new ways are fraught with unintended problems, your capacity to navigate them befits a far older person. Your father did not attain this status on this Council until he was three years older than you, despite having been on the Council for a year longer.

"I will not lie Ruarnon, I prefer men in leadership. But every now and then people like Takanis and my granddaughter keep me in check with how they navigate what used to be a man's world of the army and a man's world in government. You are not who I would have chosen. I would have had Parmoran as regent. I would have asked Lenaris to persuade you to appoint him as such. I would have been short sighted to do so."

"You cantankerous old bastard!" Lenaris yelled. "You were testing us all along?"

Monin smiled at her, a wild, hardened smile that would intimidate almost anyone else, but only seemed to antagonise Lenaris.

"You were overheard," said Ruarnon, unsure of their footing, but sensing it was time to air this unspoken secret. "Arlian heard you talking to Pamoran and he told me everything."

Monin shook his head. "I can not decide whether my son plays his cards too close to his chest, or whether he just makes things up as he goes along. I knew Lenaris was concerned. But when I put her in a position of compromise, she remained loyal to you, as a true Companion should. She passed her test to become Companion.

"As for Linh, I saw how frightened that girl was of the sorcerers. But not only did she speak to them and dare challenge me when I would have silenced her, she dared argue with people she feared. She dared press reason on Poran even when she feared he may crack. She too displayed courage and a commitment to doing what she believes is right, not to mention outstanding judgement of how far she could push Poran."

Ruarnon took a nervous breath. "And what of me?"

Monin sighed. "When you suspected I, the most senior man in Tarlahn politics after the king, may be a threat to your position, at first I thought you feared me and dared not act against me. Then I realised you had the tenacity to try and win me over. You strove to prove yourself to me, to this Council, the army and all Tarlah."

Tor had gone pale. He hadn't known. Even General Aza blanched. General Takanis' eyes widened. None of them had known Monin had spoken to Pamoran of persuading Ruarnon to appoint Pamoran as Regent, for Ruarnon's reign to be delayed indefinitely and Ruarnon and Lenaris to marry, ultimately putting Monin's great grandchild on the throne. Advisor Monin, the old soldier, had kept the true intent and extent of his scheming to himself.

But there was pride in his tone. "When I pushed you, you pushed back. You took risks. You countered my reasons with reason, as you have done today. Had it been up to me, Tarlah would not rule the Realm. There would not be peace. And our future would not be so bright. I never expected to be so glad that it was never up to me."

"You allowed Ruarnon and Lenaris believe that you wanted Poran as regent, until the King returns?" Tor asked.

"I was genuinely concerned about Ruarnon's leadership initiatives. I let that play into an ultimate test of character."

Tor turned to Ruarnon. "And you didn't tell me?"

Was that hurt in Tor's eyes? Or was it concern?

Ruarnon sighed. "I never told anyone how inadequate how I felt. I didn't even admit it to myself. I just rode the chaos out, until I proved to myself, and everyone, that I could."

Monin nodded. "What I misinterpreted as lack of fight, or lack of courage was a quiet commitment to never give up, regardless of the odds. I still think that to recover the Zaldeaan army, even were that a good thing for us all, you would need the aid of Chaos himself. But nothing will hold you back from your family, or my son, myself included. I do not like trusting these hidden sisters, of whom we know almost nothing, precisely because they are so secretive and so powerful and I do not know what drives them.

"But I know that Linh and her friends wish to get home. I presume they believe sailing east will assist them in that and assist your western expedition. And I suspect that if the sorcerers we met are representative of those Narz recruited, Linh doubts half of them would attack our ships, should we be caught in the crossfire. She may well be right.

"I think we all agree that any assistance from the east to aid our western expedition is vital. But in the west, the distances on Poran's map suggest that by the time we have freed the Zaldeaan army, an estimated seven thousand men, Narz's ships may have sailed from Azula to combat us at sea. The King and Queen and the others we might recover by stealth, but not the army. Were it possible, your Uncle Karmarn would have brought them home already. I half expected him to."

Aunt Telena had told Ruarnon to consider the price he was willing to pay in the Zaldeaan Realm. She had meant, how many of your own soldiers are you willing to let die? To free Ruarnon's family, ideally none, though many may volunteer. To free Zaldeaans so soon after the war... no Tarlahn should die for that.

"I intend only volunteers to sail west," said Ruarnon. "And I would include Zaldeaan volunteers in that. Some may leap at the chance to fight for their fathers', brothers' or uncles' freedom. I can give them that opportunity."

That may be the most Ruarnon could give them. They simply didn't have the resources for more. Rescuing seven thousand men had been a naïve, optimistic dream, perhaps even before it became clear sorcerers may hold the Zaldeaans captive. They had wanted their family back so much, and wanted to give their Zaldeaan subjects, who carried the same fears and doubts, the same hope, the same love of their family members, the same gift. But while the odds had turned in Tarlah's favour in the Realm, the odds were stacking ever more heavily against them in the west.

"I wouldn't advise planning anything about the Zaldeaans until our scouts have gathered more information, moving ahead of the expedition," said General Aza, and everyone else inclined their heads in agreement.

Of course. They couldn't just trust Poran's map. Even if he had drawn it up in good faith, they didn't know how accurate it was. The only way to obtain accurate geographical information was via Tarlahn scouts and spies after the recovery expedition set sail. The scouts would report to Tor as the expedition's leader, and Tor would decide whether to free the Zaldeaans, their commander, Ruarnon's Uncle Karmarn, Aunt Merlah and cousin Coroth, if those three *were* with the army…

"Between scouts, and enough soldiers to rescue the royal family," said General Takanis, "I agree with the regent that we should take three ships, west, and east."

"That sounds excessive," Monin protested.

"I believe our soldiers need not only practical experience at sea," she continued, "but mental experience. Companion Noma nearly had a mutiny on her scouting expedition. The soldiers will be terrified when we confirm that they will likely have to confront sorcerers in the west. We need to prepare them for what they will face on the western expedition. This voyage should give us at least two months to do so."

Ruarnon's gut twisted. Tarlahn soldiers had faced the unknown before, but Ruarnon had led the army against damars themself. Uncle Omah had led them in their fear and uncertainty in the first pitched battle in a generation. But there would be no royal family member sailing west to boost morale.

"I do not believe there is much else we can decide now," Tor said into the silence.

A single sentence, but Ruarnon heard a lot in it. It would be Tor who led the expedition. Tor who would hear the scouts replies, and plan and carry out the plans, or not, to recover Ruarnon's family and the Zaldeaan soldiers. All they could do here and now, while Ruarnon was present and in charge, was speculate. And while the Council's speculation could be valuable, Ruarnon had no desire to sit doing nothing while they speculated.

"While I sail east," Ruarnon told the council, "I want you to write up what we know, what we suspect, circumstances you anticipate us facing and what you consider to be acceptable risks under each circumstance. I won't have the information I need to make final decisions for the expedition, but I want all of your wisdom and logic to inform the orders I will give Companion Tor when he leads the expedition."

The council bowed their heads as one. They would be logical and discuss and elaborate upon and challenge one another's thoughts. Facing the unknown as intelligently as possible was the Tarlahn way of life. Ruarnon had every confidence in them. So what had stopped Ruarnon's appetite? Tightened their throat? Made them avoid everyone's gaze as their advisors and Lenaris departed? Why did Ruarnon feel as if someone had died?

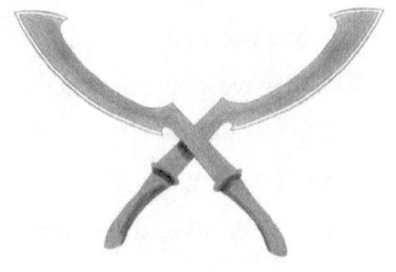

CHAPTER 14

COMMUNICATION ~RUARNON

Ruarnon?"

Lenaris' voice drifted through Ruarnon's cabin door. Curious about why she didn't wait for them to join their friends on the foredeck, Ruarnon opened it.

"Can I speak with you?" she asked, her expression serious.

What did she have to talk about when the voyage had barely begun? Ruarnon opened the door wide enough to admit her, then gestured to the delicate wooden table and seats built into their cabin wall.

"When you made me Companion," she said as she sat, "I thought we would be discussing Council meetings and chewing over everything together, like before you became coregent. But we've hardly spoken in recent weeks. We talk to each other less. Yet we've learned so much about Narz's sorcerers and you have such a decision on your shoulders. I wanted to tell you that if you wish to talk the way we used to, I am still here. And Mawana driving me to distraction doesn't change that," she added with a smile.

Ruarnon smiled at that last. Then their gaze drifted away, as they processed the rest. She was right. She knew them better than their other friends. And they were talking to her less. Because they did most of their thinking on their own. Unless the Australians barged in, which they were good at doing.

"I'm sorry," Ruarnon said. "Ever since I first attended Council meetings, Tor made it clear that I had to prove myself. That my thinking could rival theirs and I could lead them. I'm used to being distant with them and relying only on their intelligence. I didn't mean to push you away. I suppose, I've felt I must prove myself to you too. You're part of the Council now, and every decision I make requires your approval."

Lenaris shook her head. "First and foremost, I am your friend. That is the whole point of Companions versus Advisors. We're to be the ruler's age, to understand them, to provide the emotional support advisors are not supposed to provide, because they are supposed to be logical, calm and objective at all times. Companions are allowed to be subjective. We're supposed to be here for you to blow off steam with. Your father and mine used to get drunk together, early in your father's reign."

Ruarnon's mouth dropped open at that mental image.

"Behind closed doors," she added, "I saw it once, when I should have been in bed. And Omah had Telena."

Ruarnon sighed. "I've… stopped confiding in people. I did a little at Cauldron Island, but only because Tor saw me sinking and pressed the advice I needed on me, because he sought me out. I don't know Mocco or Mawana well enough, and while the

Australians have a blunt way of speaking, I only tend to speak freely to them when they invite it. I guess, I've become used to keeping everything in. To not reacting, to processing everything first, that I've stopped speaking to you the way I did before I became regent. That's what's changed."

"What hasn't changed is that you seem no more interested in falling in love and having a spouse to confide in, so friends are the only confidants you've got."

Ruarnon nodded slowly. "It's just... no one teaches you how to be focused, calm, collected and decisively ruling a kingdom one moment, or picking up a spear and leading an army to battle, then letting all that slip away, and being vulnerable, a person instead of a ruler, the next moment. I love my work. I love the challenges, the intricacies of solving a nation's problems. But I guess, I am doing that by stepping back from my feelings. By being regent all the time. Being myself less."

It was exactly the trap Uncle Omah had warned them of. But they hadn't fallen into the trap of being fearful of opposition like Kyura. They were forging relations with Zaldeaans, had challenged Monin, and led the Council, instead of letting it steer them. But since damars had been sighted off the Urai coast, they'd hardly spoken a casual word to Lenaris. Everyone else had been talking and bonding, especially the day Selenia took them to see the cave paintings. But Ruarnon's mind was always busy, processing, thinking, calculating and making connections between their knowledge. Their mind was elsewhere, causing them to drift from their friends.

"Thank you for raising it," they added to Lenaris.

"That's the sort of thing I'm here for," she replied. "Grandfather also said a Companion's job can be using banter to ensure the ruler doesn't get too big a head, but it seems more likely my job will be reminding you of the present, that you have friends as well as responsibilities, and that this voyage is a good time to enjoy our company and take the break you've very much earned and likely need."

Fiona had asked when they'd last had a day off. The Australians didn't seem to understand that regents didn't take days off. But now they weren't defending Tarlah, or reforming and trying to keep the peace in the Tarlahn-occupied Zaldeaan Realm or rushing to defend Tarlah against damars or question sorcerers, maybe it was time to rest and enjoy the company of friends, at least for a little while.

"I will try not to keep my thoughts to myself so much," they told Lenaris. "I should have made you Companion sooner, so I saw you as my ally on the Council and not just another advisor I had to win over."

"Well," Lenaris added with a smile, "you have the chance to get that right from the start with the Australians now. Though I must admit, I was surprised, even after the questions he asked me, that grandfather was happy to make Fiona and Troy your companions too."

Ruarnon smiled. "I suspect Tor had something to do with that. He knows them better. And you and Tor helped them understand their role?"

Lenaris shook her head. "Troy refuses to see the formality of it. Even Michael seems to understand it in terms of being a good friend and watching your back. I think I will need to continue to educate them."

Ruarnon smiled, picturing spear lessons with discussion of how to be a good companion to the regent taking place while the Australians swung weapons at each other. It ought to be good practice.

"For now," said Ruarnon, "I think I need a break. How would you feel about duel?"

Lenaris' eyes glinted fiercely as she smiled. "I'm always happy for one of those."

Ruarnon took a spear off a holder on the wall for them both. Lenaris led them to the foredeck more slowly than they expected. Slowly enough that they could smell the salt on the sea, feel the hot sun beaming down overhead and the cool of the sea breeze on their face.

Sails flapped overhead and a large shadow advanced on their right, matching the Iylena's speed across the sea. General Takanis acknowledged them from the Meera's foredeck with a bow of her head and they smiled, as soldiers sparred on her foredeck, training for the western expedition. The levied soldiers normal job was sailing, so that the crews on all three of Ruarnon's ships in this voyage doubled as soldiers.

As they crossed the main deck, part of Ruarnon was still uneasy. Just before their departure, a report had arrived from the Zaldeaan Realm, saying that retired soldiers had tried to kill Regent Armar at the Feast of the Mother Goddess. The act of sacrilege had provoked Governor Syenne to cut down most of the would-be assassins herself, bringing calm, and likely the fear of the gods to the Realm. Not wanting to be outdone, Governor Iagl had invited malcontents with Tarlahn rule to a duel with him. One of late Governor Derlan's friends had taken him up, and Iagl had publicly fought the man to the man's death.

Iagl was still recovering from his wounds, but the governors, Ruarnon's generals and Monin were all convinced that Syenne and Iagl's apparently united and fierce crushing of opposition would calm things in the Realm for a while. Monin's regency in Ruarnon's absence ought to be a quiet affair. Ruarnon was confident they'd left a very capable regent behind them, but part of them still twinged with guilt as they climbed the foredeck stairs, pursuing aid and resources to recover their parents, while leaving the Realm in an uncertain state in their absence.

"You cannot do everything all the time," Tor said quietly as they stepped onto the foredeck, reading their slumped posture well. "Your father was one of the most energetic young rulers Tarlah has seen, and even he couldn't be everywhere at once. Try to stay in the present on this voyage."

Lenaris' comments on Companions fresh in their mind, Ruarnon realised the line Tor walked. As Ruarnon was regent, but not king, Tor had retained the title 'Companion', but technically he was King Urmilian's companion, and Ruarnon's advisor. Yet somehow, he managed to address Ruarnon's worries and uncertainties, to help them manage their emotions, as a companion should, while wisely advising them like the impartial advisor he was supposed to act as until Ruarnon's father's return.

Ruarnon smiled and bowed their head in acknowledgment of his words.

Mawana eyed Lenaris and Ruarnon with interest when he saw them holding weapons, as did Selenia.

"Companions, out of the way, the regent wants to duel," Mawana warned the Australians, who stepped back, Mocco shaking his head at Mawana's casual use of the title. But Troy grinned and the others smiled. Ruarnon smiled back, knowing they would be quite happy to be formally permitted to attend any Council meetings or conversations of similar status for the rest of the voyage. They tended to like knowing what was going on.

Then Lenaris was facing Ruarnon. She flashed a smile and her spear tip glinted towards them. That was all it took. Everything crowding their mind and tightening their shoulders slipped away. As they ducked, danced aside, thrust their spear butt forwards and countered Lenaris' spear tip. She fought with grace and speed and so did they.

The world was reduced to rapid, violent, graceful movements of weapons, spear butts thunking, spear tips clashing together, weapons slashing empty air as either opponent danced out of the way. Training fighting was a dance, one that sped up Ruarnon's heart and made them smile, as they let their body flow into the rapid rhythm of the dance.

"We've a letter!"

Mawana's cry broke the rhythm and Ruarnon and Lenaris paused. For a heartbeat Ruarnon worried it was a warning Narz's ships had been sighted nearby and that they would need to change course. Then Mawana said, "It's for you cousin," as he retrieved a scroll from the talons of a large bird with dark blue feather's hovering over the railing.

Ruarnon sighed as Mawana passed the scroll on, then pet the bird's neck as it landed, showing no concern about its wickedly hooked beak. He fed it something from his pocket, which the bird gobbled up.

"It gives them an incentive to deliver letters," Mawana explained, noting Ruarnon's gaze. "Beyond getting to visit me," he added.

"You trained that one?" Troy asked and Mawana nodded.

"It's from Mother," Mocco reported as he scanned the scroll. "She says a damarian fleet has attacked the Island of the Guardians. The island is the other sanctuary for creatures like Flariah's, and they fought off damars successfully, but two ships escaped. We need to keep a look out for them in case our ships cross paths."

Perhaps they weren't out of danger yet, but at least it was only two ships. Ruarnon nodded to Tor, who moved to the side of the deck to signal a warning to General Takanis.

"There's an army bred for the Sorcery War, on an island called *the Island of the Guardians*?" Troy asked, raising an eyebrow.

Ruarnon sighed. "My parents could have told Narz that's what the Timbalens named the desert island their traditions say Guardians were last sighted on. But my parents don't know where it is, just that it lies east of Tarlah. Timbalen records say it's another inhospitable, uninhabited wilderness. I wonder if the ship that dropped damars on Timraith Island went further east, to explore Cauldron Island and locate the Island of the Guardians."

"That may have told him more about the Sisters' creatures than my people could," said Mocco. "The creatures behave like normal animals during peace time and neither Lylah nor Flariah told our people what truly wandered the plains or hid in the caves."

He shivered, making Ruarnon think that perhaps only Flariah, the faeron and gorans had known the true nature of Cauldron Island's other inhabitants.

"Flariah wouldn't have let your people wander near creatures that could harm them," Selenia assured Mocco and Mawana. "Gorans and faeron keep watch over humans on the island."

Mawana shifted uneasily. "I thought the reptiles were especially dangerous. I didn't need to get close to see that, but I'd never have guessed..."

Mocco's face clouded over. "You snuck off to watch them when you and your father shipped Urai to the island?"

"I kept my distance," Mawana replied calmly. "The dragons saw me once. They were hunting dinner on the plains. But none of them went for me. Though the lizard I saw, I had to run like Chaos himself to get away from it. No creature I've encountered in the jungle made my instincts scream at me to flee like that one did. But it never occurred to me they could *all* be that hostile. Or magically controlled."

Ruarnon shook their head. "Is Flariah certain the ship that sailed east of Tarlah didn't have spies on board, watching and gathering information about the creatures directly?" they asked Selenia.

"It never landed on our shores," she replied. "And the people on it would have seen nothing through the mountains unless they somehow used magic. And even if they did, they would just have seen a bunch of reptiles sunbathing or wandering about. They couldn't have guessed the creatures' potential by observing them in peace time."

"And the Gateway of Umarinaris there has been broken for a while?" Michael asked.

"I suspect Flariah broke it long ago," Selenia replied, "to make it impossible for anyone to transport the army off her island by gateway. If there is a gateway on the Island of the Guardians, I suspect it will have been destroyed for the same reason."

"So he can't have sent spies by gateway," Michael finished.

Ruarnon shook their head. Only Flariah and perhaps Lylah knew of the army's existence. And Narz hadn't had physical access to the island, yet Lenaris and Linh agreed he somehow knew how many damars would be needed to in theory vanquish Flariah's army.

"I wonder if Narz knew something dangerous lay east of Tarlah and put damars on board to attack it," Ruarnon said. "But what drew his attention east, beyond what Azula would see as the ends of the known world in the first place?"

"Why think an army halfway across the world, that had kept to itself for centuries, suddenly needed to be wiped out?" Troy asked.

"When he captured the Zaldeaan army to coerce it to occupy the Galvations, and could have used Flariah's army to keep the rulers he fears will ally against him at bay," Ruarnon added, nodding.

Why respond so differently to a creature army, than to the most powerful human army in the east? Nothing Poran had claimed or believed about Narz's eastern incursions made sense. Ruarnon had been convinced Narz was lying to Poran, yet Narz *had* tried to annihilate the army on Cauldron Island.

"Humans can be controlled by threats, bribes and fear," said Tor. "Seven thousand men do not require direct control. But damars do. And it sounds like Flariah's army does."

"If he can control damars well enough to create them, ship them far away, and successfully launch attacks on two islands," said Lenaris, "then he has the resources to do the same with Flariah's army. I saw the way hundreds of damars marched to battle as an army, with Tyrook controlling them. I saw damars cluster at the base of the rigging and start climbing it when Tither and Tarata went after the sorcerer. Narz has the means to control Flariah's army. But he didn't even try. He seems to have thrown everything he could into destroying it."

"The sorcerers claim he hasn't used damars in conflicts at home," Tor added. "That he hasn't risked his sorcerers losing control of damars on what sounds like a densely human populated continent. That tells me he fully acknowledges the destructive power of damars. The same must be true of Flariah's army. But his response was to devote considerable resources and sacrifice one of his own armies trying to destroy hers.

"I have only ever seen mighty and powerful rulers try to crush what they perceive as opposition with such force for one reason: because they *are* afraid. I lived through the last Zaldeaan occupation of Tarlah. The gallows were a busy place. Every royal family member the Zaldeaans identified was murdered. The Zaldeaans garrisoned in Tarlah City conducted regular raids on private homes, seeking evidence of rebellion or opposition.

"It was hard to believe the governor could fear us, when the Zaldeaan army greatly outnumbered ours, and armed guards patrolled our streets day and night. But Monin said that while the

Zaldeaans had the military upper hand, if you counted every Tarlahn aged ten to seventy, we outnumbered that garrison many times over. If we were prepared to rise up, he assured everyone he trained it was achievable. And we *did* throw off Zaldeaan rule, in the Great Rebellion.

"The governor knew that was possible. He knew that was the risk and possible price of his position. That's why he killed so many Tarlahns and instructed Zaldeaan guards to turn so many homes upside-down. To counter his greatest personal threat. He dedicated most of his resources to it. At Cauldron Island, Narz appears to have done the same."

Ruarnon couldn't argue with that. But why on Umarinaris, with so many enemies at home, would Narz dedicate so many resources to destroying threats no one else had detected in the east? His actions on Cauldron Island suggested fear was truly his motivation, just as Poran claimed. It sounded like he'd attacked the Galvations, or they had attacked him, because of their hatred of sorcery made them obvious enemies. And he was using the Zaldeaans to keep the Galvation threat at bay.

If other rulers did oppose him, if they allied against him, it made perfect sense for Narz to seize Flariah's army for himself. The fact he hadn't attempted it suggested he truly feared her army. Who did Narz fear would use Flariah's army against him? Did he really think his enemies at home had the resources and information to locate the creature armies, and his capacity to seize an army from across the ocean as Poran claimed? But from everything they'd learned so far, it seemed the only people who had the capacity to transport creature armies halfway around Umarinaris were Guardians.

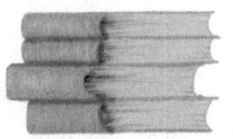

CHAPTER 15

DESRIAN'S PALACE ~LINH

T he shallows lapped coolly around Linh's sandaled feet as she, her friends, Ruarnon and their companions waded from the Iylena's boats to the Island of the Guardians. Sandy white beaches stretched before them, while formidable red cliffs barred the island's interior. As they crossed the sand, each carrying a pack on their backs, all Linh heard was breaking waves. A cool breeze blew in off the sea, ruffling her clothes and hair, and gulls spiralled upwards, following an updraft high into the sky.

"These beaches are as nice as at home," Fiona said quietly. "I wonder why the Timbalens didn't want to settle here?"

"Maybe the island's interior differs," Linh replied.

Ruarnon led them towards steep steps carved into and between the cliffs. They were high cut to Linh and Fiona, who let their longer-legged companions go first, though some of Ruarnon's bodyguards insisted on marching at their backs and were patient as the pair laboured up the steep steps behind everyone else. The climb soon had Linh sweating. She was grateful for the sea breeze, which cooled them each time they climbed up onto the next ledge.

Gradually, they left the Iylena, Meera and Saeron, most of the soldiers and the inviting beaches below behind.

Linh reached the top of the pass with aching legs and her tunic sticking to her sweaty back. She and the others gazed down a steep rocky hillside across dry plains of orange, shrub-scattered soil spanning to the horizon on their right, where tiny hills marked a border with grasslands. Much of the orange land to the left was hazy below heat waves, and large patches of mirages gave the illusion of lakes near the horizon.

"Maybe this is why they didn't settle here," Linh answered Fiona's question, as the fierce heat of the sun beamed down on her from above and reflected up from the rock under her feet and the desert plains far below.

"Don't tell me we have to walk across that," said Troy.

"Desriah's letter said she will provide transportation," Ruarnon replied, and Linh exhaled, her posture relaxing slightly.

As they moved down the far side of the pass, the desert seemed larger, warping and blurring among heat waves, a hot breeze wafting up from it adding to the sweat trickling from her joints. No one spoke as they laboured their way down towards what felt like a giant orange oven.

"What are those things?" Troy asked as the bottom finally drew nearer.

"Desert gorans," Mawana replied.

"They're different from the ones at home," Selenia added.

Linh squinted through the heat haze at tall, well-built figures and an indistinct mass behind them. As she walked towards them and the mass moved closer, she made out orange scales and angular faces; a new species of goran.

"We from Desriah," the nearest goran announced, its voice deep and grating, as Ruarnon stepped onto the edge of the desert plain. "She want us bring you palace. You get in wagon."

The mass behind them resolved into two giant, docile-eyed lizards pulling an enormous wooden carriage.

"You're sure they're not carnivorous?" Troy asked.

The goran frowned.

"They're not showing much interest in us," Mawana assured Troy. "And I have seen herbivores of a similar size on Cauldron Island."

Mocco shook his head, probably because Mawana had seen them where he shouldn't have been. Linh wasn't quite reassured.

Mawana vaulted the giant steps into a wooden construction a storey and a half high. It was more of a bus-sized carriage than a wagon, the right size for Mawana, comfortable looking for Ruarnon and the others, but Linh suspected it was cavern-sized for her and Fiona.

Mocco and Ruarnon followed stiffly, Lenaris and Selenia moving cautiously behind them, Tor, of all people, mimicking Mawana's interest, peering intently at the giant lizards. Linh smiled when Troy and Michael gave the lizards a cautious berth, and she and Fiona kept their distance as they boarded. She chose a goran-sized seat in the front row, and she and Fiona placed their packs at their feet and pushed themselves up onto wooden benches so high their feet hung above the floor.

Linh dozed as the carriage trundled forwards and the blazing sun mercifully descended. She should be more concerned about trusting giant lizards to get them to their destination. Even Troy was eyeing the creatures as they trundled across the desert plains.

But it was too hot to think clearly, or much at all. Though if this was the welcoming committee Desriah had sent, Linh wondered at her power, her control of magical creatures and what sort of aid such a formidable person may offer Ruarnon's western expedition.

She drifted to sleep eventually, finally waking in blissfully cool darkness to a four-story castle lined with windows stretching before her, some glowing with lamplight. On the ground floor gorans stood at double doors, which opened to admit the carriage into a corridor of polished sandstone.

"And the Timbalens thought this place was uninhabited," Michael said softly behind her.

"Maybe they couldn't see it through the heat haze," said Troy.

Linh grabbed her pack and climbed out to find a goran waiting for them. She tried not to stare at it as her companions climbed out of the carriage. It was so tall and broad, and stood so still that it could have been a statue, if not for its occasional blinking. It blinked sideways. She was staring now. She dragged her gaze away.

A high ceiling rose overhead, above smooth stone walls, on such a scale that Linh felt dwarfed by them.

The goran bobbed its head to Ruarnon, then began leading everyone down a corridor lit by burning torches, towards double doors opening into a hall lit by candled chandeliers. Linh blinked. Beside the double doors, a tall woman studied them with sharp blue eyes. Her inquisitive face was framed with auburn hair blowing in the evening breeze, her elegant purple dress fluttering in the hall's entrance. Her eyes were blue, but she had the same slender nose and firm cheek and jaw bones as Flariah. The word 'sisters' had seemed an odd expression between Lylah and Flariah, but the resemblance made Linh suspect Desriah and Flariah were biological sisters.

"Welcome, I am Desriah. Join me," and she gestured to a table behind her that came up to Linh and Fiona's elbows.

"Doesn't fret about niceties and gets straight to the food. I like her already," Troy said quietly.

Linh poked him in the ribs in case he offended Selenia or anyone else. He flashed his usual grin and she rolled her eyes. Mocco, Mawana and Selenia were already pulling up blocky wooden chairs on one side of the table, Ruarnon, Lenaris and Tor sitting opposite. Desriah nodded for the guards to sit, and at a bow of Ruarnon's head, the guards moved to seats at its end.

Linh pushed herself up onto a chair next to Selenia, and her feet dangled awkwardly. An approaching goran towered over them, making Linh flinch back, until she saw the tray in its hands. It was handing out plates of rice topped with crispy looking vegetables. She smiled at a meal that resembled her mother's cooking, her smile broadening as she picked up familiar feeling chopsticks and began to eat in a way that reminded her more strongly of home than anything she had encountered so far in Umarinaris.

"Whose style of food and eating utensils is this?" Michael asked, breaking the silence of the vast, mostly empty dining hall.

"It comes from the East Islands," Desriah replied. "There was trade between them and this island, once."

So that *was* where Umarinaris' Asian descendants were hanging out. Linh wondered why they were so insular, but she supposed if Timbalens mainly sailed west to aid Tarlah in its endless wars with the Zaldeaan Realm, perhaps they preferred their island end of the world to the war-torn rest of it.

Linh's shoulders tensed as another intimidating, bulky figure with a grey hide face and too-knowing eyes passed by, handing out glasses of fruit juice. The silence was broken again by the two gorans speaking to each other, in their gravelly-voiced way.

Linh's mouth opened and even Michael's eyes widened. She didn't understand a single word. Maybe the spell that let them understand Umarinaris' languages was limited to human languages? From Michael's frown, he was probably drawing the same conclusion.

Finally, Desriah spoke again.

"Lylah's insights into the future of the west have persuaded myself and my sisters to break an oath we swore long ago. She has persuaded me to tell you a secret that has been kept in the east since she first began teaching Urai shield magic. A secret we believed worth maintaining, when the North Landers kept their oaths not to use magic to harm others and stayed out of the Zaldeaan Realm's wars. And the Timbalen Elite Guard strengthened and kept their code.

"You have fought Narz's damars and have some idea of his power. But the damars you have fought are as nothing to the forces he will unleash if war on his continent progresses as Lylah *Sees* in multiple futures that it will. In some futures she has seen, the Galvations may not survive."

Linh tensed. *Genocide*? Lylah *Saw genocide* in Azula's future?

"So I will tell you, sorcerers are not fundamentally different from other humans."

Linh gaped, but Mocco and Selenia relaxed in their seats at the revelation.

"If everyone can wield magic, why don't they know it?" Michael asked, and Tor frowned at his interjection.

Desriah's gaze lightened. "Any soldier who has fought in enough wars can tell tales of arrows they were sure would kill them, or a blow they were convinced would be fatal. Farmers can tell you of accidents where people miraculously moved out the way of broken or falling equipment before it crushed them. Perhaps they felt something strange or suspected they did something impossible, but the heat of battle, the panic of the moment obscures it.

"Then everyone thanks Mijora for protecting the lucky survivors or Esla for sparing them watery graves. In the Zaldeaan Realm they thank the Mother Goddess for keeping her children safe. In Tarlah, they thank the guiding wisdom and strength of their ancestors. They attribute it to the higher powers they would collectively prefer to believe in.

"Few people on Umarinaris believe they can wield magic because few people want to. But in extreme circumstances, many have strived beyond what muscles and wits can achieve, and crafted magic out of desperation. Only a few realised what it was, and fewer still moved to the North Lands seeking guidance on exploring their suspicion that they are sorcerers."

"But, I don't…"

Ruarnon gently cut Lenaris off. "Did you see how many soldiers we cut down in our efforts to reach Arlian?" they asked. "Our speed, the number we killed… and we did not tire. We should have been exhausted. Someone should have been able to stab us in the back halfway. But they didn't. We fought on until we reached Arlian's side, cutting down tens of soldiers, and suffering no serious wounds ourselves. It shouldn't have been possible."

Tears sprang to Lenaris eyes. "But if anyone can wield magic... why didn't..."

Ruarnon slumped in their chair. "Perhaps he did. Perhaps Ethlin did too. There were a great many dead Zaldeaans around where they fell."

"But, then why are they... why did we survive, when they did not?"

Tor sighed. "You were training with Tarlah's most skilled warrior since you were three years old," he told Lenaris. "And Pamoran instructed Ruarnon for many years. You two have had more training and time to develop greater focus, stamina and skill than many Tarlahns. I assume these qualities are also an advantage with magic."

Linh's face went slack. Ruarnon and Lenaris had somehow used magic to help them fight during the siege of Tarlah City? Was focus and discipline all it took? The rational part of her mind protested at the top of its lungs that that was impossible, not to mention insane.

"Magic is part of the fabric of this world," said Flariah. "It is connected to every living thing and developing an awareness of that connection allows anyone with an open mind and sufficient will power to craft it. The only thing separating sorcerers from everyone else is that their ancestors didn't deny their abilities. They explored, experimented and honed them. They taught their children. Knowledge, teaching and magic training were passed down through the generations, overcoming all doubt and fear, consolidating and extending the extent and manner in which sorcerers and their children craft magic.

"All it would take for supposed non-sorcerers to wield magic is to overcome their fear, control their emotions, discipline their minds, and do so with sufficient determination and courage to succeed in intentional magic craft."

Troy's cutlery clattered to the table as his brows disappeared up under his curly fringe.

"People still suspected as much when my sisters and I agreed that Lylah could teach some Urai shield magic craft, in case migrating sorcerers and their descendants spread the war into the east. But they did not."

Linh gazed unseeing across the table, her mouth dropping open slightly. How *old* were the sisters? Had Lylah begun teaching Urai magic at the end of the Sorcery War? Everyone kept saying there was no evidence of Guardians in this world, but if the Guardians weren't a myth, a small voice at the back of Linh's head told her she knew two of them and may be listening to a third. The thought made her tense from shoulders to toes and she shoved it away.

"The situation in the west is different," Desriah continued. "Magic is known and wielded on one side. If we do not teach the Galvations magic, one future Lylah has foreseen is that most Galvations will not survive Narz's war. And your chances of recovering your family Ruarnon, are negligible without magic."

"Hang on," said Troy, "Poran said most Galvations hate and fear magic. But you want to teach *them* to wield it?"

"I will not be teaching them anything. Flariah and I hold the bonds to creature armies, bonds that would break should we sail too far from our creatures, leaving our armies free for Narz's forces or his rivals to claim. Such sorcerers will visit us in time, if Narz's war drags on too long.

"Lylah, on the other hand, would be detected by those powerful enough to block her *Sight* the moment she arrived, and her presence and the extent of her power would prompt the mobilisation of armies and battles that may otherwise be forestalled or prevented. This she has *Seen*."

Linh's head spun at Desriah's implications. The hair on the back of her neck stood up in protest.

"You would trust us to learn magic from you, and teach it to the Galvations?" Ruarnon asked.

Goosebumps rose up Linh's arms and legs. Travelling and eating dinner with two men who could craft large shields out of magic was enough to be getting on with. But Desriah wanted Linh to touch the stuff herself?

"Only defensive magic," Desriah replied. "Only if you agree to use it defensively and to teach only those Galvations who agree to the same. Lylah has watched you more than you know Ruarnon, and you are her preferred leader based not only on what she has *Seen* but what she knows and predicts of you."

"You think the Galvations may be desperate enough to overcome their fear and distaste of magic, to learn it from us?" Tor asked.

Desriah sighed. "Lylah cannot yet *See* what will happen but that is what she predicts."

"Can she tell me if my expedition will succeed if I do not go?" Ruarnon asked earnestly.

"In multiple futures, your parents are released, even if you do not lead your expedition. But your aunt, uncle and cousin's lives hinge on your decision, and in some futures, your parents are unlikely to survive the devastation that sweeps the continent if all we hope for fails. Though you are not the only factor favouring better outcomes."

"Surely *we're* not the other?" Troy asked, frowning.

Linh went very still and forgot to breathe. How was everyone suddenly speaking and contemplating the impossible as if it were possible?

"Not the only other. Others may help you. But there are many decisions yet to be made, and Lylah *Sees* many futures at present, too many to speak in more than vague terms."

"Will you teach us shield magic, even if I do not go West?" Ruarnon asked.

"On Lylah's advice, I will."

"Then we will abide by your conditions, as will whoever leads the recovery expedition."

"I shall begin teaching you in the morning. When you master enough basic aspects of shield magic to no longer be a danger to yourselves, we can begin training your soldiers."

Linh lay staring at the yellowish light shining against the thin curtains of the room she shared with Fiona. It was very late. Tor had advised them all to go straight to sleep. But she couldn't imagine sleeping. And for the first time, she hesitated to speak to Fiona. Hesitated to drown her friend in the uncertainty, disbelief and dizziness she was sinking in.

She didn't know what part of what she'd just heard to try to swallow first. But the moment Linh lay still, a truth she'd been skirting for months burst through the surface of her thoughts. It was the vague notion she'd had of sailing safely west with Ruarnon's soldiers, travelling by night to avoid detection, skirting all conflict until a sorcerer opened a gateway of the world and they slipped home while Narz wasn't looking. That was an oversimplification. Because they intended to travel with Ruarnon, who would attack Narz's sorcerers to free their parents and intended to ally with Narz's enemies, the Galvations, to do so.

Linh had refused to consider what that quest might look like in any detail. She'd only allowed herself think naively about it, because deep down she knew it was the most dangerous place she could step foot in this world. Everything they were learning about Narz and the brewing wars in the west said as much. The only way to survive sorcery seemed to be hiding from it and dodging and avoiding it at all costs.

But the battle in Blue Bay had proved how naïve that idea was. No matter how much intelligence Ruarnon gathered, they couldn't know the whereabouts of every sorcerer, especially if plenty of sorcerers didn't openly serve Narz. In the West, it was possible that magic could hit her at any time, shaped by anyone, and she may have no way of knowing by who, where or when until it happened. Magic may be impossible to avoid.

Developing skills remotely like Mocco's and Mawana's with defensive magic may be necessary for her, Fiona, Michael and Troy to get home safely. Just like learning to wield conventional weapons had been. But *how* could *she* control magic? How did she even touch the stuff? What would stop touching it from setting it

206

on fire, the way Jandar's flames had burned through the air of Blue Bay?

"Flariah will need to explain a lot more, won't she?" Fiona asked.

Linh sighed. "I wasn't sure you were still awake. Damn right she will. I don't want to try to touch, let alone wield magic until I know how, what it can do, why, how it can go wrong and how to stop it from going wrong. Is there truly such thing as a *safe* way to touch such a substance?"

Fiona sighed. "I suppose it depends on what magic can do in Umarinaris. We only know it can make things burn, shield things, and that it somehow transported us to Umarinaris. I'm not sure how it helped Ruarnon and Lenaris during the siege of Tarlah City. Perhaps with strength, or speed, or redirecting blows that should have killed them?" she shuddered in the dim yellow light, then stilled.

"The Tarlahns don't seem too worried about it," she added.

Linh grimaced. "They don't know about molecules. They can't be afraid of accidentally disintegrating themselves —or someone else— at a molecular level."

Fiona gazed at the ceiling. "Maybe the faeron do. They once had metallurgy and science. Yet they didn't seem frightened of stopping the sorcerers Flariah captured from using their powers, however they did that. It's not easy to imagine us calmly wielding magic like that. Or like Flariah. I wonder if the sisters are human."

"I suspect they're not," Linh replied with a shiver. "Maybe magic made them that way."

She shivered again.

"It doesn't seem to have done Mocco and Mawana any harm," Fiona countered. "And while Mocco may have used magic in ways most people would define as safe, Mawana likely hasn't, and he's alive and well."

Linh exhaled and some of the tension went out of her shoulders. "How do you have such a good perspective?" she asked.

"I've got older siblings who help, as well as my parents. And there's so many people in my house with so much to say. I've done a lot of listening and learned a lot from everyone around me."

"Instead of worrying about anything the moment you see how it could endanger you," Linh added with a shake of her head. "Magic feels *way* outside my comfort zone."

"Think of the good it could do," Fiona countered. "I don't think what Poran said was just propaganda. It really can be used to heal illness. To help women give birth safely, without the help of modern medicine. And Mocco and Mawana have shown us it can save lives and defend us from sorcerers."

Think of the good it could do. There was a phrase that captured Fiona's spirit in a nutshell. She always seemed to be thinking about the good that could be achieved. Often for other people. And when so much was at risk; she was right. Focusing on what could go wrong could paralyse Linh from wielding magic. And what if she *did* need magic in the west? What if Fiona, or Michael or Troy's life depended on it, and she hadn't overcome her aversion to touch the stuff?

Come morning, she would have to rely on her favourite life strategy; stubbornly insist on doing what she thought needed doing, until she succeeded at it. And if anything made her doubt, or resist the idea, she would remember the importance of having magic at her fingertips, in case she ever found herself in Mocco or Mawana's position in blue Bay.

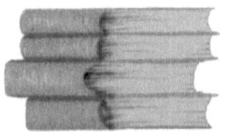

Chapter 16

A Touch of Magic ~Linh

Linh and the others followed Desriah down a sandstone corridor lit by morning sunlight pouring in through large, glass-less rectangular windows. The air was cool inside, but the sunlight was already hot.

"We're going to learn *magic*," Troy said, gazing into space.

"I don't understand how it's possible," said Michael. "Magic doesn't exist in our world, so how can *we* wield it?"

"You've been ingesting it," Mawana said on their right and Linh frowned. "You've been eating and drinking our food since you arrived, so if magic is part of everything here, you've been consuming it since you arrived."

"And breathing it in, I suppose," Michael added.

Linh shook her head. "There I was warning Troy not to chase after Red Cloak when he could be dangerous, while I was breathing in magic particles." She shivered. "I seriously underestimated how dangerous Umarinaris could be."

"You were right all along," Troy added, surprising her with the sincerity of his tone.

"Does this mean you'll take absolute care with magic and not blow our heads off?" Michael asked Troy solemnly.

Fiona smiled first. Troy opened his mouth to protest and Linh laughed. Only then did Michael smile.

Troy shook his head. "If I do anything silly, Mawana, feel free to knock me out. Michael says you're good at it."

Michael clapped Troy on the shoulder. "You'll be right mate. You're more responsible than you like to admit."

They exchanged smiles and Linh shook her head. It wasn't just Michael, who nearly seven months ago barely smiled at all, and didn't joke with anyone, winding Troy up *and* calming him down so easily that surprised her. It was the fact she agreed with Michael. What had the world come to that the prospect of Troy learning magic didn't turn her insides to ice?

She shivered. The scary part wasn't just that Troy would wield magic. It was that *all* of them would. It was that *she* would have to touch the same power that had tried to burn the ship she stood on not so many weeks ago.

"I think we should all spread out," she suggested. "Just in case."

Troy grinned.

A courtyard loomed ahead and Linh's shoulders tightened. "How many ways can magic go wrong?" she asked, loudly enough for Desriah, who walked ahead, to hear.

Desriah slowed. Everyone else fell silent and all eyes turned to her. Even Ruarnon looked a bit nervous.

"If for example, we set something on fire, instead of shielding it?" Linh elaborated.

"A mistake like that is more difficult than crafting a shield. Crafting magic into any form requires great concentration. Subconscious casting is very rare."

Linh sighed. Desriah's style of instruction didn't seem to take the fact her students were human and had a *lot* of feelings about wielding magic into account. And yet self-belief was apparently the first thing they needed to achieve. Linh supposed not being terrified of setting her own hair on fire was the second. How exactly was this going to work?

"You'll be right," Troy called to Ruarnon. "I'll be watching you to prove it's possible. No pressure," he added with a wink.

Ruarnon smiled. They were the most open-minded, capable person Linh had ever met. Ruarnon had no reason to doubt, and Lenaris and Tor little more. Selenia's imaginative spirit would probably thrive at magic. Meanwhile Mocco and Mawana were already accomplished. It was just her and her Aussie friends likely to be bumbling.

They followed Desriah into a large courtyard, with cacti growing around dry beds against its interior walls and sunlight shining through its open roof. Sandstone floor levels rose above the walls on every side, and distant bridges spanned between floors overhead. It was huge, but the bridges were deserted, and she hadn't heard another soul in the place, aside from a few gorans. Did the faeron build all this? Or the Guardians?

She stopped before one of several sturdy square columns rising from the courtyard's floor to support bridges at varying heights above and faced everyone.

"You will need to train with me for at least four weeks. I will show you how to form shields that remain around you, fix shields to a location, and block moving objects. Be warned; the effort required to shape magic continuously can be very tiring, especially for inexperienced users. It will wear you out quickly in battle,

212

leaving you defenceless amidst enemies. It is best used briefly, in extraordinary circumstances, such as rescuing Ruarnon's parents or defending yourselves against sorcerers.

"Today, I will teach you to shield yourselves. Focus as much as possible. Hold your hand forwards, project your will for a shield to exist out from it, and you will begin crafting a shield, like this."

A white substance seeped from Desriah's hand and spread like a wall of mist. Linh gaped. Stand the right way, do the right action, anticipate something that had been impossible for most of her life would happen and it would just *happen*?

"Concentration is key to shaping magic," Desriah continued. "If your attention wanders, the magic will revert to its normal state of formlessness. To maintain a shield, you must remain focused on every part of it at once. Physical gestures may help you direct the magic within to hold the magic without in the form you impose on it."

Linh's mouth dropped open.

"It's a physical substance we can manipulate with telepathy?" Troy asked softly. "*Any* way we want?"

"Supposedly, though she's dead keen on defence only," Michael replied.

Linh's disbelief had barely lessened when Desriah demonstrated again, while Lenaris, Ruarnon and Selenia asked questions. None of the answers soothed Linh's memories of fire pouring out from a sorcerer's hands. She gave the memory a mental shove. That was *not* going to happen today. Flariah was confident. And seemed adept at magic herself. Perhaps she was adept enough to counter everyone's magic if it went awry.

It was time to begin. Linh stared at air. *How* could it have magic in it? But the air above Blue Bay had burned, when air couldn't do that. There really must be an invisible substance in it, perhaps tiny particles floating invisible to the naked eye. How did you connect to particles? And even if you somehow managed that, how did you *shape* them?

Linh raised her hand doubtfully. Nothing looked, sounded or felt different. There was no outward sign the impossible was now achievable. Frustrated, she pushed her hand a little further, wanting to feel *something*. To know this wasn't a trick or a waste of time. She screwed up her courage and pushed harder. Trying to feel a magic shield wall that wasn't there. Its hardness. Its strength. The protection she and any of her friends may need in the west.

"Holy shit," said Troy. "Your palm's going white. What are you pressing against?"

But she couldn't… for a split-second Linh *felt* the shield she was imagining her palm pressing into. Then her palm pushed through ordinary air, and she stumbled, gasping for breath, sweat dripping down her forehead.

"I thought I was imagining it."

Troy slowly smiled. "You're the strongest willed of us all. If will power is the key ingredient, you're going to ace magic."

Linh quirked an eyebrow and he smiled in a way that told her he *was* saying the ace was ace at magic.

Michael shook his head. "I get willpower, but what about the laws of physics? They don't seem to apply to you as much as they do to me. I *know* that's logically impossible, but I can't seem to believe otherwise.

Linh raised a finger. If it wasn't just a fluke, just imagination, she should be able to do it again. As she reached out, something tingled at her fingertip. As if something *was* there. The same tingling she'd felt in Mocco's cabin, as a spearhead ground against her chest armour, but the tip didn't cut her.

Linh gasped. Desriah was right. The heat of battle had concealed it.

"I think I've done it before," she said slowly. "When we were fighting damars in Mocco's cabin."

"And on my deck," Mocco said, approaching on her right. "When my shield was failing against that sorcerer's blows. You were worried I was overexerting myself. And I was. Your touch on my arm slowed my racing heart. You calmed me down. I relaxed too much and that's when and why I fainted."

Linh shivered. "I'm sorry. I didn't mean to endanger you."

Mocco shook his head, then looked down at her, his expression more open and vulnerable than she had ever seen it. "You may have saved my life."

Linh's spine tingled at the idea.

"When we sail west, I'm staying near you," Troy said fervently, with his usual grin.

Michael was staring intently across the courtyard. "It sounds like projection. Like you projected your desire for him to stop overexerting himself and somehow slowed him down."

Linh shivered. "I was worried you could die saving us," she told Mocco, "when you barely knew us. I was determined for that not to happen."

"And you pressed your will onto magic and ensured my cousin didn't operate beyond his limits," Mawana added, a fierce

215

smile on his face. "We are as much in your debt as you are in ours."

Linh smiled back. Magic could *save*. It h*ad* saved. *She* may already have used it to save a life. But both times she thought she'd wielded it her heart had been pounding out of her chest. Her body had been trying to flinch away from reality. She'd been scared out of her wits. Perhaps it was easiest to be clear headed, highly focused and to direct your whole will into crafting magic when someone else's life depended on it.

She didn't want to wait till a friend was about to die to craft magic. Because if she missed anything, one of her friends could be dealt a death blow before she noticed the danger. She needed to wield magic before then. To act pre-emptively against the danger, not at the last second.

But when she extended her hand, reaching out with her mind, felt the tingling and acknowledged what it was, it vanished. As soon as Linh accepted her fingers were touching magic, she stopped touching it. The idea was unnerving.

Fiona wasn't hesitating. Her eyes were closed and tiny specks of white glowed at her fingertips. It was disconcerting, but maybe shutting her eyes, so she didn't see the stuff she'd had the capacity to shape for eight months, without noticing it, would help.

Linh tried again. It took several moments, and the tingling faded immediately when she sensed it. But she hung on. And nothing blew up. Nothing caught fire. All that happened was the harder she held on, and pressed against something solid at her fingertips, sweat trickled down her brow and she forgot to breathe.

She sighed, letting go. She could do this. But it was going to take time, effort and she would need to truly believe the magic she shaped wasn't going to tear her or anyone else apart. Not that it had done anything she hadn't made it do yet.

She sighed and sat down with Troy and Michael. Fiona joined her.

"How does it feel to you?" Linh asked Fiona.

"A tingling at the tip of my fingers, when I really try. Almost like magic is alive. But it feels kind of wrong, trying to make it do something. I don't even know if it's sentient, let alone self-aware, but I don't..."

"You don't want to impose on or bother it," Troy said with a smile. "Fiona Dolberry, never wanting to bother or inconvenience anyone, even magic."

"You think I'm... too considerate?" she asked shyly.

"I suspect your consideration is misplaced on magic," Troy replied diplomatically.

Linh smiled at the sincerity in his eyes and the relief in Fiona's. Fiona was sensitive and too considerate of others, too quick to put them first. Fiona lowered her head and smiled shyly back at Troy and... *oh*. There was affection in his gaze and something more when it was directed at Fiona.

Light flashed on her right, at Ruarnon and Selenia's hands. A shimmering white substance the size of a small plate hovered before Ruarnon's extended hand. It rippled and shifted as if blown on the wind, then vanished.

"Maybe you could do that too," Troy said seriously to Fiona. Then his lips curled in a smile. "If you didn't worry about hurting magic's feelings."

"I reckon it's going to be a while before any of us can do that," said Michael. "Ruarnon's mind's in a league of its own."

Linh surprised herself by sleeping soundly that night, though she followed the others to the upstairs bridge Desriah wanted them to train on the next morning with footsteps slowed by the weight of apprehension.

"Desriah's going to let us coach you," Mawana announced, as Linh and the others zig-zagged up an internal stone staircase after Desriah the next morning. "I'll coach you lot, and Mocco will help Ruarnon, Lenaris, Tor and Selenia. Desriah's going to watch over them too. She says Ruarnon is already capable of shaping magic sufficiently to accidentally get themself in trouble."

"And what do you advise, o teacher?" Troy asked in mocking tones, with his usual friendly grin, as Desriah led both groups through an empty room and out onto an open-air stone bridge, shaded by a parallel bridge above.

Troy's grin vanished and Linh moved apprehensively, realising she was a few stories up, but couldn't see any framework supporting this bridge, which appeared to hang from both the walls it linked.

Mawana smiled at Troy's tone, leading them to the far end of the bridge, a fair distance away from Mocco and the others. "Michael, you need to let every thought go, then reach for magic. I'll keep a close eye on you, in case that results in you doing something unexpected.

"Fiona, don't worry about it being rude to push magic around. I don't know if it's alive or not, but if it has any sort of consciousness, I think it enjoys the challenge of being pushed to hold states of being that aren't its natural state.

"Troy, I suspect you need to treat magic wielding like bathing your younger siblings. Gently and with care, but less hesitation you're going to break something. You can't break magic and it's incredibly difficult to break things *with* magic.

"Linh, you need to learn to push your will on magic when your body is relaxed. And all of you need to remember that you won't be able to shape magic much beyond your fingertips at first. Basically, you're not competent enough for things to go wrong yet."

"You mean we're so incompetent we can't achieve enough to screw up?" Troy asked, frowning.

"I am unfamiliar with that expression, but from your tone, yes," Mawana replied.

Troy shook his head, grinning and Michael smiled too. Linh sighed, relief flooding her.

"Shall we begin?" Mawana asked enthusiastically.

Linh and Fiona stood side by side, their backs to Michael and Troy. If anything went wrong, it would be moving off the bridge, away from them. Linh stared into the distance, letting her eyes glaze over, her breathing slow and her body relax in the knowledge she wasn't skilled enough to screw this up.

She raised her arm, kept her breathing steady and reached into the air. Magic tingled at her fingertips. She took a deep breath, bracing herself, and pushed slowly against it. Air hardened at her fingertips. She gasped in excitement and her fingers reached through ordinary air. She *could* do this. She had to stop fearing what magic *could* do and focus on and believe in what she *wanted* it to do.

It was slow going. Often, she'd focus so hard she forgot to breathe.

Michael swore and Linh whipped around. He was falling forwards, having overbalanced. Mawana caught him around the waist and set him on his feet.

"What happened?" Troy asked.

"I made a shield," Michael replied. "I tried to make it stronger, pushed too hard against it, broke it and fell."

"Mine don't feel right," Troy grumbled.

"Try again," Mawana instructed.

Troy held out his hand, grimacing with the effort of focusing. Mawana moved his hand as if to high five Troy's. And kept reaching until their fingertips almost touched. Troy frowned.

"You my friend, have made shield fingertip gloves," Mawana explained. "You'll have to reach further with the magic, to shape the magic in the air, instead of the magic in your fingers."

Troy sat suddenly. "As you were everyone," he added. "I'm just taking a break to process that there's magic in my fingers and I'm using it to give them an exoskeleton."

Linh laughed. The idea was so absurd, and he was genuinely finding it difficult, but Troy was grinning too.

Something moved at the edge of Linh's vision. White particles glittered. It was perfectly flat, a circle roughly the size of Fiona's raised hand. Sweat beaded on Fiona's brow, and her face tautened with concentration. The shield remained in place for two heartbeats. Then it vanished.

"How are you doing that?" Troy asked. "Isn't it disconcerting, seeing the magic you're shaping?"

"I'm guessing that's why the rest of our shields are invisible," said Michael.

"You'll need to work on making visible ones over the next few days," said Mawana. "It will make casting larger-than-fingertip shields easier, seeing what size they are."

"You want us to look straight at an impossible substance, as we impossibly shape it?" Troy asked, gaping.

It took them the rest of the week to form visible shields for more than a split second. Michael and Linh both managed to form hand-sized ones a few times, and Fiona's were bigger. But Troy was having trouble connecting the pieces of shield before his fingers. Finally, he growled and his hand balled into a fist. Sparks burst like miniature fireworks at the tip of his knuckles.

"Shit!" Troy jerked his hand away and he and Michael leapt backwards. The sparks vanished.

Linh couldn't help smiling. "You got angry and wanted something to explode, didn't you?"

Troy grinned sheepishly. "Apparently losing your temper is the easiest way to do magic. Pity you can't lose your temper *and* control how you craft magic simultaneously."

"But if we channel our frustration at how long this is taking *into* crafting magic…" Michael suggested.

He extended a tense forearm, a tendon standing out, and stood patiently. Something rippled before his palm. It was rectangular. Then circular. It vanished, then reappeared as a square, rippling from one semi-transparent white side to the other.

Linh's breath caught. She stared at the erratically extending and retreating substance, hardly believing her eyes. But was it solid?

Troy reached out, tentatively, and pushed it with his fingertips. It moved before his fingers, maintaining its square shape.

Michael gasped and his shield vanished. "I sensed it," he said. "When you tried to touch it. Wasn't it solid?"

Troy started. "I was uh, kind of scared to actually touch it. I think I might have used magic to push it away. You weren't trying to keep it in place were you?"

Michael shook his head.

Troy shifted, took a deep breath and raised his hand, his features scrunched in discomfort. Time passed, and Troy's features gradually narrowed in concentration. Linh couldn't see anything. Michael reached out and rapped his knuckles against solid air.

"Ouch!"

Michael was clutching his hand, his knuckles bleeding. "That was a shield, but it was sharp as a knife!"

Troy flashed a sheepish grin. "Sorry.

Mawana came over to bandage Troy's knuckles. "It appears we're at the point where seeing shields is crucial, because you're making ones strong enough to hurt yourselves. Don't touch them anymore," he instructed cheerfully.

Fiona stood on Linh's left with her eyes closed and a shimmering substance extending steadily outwards from her upraised hand. It was as big as Fiona's hand, with all five fingers extended. Fiona opened her eyes. The substance wavered. Fiona's face screwed up in concentration, and the edges crept out sideways, but the top and bottom started to shrink.

Linh's mouth dropped open as *all* sides of Fiona's shield expanded outwards slightly, the largest and most controlled any of them had managed in eight days. Fiona was panting, her face dripping with sweat.

"Let go, Fi! You don't want to knock yourself out!" Linh warned.

Fiona's posture relaxed as her shield faded to nothing, and she stood catching her breath.

"That was brilliant," said Mawana. "The others are forming solid shields of a consistent size, but you're ready to focus on making larger shields. Try making it bigger all at once next time, like Ruarnon does. That might be easier."

"It was?" Fiona asked, only appearing to have taken in his first three words. She was blushing.

It occurred to Linh how rarely Fiona was the centre of attention. That was partly Linh's fault, her tendency to speak her mind drew attention, and Fiona didn't speak up as much.

"You do realise you're clever?" Troy asked Fiona softly.

"I'm *ok* at school, but I'm not really…." Fiona replied uncertainly.

Linh's mouth opened in protest. Didn't Fiona realise the only reason Linh got better grades was that she spent her spare time reading, whereas Fiona spent hers caring for younger siblings?

"You *don't* realise? You realise Linh's as smart as Mic?" Troy whispered, probably more loudly than he realised, as Linh could still hear him. "I don't bang on about it like I do with Mic, because she knows it and isn't so hard on herself."

"I know but, it's not like… I'm anything special," Fiona replied. "I mean, I'm just, ok at everything."

Linh opened her mouth to object again, but Troy got there first. "Fiona Dolberry, you are more than ok. And you always seem to understand Linh and Mic when I struggle sometimes."

"You don't know what they're going to say before they say it?" Fiona replied.

"No. Have you been holding out on us?"

She had. Fiona often let others speak up, except for those rare occasions when no one else had her thoughts. Linh frowned. How had Troy spotted at that? Maybe because of the way he looked deeply into her eyes, as if drinking them in.

"I hear there's lots of interesting statues up on the roof and the sunset views are quite pretty," Michael told the air loudly.

Troy turned to him thoughtfully and Linh's brows raised in confusion.

"Should you two need a location for a date," Michael added bluntly, with a mischievous smile worthy of Troy.

Fiona blushed.

"Tonight?" Troy asked Fiona.

She smiled. "Tonight."

Linh sighed. They could all craft magic now, and Fiona and Troy were planning a date among statues Linh suspected depicted the Guardians. Life was moving forward; magic was returning and Umarinaris' past was coming to light again.

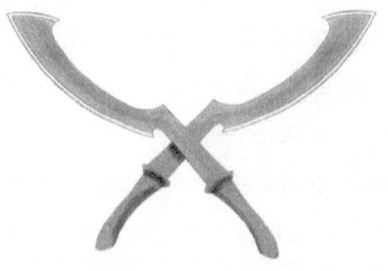

Chapter 17

Forgotten Powers -Ruarnon

T hree weeks into magic practice, Ruarnon had mixed feelings about it. Could they have broken the chariot's axel, made it lose a wheel and forced it to stop, when Zaldeaans abducted their parents so long ago? The fighting had been too strained, and there were likely too many threats for magic to have saved Arlian or Ethlin. But could magic craft have deflected the blow that killed Uncle Omah?

Ruarnon shook their head. Companion Tor had advised them and Lenaris not to think this way. Not to torture themselves by considering their losses, and how knowing magic craft earlier might have saved people they loved. "Look to the future," Tor had said. And Ruarnon had thought of how magic shields would help them, Governor Armar and Governor Syenne ward off assassination attempts in the Zaldeaan Realm.

But what else did Ruarnon have to think of? They had accepted the challenge of magic craft because it challenged their mind and body in ways they had never been challenged before.

Because it was fun to compete with Lenaris, to see Selenia's enthusiasm and from his thoughtful feedback, Mocco was enjoying helping them hone new skills. But as Ruarnon watched Tor focus, blocking out the world, his shields not faltering even when Troy cried out… Ruarnon lost their enthusiasm.

Their attention wandered far from the sensation in the air, that beckoned to be shaped when they reached for it. Away from the shaded bridge, and the hot dry air of the desert below. To the Far West, where Tor would use magic craft to rescue Ruarnon's parents. To help Uncle Karmarn, Aunt Merlah and cousin Coroth get out alive. Where the soldiers assisting Tor could depend on magic to save them when weapons, armour and wits failed. While they faced unknown dangers. And Ruarnon stayed home. What did Ruarnon need magic for?

They raised their hand distractedly. And reached out again as something pressed into their brooding. But the thing became harder, then another. Ruarnon turned, frustrated. Lenaris was throwing a leather ball at them. Ruarnon reached, strained and it fell to the ground.

Lenaris stared. "You weren't even trying. I threw a ball to get your attention and you… blocked it without looking."

Ruarnon looked down. Five leather balls lay at their feet. Five. Their mouth fell open. "I was thinking. It was like something pressing at me, trying to distract me, so I pushed it away. I was so distracted… I didn't realise that mental push wasn't intruding thoughts, it was physical objects."

Mocco shook his head. "You are learning faster than Mawana. Lylah said he was the most reckless, rapid learner she has ever taught."

"You sensed the balls, didn't you?" Lenaris asked.

"They were disturbing the magic in the air," Ruarnon reflected. "So I half-consciously reached towards them, felt them coming at me, and pushed to stop them."

"Half-consciously?" Mocco asked. "You dropped two balls that hit your shield forcefully, with half your mind focused elsewhere?"

Ruarnon smiled slowly. "That is what being regent is. Doing one thing, while half your mind is on one of ten other things you should be doing. I frequently do things with only partial attention."

"But your focus is incredible when you give things your sole attention," said Lenaris. "Yet it seems you're still impressive with a split focus. You're the best of us with magic."

Selenia's shield curved inwards and sweat trickled down her face as she strained to shield a ball that slowed, then rolled, rather than fell to the floor before her. Mocco threw one at Tor, and it slowed, but still came so close he had to catch it at the last moment.

Beyond them Michael was laughing, throwing ball after ball rapidly, at Troy, who was ducking and catching with a large grin on his face, as if his muscles were programmed that way and he and Michael had decided the exercise was silly and had given up. The ball Linh threw at Fiona slowed, then Fiona caught it, as it burst through her shield.

The Australians swapped. Fiona threw the ball gently, and Linh strained. It fell rapidly, and Linh hunched forwards gasping for breath. Troy threw a ball slowly at Michael, whose face scrunched up in determination. His ball slowed slightly. Then he swore and kicked it aside. Mocco caught Lenaris off-guard. The ball redirected into her hand. She'd steered instead of blocking it. Then she sat down, panting rapidly.

Ruarnon was best at magic. Every daunting challenge they had faced, the act of will it took to smile, raise their chin and walk about with confidence while they had feared Tarlah would fall down around their ears during the Zaldeaan invasion, or assassins would kill them in the Realm, while they privately battled stress and uncertainty about missing family members for months on end… all of it made them excellent at magic. They were running circles around their friends with moderate effort and half their focus. And it was all a waste. Because they weren't sailing west.

Ruarnon remained distracted. They tried to focus more, and excelled in speed, control and capacity beyond the others. Partly because overcoming their catching reflexes to block balls with shields was a serious obstacle to Troy and Michael, but everyone gradually got better.

Ruarnon was the first to practice blocking balls blindfolded. Desriah sent them and Lenaris to the next bridge, where nothing else would disturb the magic in the air, and it was quieter. After a week of that, Ruarnon was blocking their own and others balls while people talked and moved around them. Mocco and Mawana tried making loud noises at random, and when Mawana startled Ruarnon by jumping loudly, Ruarnon instinctively seized him around the middle with magic, giving him a scare and making everyone laugh at his attempt at sabotage backfiring.

Then, mercifully, instead of being brilliant at something they'd never need to do, Desriah asked Ruarnon to help Mocco, Mawana and General Takanis train the soldiers. The first time Ruarnon crafted a visible shield in front of their soldiers, the size of a bronze one, jaws dropped and the soldiers stared in silence. But as Ruarnon and Mocco talked them through sensing, touching and crafting magic and mentioned situations soldiers may have unconsciously crafted it, Ruarnon saw recognition in many veterans' eyes.

The soldiers responded differently, the most determined casting hand sized shields from the outset. With Ruarnon's encouragement they took their time, and soon many applied enough focus to touch and craft magic. Their focus from regular arms training enabled most soldiers to progress more swiftly than Ruarnon's friends.

In a few weeks, Desriah was satisfied they had learned basic lessons, and could cast shields with sufficient control and intent to continue practising without her.

"Practice whenever you can," Desriah told the soldiers and Ruarnon's companions. "Especially in the time you have at sea. Distract each other by talking, singing, and making loud and sudden noises, to hone your focus and control of magic craft. When you are ready, throw arrows at each other instead of balls. They are heavier and will be moving faster. When you can block multiple thrown arrows at once, you will be in good stead for the west."

Then Desriah led Ruarnon and their companions down a flight of stone steps through an archway into a dark cavern, along a wide path lined with tall rocky pillars. Water trickled through stone gutters along sandstone walls lining both sides of the path, making the room feel even cooler, as Desriah led them towards daylight.

As she stepped outside, sand rose in scorching sunlight beyond the guttered walls and Ruarnon was grateful for pillars supporting a stone roof and providing shade overhead. The desert seemed motionless and silent, nothing but heatwaves and an endless sand sea stretching beyond the trickling water. Hot, dry air blew past, and Ruarnon heard the occasional call of a bird flying overhead towards palms lining the mountains bordering the desert on their far left.

They reached the end of the path, walking down several steps to where the walls joined in a circle, the gutters breaking off into waterfalls flowing into a small, stone-lined pool.

"This is a place I often come to think," said Desriah. "I want you to drink in the calm, quiet and peace of it. Remember it, and if ever you have trouble forming shields in your travels, if you are stressed or distracted, close your eyes, picture this place, and use its peace to ground yourself."

It was beautiful. Ruarnon would think of it if ever they had a stressful day in a Council meeting, or the Zaldeaan government officials gave them grief. It was hard to keep bitterness from rising within them, even as they stood in that oasis of desert calm.

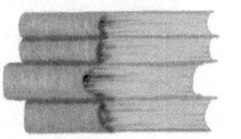

CHAPTER 18

To See-Linh

L inh sat in a goran carriage beside Fiona, a face sized shield hovering before her as they trundled through the desert heat, her fingers gently pressing against her shield. She could see, feel and shape it, but even now, if she thought too much, she lost her grip and the magic reverted to its usual state of invisible formlessness.

"I can't quite believe them either," said Troy from the seat across the aisle. "But I'd rather not make them outside official practice –they do my head in."

Linh smiled sympathetically.

"Bad news Troy," Michael said from Troy's left, "I suspect it's exactly the way Linh throws herself at it that's making her so good."

Fiona was still better. She could cast larger, more powerful shields, for longer, which resisted more objects, despite more distractions. But if Fiona was surprised, hesitancy could still hold her back. Whereas surprise or extra pressure improved Linh's shield magic. It motivated, even honed it.

"I think so too," said Linh. "And I'm beginning to understand why most people on Umarinaris aren't wielding magic. They have to *really* want to, to overcome disbelief, fear of the unknown and fear of what can go wrong. Only for a very clear and important purpose would you keep attempting and let yourself succeed at magic craft. Though I do wonder why more soldiers haven't honed it."

"Because it is a last resort," Tor said from the seat in front of Troy. "Offensive and defensive blows and physical reflexes keep soldiers alive and are all-consuming. Only when those ordinary skills fail can I see soldiers reaching into the unknown to hold off a death blow. And many would be cut down by blows they didn't see coming."

"Our family were chosen to learn shield magic when Lylah detected Mawana shaping magic, as a child," said Mocco, from behind Linh. "If the way she managed us is anything to go on, she looks for children who are going to discover their ability, then trains them and their parents, so the parents can monitor, help and conceal their child's magic craft from the rest of us, as well as defend our people."

Mawana smiled beside him. "I suspect her ability to *See* isn't just influenced by magic. She's very good at reading people. And predicting what they'll do next. I wonder if her ability to *See* futures is a magical extension of ordinary skills she's been honing for who knows how long."

Linh sighed. "That's a relief. If the sisters are older than most humans, then most of Narz's sorcerers shouldn't have anywhere near their ability with magic."

Mawana sighed. "If some can control damarian armies, I think you will find them formidable enough."

Linh shivered. The slow, tiny steps she and her friends had taken in learning magic suggested that Tyrook was as formidable as Flariah herself, given his ability to force hundreds of damars to attack the same target. Precious few had that power, and she sincerely hoped the number with Poran's power to support a damarian army's control was similarly limited.

Magic shield practice continued on-board the Iylena, Saeron and Meera, where some crew still averted their gazes or whispered prayers to the Ancestors at sight of magic craft.

Over the next few days, they sailed past hazy desert and dunes. Then desert mountains gave way to grassy hills and plains. The remnants of an ancient stone pier came into view on Linh's left, before a tangled mass of trees and grass. All three ships dropped anchor, and the Iylena's boats were lowered.

A woman awaited them in a small clearing on the edge of the sand. She wore a green, elbow length linen tunic, and ebony linen pants that fit like leggings, over soft brown leather boots. Her straight black hair was braided around her head, her cheek bones were fine, her nose delicate and her angular black eyes were full of curiosity.

Ruarnon led everyone towards her.

"Welcome to the grasslands," she said. "My name is Sryah, and I shall lead you to my residence, the City of Peaks. Do not stray too far from me or the path, as my animals are not tame, but will not threaten you while you are on or close to the path."

"If the castle is your residence, where is home?" Mawana asked.

Sryah smiled. "We are walking through it." She gestured with both hands at slender trees with delicate clusters of leaves, taller trees branching out in all directions with their own dense canopy above, creepers and long grasses rising and winding over branches and birds flapping through the treetops.

Mawana returned her smile. He surveyed their surroundings eagerly and Mocco's posture relaxed as they followed Sryah into the forest. Linh couldn't name the foliage around them, but it reminded her very much of gum trees and familiar small plants with little pink and yellow wildflowers resembling ones she'd seen in the mountains at home.

"This is more like home than anything we've seen since Oval Island," said Fiona, channelling her thoughts.

"The only way to 'find' Oval Island is to step onto it via a Gateway of Umarinaris," said Sryah. "But if it was possible to find, I think you would find it in this zone of climate."

Troy shook his head. "We've come full circle."

"I don't think you will achieve that until you see the man you call Red Cloak again," said Sryah. Her gaze was distant, her expression almost dreamy. "He is reaching for you. I make him nervous, but he seems curious about how you fare."

Linh stopped in her tracks. So did Fiona, Troy and Michael.

"They are a little startled now, but they are well," said Sryah.

Troy's mouth dropped open. "You're speaking to Red Cloak?"

"I was. He is as surprised to be detected as you were to be reached by him."

Ruarnon frowned. "The sorcerer who brought my friends into this world can reach them by magic? Across the ocean?"

"How is that possible?" Lenaris added.

It struck Linh that despite that everyone had stopped and the tension in the air, Sryah was calm. Her features were open, her voice almost dreamy. Something radiated from her. Something tingled in the air around them. Was Sryah touching the magic in the air as they walked? Hairs on the back of Linh's neck stood up. She was shocked, but no fear rose in her. There was something calming about this setting, about the shade of the trees beneath the hot sun, the buzz of bees around the wildflowers. It was as if the *magic* in the air was calm.

"It is my gift," Sryah replied. "It is the reason I was asked to come here and guard what you call a creature army. I was the one who told Lylah of your arrival in our world," she added and Linh's skin prickled. "It was me who warned everyone via Umarinaris Book that the Gateways of Umarinas' had been opened once more. But you didn't need to know that unless you needed to know me."

She seemed to add the last in response to Linh and Michael's brows rising in surprise that Lylah had lied about being the one who wrote in the Umarinaris Book.

"I have *Seen* Red Cloak open other gateways, in recent years. He has been mapping them. But it is normally only while he works on the Gateways that I *See* him. He hides his presence at all other times. He must not have realised you were near me, otherwise I doubt he'd have reached out. But he seemed to sense that I mean him no harm."

She began walking again, and Linh and the others followed, transfixed, as if the magic she touched in the air invited and ushered them on. But Linh knew it was the knowledge Sryah was sharing so freely that drew her forwards.

"May I ask why you are, so forthcoming?" Ruarnon asked. "Your sisters seem determined to tell us only so little as they think we need to know, when they think we need to know it."

Sryah smiled. "They do not remember the days when people with my gift and Umarinaris' World Books freely kept each other informed, warning of the approach of bad weather, or bandits. Sharing our knowledge and insights. In those days, people with my gift and Red Cloak's had a special language with our hands. We could *See* each other and speak that way across great distances."

Linh stared. Was she describing the age when the Guardians were still part of the world?

"My sisters know I have always believed in the benefit of *Seeing* and sharing. While they would stunt magic craft in the east out of fear, I see you as no different than my sisters and I were once, a lifetime ago. You have the potential to learn, you are already connecting and working together. These skills must be strengthened, these potentials honed, if you are to succeed in the west. I have *Seen* how collapses in communication have failed people, how battling alone endangers some. I would not have you repeat the mistakes the westerners are making."

Tor eyed Sryah keenly, and Lenaris nodded, but Linh and her friends were distracted.

"Why was Red Cloak looking at *us*?" Troy asked. "We haven't had *any* communication with him. Has he been watching us this whole time?"

Sryah shook her head. "I suspect he can detect Lylah's and Flariah's magic. Most people with his gift and strength could. And their aura's would put him off, no matter how far away he is. He would not *Look* at you while you were anywhere near them. But while you were on Myleth Island, and perhaps in the Zaldeaan Realm, I wonder if he did *See*. And while he must have sensed my magic, I suspect it was welcoming enough to make him curious.

"He looks to you with hope. I *Saw* some great task. Some darkness near him. But it was hard to *See*, because when he *Looked* to you, he pushed that all away. He turned with wonder and some amount of concern, to see why you walked with such a powerful magic crafter as myself."

"What sort of man do you think he is?" Fiona asked.

"He seems young. Not much older than Lenaris. But his ability to set aside everything, the darkness that surrounds him and his fears, to *See* all this way, and the power and control with which he does so are extraordinary. If he is anywhere near as young as he seems, he is likely the strongest magic crafter of this age."

"Then why is he messing about with gateways?" Michael asked. "You haven't seen him use them for anything?"

Sryah paused, then continued walking. "You have some inkling how terrible the greatest sorcerers' powers are. Their families have taught and honed their powers over many generations. You know the legends of the Sorcery War and you saw how frightened the sorcerers who surrendered to you are of sorcerers in the far south. Do you see the threat that poses?"

Ruarnon sighed. "Poran said Lord Vye is representative of the southern sorcerers and if they are drawn into Narz's war with allied southern rulers…does he fear a sorcery war?"

"Or the end of the world," Troy added. "They don't sound too different from each other."

Magic tingled at Linh's fingertips at that thought, and around her hands, across her chest. She was connecting to it, probing the air, feeling for disturbances in it. She sensed nothing. There seemed no threat for her new magical fight-flight response to meet.

"When he first *Saw* you," said Sryah, "his eyes were filled with hope."

"*You are greatly needed, and not just by Ruarnon. To someone, you are the balance between order and chaos,*" Fiona said softly. "Lylah said that. Does Red Cloak need us too? But why would we be the balance of order and chaos to him?"

Linh shook her head. Nuard had told them Myths of the Strangers. Of people from faraway lands, who appeared when the Timbalen Empire was in peril and saved the world. People he sincerely believed Linh and her friends could be. They had never truly bought the idea, even when most lost and confused about how and why they had come to be in Umarinaris. But in naming them catalysts for peace in the west, hadn't Lylah said much the same? She'd even *Seen* it... And Red Cloak was watching them across the ocean, with hope...

"Could he know Lylah thinks we're catalysts for peace in the west?" Linh asked. "Does he hope we are?"

"I still think anyone who thinks we're going to save the world is out of their mind," said Troy.

Linh smiled at a hint of his reaction to Nuard saying the same thing on Myleth Island. But they *had* persuaded Ruarnon to occupy the Realm, ending its civil war and purging it of damars. And if Ruarnon or Tor sought an alliance with the Galvations, she and her Aussie friends would likely get to speak to Galvation leaders too. Maybe they could make some small difference to an entire nation in the Far West.

They walked on in silence. Through warm air, leaves rustling in the breeze. Dried leaves rustled or scrunched under the feet of lizards or small mammals concealed under grasses and bushes in the undergrowth, as they went about their business. If Red Cloak had any ability to read people, like Sryah, and he carried the burden of saving everyone in the west on his shoulders, maybe the hope on his face had been at a personal level. As he gazed at a peaceful place, where a group of good friends wandered through a temporary oasis of calm.

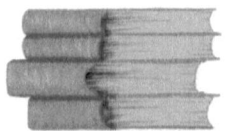

CHAPTER 19

THE GRASSLANDS ~ LINH

As they walked, Linh inspected surrounding grasses and creepers for any sign of creatures that may be part of a creature army, until Mocco drew her attention ahead. "That looks like a change of scenery," he asserted, pointing at spires rising above the overgrown forest.

"That's one gargantuan castle," said Troy, as patches of stone wall came into view between the trees.

"It looks city-sized," said Linh. "Does anyone else live there?"

"Not for a long time," Sryah replied. "It was built around the end of the Sorcery War. Those towers are high enough to provide views of the grasslands, scrublands, and to monitor the pass into the desert. It was once a watchtower, from which lookouts kept watch for sorcerers."

"The Guardians actually lived here?" Troy asked.

"Once," Sryah replied, "Long ago."

"But what happened to them?" Selenia asked. "Why won't the faeron tell me?"

"Their peace was harder won than you know. They paid for it dearly, and their descendants are entitled to it."

It had seemed strange they had disappeared entirely after the Sorcery War, when sorcerers lived on in the West and the North Lands. Linh was beginning to wonder if an island in the far east, like Oval Island, perhaps screened by magic, hid a Guardian civilisation. If refugees from the war had fled northeast of here, perhaps the Guardians had retreated beyond human settlements, to a place where no one feared them, or held them in awe. Where they could live normal lives, just like the North Landers.

A series of towers surrounded the enormous building ahead, giving way to spires and one thick central tower. Judging by the window spacing, each storey was twice the height Linh was used to.

She followed Sryah through a garden of small trees and hilly lawns around the city. Her skin tingled. Especially her fingertips. "Is the magic in the air here active?" she asked.

Sryah paused atop a small hill, nodding. Linh noted how high the towers rose. There were no windows on the ground floor, and the stone steps to a nearby door were less faded, less cracked than the castle walls, making her suspect they were newer. This place looked heavily fortified. Flariah's castle had more of a sense of leisure about it. But this place looked designed to weather attacks, its towers positioned to provide views to every corner of the continent, a heavily fortified watch tower.

"What kind of enchantments are on the walls?" Selenia asked.

Linh frowned. Mocco and Mawana stood fixated on the walls, and Ruarnon seemed unsurprised by the question.

"Defensive enchantments. To prevent any hostile force from entering this building, killing the people who held the bonds of the creature armies of this island, and taking the bonds and armies for themselves."

"There was no need to teach us here," said Ruarnon. "You could have come to Flariah's palace, instead of letting us see this place. Letting us see how the founders of this island once feared attack, how, I'm guessing, they protected even themselves from these armies. So why are we to study with you here?"

"Lylah *Sees* that you will seek an alliance with the Galvations. But *Seeing* what I have of the westerners, and of your friends and self, I see people in this party meeting others in the west. I think your reach in word and deed has potential.

"In another lifetime, my parents were farmers in a new land, with limited knowledge of the soil, the climate and what would grow there. They brought with them seeds of every type of crop, and planted some of each seed widely, noting which soils and climates they grew in, which plants competing for sunlight, soil and shade they could take root in, and grow alongside.

"Even with my *Sight*, and Lylah's of the future, I regard the west as unknown soil. I do not know which seeds of information and experience I give you will take root, and flourish into trees that will aid your role as catalysts of peace. So I will give you as many seeds as I can. I will satisfy your curiosity, that you may better focus on honing your magic craft, and understanding the consequences of the previous sorcery war, how terrible its weapons were, how great the defences required against them.

"I would ask you to tell anyone in the west you think needs to hear it, what you saw here, how it felt, that the people of the west may know the power that saved the northern half of the western continent once. That should that continent become the dark and fearsome place we fear, they may hope it will save them again."

"But not the Guardians?" Ruarnon asked. "Who could non-magic wielders in Narz's path turn to with hope?"

"I see multiple candidates in the west already. Your cousin Coroth is one of them. His lover is another. And there are independent sorcerers in the west. It is not divided evenly between Narz and the God Kings and Queens. But should every other power appear to be failing, Umarinaris will see that the Guardian's descendants never truly left."

"But Flariah and Desriah hold the bonds of armies, and can't leave their islands, and I'm guessing you're the same," said Linh. "Who else will come, if all other hope is lost in the west?"

"If the Guardians' descendants are needed, I suspect you four of all people, are likely to meet them. But they are not as pure and superhuman as the legends claim. They are not infallible. Even they may do with reminding of this castle, its fortifications, its enchantments. Of how its original founders feared not only sorcerers, but the armies they smuggled through a gateway in the west long ago."

"Why not destroy the armies?" Ruarnon asked. "If they were such a terrible threat then, if Narz fears their potential so much now, why not kill every creature?"

Sryah's head lowered. "We hadn't the resources. Or the strength. It was two generations before such a thing was possible. And in that time, we proved they could be kept on these shores. No one came to claim them. Contact with the western lands was lost. And those who fought, in their old age, did not wish to see more slaughter. Did not wish to perpetuate more savagery.

"With no one strengthening or renewing the enchantments on the creatures, most began to weaken. They became less of a threat. And while some were impossible to control, the faeron, in their final act before their total seclusion, took those creatures in, taming the creatures with their magic. They sterilised the most dangerous ones, so none could reproduce.

"Of the original armies, all that now remains is animals prone to perceive things that approach them as threats and to attack them, instead of fleeing. They do not hunt the way damars do. They only attack based on proximity. They are still a threat, but they have been breeding with normal animals on this island, which lessened their aggression.

"We had thought to sterilise them all, but time and mixed breeding is rectifying the mistakes of desperate magic wielders. Nature is reclaiming its course. It gave people hope in the early days after the Sorcery War. But now, more than ever, it is a testament to what must never be again."

Sryah motioned everyone to be still. Bark scraped. A large snake was spiralling along a tree branch uncomfortably close to the ground, a few meters on their right. Linh felt a distant tingle of magic that gave her goosebumps. But the snake paid them no heed. It slithered onto another branch, up a trunk, a third branch, then over the garden wall. And Linh wondered, could damars one day become like that? Predators fled by other creatures, living in the wild, only attacking things that came too close to them? Was Sryah showing them what she hoped the future would be?

Sryah led them to a clearing beside the castle walls for their first lesson. They sat close enough to the walls that even Troy noticed a faint tingling sensation, which made Linh wonder at the power in the enchantments that had helped fortify those walls so long ago. It was almost a welcome distraction from the long, unmown grass around the castle, and what might be slithering through it.

General Takanis saluting Ruarnon as she marched the soldiers into the garden gates and onto the lawn made Linh feel better. That many people stomping about and talking in low voices ought to scare any wildlife away.

"The magic I will teach you is more dangerous than shield magic," said Sryah. "Cast properly; it is a sleep spell. With too much power and force, it can be impossible to wake the sleeper. Cast with excessive force or ill intent; it can kill the sleeper. Most of you lack the focus and power for unwake-able sleep or death to be a possible risk —yet, so I want you to develop your abilities gradually, and with care.

"Notice the effects of the magic you are crafting on the body. Monitor posture and the relaxation of muscles. Notice the rate of their breathing slow. Watch their eyes close as they drift off to sleep. Ease your push to shape magic as their body relaxes. Release your grip on the magic as their eyes close.

"If you have crafted the magic well enough, they will stay asleep without magical encouragement. That is the stage I would like most of you to reach before I take you to a final location, to learn your last skills on this island."

Linh's heart sped up as Sryah spoke. But her shoulders didn't tighten in quite the way she anticipated. Her tension from Blue

Bay had a rival now, the fierce determination burning in her chest. This magic could harm if handled wrongly. But it could help people sleep on stressful, sleepless nights. It may even put enemies to sleep as she and her friends snuck towards a certain gateway. It was valuable, and it was her best chance in training to conquer her fear of magic. She needed to face it head on, again and again, until her shoulders no longer tensed, and she no longer wanted to flinch away from the idea of crafting magic.

"Work in pairs. Relax your own body, breathe slowly, then visualise the other person's body relaxing, slumping, their breathing slowing and eyes becoming heavy. I find crafting sleep magic is like meditating on sleep, then projecting it onto yourself or another. Today, I want you to shape the magic inside yourself. The idea may be unnerving," she added as a dozen soldiers shifted and murmurs rose, "but you need to feel the effects of the spell to help you gauge them. To develop your sense of what it looks *and* feels like when someone else has been put almost to sleep. Developing that awareness will help you safely practice."

Everyone spread out across the lawn and lay deep in the high rising grass. It took Linh a few moments to get used to grass rubbing against her bare calves and forearms, and her neck and to the view of stalks rising up in all directions around her.

After six weeks of magic practice in shady spaces above desert heat, she was *tired*. Her limbs and spine were quite happy to relax into the grass as she lay flat on her back. Patches of direct sunlight still spilled over the blades of grass, making her feel warm and sleepy. She closed her eyes, giving in to the comfort of her grassy bed and the warmth of the sun. Magic tingled around her hands. But that didn't seem right. She breathed slowly, imagining her limbs relax more. And felt the tinniest tingling's elsewhere, which made her jerk and almost prompted her to sit up. The tingling vanished.

It was a strange process, allowing magic to activate across her body. It was like lying on the sandy shore of a beach as the tide comes in, flat on your back, not being at all worried or disturbed by the tide creeping up your chest, then over your mouth and face. That was partly because she kept holding her breath, a bad habit.

But between warmth, comfort and growing mental discipline, Linh managed to relax as magic tingled across her chest, down her legs, but not quite up to her shoulders, neck or head. Hesitation always made her shiver, and the tingling cease, as she mentally flinched away from the idea of activating magic in or near her face. It felt too like letting someone poke you in the eye.

Three days later, she was frustrated, determined and managing to stay relaxed as the magic tingled all the way to her neck. But the idea of letting magic switch off her brain kept her eyes wide open and would not let her sleep.

Mocco and Mawana were putting each other to sleep by then. Their experience with and control of shield magic seemed to make learning sleep magic second nature. When Mawana started putting two people to sleep at once, Sryah asked him to help her supervise. He watched Linh carefully, then said, "I think you and Fiona are ready to practice on each other."

Linh frowned.

Mawana smiled. "Try putting Fiona to sleep."

Linh grimaced. Shape magic particles *inside* someone else? Especially when that person was Fiona...

Fiona smiled. "I trust you. You'll be fine."

247

Fiona closed her eyes. Linh took a deep breath, bracing herself. She reached with a tingling sixth sense for Fiona's limbs, imagining them relaxing, ever so carefully. They slumped into the grass. Linh took a ragged breath, focusing on Fiona's torso, feeling Mawana's gaze and not wanting to stuff up.

Fiona's torso gradually relaxed. Sweat began to bead across Linh's forehead. She was shaking slightly, and the tingling in her head seemed to be buzzing. She exhaled carefully and sensed her grip on the magic in Fiona's legs. That was how to do this, relax different parts of Fiona's body one at a time, because she wasn't strong enough to put all of Fiona instantly to sleep.

Fiona's breathing deepened and her chest rose more slowly, as Linh's tingling fingers shifted and she directed magic towards Fiona's face, imagining her eyes drooping, her breathing slowing.

"You've done it," said Mawana.

Linh started and some of the magic she was holding winked out. But not all of it. She had to consciously let the rest go.

Mawana smiled. "That's why I wanted you to try. Your dread of surrendering to magic distracts you and holds you back when you cast it on yourself, but you're good at crafting magic in other people. You might be putting Fiona to sleep in one go, her whole body, by the end of the week."

He was right. As Linh's sense of magic within somehow connected, and her awareness extended to the magic without, she slowed Fiona's breathing while making her eyes droop closed. Linh did crafted sleep magic tensely, the strain made her sweat and she was often short of breath and had to rest after, and eat twice as much as usual, but she could do it.

"Damn," Troy said, shaking his head. "You're still not comfortable with it, are you?"

Linh shook her head.

"But you're still better than me," he added.

Interestingly, Fiona wasn't better than Linh at sleep magic. She was probably too worried about harming her friends. Michael and Troy just… struggled. They got sweatier, and pale, and started shaking with the strain of it earlier than Linh, and Troy especially took longer to recover. But Ruarnon could cast magic with a smile, on Selenia and Lenaris both. Mawana accused them of showing off, and they peered intently at him. Mawana's eyes began to droop and Mocco laughed and rushed to catch him. Mawana started awake in Mocco's arms.

"That will teach you cousin!" Mocco chided.

Mawana just grinned.

"It is time to take you to the last site we want you to visit here," Sryah announced. "Some of you are impressively skilled for how new you are to magic, but don't get cocky and don't let that tempt you to take risks. The soldiers will need to continue practicing on board their ships. I should like to see more showing your strength," she added to Takanis, who had developed a habit of putting more people than she intended to sleep at once, often into a deeper sleep than she intended, though thankfully no comas.

General Takanis smiled and at Ruarnon's nod, she had the soldiers form rank and follow her out of the castle gardens, back to Ruarnon's ships. Sryah led Ruarnon and their companions the other way, south of the castle gardens, through more trees, then across open grass lands, in which trees were scarcer, and small creeks flowed, small enough that even Linh could leap them.

"I suppose there isn't much rain here?" Troy asked.

Sryah shook her head. "Not enough for Timbalen crops, conveniently."

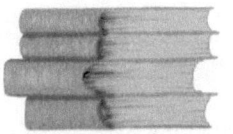

CHAPTER 20

SRYAH'S SCRUB LANDS ~LINH

They followed Sryah onwards, across grass-covered hills scattered with flowering gum trees, scraggly tea tree bushes and wildflowers. Linh wondered which magic could come next. Some of her companions talked, but eventually the only sounds were birds flying overhead or fallen leaves rustling as the occasional lizard scampered away through them. The smell of dried grass and strong scent of eucalypt gums, and reminders of home on every side helped her to relax, despite one more challenge not far ahead.

They wandered uphill, up steps of blue-grey stone onto a large platform with pillars at its corners, supporting a vast slate roof.

"Welcome to Mijora's Dwelling," said Sryah.

The pillars were engraved with elegant, unintelligible symbols, different to the faeron script, but just as unreadable. The platform was bordered with stone reliefs, depicting fanciful cities with graceful spires, towers and bridges spanning them, and people in strange flowing clothes with long hair. Above them, the underside of the ceiling was carved. In the centre, the face of a beautiful woman was surrounded by fields and forests. In a corner stood a man emanating the sun's rays. In the opposite corner, a man walked on wind-blown clouds, and in a far corner were waves, rocks, fish, and a woman riding a sea creature, the four gods of Timbalen creation myth.

Sryah led Ruarnon and their companions down steps on the far side to the grass in the monument's shadow.

"This is the idealised worldview many people held before the Sorcery War," said Sryah, "carved here after the war, so it would not be forgotten. In those days, people worshipped Esira for the gift of sunlight, Erhmun for the gift of rain, Mijora for the fruits of the earth and fishers and seafarers prayed and made offerings to Esla to keep them safe as they skirted her wild seas. Death was the jealous rival of the creator gods, blighting the land with illness, injury and attempts to claim for himself his siblings' creations. There was balance.

"Now, some humans craft magic like godly power, while others feel defenceless. But magic is not the only way to fight magic, nor the only form of power. It should not be humanity's greatest source of confidence. Non-magic crafters in the west need to learn their value, and non-magic means of countering magic craft. Until there is a balance of power in weapons, in confidence and perceptions of safety, I see the west being volatile and a likely war zone.

"I believe people's power and capacity are far closer to those carvings on Mijora's Dwelling than either will feel or look in the west. And it will not be magic alone that helps you be the equal of those who threaten or obstruct you. Your wits and physical strength and skills may prove just as crucial. I want you all to remember that.

"My sisters would have you ask yourselves only, is this an emergency? And magic my last resort? I would have you ask more. Because magic craft for emergencies is like starting a fire to cook a meal, without considering who else could be impacted, or how, so your cook fire becomes a bonfire or worse, a raging forest fire. My first rule of magic craft is think ahead and no forest fires. Is magic the only or best option? Is my second.

"I want you to consider those questions, and soak up the peace of this place, as you practice shield magic again, and sleep magic."

Linh didn't just cast a shield in front of her hand this time. Instead, she pictured an arrow whizzing towards Fiona and shocked herself with the speed at which she crafted a shield before her friend. Under Sryah's guidance, everyone shared ideas of imaginary scenarios they may face in the west and took turns crafting shield magic in immediate response. At Ruarnon's lead, they discussed what action they could have taken differently, or more effectively to hone their magic and minds.

The ships sailed around the coast in time for them to sleep on board that night, and they created scenarios and assessed each other's responses for another week. When everyone ran out of ideas, Sryah tested them with her own scenarios. Then she surprised them with one last task, after Ruarnon sent the soldiers back to the ships. She led Ruarnon and their companions into the trees, to a large boulder.

Linh gaped.

"The sword in the stone?" Troy asked with a frown.

It was a bronze sword, and its blade was impossibly embedded in the middle of solid rock. Surely magic had put it there?

"My sisters and I were undecided on showing you this," said Sryah. "This sword has not been touched since immediately after the Sorcery War. Touching it takes you away, tests you, and should you pass the test, it may give you tools of terrible power, which will aid you in the West. Should you fail, you will return empty-handed."

"Devices from the Sorcery War are stored here?" Ruarnon asked.

Sryah nodded.

Ruarnon studied it with worry-filled eyes and clenched fists. Mocco made what Linh assumed was a sign against evil, and even Mawana kept his distance.

"Why would *we* need devices from the Sorcery War?" Troy asked. "Do you want us to give them to the Galvations?"

Sryah shook her head. "These must be wielded by those who retrieve them."

"Is it safe?" Lenaris asked.

"It cannot cause physical harm."

"What happens if we touch it?" Ruarnon asked.

"Nothing you cannot handle. The enchantments on this sword are some of the most complex now existing, almost as complex as the enchantment in some of your minds that lets you understand most languages."

"*We're* under a *Guardian* enchantment?" Troy asked, frowning.

"Informed by the faeron?" Fiona added, and Sryah nodded again.

"The spell on your minds is of Guardian devising. As is this one."

Linh wasn't really listening. She was taking a deep breath. One last challenge. Involving magic. One last chance to face her fear. She grit her teeth and strode forwards, before anything could counter her will. She reached for the hilt with her right hand. The world vanished.

Linh stood in a courtyard with great towers rising around it. An archway rose ahead. Someone yelled beyond. She crept to the archway and peered cautiously around it. Brightness and movement at the corner of her eye. She jerked back reflexively and trembled as a line of fire burned through the air beside her. A *sorcerer*. And *she* seemed to be his target…

There was another exit. On the far side of the courtyard and archway, the far side of the sorcerer's line of fire. She had no confidence in sustaining a shield against fire magic while *running*.

"Where are you?" a man's voice demanded.

Linh backed up along the wall, keeping both archways in sight. Magical fighting and resistance were going to go poorly. Dared she try talking her way out? Troy would. With his easy-going swagger. Worst case scenario, it was unlikely to result in instant death.

She steeled her courage and said the first thing that leapt to mind. "What do you want?"

"*Want?*" came the man's voice.

"Why did you attack me?" Linh asked.

Everything became hazy. The ground appeared to ripple, yet it felt solid under her feet. There was a flash of colour. Her breathing quickened, and she clutched at the wall, wondering what the hell was going on. Then everything cleared, and her hand pushed through empty space. She stood on an open plain, with men all around her, in armour, with swords, clashing, slashing. It was a battle.

Linh's heart raced. She turned for a way out, and at the corner of her eye a naked blade moved. *Her* sword, which she held in her right hand. She wore armour too and was surrounded by fighting in all directions, save the direction a soldier approached from. Why couldn't it be spears, like Lenaris had trained them with?

Taking a deep breath, Linh strode forwards. Her armour was lighter than she expected, her heart pounding wildly inside it. She didn't let the man out of her sight. He slashed. She ducked and ran under his blade, vaguely aware of the tingle of her magic as she willed herself faster and everything blurred as she sped up. She was free!

Two men stepped out from the fighting, blocking her path.

"Shit!"

She couldn't fight both. Not with a sword. She'd have to take one out.

Linh focused hard on the man on the right and pictured him breathing slowly. His chest rising and falling gradually, eyes getting heavy. The man stopped. He slumped, and Linh tried to hold her crafting.

She raised her blade, instinctively, as the other man's flashed towards her. She ducked a slash. The ends of her ponytail fell through the air with her, sliced off. He was *too* fast. Panic gripped her chest and her breathing came in rapid gasps. She stabbed at his hand. He cried out and dropped his sword. She tried to run, but he reached for her with his left hand. She hit him with the flat, and he cried out in pain. Then she was past.

Another man stepped in her way, and panic took hold. Breathing got harder. There was no air. The man had stopped. At the edge of an invisible shield tingling before her, that Linh had cast instinctively.

She tried to slow her breathing. Every man fighting on either side was ignoring her. She could charge him with the shield in place, but surely the force of his body crashing into the shield would knock her out...

Anger boiled inside her. Corner her like a hunted animal, would he? She would show him! She released her shield and charged. She countered his first blow and a second. She side-stepped instinctively and copped a winding blow to the chest. He could *kill* her. She lashed out, lopping off his sword hand, running past as he cried out in pain. She ran blindly, as fast as she could. What had she *done*?

Everything rippled. She slowed, then sunlight shone down around her, and she stumbled into a clearing ringed by gum trees, whose long, curved leaves rustled in a gentle breeze. She turned wildly, but there were no more men. There was no battlefield. She was back in Sryah's Scrublands, her ponytail whipping behind her as she turned, at its normal length again. As if nothing had happened in... wherever that was.

A weight dragged on her right hand. The sword was still there. But here, under a hot sun, with the warble of what had to be magpies somewhere behind her, the sword felt cold and hard in her hands. And it had weight. It was somehow more *real* than a moment ago. And its colour was different too. A strange mix of iron and bronze, as if streaks of liquid both had been poured together in a mould, then set as a single peace. But that wasn't the most startling thing about it. She could sense the tingle of magic from the base of the blade to its tip. The sword was enchanted.

"Linh? The fuck is this?"

Michael stepped out of the air opposite her, his face pale and eyes wide.

"I don't know if it was real," she said. "My ponytail got cut off by a soldier, and now it's back again. And there was blood on my sword," she added with a shiver, "but now the blade is clean."

Michael moved to sit on a fallen log, gasping for air, and Linh sat beside him. He shook his head.

"Wasn't it Ruarnon's uncle who told them 'Dangerous times call for decisive action.' And here's us blundering into a *Guardian* enchantment at the first opportunity."

"We're in *way* over our heads, sailing west," said Linh. "Even if Red Cloak does play nice. Yes we can craft magic now, but our crafting is like toddlers learning to walk compared to Mawana. And I have a bad feeling anyone Narz has trained is going to be a lot more like Mawana, or Flariah in their crafting."

She shivered, but if they were going to sail west, confronting facts head on *before* they faced that kind of danger was likely necessary to survival.

Michael nodded.

"It's good to see you two."

Ruarnon stepped out of nothing, sweaty faced but smiling and holding a sword. Linh gaped. "Did you face a fire throwing sorcerer and a battlefield?" she asked.

Ruarnon nodded. "I wouldn't have been able to hold off the sorcerer for very long, but luckily I didn't need to. And those poor soldiers didn't stand much chance. What or who did you two face?"

"The same, by the sounds of it," Michael replied.

Linh bit her lip. "Why put us in *two* life-threatening situations? Why corner me on a battlefield and make me face multiple soldiers, one after another?"

She remembered a severed hand and shuddered.

"I didn't think the sorcerer was after me," said Michael. "There was a woman in the corridor and she was frightened. She didn't want to move when we had a moment, and then he sent fire burning towards us, so I shielded us both. I don't know how I held off the fire, but I doubted I could do it for long, so I tried to reason with him."

Linh frowned. "I was going to try the same, but the moment I asked what he wanted, everything just faded away."

"We both acted to defend instead of attack," said Michael, and Linh could almost see the cogs of his mind beginning to turn, puzzling it all out. "He wouldn't listen to me, but he followed when I tried to draw him upstairs, where a little girl was making wooden toys fly. She saw me, smiled and kept playing.

"Then the sorcerer came up. He was furious, but I think he was frightened too. He shot fire at me, and I somehow held it off. He stared at me, and I said I didn't want to hurt anyone. Then I went to the battlefield."

Troy staggered out of nothing behind Linh, breathless, his eyes wide. "Thank God!" he said. "I thought you were all in that battle somewhere!"

Michael frowned. "What did you do in the battle?"

"I fought off the first bloke, disarmed him and punched him out, then two others got in the way, and I demanded to know what they'd done to the rest of you. And they wouldn't tell me, so I looked around, but I couldn't see you."

Linh blinked. Those were tears in his eyes. Men had been trying to kill him, and his first thought was *where are my friends?* Had she *ever* given him enough credit?

She stepped forwards and his eyes widened in surprise when she hugged him. "We're ok."

He hugged her back, his knuckles tapping her, not seeming to have registered that he was holding a sword. He was breathing heavily, in near sobs.

Another arm wrapped around Linh's across Troy's back. "We're all right mate," said Michael. "You're not free of my theorising or Linh's cheek just yet."

Troy and Linh broke apart laughing.

Troy shook his head, wiping tears off his face. "There I was thinking you're *so* thoughtful," he said to Michael. "You're a right prick."

Michael smiled sweetly.

Troy's expression turned serious. "It's just as well Andy asked you out first. I wouldn't know what to do with you."

"Maybe you two can gang up on me when we get home?" said Michael. "And stop me running circles around you."

The smile on Michael's face almost invited retaliation. Linh shook her head. "Troy, what have you done to Michael?"

"He winds me up and it's *my* fault?" Troy asked.

He turned imploringly to Ruarnon, who was no help, because they were quietly laughing hard.

Linh smiled warmly at Troy, seeing that he'd partly taken her seriously, not realising he'd rubbed off on Michael *and* her. Then she said more seriously, "Michael thinks that was a test. But what was whoever set it looking for?"

"Testing our reactions," Ruarnon said, their expression serious again. "We've already seen what happened with magic when Troy got frustrated while crafting it. It's dangerous if you allow extreme emotions to govern it. And these swords," Troy's eyes widened as he registered the presence of a sword in his hand, "are enchanted. As if the enchantment of that place was testing whether we could be trusted with these swords."

"How did you react to the sorcerer?" Michael asked Troy.

Troy blushed. "He was right in front of me, so I punched him in the nose instinctively when he raised his hand. I thought he was going to cast fire magic."

"He was," Michael replied. "Good call."

Linh saw a severed hand flying through the air again and shivered. "It wasn't... real, was it?" she asked. "That place? I panicked and I... I *cut* a soldier's hand off! His blow nearly cut my chest armour in half!"

Troy gave her a sympathetic grimace.

"I don't think it was," said Michael. "Not if it we all went to the same place, with the same or very similar people, at the same or a similar moment in time."

"Am I out? Where's..." Fiona stepped out of nothing, crouched almost double, then straightened and turned.

"It's ok," Michael assured her.

Fiona relaxed and stumbled. Linh stood to offer her a hand, and Fiona leant heavily on Linh's arm as she staggered to the log and sat.

"What happened to you?" Linh asked.

"I'm fine," Fiona replied, panting for breath. "There were too many soldiers blocking my path, so I made a shield tunnel. It wasn't very long, but two soldiers crashed into it. I'm just really tired."

"They put us in two situations in which we were terrified, one against a sorcerer, one a battle with more than one enemy and wanted to… see if we were *merciful*?" Linh asked. "Why do *I* have a sword?"

"Because you did what you thought was necessary to save yourself, and no more," Michael replied.

Linh almost smiled, grateful that Michael's mind worked so fast.

Troy nodded. "Whatever's so special about these swords, it's like whoever left them here wanted them to be used with restraint."

"What did you do in the battle?" Michael asked Ruarnon.

"I disarmed the man who attacked me, demanded to know where we were and what was going on, then fought him off with my bare hands, and then I was here."

"You fought with your fists when you could have used a sword?" Michael asked, and Ruarnon nodded.

"Are you going to need that sword?" Fiona asked Ruarnon, and Linh was surprised to see Ruarnon's features twist in distaste and Ruarnon examine their sword as if it was diseased.

"I wanted to know what power needed such elaborate protection."

Mawana stepped out of the air frowning, studying the sword in his hand, then eyed everyone. "What have I just signed up for?"

"We were just discussing that mate," Troy replied.

"Will the others come too?" Linh asked.

"I think Mocco will follow me," Mawana replied seriously. "We have never really seen eye to eye, but I do not back down from challenges and with all of you through…."

Mocco arrived soon after, both cousins having escaped with their shield magic, which Linh envied. She stared when Lenaris came. Lenaris seemed surprised herself. She caught Mawana's eye, and in the face of his smile, her uncertainty gave way to a smile.

"This doesn't mean we're *all* going West?" Troy asked.

"Probably," Michael replied.

The nothing behind them vanished. Tor stood rigidly opposite, his gaze fixed ahead, while Selenia eyed them curiously, and Sryah smiled proudly. Linh and her friends walked towards them, the others showing off and examining their swords, but Linh didn't know what to make of hers or if she even wanted it.

She was vaguely aware of Troy swinging playfully at Michael, who raised his sword to deflect the blow. The blades froze in mid-air, several centimetres apart.

"The hilts have gone cold," said Michael, frowning.

"My skin's tingling," said Troy.

Sryah eyed them sternly. "They are weapons of the Sorcery War, and there is powerful magic operating upon them, dangerous because it is forgotten, but I know that they will be effective against magic. I never thought to see these swords in human hands again, after what they were used for during the war. Use them only at your greatest need, only with the greatest of care."

Linh shivered. The sisters said much the same about magic, but there was something more terrible about these blades, which seemed completely lost to memory, until now.

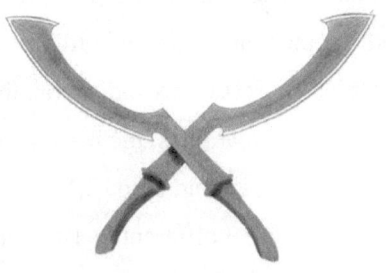

CHAPTER 21

NARZ AND THE EAST-RUARNON

Ruarnon followed Sryah back through strange trees towards the Iylena, lost in thought. Leaves rustled around them. Birds chirped in branches or screeched as they zoomed through gaps in trees. Butterflies fluttered lopsidedly about and everything seemed so peaceful.

"Tyrook had one of these," Lenaris said into the silence, gazing at her blade as she walked beside Ruarnon on the narrow trail everyone followed Sryah down. "Flariah crafted magic to lift him into the air, and he slashed the air with his sword and began to fall. As if his blade cut her magic grip and released her magic back to formlessness."

Ruarnon tensed, and let Tor, Selenia, Mocco and Mawana wander ahead of them, so they and Lenaris could speak without Sryah overhearing.

"Do you think these swords can cut through magic shields?" They asked softly.

"I suspect so."

"And Sryah alluded to them being used for something terrible during the Sorcery War." Ruarnon shuddered. "You don't think… they were used to cut through the shields of sorcerer families?"

Lenaris paled. "If the fear Poran said ordinary people still have of magic craft in the west is any indication, they may have." She shook her head. "The Guardians, the heroes who saved the world, murdering sorcerers, in cold blood…"

Ruarnon sighed. "Is it that different to Tarlahns attacking an Urai man's shield until the strain of maintaining it killed him, in their struggle to demand aid against invasion? Just because you're trying to do a good thing doesn't mean your actions can't go to Chaos."

Ruarnon stumbled. Desperation had led Tarlahns to attack Urai, and perhaps Guardians to murder sorcerers. Ruarnon had felt that desperation while Tarlah City lay under siege. But Tarlah had allies. Omah had called them. As the might of the Zaldeaan army smashed into Tarlah City's walls, Ruarnon had *known* help was coming.

"What is it?" Lenaris asked.

"When I first heard of Narz, a king with damar armies, the resources to ship them across the world and devastate the Zaldeaan Realm, he seemed so powerful. I didn't realise how similar his position is to Kyura's. Narz doesn't have the Timbalen Empire as allies. He may have no one to call upon, as half his continent turns against him as sorcerer king.

"Perhaps he stole the Zaldeaan army because he thought it was the only way to secure Galvatia, and his northern border. Perhaps he overlooked Vye's capacity to unleash damars and commit murder because he *need*ed him, just as Kyura trusted the uncle he needed, not realising Derlan was a murderous, warmongering traitor who probably aspired to usurp his throne.

"Kyura was terrified of glory-seeking opposition. Narz seems terrified of magic haters. Magic strengthens Narz, but what if he knows there are weapons that can cut through it like cobwebs? Weapons like the ones we now carry?"

They turned back to the Australians. "What if Narz didn't wash his followers' minds of all that contradicts his claims? What if it wasn't reason or trickery that convinced Poran and Dargus, but the sincere feelings of a leader they admire and wanted to see good in? A frightened leader wanting to protect them, their families and everything they have ever feared for?

"I was surprised at the true extent Kyura felt insecure on his throne; because I didn't know the opposition he feared had already murdered his father. I believed, like most people, that Kyomi died of natural causes. But he didn't and Kyura suspected the truth all along. We don't understand the extent of Narz's fear, but what if it's because he too knows something we don't? Something that validates his fears?"

Before them, Tor nodded as he walked. "Narz is winning the devoted support of sorcerers and I doubt his subjects would dare revolt against a sorcerer-king with more sorcerers at his command. To do so sounds more dangerous than participating in the Great Rebellion in Tarlah. But if Narz has acquired two kingdoms already, then invaded a third... other kingdoms may fear he wishes to conquer an empire. And if his handful of sorcerers finds itself outnumbered against the might of multiple armies, perhaps his sorcerers can be defeated, just as a band of ordinary Tarlahns defeated the Zaldeaan garrison."

"And if any of his opponents *did* ally with Flariah, Desriah, Sryah and their armies…" said Michael.

"I do not like where this is going," said Mawana, falling back beside Tor. "Narz surrounded and lashing out with damar attacks, like a frightened animal. Yet, that makes sense of him creating the damars. Were his enemies to surround him on all sides in his capital, unleashing damars hunting by sound may be an effective last line of defence. Especially against enemies who have never encountered damars before."

Ruarnon shivered. If they had had damars to unleash on the Zaldeaan army, and the Timbalens had not responded to their uncle's call for aid, and they stood alone against siege, would *they* have unleashed damars on their enemies? Could sheer desperation silence the horror a person would feel at the prospect of creating such creatures?

"Poran said damars were made to face something no man should face," Linh reminded. "They sound like a product of fear."

"You mean he's so terrified that he's lost his grip on reality and is breeding armies to slaughter anything that keeps him awake at night?" Troy asked.

"It looks like he could be," Michael replied. "Everything he's done looks rational as a product of fear, and paranoia might do away with the need to confirm the validity of his fears. But either he has reason to think someone who opposes him can access and control the creature armies, or we're missing what prompted him to turn his paranoid gaze east in the first place."

It made sense, Narz's actions as the product of intensifying and extreme fear. But what drove the full force of that fear? What did Narz know that Ruarnon and their Companions didn't?

"Red Cloak can *See* the east," said Linh. "Is that what turned Narz's attention east? Did Red Cloak *See* gorans serving Desriah dinner? Or Flariah chatting to faeron? What if Red Cloak believed he *Saw* Guardians in the east and he told Narz?"

Lenaris' mouth dropped open as she fell back beside Mawana. That was a brilliant explanation. Tor caught Ruarnon's gaze and bowed his head.

"Perhaps Red Cloak *Saw* enough of the Zaldeaans for Poran to think them a selfish, destructive bloody race," Ruarnon added. "And while Narz sent ships and damars to coerce the Zaldeaan army, he sent a ship to investigate Red Cloak's claims of Guardians further east. Perhaps Red Cloak *Saw* the creature army on Cauldron Island."

"Did you just make Narz make sense?" Michael asked with a smile.

"If Red Cloak told him three Guardians lived in the east, with creature armies at their command…" Ruarnon continued, lost in thought, "Lylah said Narz could block her *Sight* of other people's futures. He may have felt her magic reaching for him, the same way Sryah felt Red Cloak reaching for you. He may have consciously blocked Lylah's magic craft. That may have been what convinced him Red Cloak's reports were accurate."

"It is still a leap of imagination," said Tor, "from knowing a sorcerer who controls an army is watching you, to assuming they will cross the ocean with that army to invade you. Even if Narz believes the myths of the Guardians, why is he certain the sisters embody those myths?"

Ruarnon sighed. Narz seemed better informed than perhaps anyone but the sisters themselves, and three of the four sisters seemed bent on saying only what the sisters thought anyone else needed to know. It may be impossible to confirm what brought Narz's damars east.

"How does Red Cloak fit into all this?" Michael asked.

"What's wrong?" Troy asked.

Fiona had stopped walking. "If Narz feels like he faces opposition on every side, and he fears the creature armies and for all we know, the Guardians themselves, what if all his enemies *did* attack him? If sorcery war erupts again, and thousands of lives are threatened, and you wanted to get lots of people to safety, swiftly..."

"An evacuation plan," said Michael. "You'd need to know what sort of terrain you were going to. Depending how long ago the Sorcery War was fought, you might need to ensure none of the gateways transported you underwater because of rising sea levels, or into buildings sunk by earthquakes in the intervening centuries. You'd need to know where each gateway took you, to see if it was still safe. That would make sense of Red Cloak leaping in and out of gateways."

"And if things got as dire for people caught up in sorcery war in the west as the climate here became for the faeron, you could always check out our world," Linh added.

All three of her friends stopped walking.

"You could open the gateway," Michael said breathlessly, "spot four clueless teens wandering nearby. Find the strain too much, estimate how long they'll take to reach the gateway, then open it again. And when they stepped through alive, and unharmed, confirming that the gateway was fully functional and safe to use, you'd know that should this world be ending and you need to evacuate your people far away, that *was* an option."

Silence fell. The past six weeks had shown just how much focus, discipline, will power and emotional regulation magic craft required. If it was Red Cloak who brought their Australian friends to Umarinaris, Ruarnon suspected he was the most powerful, capable sorcerer alive.

"And if you really were scared the end of the world was nigh," said Troy, "and other people with the same fear knew you had a plan to save them, and you discovered the plan worked, you wouldn't stick around to chat to the clueless teenagers, would you?"

"You'd run off to report to your people that even under the worst circumstances you could still save them," Michael finished. "*That's* what he was reporting to someone."

Everyone had stopped walking now, and Sryah had turned back down the track towards them. She bowed her head. "I agree, based on what I have *Seen*."

Troy shook his head. "There was good old Nuard thinking we were figures of Timbalen myth, and we really *were* guinea pigs in a science experiment."

Linh frowned. "Why not make certain the gateway was safe to travel both ways by sending us home? Why lead us to the castle, leave the gateway to Myleth Island open, with Nuard waiting to welcome us?"

Michael nodded. "He could have just abandoned us on Oval Island. Why bother leading us to a safe place?" He shivered. "Why not kill us, to keep his master evacuation plan secret?"

Linh's mouth dropped open. "He opened a gateway to a backwater of the Timbalen Empire, which had had no contact with Tarlah for fifteen years. How was Red Cloak to know warlords would succeed in manipulating Kyura to war, or that the Empire would answer Omah's call for aid? For all he knew, he sent us to a quiet corner of the world and stranded us there, where we had no one important to talk to."

"Why didn't he stop us?" Troy asked. "When we went to Tarlah?"

Michael frowned. "Narz sent a ship to the mainland to retrieve Ruarnon's parents and Pamoran, but no one else from the west had access to or contact. We'd only be a liability… if *we* sailed west. And he keeps checking in on us, and our location…"

"Should Red Cloak magically pop in on us again," Troy said to Sryah, "would you mind telling him we promise we won't tell anyone in the Far West about gateways, and could he possibly find a time when it's convenient to maybe send us home?"

"As I said," Sryah replied, "I believe you have not seen the last of him. I think your paths will cross in the west."

"If Red Cloak's been exploring Gateways," said Linh, "has he told Narz the one we arrived in this part of the world via isn't far from this island and its creature army? Or that there's a gateway in the jungle? If that jungle Gateway works, and Red Cloak thinks Flariah, Desriah and Sryah are Guardians, all they'd have to do is sail their creature armies to the island we arrived on, or the jungle, and the Gateways could have them on Narz's doorstep in a week."

"Giving him little time to move soldiers, sorcerers and prepare his defence," said Tor. "If Narz is in contact with Red Cloak and as well informed as we suspect, that may have factored into his eastern attacks. And if he could not fit his ships through a gateway, and by sea was the only way to attack the east, perhaps that is why he sent both fleets as soon as he learned of 'threats' here and how speedily those 'threats' could attack him."

It all made sense, if Narz *was* protecting his people, and Red Cloak *was* reporting to him and he knew something that convinced him the eastern creature armies would appear on his doorstep via gateway, perhaps led by the sisters or Guardians at Selenia's behest. Perhaps the man was taking calculated steps to secure his power, or worst-case scenario, to make a highly efficient evacuation plan. If Narz was so well informed, did Ruarnon have any chance of recovering most of their living relatives, let alone *any* Zaldeaan soldiers from Narz by stealth?

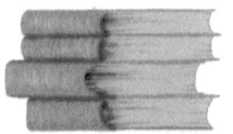

CHAPTER 22

RUARNON'S CHOICE

Ruarnon was content to walk in silence along the rest of the narrow trail through bushes, crunching on dried fallen leaves and watching bright orange butterflies with black lined, yellow spot tipped wings fluttering clumsily off the grass as they passed. Insects the Australians called dragon flies dashed through the air on shiny, clear wings. For a few precious moments they soaked up the peace of the Island of the Guardians, a refuge near the eastern end of the world.

Then Lenaris broke the silence, speaking quietly and close by their side. "I do not like the Australians going west. It sounds like a brewing war zone, far more dangerous than the war they arrived in Tarlah during. They would be much safer waiting until Narz consolidates his kingdoms, or is defeated, and sailing west in calmer times. And they have their new duty as Companions to occupy their time while they wait."

"Who would be sailing to the Far West then?" Mawana asked.

"The Timbalens want to re-establish trade in the Far West," Lenaris countered. "Commander Imphin said so himself."

"After so many months of doubt and waiting, you would have them wait and doubt longer?" Ruarnon asked.

She frowned, but they both knew of fear, doubt and waiting, for word Ruarnon's parents and Lenaris' father still lived in the Far West and for hope of recovering them.

"I will *not* have them die trying to get home," she replied.

"Duty will keep me in Tarlah," said Ruarnon. "But why shouldn't they take the first path to their loved ones, after so long?"

Lenaris' voice softened, "You would let them do what you wish you could?"

Ruarnon nodded.

"But the danger," she insisted.

"Go with them," Mawana said quietly, dropping back. "If they are bound to a fate that puts them in great danger, but not necessarily the same situations as Ruarnon's expedition, then they need someone they trust to advise and protect them."

"There is no telling when this storm will calm," Tor quietly added ahead of them. "This brewing war may take years to resolve. If you date its start to Narz's war with the Galvations, then it has already begun, and shows signs of escalation.

"I can only protect them while they travel with the force Ruarnon sends. If their quest takes them off into the wilderness seeking gateways, I am sure Ruarnon and I can plan to spare them guards, but I cannot provide older, wiser, more level-headed, battle experienced people to guide them."

"I'm not letting them wander the wilderness alone," Lenaris said firmly. "Whenever they sail west, *I* will be there."

Ruarnon slumped. They couldn't be there. They couldn't make that promise of commitment to the friends who had helped persuade them to occupy the Realm and were helping them understand the man who held their parents' captive. The Australians were really just along for the ride in the east. When this voyage ended at Tarlah, Ruarnon and the Australians would part ways. Ruarnon dawdled after that, in no hurry to reach the Timbalen Empire, because as soon as they turned back for Tarlah, the countdown to say goodbye to their Australian friends, and newest Companions would begin.

"I overheard you."

Ruarnon started, having forgotten Selenia trailing behind everyone, drinking in the scenery as she walked. She carried sheets of papyrus with her and had sketched the unfamiliar vegetation and wildlife between magic practice in recent weeks. It she seemed she was spending their final walk on the Island of the Guardians committing images to memory so she could sketch them when Tither's ship brought her back to Cauldron Island.

"Flariah has been too protective," Selenia added. "Your friends have been in more danger than I since they arrived, but they knew the dangers they faced at each step and made informed decisions, like you do as regent and king. I have often wondered what sort of enchantment binds my family and how and why exactly Narz threatens me. I think it is time to ask Flariah to tell me everything."

"I agree," Ruarnon replied, "But I doubt you will like the answers."

"Since when have you avoided asking questions because the answers were unpleasant?" she replied with a smile. "You ask about everything because you need to know as much as you can to form wise policies. Why shouldn't everyone govern their lives that way?"

Ruarnon smiled, and they walked together until the stunted, tree-covered hills gave way to sand, and the Iylena rose before them. Ruarnon thanked Sryah for her teaching and the knowledge she had shared so freely, then turned to Selenia, who would stay with Desriah until Tither's ship took her home.

"I will be safe on Cauldron Island," she said.

"What if Narz attacks again?" Ruarnon asked. "The ships that escaped this island will tell him his attacks have failed. Would you be safer in Tarlah or Tree House City?"

Selenia's gaze warmed. "I shall suggest it to Flariah. I wish I could come with you. I should love to see the Timbalen Empire. Can you write and describe it to me?"

"As soon as I know where to send my letters," they replied, returning her smile.

Ruarnon had got used to her companionship, to the way she teased their magic-wielding, pointing to imperfections in their casting and saying she did so because they didn't need another over-confident shield caster like Mawana on their hands. She made them relax and smile, like their Australian friends, but she had more of Lenaris' maturity, and their family situations were even more compatible than Narz holding only Lenaris' father captive.

"I am sure there are plenty of attractive girls in the jungle," they added.

"All the more reason to relocate," she replied with a smile they would miss.

Ruarnon reached down to hug her goodbye.

"Take care of the Australians, and don't let Mawana get them into too much trouble," she added teasingly, seeing Mawana watching.

Mawana grinned.

It was time to board the boats. Ruarnon did so reluctantly. As sandy shores fell behind, and Selenia and Sryah shrunk away, Ruarnon sighed and climbed a rope ladder back onto the Iylena. They didn't notice the wash of waves, feel the sea breeze on their face, or smell the salt of the sea this time. They felt only dread, as a decision they had postponed loomed over them.

Delegating the decision to recover the Zaldeaan army or their parents galled Ruarnon, but Tor was their father's closest friend. He had filled Uncle Omah's position of watching out for and advising Ruarnon, more so than anyone else. Ruarnon trusted their former tutor with the fate of the Zaldeaans and their family and to watch out for the Australians.

They could delegate leadership of the recovery expedition. They had to, because they couldn't abandon their duty to ensure stability in Tarlah and the Realm, and if they were killed in the west that abandonment would be permanent. Nor could Ruarnon give their people reason to fight each other for the crown, as the Zaldeaans had. They must stay in Tarlah and trust that Tor could lead and preserve morale as well as Uncle Omah had done.

They called everyone into their cabin, where their elder friends and Tor sat at the table, and their Australian friends sat on their bed, to Lenaris' chagrin at what she saw as disrespect. It would have made Ruarnon smile once, but now it twisted their gut.

"You are all agreed on accompanying my expedition West?" Ruarnon asked.

Linh frowned, but Michael eyed Ruarnon critically.

"It's not just about getting home," Fiona said quietly. "If there's any chance we can make a difference, I want to be there, and I suspect the rest of you feel the same."

They nodded. Troy swallowed but said nothing.

"Do you realise what you are risking?" Lenaris asked. "Even if you stay with Tarlahn soldiers, Ruarnon intends them to seek an alliance with the Galvations, Narz's sworn enemies. Ruarnon anticipates skirmishes and raids. Sorcerers will be involved. It is possible that instead of finding your way home, you will find your deaths. Do you still wish to go, knowing that?"

"My other half is at home," Michael replied. "I'm not giving up on Andy, not after everything he's helped me through."

"What if you do not find a way home?" Lenaris asked. "Even if everything else in the West succeeds, what if you are still here at the end?"

"Easy," Troy replied. "We go to find out. That's infinitely better than waiting in Tarlah and never knowing whether or not we passed up our only chance to get home."

"Are you coming with us?" Fiona asked the room at large.

"You *are* decided?" Ruarnon pressed, forcing down guilt, and they nodded. Ruarnon didn't blame them. They would rather send another expedition West to recover their missing family members, and have it fail than not send one. Yet, they suspected their Australian friends didn't truly appreciate the risk they were taking.

"Are you?" Michael asked.

It felt like a physical blow. Ruarnon took a deep breath and forced the words out. "My duties do not allow it."

Linh's eyes widened. Fiona's face fell, but Michael's expression was as unreadable as ever, with a dark edge to it Ruarnon hadn't seen before. Troy's sturdy frame stood listless. Ruarnon was abandoning them. They turned away, blinking back tears, knowing that if the four Australians achieved what they hoped in the West, Ruarnon would never see them again.

"And the rest of you?" Troy asked pointedly.

"I am not letting you wander into the West without me," Mawana asserted. "Not if I can help it."

Ruarnon snuck a look. Troy's face split in a relieved grin.

"The Council of Elders may not permit you," Mocco cautioned. "Our people have no interest in the West, and they will not want you to risk being caught up in a war."

"They *do* want me to take on more responsibility," Mawana replied. "This is how I choose to do so."

"And if the Elders forbid it?" Mocco asked.

"I care more for the safety of my friends than the Council of Elders' authority. That is what it comes down to."

To Ruarnon's surprise, Mocco bowed his head. "I can ask their permission. But they may say that my time on this voyage has detracted enough from my studies as an apprentice Elder."

Mawana's determination and Mocco considering an extended absence from his studies to support their Australian friends made Ruarnon's stomach roil with guilt.

Lenaris eyed them all sternly. "Someone needs to balance Mawana's influence. I will go too." Her tone was challenging, but her eyes and mouth smiled, and Mawana smiled back.

Ruarnon's older friends would help and protect their younger ones, who may never return, while Ruarnon abandoned them. But

Ruarnon could not risk leaving Tarlah without an heir, pursuing their parents like a private person, as if they did not carry the weight of two kingdoms on their shoulders. The guilt they had felt sailing east would be far worse if they sailed west. Duty would separate Ruarnon from their friends again, as it had during the siege, only this time, it was their friends who would travel into danger.

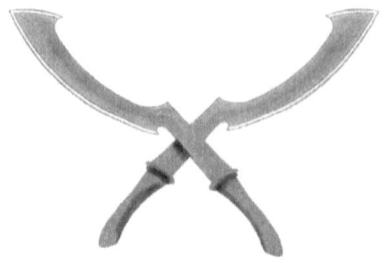

Chapter 23

Sorcery ~Linh

Linh kept her eyes on Fiona as they circled each other, wooden practice swords in hand. She attacked again, and Fiona parried, side-stepped her thrust, ducked Linh's blow to the head and leapt Linh's slash at her feet. Linh suggested they take a break.

"I keep thinking about that sorcerer and battlefield," she confided. "The fear I felt there was real, and we might face things like that in the West. If Ruarnon doesn't come...."

Fiona nodded, leaning on the foredeck railing and watching a Timbalen patrol ship sail past. A serpent's head rose from its prow, its jaws open and a pointed tail angled away from the stern, a large yellow flag flapping atop the ship's mast.

"I think we need to start practising magic with distractions," Fiona replied. "Noise and people getting in our way, even casting shields against practice sword blows. We need to learn to respond well under pressure before we reach the West. To develop the right instincts, so we can shape magic when we're in danger and not get paralysed by fear."

Linh nodded, as they sailed alongside an island on their left. Troy ran over, followed by Michael.

"Is that Myleth Island?" Troy asked.

Linh stared as they drew nearer. She made out a familiar walled barley field on her left, the wall turning a corner and running away from them along the sand. A hill rose behind it, and the four towers of Myleth Island's square castle rose above. So much had changed since she last saw those shores. So much had happened. But she still had a sword from her first weapons instructor, Familon, in her trunk. And Familon's father Nuard may have been more right about their purpose in that world than any of them had believed possible.

As the Iylena drew closer to the pier, a woman ran out the village gate, across the sand, and continued down the pier.

"Familon!" Troy called, waving.

Familon waved. Then she drew an arrow from her quiver and bound something to it. She knocked the arrow and aimed above their heads.

"Danger to port!" a lookout yelled.

"It's all right!" Troy yelled back.

Familon loosed the arrow, and it soared over Linh's head and lodged itself in the mast. Fiona went to retrieve it.

"Father wanted you to have the key!" Familon yelled. "He guessed you were coming because the ancient bird in the forest left its perch. He thinks you arrived so near our island to take the key the bird was guarding."

"What's it unlock?" Troy asked.

283

"No idea. Father thinks the Guardians sent it here through an archway to keep it safe. It must have decided now is the time to give the key to you."

Fiona carried the arrow over and held up the key. It was made of indistinguishable metal, of a strange colour, like the swords belted at their sides, iron, with a bronze sheen or the other way round. If the enchantments on their swords were cast during the Sorcery War, surely the enchantments on the key were too?

"Thanks, Familon," Fiona yelled, waving, and Linh realised the pier was already behind them.

"Best of luck!" Familon called faintly, and everyone waved, as the Iylena moved beyond Myleth Island.

"What do we need a key from the Sorcery War for?" Troy asked.

"I wonder if Red Cloak's finally decided to have an input," said Fiona. "If he realised we were sailing this way when he *Saw* us on the island of the Guardians and he opened the gateway we came to Myleth Island on to call the bird back, so we could retrieve the key."

"But how did he know Familon would give it to us?" Troy asked.

Linh shivered. "He may have *seen* Nuard greet us on Myleth Island and heard Nuard's theory that the Guardians sent us and guessed Nuard would send us the key."

They speculated on the key as the Iylena approached larger islands with fisherman's huts and small boats arriving or departing from different shores. Barefoot children ran along beaches, pointing excitedly at three foreign ships sailing past, and Linh and her friends waved. The children waved back enthusiastically.

The islands became larger. Stick huts with thatched roofs gave way to stone buildings with slate roofs, while small boats in the channel between the islands gave way to merchant ships with birds' head prows and bulky leisure craft from which music, laughter and chatter streamed. Gradually, the islands rose higher above sea level. Hills and cliffs stretched up to multi-storey stone buildings, surrounded by leisure gardens, orchards and fields. The country houses of wealthy officials blocked Timbalen Island and the empire's capital city behind them from view.

"Two Imperial Navy ships approaching!" a lookout cried from the crow's nest, and a bell tolled overhead.

Linh looked back to where two Timbalen ships manoeuvred to overtake the Iylena. They had every sail lowered and passed swiftly, a man on deck shouting, "TURN BACK! THERE IS WAR!"

Dread panged in Ruarnon's chest at the words. They ran up the foredeck stairs with Mocco, Mawana, Lenaris and Tor. Surely there was only one person the empire could be at war with? Why hadn't damarian ships overtaken them while they spent six weeks learning magic on the Island of the Guardians? Or had the ships sailed beyond sight, like the two that escaped Desriah and Sryah?

"The Timbalens said the Tarlahn Trade Route was safe yesterday…." Lenaris objected.

"Narz knew they were watching the West," said Tor. "Perhaps he invaded from another direction."

The Iylena glided around cliffs. Ruarnon gazed ahead and stared at something orange glowing in the water. Fire. They frowned at flames lapping the bulwarks of a ship, climbing towards the prow, above which a serpent's head rose. The sails and a yellow flag atop the mast were aflame, and a rowboat full of soldiers paddled beside the ship.

Lenaris and Linh said the sorcerers could wield fire. And the burning ship was Timbalen. Narz was attacking humans this time...

A bell began to toll repetitively overhead.

"LOOK SHARP SAILORS!" the captain bellowed, as a constant thud of footsteps began on the main deck below, soldiers emerging from the hatches.

The burning Timbalen ship wasn't alone; a dark-timbered vessel behind it was also alight.

The Iylena turned further round the cliffs, and the sea opened before them. Beyond the burning ships, the stern of a charred vessel and its serpent's tail angled out of the water, sinking. On Ruarnon's left, a black vessel and an imperial ship sailed towards each other. Orange balls of light flashed between them. Ruarnon gaped, and time slowed.

Alongside the Timbalen ship, fire flared against a flat, vertical expanse in the air. Yellow cloaked people lined the deck facing fire burning through the air. Some flames burned in straight lines, others arcing like arrow fire, all blossoming against the faint white of a magic shield before a damarian ship. Small fires formed outside the damarian shield, opposite short grey figures lining the damarian deck, which raised their arms and gestured, causing fire to burn arcs across the air towards the Timbalen ship.

Ruarnon sagged into the railing. *Sorcery*. And not human sorcerers, *damars* that could craft sorcery. They felt weak at the knees.

Further left, two black vessels floated either side of an Imperial ship, lines of flame streaking between them, fire blossoming against all three ships' shields, but mostly the Timbalen ships. A second Imperial vessel sailed to its aid, fire lines blazing ahead. More dark vessels and Timbalen ships dotted the water beyond, and fire lines and bright bolts of light shot between them while more ships burned and sank.

Amidst the chaos, shouts of fear and shock, and prayers to the ancestors from sailors and soldiers on deck behind Ruarnon, what had never made sense clicked into place in their mind, the evidence Narz had that they did not. Narz's reason for abducting Ruarnon's parents.

"The information Narz sought from my parents," Ruarnon said softly. "He wanted to know about the Elite Guard, the most powerful soldiers in our allies' army. He perfected damars to fight *them*. They're his enemy no man can face… But if his sorcerers don't want to fight other sorcerers… does he think they're Guardians? Did Red Cloak *See* that they could do all this?"

They gestured at the enormous, presumably immensely powerful shields blocking fire magic streaking through the air beside the Timbalen vessels. And fire burning towards damarian ships. It all made sense. And the truth was horrifying.

"ORDERS BENEVOLENCE?" General Takanis bellowed from the Meera's deck.

There was only one thing to do in the face of this chaos. "RETREAT!"

"DANGER TO PORT!" a lookout bellowed.

A black vessel sailed out from behind a rocky point less than a league away. It moved as swiftly as an Imperial ship. They had no hope of outrunning it.

"*Bloody hell*," Troy swore.

"Benevolence?" Tor asked.

Ruarnon shouldn't be on deck. But how did you stay safe on a ship when damars that could craft fire magic were trying to burn it down?

"It's too late," Ruarnon replied. And if they couldn't fulfil their duty of safety, there was only one other thing to do.

"ARCHERS TO THE FOREDECK!" Ruarnon bellowed. "ARCHERS TO THE RIGGING! LOAD THE POWER BOWS. FIRE AT WILL!"

"How do we defend ourselves against *that*?" Troy asked.

"I'll shield the prow," Mawana said to Mocco. "So they can't sink us with fires below deck. You shield the masts."

"*We* have to help!" Lenaris insisted.

"I need to watch the soldiers as well," Ruarnon replied, nodding and gesturing to soldiers spreading out across the foredeck and climbing the rigging. They needed to oversee the defence of the whole ship, but their shield magic was the next strongest.

"If your magic weakens, I'll back you up," they told Mawana. "Tell me if you need help."

Mawana nodded, then turned to the Australians.

"Do you know how to merge your shields?" Mawana asked.

"We can try," Linh replied.

While they all focused, and magic tingled in the air around Ruarnon, Ruarnon reached out beyond the Iylena, towards a disturbance in the magic moving towards them. Fire streaked through the air from a distance. Soldiers pointed and cried out. Some trembled. Others murmured prayers to the ancestors. It couldn't be. But it was. And it could burn any of Ruarnon's three ships, killing everyone on board.

But that wasn't going to happen. Ruarnon seized magic in the air before the fire magic, groaning as they locked magic particles into place. The fire halted before their invisible wall. It pressed softly, futilely against it. Then Ruarnon sensed magic tingling in a different direction, as the fire tried to burn up over their wall. They seized it, wrenched it and it puffed into smoke.

Ruarnon gasped, as sweat trickled down their neck, face and back. They were short of breath and felt like they'd been running, but they could do that again if they had to.

"What happened to it?" a soldier cried.

"I did," said Ruarnon, turning to face their soldiers. "Those damars can wield magic. So can we. Their magic feels… flighty. I bet it is as instinctive as their physical attacks. They don't have our will to win. It's our will versus their instincts. Show me your willpower!"

Some soldiers hesitated, but a few veterans smiled grimly, leading a return salute as Ruarnon gave them a one-armed salute. Then they turned back to the oncoming damarian ship, wondering how much fire they could stop in its tracks before they passed out. How many damars would be throwing it at them?

They decided to snuff out the flames only if they targeted an unshielded part of the ship, or if the other's shields were weakening, a thought that made them deeply uneasy, letting dangerous magic get so close to timbers that it could burn beneath everyone's feet.

But as the damarian ship came closer and more fire flared, Ruarnon had a strange realisation; this was where they wanted to be. At the front of the deck. First and final defence of their people against fire. Facing danger beside their friends. In command of their own expedition and leading all those who volunteered to face that expedition's challenges head on.

Fire flared again and monitoring magic to defend their ship and leading their soldiers claimed all Ruarnon's attention.

Sweat trickled down Linh's back and her chest tightened. The very idea of a magic battle turned her insides to ice. She had no idea how to merge her shield with someone else's. None of them did. But that ship was gaining on them, and the Iylena was turning too slowly. This was what all their training had been for...

She gripped the railing with both hands, drew a deep breath, and concentrated hard on projecting a Tarlahn bronze-sized shield onto reality. Her shield formed thick and misty before the railing. It was her biggest yet, but it wasn't enough. She exhaled, holding the shield tightly, and extended it slowly. She stopped when the misty sheen of Troy and Fiona's shields reached towards hers. How did she join them?

Troy's shield pushed against hers, and she instinctively loosened her hold. The edge of her shield rippled. Troy's shield edge rippled into the reverse shape and expanded until their shields touched. They'd done it!

She smiled, and Troy returned her smile, concentrating too carefully for speech. Something nudged her left, and she instinctively took hold of Fiona's shield, then smiled in surprise, barely maintaining her grip. Fiona smiled back. Mawana's shield reached down and aligned with the tops of theirs. She reached for the edge of his magic, and her awareness narrowed to the parameters of her shield and the three edges she gripped, her arms extended to either side, hands angled towards the shield, muscles from shoulder to fingers tensing.

She flinched at a strange sensation. Fire flashed in the right corner of her eye.

"They must be five hundred meters away!" Troy yelled. "How can they reach us?"

"They're strong," Michael replied quietly. "That's how they sunk those Imperial ships."

Linh kept a firm hold across the shield with her mind and peered through its fog-like substance. On its far side, lines of flame burned towards her. She gripped tighter and stared at lines of different heights, streaking towards her at varying paces until several struck simultaneously. Fire blazed before her, and she gripped hard as heat struck. Orange glowed for seconds, a tense, sweaty eternity and then flames dissipated to smoke. She sighed and let her shield thin as her arms relaxed a little.

"ARCHERS, LOWER BOWS AND FORM SHIELDS INSIDE THE MAIN SHIELD!" Ruarnon bellowed.

At the corners of her vision, new shields formed. Flames roared, and the shield Linh and her friends maintained was enveloped in fire again. She held tightly, the heat making her sweat as fire gave way to smoke.

A misty second shield expanded before her. Another shield formed before Troy's and a third before Fiona's. The new shields reached towards each other and shields overhead reached down. But they didn't join. They left gaps wide enough to let fire through.

"Soldiers hold hands!" Ruarnon ordered as fire flashed.

Linh's muscles tensed as she thickened her shield against the fire burning before her, shaking with strain.

"Feel your allies," said Ruarnon. "Cast your shields as one! Open them to shields around you and let them join!"

Shields before Linh began to merge. She and Fiona sighed, and she let her body relax and her shield thin again. For a few precious moments, her lungs filled with fresh air, and she could just breathe. Then orange glowed towards her again. She thickened the shield, trembling as fire blossomed against it. This time she felt the fire pushing. As if the damars were trying to force her to let her shield go and turn it into fire.

Sweat trickled down her sides as she resisted. She leaned heavily on the railing. Her sense of carrying weight lessened, but every muscle felt tense with strain. Pressure built in her head.

Something large moved into her peripheral vision, the Meera, trying to draw damarian fire. The blur on her left must be the Saeron. The next volley of fire lines divided between the three ships.

Ruarnon tensed as lines of fire streaked towards all three of their ships. Shields misted before the other two ships' decks. The first fire to get near General Takanis suddenly streaked off course. She grinned at it.

They were going about this wrong. When it was powersling fire during the siege, they didn't try to knock balls of rock off course. They tried to destroy the enemy power slings. They should be attacking the damars. But the sisters hadn't taught them how and it was a dangerous time for experimental magic.

"Sleep magic!" Ruarnon cried. "Soldiers, maintain the shield before the ship! My friends and I will target damars on deck with sleep magic. That ought to disrupt their fire and if we are lucky, set fire to their own ships."

"Brilliant," Mawana replied.

Tor inclined his head, and Ruarnon's companions shifted their focus to the damarian decks. Ruarnon reached out, ignoring feeble tingling pushing against them and projecting calm. They dropped a half dozen damars at once. Creatures screeched and hit each other. Fires cut out part way from the damarian decks, some flaring among the damars.

This was a good strategy. Would Tor or General Takanis have thought of it in the west? Could any Tarlahn craft magic with Ruarnon's singular focus and power of will?

More damars dropped on the black decks. But in ones, or twos. No one else could project their will on magic like Ruarnon could. Mawana dropped four damars with a groan, but even Mocco could not equal Mawana in magic. Had Ruarnon made the right decision about who should lead the western expedition?

Linh released her grip on the edges of Fiona's and Mawana's shields, her body slumping with relief. Her shield shrunk into a ball before her, and her muscles relaxed. Her shrunken shield vanished, and she sank into the railing.

It took several moments to catch her breath. Then her sense of danger sparked adrenaline, and she resisted the urge to shape the shield again. Instead, she peered through the misty, patchwork curtain of soldiers' shields at the dark damarian ship beyond, seeking a target.

The aft, main and foredecks were crowded with damars. Some stumbled under other people's sleep magic. Her sense of magic tingling as others crafted it was chaotic. She tried to block it out, and visualised pairs of damarian eyes shutting, chests rising and falling slowly. She squinted, trying to focus on a couple of damars on the main deck and put them to sleep. Two fell. Her mouth opened in surprise, and they flailed, knocking damars around them. Two fires outside the damarian shield turned to smoke, and a damar caught fire.

Linh tensed as flames blossomed before her against the soldiers' shield. Then she visualised sleep and mentally gripped damars raising their hands to cast magical fire along the damarian railing. Pressure tugged at her magic. She released it. Damars it had bound thrashed under a fire floating in the air.

Thrashing damars knocked others down across the main deck, distracting those casting magic. Some fires smoked out, but others began to burn inside the damarian shield. Burning creatures pushed through the crowd, shrieking and spreading fires from damar to damar. It was working!

Linh took another breath and strained. She put two damars to sleep and released her grip as they fell against the railing. They were smashed through it by panicked neighbours fleeing the main deck. Half a dozen damars fell into the water.

Linh smiled wearily, then noticed the trickle of sweat all over her body and that she was shaking. She frowned. The pressure around her head and tension in her muscles had returned. A light shield floated before her, and she was maintaining it. Troy and Fiona had recast their shields too. It had become a survival reflex.

Damars pushed their way up the fore and aft deck stairs on the dark vessel or leapt overboard as the wind whipped flames towards the mast. Sporadic fire-lines streaked towards the Iylena, Meera and Saeron from the fore and aft decks.

Linh's body shook. Her shield was thinning. Her vision blurred. She sat instinctively as everything got dark. Alarm spiked her adrenaline, and she let go of the shield. She sat panting, gripping the railing with both hands and leaning her face against it, blinking to clear her vision.

When dark patches obscuring the railing and deck before her cleared, and Linh had the strength to turn, she checked on her friends. Fiona's gaze was focused, her face lightly sheened with sweat and cheeks pink, but Troy slumped against the railing. He was shaking and sweat trickled steadily down his face.

"Troy," she said weakly. "Let go. You'll knock yourself out."

Troy gasped and sat, panting heavily. "Thanks," he said.

Ruarnon surveyed the damarian ship. Damars fell on dark fore and aft decks, fires landing on some, setting them alight. But the

295

Iylena's shield was thinning, and the occasional fire still flared before it.

"Relief soldiers to the foredeck!" Ruarnon ordered. "Relief soldiers, cast your shields!"

The damarian main mast was on fire. If those creatures started jumping overboard and any survived a swim to the islands with children playing on their shores not so far behind the Iylena...

"Archers ready!" Ruarnon yelled. "Lower the shields! Kill them all! Loose!"

Arrows plummeted into the sea or struck damarian bulwarks. Perhaps there was a sorcerer on board, shielding the ship and letting the damars lead the attack.

Damars rippled as a power bow bolt crossed the dark deck. Another ripple signalled another bolt, and Tor shouted encouragement. Flames consumed the main deck and sails, climbing the wooden stairs to the fore and aft decks, from which damars flung themselves overboard or fell to arrows.

Soon, the only movement came from the water. Damars flailed, arrows raining among them until they floated limply, and their entire ship was ablaze. Archers cheered and soldiers laughed, clapping comrades on the back. It was over. They had fought sorcery crafting damars with magic and they had won. Ruarnon stared, not quite believing it.

"We beat sorcery-wielding damars," Linh said weakly on their left.

"Yeah," Troy said quietly. "We're awesome."

Mocco and Mawana were sitting slowly, exchanging smiles. Ruarnon's other friends sat in sweaty heaps on the deck, exhaustion plain on their faces. Ruarnon's tunic was slick with sweat, but they could stand well enough while leaning on the railing.

On their left, the nearest damarian ship was engulfed in flames, and the Timbalen ship that had fought it smoked towards two comrades, each battling a damarian vessel. The burning ships they had seen earlier were sunk, but rowboats floated near them. Yellow-cloaked soldiers in rowboats sent lines of fire streaking at damars in the water and hauled yellow-cloaked soldiers on board. More Timbalen ships battled dark vessels beyond.

A damarian ship before them became engulfed in flames. Its Timbalen opponent aided allies against the last nearby damarian vessel, bombarding it with volleys of linear fires and flashes of bright light that streaked like lightning, hitting and only partially penetrating its shield.

Ruarnon watched open-mouthed. The Elite Guard's power was astonishing. The damars were frightening too, but Ruarnon suspected the damars outnumbered the Guard. That one Guard could craft five times the amount of magic. Had Red Cloak *seen* the Elite Guard training? And mistaken them, understandably, for Guardians?

Gaps opened in the nearest damarian ship's shield. Fires shot towards Timbalen ships, flaring against small shields in mid-air. Lightning pierced the damarian shield, setting its mainmast and deck on fire and damars fleeing. The fire gradually ravaged the damarian decks, climbing the mast and sails, and the fighting was reduced to Elite Guards watching damars flail in the water. The damars soon drowned.

In the relative quiet that followed, Ruarnon noticed shouting from a boat in the water. "I'm told the fighting ashore is heavy and may last days. Your Benevolence's best option is to wait on Merchant Island west of here until it is safe to approach Timbala City."

A Timbalen messenger.

"Thank you," Ruarnon called back. "Captain, make for Merchant Island."

The Iylena creaked as it continued its interrupted turn around the cliffs. Ruarnon gazed beyond the floating battlefield on their left, at the horizon, on which a strip of white was visible above a crowded dark mass, with fire and strange lights flashing amongst it, a land battle. Sorcery War had returned to the world.

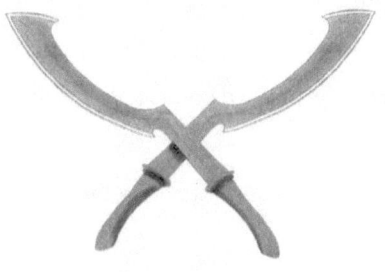

CHAPTER 24

BATTLE BEFORE THE WHITE WALL ~ RUARNON

Ruarnon stood on the Iylena's aft deck, forty paces from the shore of Merchant Island, after breakfast. Tor and Lenaris stood with them, gazing at the battle raging between damarian and Timbalen ships across the sea. Damarian shields were failing more swiftly now, suggesting that Ruarnon's message about using power bows against them had been received.

"We're still missing something," said Ruarnon. "If Narz thinks the Elite Guard are Guardians and that they'll return west to oppose a sorcerer-king, I can understand him seizing the Zaldeaan army as a buffer against the Guardians. I can understand him trying to destroy the creature armies before the Guardians wielded them against him. If he thought the Guardians were going to wipe him and his sorcerers —and their families— out, perhaps he could even be scared enough to breed damars to defend his people. But to launch this attack out of fear, with no evidence the Elite Guard know of his existence seems utterly irrational."

Troy slumped into the railing. "So much for being catalysts for peace," he said, eyeing burning ships on the horizon.

"Lylah didn't say we could prevent Sorcery War," Michael said quietly. "She only said we could help contain it in the Far West."

"How about helping your allies win their battle?" Mawana offered.

Mocco caught his cousin's eye and nodded.

Ruarnon turned to them enquiringly.

"The Timbalens are relying too heavily on magic," said Mocco, his gaze fixed on the battle at sea. "They risk dying from magical overexertion when conventional weapons will suffice. I suspect that both sides stand under magical shields onshore, using magic to penetrate each other's shields. If a sorcerer punching my shield in Blue Bay nearly knocked me out, imagine what an infantry charge with bronze shields could do."

"That would leave Timbalens vulnerable, while they charge," said Tor, crossing the aft deck.

"But soldiers can shield themselves overhead and in front while they charge," Mawana objected. "They would not face fire until they broke the damarian shields. Then archers and spears would make short work of the damars."

"You are right," Tor conceded. "But the Timbalens are unaware that we know anything about magic. And as your tactic will place Elite Guard in danger, our allies may not listen."

"We can show them," said Mocco. "I know what sort of strain they labour under. I felt it in Blue Bay, and I can't rest knowing others may be dying of it onshore. Send Mawana and me with soldiers, and we will shield them while they charge."

Ruarnon's stomach churned. Intentionally pitting their friends and soldiers against sorcery-wielding damars didn't appeal. Nor did sending them to fight while Ruarnon stayed safely on board. Ruarnon doubted Mocco and Mawana's parents or the Council of Elders would approve, but Mocco thought he could save Timbalen lives, and he and Mawana were willing. And could Ruarnon deny their allies aid against damars when they had aided the Zaldeaans against the creatures?

"We will have to wait until the sea battle ends to move the Iylena closer and confirm my allies' tactics," Ruarnon replied. "Let General Takanis know how many soldiers you can shield. I will ask for volunteers to make themselves known to her within the hour."

There were only six damarian ships left in the sea battle by then. Fire burned through the air around them sporadically. At least a dozen Timbalen vessels surrounded the damarian ships, presumably attacking with power bows, whose bolts no one could make out. Damarian shields gradually failed, and dark decks burned.

Ruarnon returned to their cabin and buckled on their leather kilt, iron cuirass, iron helmet and enchanted sword, then joined their bronze-armour-clad friends on the foredeck as soldiers formed ranks on the Iylena, Saeron and Meera.

They gazed ahead, watching Timbalen ships surround the last damarian vessel. A barrage of lightning blazed against the damarian dome shield. Eventually, lightning pierced the shield, setting dark decks alight. Fire rained until, every timber above water was ablaze. Then the Iylena, Saeron and Meera set sail, following four retreating Imperial ships wide of the burning damarian wreck.

The hum of the shore battle became discernible shouts of soldiers, and damarian screeching as Timbalen Island drew nearer. Shielded damars faced off against shielded Elite Guard on sandy shores before a tall white wall shimmering with enchantments. Ruarnon signalled their captain to drop anchor and studied the battle.

The Elite Guard stood with backs to the wall in fourteen phalanxes shielded by misty domes. They faced fourteen damarian phalanxes lined up under shield domes. Fires blossomed against shields on both sides, and lightning flashed across the open space in-between.

For a moment, Ruarnon was mesmerised. Then the commander in them wondered why the Elite Guard fought from exposed positions on the beach instead of from the battlements, and why the battlements weren't lined with archers and power bows attacking damarian shields.

Timbalen infantry and cavalry tried to charge magically shielded damars at either end of the dome shield battle, but spear-wielding damars blocked them. Cavalry and infantry fought hand to hand against damarian spears.

"Their offensive magic is infrequent," said Mocco. "Both sides are tiring."

"The Elite Guard hide behind shields instead of attacking," said Mawana, shaking his head.

Ruarnon sighed. Once the damarian shields fell, would Ruarnon's archers be enough to counter fire-wielding damars? But there was no sign of damarian shields failing or Elite Guard offensive magic breaking through. They were evenly matched in a battle of magical endurance. Whoever tired first would lose and be slaughtered. Ruarnon could not risk their allies losing.

"Tor, signal the Saeron and Meera to send boats ashore."

Ruarnon turned and walked to the back of the foredeck. Their infantry stood fully clad in bronze plate armour on the main deck, holding spears in one hand and shields in the other. Every alert face peered out at Ruarnon from beneath a bronze helm, while behind them, archers held bows, and quivers hung at their hips. Ruarnon smiled inwardly at the number of volunteers.

"Our allies lack your experience. A physical charge against damarian shields could snatch victory from the jaws of defeat, but they do not see it. They cling to magic, the only strategy they know. But my friends have seen power bow bolts pierce magical shields. They have seen a sorcerer put his fist through one.

"I saw your bronze shield walls hold back Zaldeaans atop the walls of Tarlah City. I know your strength. And I do not believe sorcery can withstand a Tarlahn bronze shield wall charge. At the Timbalen Empire's darkest hour, I call upon you to return the service they did us when they drove the Zaldeaans from our walls. Who among you will show our allies the way to victory?"

The soldiers straightened, a fierce look coming into their eyes. Like the Zaldeaans, Timbalens had always been the superior force, with superior weapons. Never had Tarlahns taught Timbalens tactics, and Ruarnon soldiers' smiles suggested they contemplated the idea with pride, as well as nerves.

Spears flashed in the sunlight, raised in salute. Grim smiles of battle fury spreading across certain faces distinguished Ruarnon's veterans. Ruarnon tried to ignore the wide, worried eyes of younger soldiers as they raised their arms in a double salute, signalling that Tarlah and the Timbalens stood. Every soldier proudly returned that salute. As they would if Ruarnon ordered them to storm a sorcerer-guarded castle in which their parents were imprisoned. Ruarnon lowered their arms, emptiness swelling inside them as they dismissed their soldiers.

Tor climbed down a rope ladder against the Iylena's bulwarks, followed by Mocco, then Mawana. They would take the first boat, leading Ruarnon's soldiers as Ruarnon ought, against an enemy who could injure them horribly or kill them with unnatural ease. It should be Ruarnon going. Especially with the strength of their magic.

"Those shields will fail soon," said Michael, and Ruarnon tensed.

On Timbalen Island, an opaque shield front vanished and reappeared behind a line of damars, who were set alight. Opposite the shrunken dome, grass beside an Elite Guard dome burned, and Elite Guard repositioned.

Ruarnon waited impatiently for the boats from all three of their ships to row towards shore, the Meera's boats lagging. Ahead of the boats, waves broke and foamed to dry sand, on which hundreds of damars stood beneath magical shield domes with their backs turned.

Ruarnon gripped the railing, expecting a grey face to turn and fire to flash towards their soldiers. It didn't. Narz's sorcerers were occupied shielding damars, and the damars were intent on the shielded prey before them.

The Iylena's boats halted before breaking waves. Mocco moved left, forming a shield dome for soldiers to gather under, Mawana forming a second dome on the right. Tor disembarked in Ruarnon's stead. Ruarnon sighed, as soldiers assembled behind Tor, knee-deep in water.

General Takanis and the remaining boats reached the shore, her soldiers forming up under Mocco or Mawana's shields. Orange light flashed as a fire burned above the waves towards them.

Tor and his soldiers charged a damarian dome shield on the right, preceded by Mawana's shield. General Takanis and her soldiers charged left, preceded by Mocco's shield.

Both groups splashed through breaking waves, as fire lines streaked towards them. One fire line overshot. It sagged towards unshielded soldiers from the Meeran boats. They dived beneath the waves. The fire line hit, burning above the surface. The water rippled as two soldiers resurfaced, and the fire turned to smoke.

"Don't let this be another Gallipoli," Linh said firmly.

Both Urai shields glided over ankle-deep water, gaining speed, as Tarlahn soldiers moved onto wet sand. Bronze shields were raised along both front lines. Tarlahn soldiers roared.

The back lines of damars under four sorcerer's dome shields whipped around. Ruarnon held their breath.

Tor's spear raised above the bronze shield wall. Mawana's floating shield vanished, as roars reached a crescendo. Tor's spear stabbed through a misty white dome. His bronze shield wall thrust forwards. Spears stabbed. Shields pushed. The damarian dome shield vanished. Ruarnon exhaled.

Bronze shields ploughed down damars. Spears stabbed. Tor drew his sword and slashed his way through damars. Tarlahns at the rear of that charge halted, and arrows soared into damarian front lines. Fires winked out, and archers loosed again.

Fire blossomed over charging Tarlahns. Mawana raised his hands beside archers, maintaining a shield roof.

Tor ducked a wooden spear thrust and lopped off two damarian heads. He leapt wide of a second spear and beheaded two more damars. Soldiers around him deflected spears with shields and beheaded with their swords.

The damars made no attempt to dodge weapon blows. They had no sense of self-preservation.

Within moments, Tor's soldiers had abandoned spears in favour of swords. They danced between damars, deflecting with shields, wielding their swords with deadly grace. These damars were useless at hand-to-hand fighting, and Mocco and Mawana's shields protected soldiers from damarian fires. The Tarlahns were winning. And Mocco and Mawana still stood tall and straight, showing little sign of strain from shield casting.

Another roar caught Ruarnon's attention, left of General Takanis. A captain led a charging bronze shield wall out of the shallows from the Meeran boats. Fire turned to smoke before them as they charged an invisible damarian dome shield beside Takanis' soldiers. They halted before damars, spears stabbing sorcerous shields, men, women and midluns yelling, bronze shields pushing. Then they too ploughed into damars.

"Unbelievable," Troy said softly. "They could win this battle in five minutes!"

"Narz must have assumed fire-wielding damars do not need arms training," said Lenaris. "His sorcerers rely as heavily on magical shields as the Elite Guard."

Tor's front line faced the damarian dome shield on their right and raised their bronze shields. General Takanis commanded infantry on her left, and archers-maintained attacks to defend both groups of Tarlahn infantry.

"The Timbalens have seen," said Michael.

Front line Elite Guard charged diagonally opposite Tor's soldiers, wielding round shields and swords. A pale magic shield hung above them, patchy fire raining harmlessly against it.

Elite Guard swords stabbed forwards, and the damarian dome shield before them vanished. Elite Guard swords slashed into the damarian front line, while damars burst into flame.

Two shielded, limp men floated above the damars and disappeared behind Elite Guard lines, captured sorcerers.

A damar pack tried to flee. It was seized by tendrils shooting up from the ground, wrapping around ankles and waists, then necks, strangling the creatures.

Right of them, more Elite Guard advanced. Damars screeched, as a wall of fire spread along their front line.

Three captured sorcerers floated away. Rear damars moved back towards the sea, but the water had retreated, forming a single giant wave. It surged forwards, smashing into them. Elite Guard leapt beyond its reach, and the tide retreated, dragging flailing damars into the sea.

On either side of the battlefield, four Elite Guard dome shields merged into a shield wall and roof and advanced. As two Elite Guard front lines charged across the battlefield, a roar went up. Fires blossomed against their drifting shield walls.

Shield walls vanished, Elite Guard charged damarian dome shields en masse, and five domes vanished.

Elite Guard collided with damars. Others charged three damarian dome shields a second time. One group charged a third. The last damarian shield failed and the stalemate ended. Ruarnon's heart leapt.

Timbalen cavalry and infantry retreated from either end of the field. Thick firewalls hemmed in spear waving damars, trying to pursue the retreating soldiers. Fires pressed forwards on three sides, gradually driving both groups of damars into the sea, in which they flailed and began to drown.

Gradually, damars fell. Swords cut them down, vines strangled them, and fire cut off any that attempted to retreat, as the sorcerers binding them were also cut down.

Mawana's broad figure stepped back from what was becoming a rout. Mocco followed him. General Takanis had her soldiers form lines between them and the battlefield.

Tor slowly fought back through the damars, with the other Tarlahn soldiers, towards them. Smoke and flashes of light flared from sorcery behind him, as the Elite Guard closed a noose around the damars.

The damars fought on, likely burning themselves with fires that flared and vanished rapidly. They even raised clawed hands against Elite Guard wielding swords. They were fearless, and unyielding, as the Elite Guard circle tightened, cutting them down. Until the circle met and not a single damar was left standing.

Ruarnon exhaled. They were relieved it was over, but their body was rigid with tension. Out of fear and desperation, damars could inspire humans to treat them savagely. It was protecting an entire city. But there was something wrong here. The empire was safe, but Ruarnon had a sinking feeling no one had won.

They flinched, as roars erupted, sporadically at first, and then everyone was yelling, "All Hail Emperor Yarath! All hail the victorious army!"

The cry was repeated, and another began, "All hail Regent Ruarnon!"

"I take it they heard the tactics that won weren't local," Troy said, smiling at Ruarnon.

Ruarnon exhaled deeply. It was over. With Mocco and Mawana's aid, their soldiers had defeated at least a hundred sorcery-wielding damars on their own… and ensured their allies gained the upper hand.

They felt weak at the knees and steadied themself against the railing. Because their soldiers had just proved that with magical aid; they could overcome sorcery to free Ruarnon's parents in the West.

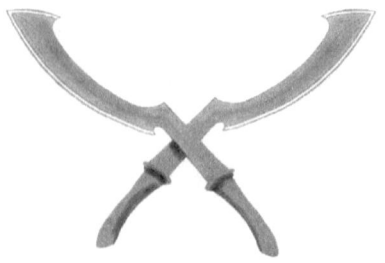

CHAPTER 25

TIMBALA CITY -RUARNON

Ruarnon stepped onto the sand of a beach covered in burn marks, with Captain Arleath and half their bodyguards. Moans rose from wounded or burned Tarlahns sitting nearby, tended by their companions. They smelt burnt clothing, flesh and the iron tang of blood. The sights, sounds and scent of what others had braved, but Ruarnon hadn't, made them uncomfortable.

On their right, soldiers carried the Tarlahn fallen to a boat, while others piled damar bodies at the end of the beach. Across the battlefield, Elite Guard bent over fallen allies. Some soldiers they tended stood and walked away, while others were carried towards chariots approaching from open gates in the White Wall.

"Benevolence," said Tor, approaching through the crowd.

Tor had a cut on his neck, a messy failed attempt to stab it, and blood seeped from his right armpit, but he seemed in good shape, his blue eyes clear and alert.

"We only lost five men and two women, Benevolence," he reported. "I feared we would lose a dozen more, but the Elite Guard are…wondrous in their healing. Mawana and Mocco shielded us well, and once the Elite Guard overcame shock at Tarlahns shattering damarian shields, they protected us."

Tor spoke calmly, but there was awe in his voice. The Elite Guard must be as accomplished at healing as the North Landers. Yet their shields were as powerful as the Urai's, and their offensive magic was as terrible as damars. The Elite Guard were well-trained sorcerers, *all of them…*

Ruarnon's soldiers gathered. Ruarnon surveyed them with a proud smile while Mocco and Mawana waved from where they lay nearby, their armoured chests rising and falling rapidly as they caught their breaths. Ruarnon smiled back at them, but their smile faltered when they met their soldiers' eyes, knowing that next time their soldiers fought sorcerers, they wouldn't even be there to praise them.

"I thought you had faced your greatest challenge against damars in the Realm, then at Cauldron Island and now here. You never fail to impress me with your courage and your efforts."

Ruarnon saluted them, and many returned Ruarnon's smile as well as their salute, but something was different, something in the way the soldiers looked at Ruarnon. They meant those words, but the words sounded slightly hollow from a leader who had not led.

Ruarnon turned and knelt before Mocco and Mawana. "I cannot thank you enough. My soldiers could not have maintained magic shields while they charged. You gave us a winning tactic, and your magic made it succeed. My allies owe their victory to you. The emperor will not realise, but I will explain."

"Perhaps this will get Mother off my back," Mawana replied with a smile, his eyelids flickering wearily.

Mocco raised his eyebrows as he eyed his cousin. He smiled, before closing his eyes and going straight to sleep. Mawana also closed his eyes, and soon his breathing slowed, and he too slept. Ruarnon wondered if they had balanced the effort of magical exertion well enough or just fought to the brink and now surrendered to exhaustion.

A Timbalen in a white tunic with a yellow collar approached, waiting for Ruarnon to acknowledge him, then bowed. "Supreme General Avarna invites their Benevolence of Tarlah and our allies to participate in a victory parade that shall begin in an hour, by the gates of Timbala City," he said, not rising from his bow.

Ruarnon thanked and dismissed him, then asked General Takanis to have the soldiers bathe and rest when they finished helping Timbalens clear the beach of damarian bodies.

"Did you realise the Elite Guard could be sorcerers?" Ruarnon asked Tor quietly, as they watched a pair of Timbalen soldiers carrying a damarian body across the beach. Nearby soldiers stared when a pile of damarian bodies magically burst into flames under the supervision of the two Elite Guard. Other Timbalens eyed the Elite Guard with open mouths or reverent smiles, but some kept their heads down and avoided eye contact.

"It seemed the remotest of possibilities," Tor replied. "Until we met sorcerers on Cauldron Island. This is the first time in Timbalen history that an Elite Guard army has assembled. I have rarely read of Elite Guard fighting in the Imperial Histories, and when they did, the details are vague. Now, it seems the true extent of their powers awes even their people."

"They seem a better-kept secret than the North Landers ability to wield magic," Ruarnon replied, "one that's been standing in the plain view to the empire and our kingdom for centuries. Narz appears to be drawing every sorcerer out of hiding, from the far west to the far east."

Ruarnon shivered. They knew that according to myth the Elite Guard played no part in the Wars of Unity that united the Timbalen Empire. Only when the emperor was established did they offer their services, which had been concealed ever since. Their caution, Lylah's and her sisters caution in teaching only a handful of Urai magic until now, and the North Landers secretive existence made Ruarnon think they had all feared and strived to evade another sorcery war. But Narz had found them and initiated that war. Where would it end?

A yellow cloak on Ruarnon's right caught their attention, and they turned to an Elite Guard healing burns down one of their soldier's arms. She stared at the woman's forearm, then the woman washed off charcoal and blood with seawater to reveal pink, but healthy, partially healed skin.

"Thank you," Ruarnon said instinctively, as the Elite Guard turned to leave. She bowed her head and turned away.

If there was any chance the Emperor could send Elite Guard West… After an attack like this, Yarath would be more determined to keep them at home than ever. Still, they could make such a difference to Ruarnon's recovery expedition.

When the beach was clear, Ruarnon had boats bring their companions ashore, and their soldiers regroup. They left a messenger with Mocco and Mawana, suspecting it was best to let them sleep, then led everyone else to where the Elite Guard and Timbalen soldiers assembled for the victory parade.

Their heartbeat quickened as they walked behind Timbalen lines towards the towering, pearl-sheened gates and the White Wall that obscured Timbala City. According to Timbalen legend, the Guardians had enchanted the walls to protect refugees from the Sorcery War. Then sailed to the eastern end of the world. Did Narz know those legends?

As Timbalen soldiers passed through the gates, Ruarnon saw crystalline, colourful buildings rising multiple stories above the city walls. They stepped through to a street lined with hundreds of buildings; some built of pale blue stone, most crystalline and every colour of the rainbow. Bridges of intricately wrought crystal linked buildings across the road at different heights, like graceful cobwebs. Ruarnon gaped in silent wonder while their friends spoke over each other in surprise.

The roadside was packed with cheering crowds, as were bridges above the parading armies and spanning side streets. Most of the crowd wore white silk with one panel of colour, others wearing gowns or tunics of a single bright colour. Women wore their hair braided into buns, with small hats pinned on top, men wearing narrow brimmed hats stuffed with feathers. Colour was linked to rank, but Ruarnon forgot how.

They followed the procession past buildings with wooden signs hanging over their doors, scissors, an anvil and hammer, herbs bolts of cloth. They soon walked past more shops than Tarlah and Falls City possessed together. Hawkers stood on street corners selling snacks; their cries drowned out by cheering crowds. Stately homes rose further down the parade route, four or five storeys high, their balconies occupied by people in silk robes, with chains of gold around their necks and wrists, and gold rings on their fingers, minor nobles.

Beyond glittering buildings of bright colours, they saw a high cream stone wall looming and the road they marched down ending at its open gates. The walls towered overhead, at least three stories high. A flight of steps rose between them, under an archway gilt with gold, with a gold gilt serpent's head protruding from its centre.

The serpent loomed overhead as they climbed the steps. Ruarnon turned to towers on either side. Each level was lined with arrow slits. History claimed the Cream Palace had never been assaulted, but its walls were better fortified than Tarlah Castle, the defences of which were designed in response to Zaldeaan assaults. They suspected the emperor's kept secret histories.

At the top of the steps, a path of a cream stone wound across green lawns lined with yellow roses, dotted with neatly-spaced trees trimmed into round or oval shapes, one cut to resemble a bird taking flight, another to resemble a horse rearing. The artistry was beautiful, but also a display of power and wealth.

Gravel paths crossed the processional route, spanned by archways covered in climbing roses, some leading to bubbling fountains or winding across green lawns with small ponds. Exotically coloured fish swam in the nearest pond.

"How posh is this place?" asked Troy.

"I love it!" said Linh.

An exceptionally long building stretched across the lawn ahead, the symmetry of its windows, doorways and statues at the corners of its roof as perfect as the garden. The entire structure conveyed a sense of order.

The Elite Guard halted before a short set of steps leading to a balcony, above which a great dome shaded people in bright silk gowns or silk tunics and leggings, some with panels of different colours and extensive gold or silver embroidery. Ruarnon halted behind the Timbalen infantry, studying a circle of people on the balcony in wide dark trousers and short tunics of yellow silk, with yellow silk cloaks at their backs, garnets encrusting sword hilts at their sides. They encircled a man and woman, the emperor's bodyguards.

Yellow silk panels and gold embroidery dominated the front sides of the emperor and empress' clothing. Two servants carried the emperor's coat tail, two more carrying the long train of the Empress' dress. They wore crowns of elegantly worked gold, the emperor's with a rearing, emerald-encrusted serpent framing its peak. From their necks hung precious stones of every colour, each stone half the size of Ruarnon's palms. It reminded them that each branch of nobility had its colour, which only they could wear.

Servants wore white silk with yellow collars indicating service in the Imperial Palace, while yellow panels on dresses or tunics signified close relation to the emperor, other panels showing houses people were descended from, while the rainbow of colours the emperor and empress wore signified that they ruled all.

Whispers around Ruarnon died as servants in white robes with yellow collars raised their hands for silence. A herald standing halfway down the steps addressed the crowd; "It is my honour to present his Imperial Greatness Yarath, who shall address you personally."

The soldiers before Ruarnon straightened, their gazes alert, and Ruarnon wondered how often the emperor addressed his people in person. Emperor Yarath looked in his middle years, his fair hair tied back with a ribbon, his crystal blue eyes sweeping the crowd, his face stern, yet somehow welcoming. He smiled, and the hard edge to his gaze faded.

"Welcome. All of you. We have fought to protect this fair city and the lands surrounding it from the greatest foe we have ever encountered, for two days. You have braved battle against creatures vicious beyond imagining and wielding sorcery besides. But thanks to the leadership of my generals, a tactic made known to us by our allies the Tarlahns," he nodded to Ruarnon, marking them, "and the bravery and skill of you all, you have triumphed.

"Before you go forth, each of you shall give your names to my scribes, and the names of everyone shall be inscribed into a monument that will stand near the gates of the White Wall, proclaiming the city's greatest defenders. From this year forth, this day shall be a public holiday. Our victory shall be re-enacted in the City Gardens. Bards shall recount poems and tales of you who fought, and we who directed the fighting. There will be feasting in the streets, as there no doubt shall be tonight. For your efforts in today's victory, all of you have my thanks."

The crowd erupted in wild applause and cheering until Timbalen soldiers began to bow their way off the pavement. Ruarnon noted that they did not cheer when the emperor paused, as Ruarnon's people did, and listened with rapt attention.

"Do you think they're happiest over winning or getting a public holiday?" Troy asked.

"They probably don't have public holidays, except perhaps religious ones," Linh replied. "That might be why they're going so wild."

Timbalen cavalry and infantry departed in neat lines, but the Elite Guard remained. Ruarnon asked General Takanis to give the soldiers shore leave, as a yellow-collared servant approached. "His Excellency wishes to receive your Benevolence," the man said with a bow. "I can escort you."

"A large retinue will not be appropriate," Ruarnon told their friends. "You may as well explore the city. I expect Mocco and Mawana will receive invitations to meet the emperor later, and I told the messenger they could meet you near the palace gates. Try not to move too far from the palace. I will send a messenger to find you when I am finished.

"Captain Arleath, his Greatness may see me bringing a full escort into his palace as an insult. My guards may take their leave; you and Companion Tor should be sufficient."

Ruarnon followed the Timbalen servant towards the palace, flanked by Arleath and Tor. The Elite Guard didn't utter a word as they walked past and climbed the steps of the balcony. Ruarnon followed the servant under a gold-gilt arch framed with a serpent and flanked by four guards into a marble hall with large frescoes of people bearing gifts decorating its walls. Wooden display cabinets held beautifully worked ceremonial gold weapons, ivory statuettes inlaid with jewels, crystal vessels, animal furs and other items given as tribute.

The servant led them past another pair of guards into a reception room with a high ceiling. Enormous glass windows let in the afternoon sunlight, and paintings of emperors and Tarlahn kings feasting and duelling lined the Tarlahn Reception Room walls. Emperor Yarath reclined in a gold gilt armchair with yellow silk cushions beside his empress, whose attention was directed at her embroidery, a serpent of gold thread. The servant bowed Ruarnon to a silver-gilt chair with red silk cushions, and Tor and Arleath onto a long sofa with red and yellow silk cushions.

"May I present to your Greatness, Their Benevolence Ruarnon, Regent of Tarlah, Ruler of the Zaldeaan Realm," the servant said.

"And may I present to your Benevolence, His Greatness, Emperor Yarath."

Ruarnon bowed, fireflies stirring in their chest. Emperor Yarath inclined his head with a smile. Servants entered with small cups of wine, fruit juices, sweet pastries, dainty cuts of roast meats, vegetables and nuts, offering them to Ruarnon, then Tor and Arleath.

"I am sorry to say that it may be some time before I can discuss our treaty with you, Ruarnon. But I should like to thank you, and I have several questions about the battle, the damars, and Narz."

"I understand, Sir," Ruarnon replied, wondering what the emperor's personal reaction to being invaded by sorcery-wielding damars was.

"I am told that ramming damarian magical shields with conventional shields was your initiative, demonstrated by your soldiers, though I was unaware that Tarlahns possessed the abilities of Elite Guard. Is shield magic something your people have learned?"

"The tactic you saw and our two main shields were the work of my Urai friends. Soon after I resumed relations with the Urai, I learned that they evaded the Zaldeaans during the Wars with shield magic. Some of my people are of Urai ancestry, and when we learnt of damars approaching, the Urai identified my soldiers who could work shield magic and taught it to them."

It was the lie Desriah had asked them to tell, and they understood her reasons.

"Remarkable," the emperor said lightly, but his gaze was penetrating, and his proud posture concealed much, Ruarnon sensed.

"Is this the only ability associated with the jungle people? For, as you know, descent from the Guardians has gifted my Elite Guard with diverse powers."

He sounded sincere, and Ruarnon wondered if he believed the Elite Guard *were* of Guardian ancestry.

"It is their only ability, but as it was their only defence against a long and bloody war, it would not surprise me that they know it well."

The emperor's smile suggested that he knew Ruarnon was holding something back but was happy to let them.

"We were surprised you came so close to the fighting, being the last of your line," the empress added lightly, her critical gaze contrasting with her tone. She was a beautiful, pale featured woman, also in her middle years, and had been so quiet that Ruarnon had forgotten her presence.

Her voice was a little deeper than Ruarnon anticipated, and her fingers and shoulders were a little broader. She smiled when Ruarnon noticed.

"I have seen a lot more danger by chance than I ought and have grown accustomed to seeing for myself what is going on," they replied, a half-smile creeping to their lips, their full smile suppressed by the fact the emperor didn't seem to have noticed anything.

"I admire tales of active kingship in Tarlah," said the emperor. "I am told you also led your men during the siege."

Conversation about the siege, affairs in the Zaldeaan Realm, the damars, and shared suspicions about Narz followed. The emperor gave the impression of making idle and polite conversation, but Ruarnon was under no illusions that he sought certain information and was concealing his tension about the attack. Eventually, the man gave another broad smile.

"You are no fool Ruarnon of Tarlah, not that I thought a Regent so young could be. And you have more subtlety than I would expect from anyone your age."

So he had noticed and was even more subtle about it than Ruarnon. And he seemed to appreciate Ruarnon taking his wife's identity in their stride.

Ruarnon shrugged. "We are as we are. I'm told the body apparently chains people to gender in the Zaldeaan Realm, but in Tarlah, gender is what it is and the body adapts."

The empress smiled. "It is almost the same here, only here, the Elite Guard and their magic craft can better shape the body to the gender."

She eyed the emperor pointedly.

"You would of course be welcome to such magics, if they appeal to you," he added.

Ruarnon suspected those were the sincerest words he'd spoken so far. They smiled in thanks to the imperial couple. "I am content enough as I am, and with the expression Tarlahn fashions grant me."

"Tarlahn fashions do seem perfect for midluns," the empress added, eyeing Ruarnon's androgynously tailored silk tunic appraisingly. "But I fear I have derailed the conversation."

The emperor's affectionate smile said he wasn't concerned. But his features firmed as he said to Ruarnon, "I confess myself every bit as curious about Narz. It seems his sorcery-wielding damars were created to combat my Elite Guard. I wonder if your parents told him of our power; he guessed my interest in extending trade and influence across the sea and expected we would become rivals in the Far West. I wonder if he attacked us before we upset his ambitions."

He spoke quietly, looking distant, and Ruarnon suspected he was wholly concealing his feelings about the attack.

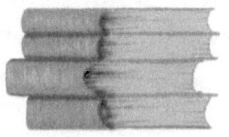

ChApter 26

The Missing Women ~Linh

L inh was only half listening to Lenaris' history of Timbala City, which was holding Mocco and Fiona in thrall. As they stepped back through the palace gates and onto a city street, her gaze followed Mawana's to the buildings opposite. The bright colours of the outer walls, four stories of angled surfaces and their balconies curving outward were graceful, beautiful, and appeared to be a made of a substance like crystal.

Michael, Troy and Mawana studied the buildings too. "The curve of the balconies, and mix of narrower and thicker buildings and bridges extending between them reminds me of the shapes of trees at home," said Mawana. "I wonder if this crystal was grown or shaped by enchantment. I think I sense magic in the walls."

Linh stared. Yes, that was the faint tingle of magic in the distance. "They remind me of the ones connecting the upper stories of Desriah's palace," she said, "and the bluestone buildings in between some of these, and statues on the rooftops, are like the ones in Sryah's city and the paintings of the creator gods at Mijora's Dwelling. I wonder if whoever built this city was inspired by the Island of the Guardians. Do you think this was a Guardian city?" Linh asked Mawana, her words drawing Fiona and Mocco towards the row of crystal buildings they studied.

"I know of no one else at this end of the world with the power or knowledge to grow a city from crystal, if that is what this place is. I wonder if this empire forgets its true origins. If the Island of the Guardians was an outpost to guard creature armies, and the Elite Guard are more than they claim."

"They don't exactly come across as human," said Troy.

"You mean they're calm, solemn and withdrawn like the Sisters?" Michael asked.

"Sure," Troy replied with a grin. "That's exactly what I was thinking."

Linh tried not to laugh. He was probably thinking they were more terrifying in their raw displays of god-like power than the sisters.

"Maybe they're what's left of the Guardians," said Fiona. "Perhaps Selenia couldn't find the Guardians because they're hiding in plain sight."

Now that was a thought. Serving the emperor with the rumour of 'strange abilities' to hush questions, concealing their true capacity. If people suspected of sorcery powers on Ruarnon's continent went to the North Lands, did anyone who found that they could do magic join the Elite Guard here?

Linh studied a stone-faced statue atop a nearby rooftop. The woman's hair was long, her skirt trailing behind her, like the fashions of the people in the stone reliefs on Mijora's Dwelling.

"They would have to have been as cautious as the North Landers," Mawana replied, "who are descended from relatives of sorcerers who waged the Sorcery War but wished no part in it. That is where the North Lander Code of Peace, secrecy and caution originated. If the Elite Guard are so ancient, they too would be nervous of the fear their powers could stir."

"I would be too," said Troy, "if all I had was ancient legends to assure me that the powerful magic-wielders in my backyard fought on the right side of the Sorcery War."

Linh wandered towards a nearby intersection, following graceful bridges spanning between buildings on both sides.

"Ses-ma!" a woman called over the cries of hawkers and loud conversation from the crystal building on her left, an inn whose patrons were celebrating victory.

"Ses-ma? Where are you?" the woman's voice called.

None of Linh's friends could hear it yet; they were still eyeing the architecture. There was a roar from the inn's balcony as a crowd of men raised pottery tankards, and others cheered them on as they drank without pause. But as they fell silent, Linh heard another voice; "Ra-sha!"

Someone else was lost. Linh didn't like that. When she turned, Michael was frowning too and Mawana looked concerned. They both heard the troubled voice from the road behind them.

"Talia! *Where are you?*"

That woman sounded frantic. Patrons on the balcony turned to her. She was in tears.

"What is wrong, mistress?" a man in linens asked.

"My daughter has disappeared," the woman replied, wringing her skirts in both hands. "She was at home in her room, working on her embroidery, but she was not there when I went to tell her of the victory. We cannot find her anywhere, and our servants did not see her go out!"

"Ses-ma!"

"Ra-sha!"

The other two voices drew nearer, a man and a woman moving from opposite ends of the road beside the palace gardens. The man and woman met at the corner on Linh's right.

"Where did you lose Sesma Darlang?"

"She was in the storage room, selecting bolts of cloth for display. I did not hear her leave, but when a servant delivered her lunch, she was gone. It is not like her to be truant in her work."

"There they are," said Lenaris, as she led Mocco down the road to the intersection.

"Something is wrong," Mawana told them. "The man and woman on your left have both lost someone, as has the woman on my right."

"Tiralea! *Where are you?*"

That woman was frantic too, running down the third road of the intersection towards them.

Mocco gathered the worried women and man, taking charge. The four missing people were young women. Two were shopkeepers' daughters in their mid-teens, one a twelve-year-old serving girl, the last a twenty-five-year-old noble.

"Not trouble, I hope?" asked a man in bronze armour, approaching from across the intersection.

His brows narrowed as they explained. "That makes five reports. We'd best go to the Captain. Come along."

He led all four distressed Timbalens away.

"Does this have anything to do with the battle?" asked Fiona.

"If some louts got drunk celebrating…." Lenaris' voice trailed off heatedly.

"No drunken lout pulled a girl out of the storage room without anyone noticing," Mawana assured her. "This is more serious."

"But they can't want a ransom," said Linh, "If they kidnapped a serving girl."

"And why take so many?" Mocco asked.

"When it's supposed to be Selenia he's after," Michael added.

Linh's jaw dropped. The idea Narz feared a girl too young to magically control creature armies had seemed far-fetched. The sisters as Guardians made more sense. But Selenia *had* escaped Narz's enchantment. Her family *had* opposed him. Had he sent people to the eastern end of the world to find her? But why else would four young women of different social classes all go missing at the same time? If Selenia left her homeland as an infant, Narz wouldn't have a clue what she looked like now.

Mawana rushed past Linh. Where was he going, with a tense look on his face? Linh followed him.

Smiling people chatted, walking past them down the street. The hum of conversation and clink of glasses drifted down from balconies. Not one face looked troubled. And Linh couldn't hear any more worried parents searching for lost daughters.

Ahead of her, Mawana strode swiftly between brightly shining buildings under graceful bridges and stepped around unconcerned people who turned to him with puzzled frowns. He reached an intersection, turned left and stopped. Linh turned the corner. It was a dead-end, barred by a bright pink crystal wall.

Mawana turned to her in surprise. "I heard someone cry out," he whispered.

327

He moved beside Linh. She heard one set of footsteps moving away. But there was no one in sight. Her skin tingled. She pointed at the pink wall. Magic tingled there.

The left side of the pink wall flickered. Linh gaped. An illusion?

Mawana ran towards it. The footsteps echoed beyond.

Footsteps approached from behind. Michael and Mocco were following them, the others trailing after.

"Where is the trouble?" Mocco asked.

"Through here," Mawana replied, nodding to the pink wall.

He reached out and Linh flinched. His hand passed through what appeared to be solid crystal. He straightened and stepped into the substance. In an instant, he was gone. He didn't cry out or give any sign of being in trouble.

Linh steeled herself and rushed through the wall after him, too quickly to let the tingling of the magic against her skin put her off.

The laneway continued beyond, and the footsteps came from another corner. Linh tip-toed after Mawana and peered around the corner. The rest of the laneway was empty, aside from a man carrying an unconscious girl over his shoulder. Linh guessed only one type of man had the knowledge and skill to create the illusion of a solid wall: one of Narz's.

The man kicked the door of a pale blue stone building open and carried the girl inside. Linh heard faint footsteps behind them.

"Do you think all the girls are in there?" Mocco whispered.

"There is only one way to find out," Mawana replied. "You should all wait outside, so Narz's man does not hear us. Linh, I think you should take yourself, Michael, Troy and Fiona to call the city guard to the illusion wall. The Elite Guard will want to hear about this."

Linh sighed. She wanted to know what was going on. But she had no desire to enter an enclosed space with one of Narz's sorcerers. And for all she knew, the man may try to abduct her as well. She turned to tell the others to fetch the city guard.

Mawana didn't like this at all. Men snatching girls from their homes in broad daylight, with so many witnesses in the streets. Even with the illusion wall, how had they gotten away with it? He supposed not everyone had his delicate sense of hearing, or his skill in tracking things that interested him by sound.

Mocco and Lenaris followed him across the street towards the bluestone building, and he pressed his hand against the rough wooden door, which slid inwards slowly, the well-oiled hinges making almost no sound. He heard men's voices ahead and crept down a short hallway with his sword drawn, ready to cast a sleep spell. Mocco followed.

The room at the end was small and deserted, with a narrow writing desk across its back wall and a half-folded carpet before it. The fold revealed a trap door in the floor, through which Mawana heard muffled sounds.

He opened the trap door and peered down steep stone stairs. A man's back shifted beyond view at the foot of them, into a dark room in which candlelight flickered.

"People are looking for the women all over," a gruff male voice reported. "It won't be safe to continue. The city guard are joining the search."

"Why can' we keep goin'?" asked another man.

"Because fool," an arrogant voice snapped, "if we bring any more girls, we could lead the city guard straight here. We can hardly demand they hand over Selenia in exchange for the girls when they can take the girls by force."

Mawana sighed. Michael was right.

"Are you sure bargaining is wise?" the gruff man asked.

"It is the only way," the arrogant man replied crossly. "There are too many damn people here. The odds of us seizing her are low, and the longer this goes on, the better the city will be watched and the greater the chance we shall be caught. We must not fail."

"*Yoo* mustn't fail coz you just wan' ya reward," the coarse voice answered angrily. "Yoo don' really care nofink for sorcerers, yoo just wan' a crown!"

Mawana heard a thump and a hoarse cry.

"Keep a civil tongue in your head, or we'll leave you here to take the fall," the arrogant voice replied.

Mawana wondered if the three were the only men down there.

"Do we join the others?" the gruff man asked.

"Yes, we had best leave now, before they get too suspicious or begin searching the sewers. Only these old stone buildings have direct access, and this will be one of the first they search if they think we are smuggling the girls out of the inner city."

Mawana turned to Mocco, nodding back to the exit. Then he darted out of the building, blinking in the sunlight as he turned to Lenaris.

"There is a group of kidnapped girls down there and three men about to take them down the sewers, which connect directly to these old stone buildings," he reported. "There was talk of demanding that the Timbalens hand over Selenia in exchange for the girls. I am going to follow them."

He turned to Mocco. "You are staying here."

Mocco was a good tracker but not as good as Mawana, and he could get them both caught. Mocco sighed and nodded, but Lenaris opened her mouth to protest.

"You don't have the skill to track them without being caught," he said firmly. "And we need to know where they are going."

Lenaris crossed her arms and nodded reluctantly. Mawana accepted their good wishes with a bow of his head, then entered the building, and eased himself through the trap door, stepping quietly down the stairs. He heard shuffling feet below, and shadows obscured torchlight on the pale stone walls. He paused. One by one, they passed the torchlight, and Mawana made out their shadows along the wall, and the shadow of ropes binding the women's wrists behind their backs, linking them in a line.

When the last shadow disappeared, he stepped down into a basement, with racks of glass bottles of dark liquid stacked along one side, flaming torches burning across the back wall, and ample empty space at the foot of the stairs, with a long trap door in the corner. He opened the second door and crept downstairs.

The trickle of running water filled his ears, punctuated by the pitter-patter of rats. Flames flickered ahead. Mawana ducked lower. Three men marched at least thirty young, fair-haired women forwards along a paved ledge beside the murky, foul-smelling sewer water. All three men walked with glowing balls of flame floating over their heads, lighting the way. What had Mawana got himself into?

Ruarnon heard voices through the open window of the Tarlahn reception room. One was a woman talking worriedly, then a man, and then a woman sobbing. Turning to the window, they saw a small party in silks and linens, highborn and low, being led down the garden path by an officer with one yellow plume in his helmet.

The emperor followed Ruarnon's gaze. "Captain Armaan of the City Guard," he said. "And as strange a group of people to bring to the palace as can be imagined."

Brows narrowed, Yarath asked a hovering servant to bring the captain in. Ruarnon listened as Captain Armaan reported to the emperor, twisting his helmet in his hands.

"One hundred and twenty-six young women have been reported missing in the inner city, your Greatness. We have guards searching all over. I fear more are missing. The abductions began in the inner city this morning and intensified as the battle onshore ended and news of victory spread. They stopped less than a bell ago."

Ruarnon's eyes widened.

"What sort of women are missing?" the emperor demanded.

"Girls aged from twelve to women of thirty," Armaan replied. "Mostly lesser nobles but serving girls and shopkeepers' daughters are also missing. Some vanished from the streets, some from inside buildings, yet the closest thing to a witness is the odd person who heard a woman cry out. No one *saw* anything."

"Sorcery," Yarath replied grimly. "Highly organised sorcerers. Narz must have more who arrived secretly before the attack. Perhaps they intended to act after the battle, but immanent defeat forced their hand. Why would he send sorcerers to abduct Timbalen women?"

Ruarnon sighed and replied, "I know a girl whose family are trapped by Narz's enchantment, who fled her homeland to live with protectors near Tarlah. Both previous damar attacks targeted islands she could have been hiding on. He might think she fled here because this is the home of the Guardians, who would offer her their protection.

"Narz does not know what she looks like and might have ordered a mass abduction of women approximately her age. But Narz has always located what he wanted before trying to seize it in the past. These abductions sound desperate. I cannot see him sending men to capture her without means of identifying her."

"Unless the means involves examining her with magic. If my guards heard of men secluding women and casting spells on them, the security measures we would implement would make the sorcerers work impossible."

Ruarnon's eyebrows rose.

"You assume they acted under his direct orders," Yarath added. "Perhaps his orders did not consider capturing Selenia if they lost the battle. Mass abduction may be a desperate action the sorcerers decided upon. A man heartless enough to pit damars against commoners would be nasty to his subjects when they fail him, particularly if he is desperate to get his hands on Selenia.

"But why go to such lengths for one woman? We have faced rebellions here. There was once a rival emperor, and the means the true emperor resorted to, to deal with him were less extreme than what Narz has done in pursuit of Selenia. Does she have a rival claim to his throne?"

Ruarnon's eyes widened. "Her protectors are yet to tell her the exact nature of danger he poses to her."

"Then I suspect she has a claim. He may fear that she will return as soon as she comes of age, rally her army, and make war upon him. So, while sending damars to kill us, he sent sorcerers to assassinate Selenia."

Ruarnon's whole body tensed. How many sorcerers did it take to abduct a hundred and twenty-six women unseen? How did Narz suddenly have so many at his command?

Yarath ordered spies to report on newcomers sighted within the city and officials to inspect the records of every public and private harbour on Timbalen Island and question people who lived or worked nearby. Then he gazed out the window as they waited for reports, and the empress' features tightened with worry.

After a silent wait, a flustered official ran to the Tarlahn Reception Room, bowed deeply and informed them that young women had gone missing from manors on Bareek Island five days ago. Anger flashed across Yarath's face.

"What happened on Bareek Island?" Yarath demanded.

"Lords' daughters, nieces and young sisters went missing from manor grounds. Calls for young women out picnicking or walking to return were sent, and the messengers found male and midlun companions and servants unconscious. The unconscious people had seen and heard nothing. It took two days for the nobles to realise that the same thing had happened at every manor and for their report to reach us. But, with the battle...."

The woman trailed off; her face flushed.

"You thought I did not need another reason to worry," Yarath finished.

There was anger in his tone, but his gaze was distant and directed out the window.

"Which was exactly what they wanted. Perhaps they thought this palace or the inner city was too obvious and that a lord's manor on the wealthy and well-protected Bareek Island would be a more discrete place to hide. So they targeted them first, but the sorcerers could not find Selenia. They assumed she was in the city and discovered it was an excellent place to hide due to its abundance of young women she could blend in with, so they abducted young women. But the palace...."

Alarm flashed in his eyes, and he strode from the room. Ruarnon eyed Tor, who nodded, and they and Captain Arleath followed, the empress saying, "They would not dare! From within the palace itself!"

Her blue eyes were alight with anger as they strode down a tapestry covered hallway, servants pressing themselves against the walls and bowing deeply as they passed. Ruarnon glimpsed a dining hall and other rooms containing tables or desks littered with paper, officials pouring over documents and dictating to scribes as they moved down the hallway.

The frescoes they passed depicted ceremonies where emperors appointed new high officials and signed important documents. Then they came to a guard room with a long table, around which a dozen men in silks sat drinking. Ten guards in full armour, armed with axes, stood across the far exit. They stepped aside, bowing deeply to the emperor, the men at the table staring as Yarath strode past.

Ruarnon followed Yarath into the corridor beyond, past closed doors. The frescoes changed, depicting women dancing, feasting, hunting and picnicking. The emperor strode to the end of the hallway, which was framed by a set of closed, silver double doors with goddesses embossed in them. Several things lay on the floor before the closed doors.

The emperor's pace quickened, and Ruarnon saw ten guards in full armour sprawled half on top of each other and the floor, while two men wearing white silk tunics with yellow collars lay before them. Their chests rose and fell, and they appeared unharmed, but falling like that and not waking… that had to be powerful sleep magic.

The emperor swept around them and pushed the doors open so violently that they crashed into the walls. Yarath stormed through, waking the confused guards. Ruarnon, Tor, Arleath and the empress followed him into a large room with frescoes of Mijora, the Earth Goddess and Esla, the Sea Goddesses on its high walls, bookshelves in the left corner, and rows of richly carved chairs on the right. A vast open space lay before them, a marble floor covered with tens of large silk cushions stretching to the far end, where an enormous fresco of the earth goddess Mijora dominated the room.

Yarath growled as his eyes swept across empty cushions.

"I do not understand," said Ruarnon.

"The Ladies of the court, aside from myself," the empress replied, "spent most of their waking hours here during the battle, praying for victory. The first servant asleep outside came to tell them of victory. The men in the guard room will be husbands waiting for them, assuming they are performing the Thanks Ritual and secret rituals. It is an offence against the Mother to interrupt, but the women took so long that a second messenger was sent.

Both messengers were put to sleep by a sorcerer, who lingered to conceal the abductions."

"This explains the gap in time between abductions on Bareek Island and abductions here," Yarath said, his unfocused eyes still angled at the walls. "They were questioning noblewomen captured on Bareek Island to plan this abduction. They probably came disguised as servants to gain entry to the women's wing."

He turned abruptly to nervous guards, who were waiting respectfully beyond the double doors.

"Tell the Elite Guard to remain outside and that I will address them in moments," he said to a nervous messenger, who bowed deeply, then turned and ran down the hallway.

"How did they get out?" Ruarnon asked.

"There is a secret exit," the empress replied, "created in the days when we still feared sorcery attack and women praying here being trapped if sorcerers defeated us. The exit leads down to the sewers, from which we could escape the city unseen. The sorcerers must be using the sewers."

Yarath led the way out of the shrine. "I will send female Guard through the Shrine of the Mother," he said, "and the rest can search the old stone buildings that have passages to sewers and the sewers themselves."

"How will they detain the sorcerers?" Ruarnon asked.

"I will have the best take what sorcerers they can alive for questioning," Yarath replied. "The rest will be killed. It is too much trouble to capture rogue sorcerers. And I will not risk them escaping when they can provide so much intelligence about us to Narz."

His face was a mask of anger and grim determination. Ruarnon's body tensed at his words. Did he think sorcerers were as dangerous to Elite Guard as damars were to ordinary people? The thought made Ruarnon cold inside.

As they approached the Entrance Hall, Captain Armaan turned to them. Either side of him stood Troy and Linh, while Fiona, Michael and two guards stood behind them, examining artefacts in the Entrance Hall.

"These youths bear news on the abductors, your Greatness," Captain Armaan announced. "They know of a building the abductors accessed the sewers from."

Ruarnon turned to their friends, their mouth opening.

"Mawana heard a girl who escaped them scream," said Linh. "And he followed them through an illusion of a wall into a building and down into the sewers. He's still following them."

"Who is the man they speak of?" the emperor asked.

"An Urai man strong in shield magic and skilled in stealth," Ruarnon replied. "You could not ask for better to find the sorcerers."

"Where is this building?" Yarath asked sharply.

"We can lead you to it," Troy replied.

The emperor blinked, and Troy blushed, perhaps at forgetting to use a title when addressing the emperor, of all people.

"Four children of another world, I daresay?" Yarath replied, interest shining in his eyes. "It does not surprise me that you find yourselves caught up in this. Follow me."

He strode away, and Ruarnon and their Australian friends followed him to the balcony where the Elite Guard were assembled.

"Narz had one last surprise for us," Yarath announced to the Elite Guard, who faced the balcony attentively. "He has ordered young women between twelve and thirty abducted, and over a hundred reports of abductions from within the inner city have reached the palace. One of our friends from Tarlah has uncovered a small party of captives and sorcerers and is tracking them through the sewers. Five of you shall accompany these children to the building they entered the sewers from.

"At least fifty Ladies are missing, abducted from the Shrine of the Mother itself. I want twenty female Guard to determine which secret passage they left by and hunt them down. The rest of you are to search every stone building in the city, entering the sewers in groups of five. Shield yourselves first. Shield the women when you find them. Take as many sorcerers alive as you can for questioning."

The Elite guard inclined their heads as one and divided into groups. None ran back through the gardens, but they strode swiftly away. Five Elite Guard approached Ruarnon's Australian friends, and Ruarnon remained reluctantly on the balcony with the emperor as they walked out of sight.

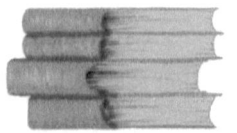

Chapter 27

The Search ~Linh

L inh, Fiona and Troy hurried to keep up with Michael and the Elite Guard on the garden path. They followed two men and three women with calm faces and a fierce glint in their eyes. The Elite Guards' calm sense of purpose seemed superhuman to Linh, and she wondered if the Guardians *had* been hiding in plain sight. It made her shiver.

She jogged down the steps. Every balcony and bridge above the road was lined with people talking, laughing or dancing. The tune of flutes and drumbeats drifted from buildings opposite her, as people celebrated their victory over the damars. The street was crowded, but people stepped back and bowed their heads in awed respect as the Elite Guard crossed the road.

Linh led the Guard through the intersection and down the laneway on the right.

"The illusion's gone!" she cried, as she turned a corner to a longer laneway than she had seen before.

"The sorcerer must be too far away to maintain it," the calmest and fiercest female Elite Guard replied.

Linh led the Guard to the bluestone building, where Mocco and Lenaris waited. The Elite Guard entered the building. Linh stopped and frowned. Mocco and Lenaris were following the Elite Guard inside.

"What the hell are they doing?" Michael asked. He rushed into the building, hopefully, to talk sense into them.

Linh followed.

"You do not need to come," Lenaris said over her shoulder as they entered the hallway, and the Elite Guard entered a room at its end. "It will be dangerous."

"Why-" Michael began.

"Our ineptitude at stealth does not hinder us in helping Mawana now," Lenaris replied.

Miss Cautious was going to follow Elite Guard to *confront sorcerers*?

"The *Elite Guard* are going!" Linh shouted. "How can *you* help *them*?"

"My shield magic is as strong as theirs," Mocco replied.

They crowded into a room with an open trap door on its floor, and the fierce-looking Elite Guard turned back.

"I am Captain Rilmar," she said briskly. "If you can form and maintain magical shields, then you may join my unit; if you stay back, do not get in our way and swear by all of Creation *not* to use offensive magic."

"We don't know how!" Troy insisted.

"Then you may come," she replied, disappearing down the trap door behind her unit.

"I still don't-" Fiona began politely.

"I am not leaving my cousin," Mocco replied, and he hurried after the captain.

"I am not letting the only man I have ever desired to marry get himself killed by sorcerers!" Lenaris replied heatedly, moving to follow Mocco.

"Do we go too?" Troy asked.

"You *should* stay here," Lenaris called over her shoulder as she hurried through the trap door, her footsteps echoing after her.

"Does she remember any of the times *she's* lectured *us* about staying safe?" Linh asked, her face going taut as her features contorted in anger.

"They need calm and focused back up," Michael replied reluctantly.

"And that's us?" Troy asked.

"It's what we *need* to be," Michael replied firmly, and Linh's mouth dropped open as Michael followed Lenaris.

"*We're* going to protect our formerly conservative friends from temporary insanity?" Troy asked.

"There's no time," said Fiona. "The others are getting further ahead, and we have to stay within the protection of the Elite Guards' shields if we're going."

He stared. "Everyone going to protect everyone else endangers everyone! It doesn't make any sense!"

"Welcome to my world," Linh replied.

"More people provides additional shields and strength to resist sorcerer's offensive magic," Fiona replied. "That's what they'll be thinking."

"It also means more people can get killed," Linh asserted.

"It's too late to tell them," Fiona replied, her eyes full of regret.

Linh's hands balled into fists. "Let's stick together," she said, waiting a second for both her friends to nod before she went down the trap door.

At the bottom, she hurried after Michael and the others, along a narrow stone platform beside the most disgusting smelling stream of she did not want to know what she'd ever smelt. Three Elite Guard led the way, two walking behind them. A globe of light floated above the water on their left, lighting the sewers.

Troy and Fiona's nervous faces moved up beside her, but everyone was silent, because enemies could overhear them talking. They'd missed their chance to talk the others out of this. She braced herself, marching in tense silence, her right hand gripping her enchanted sword hilt.

Captain Rilmar flung up her hand, and everyone halted. Linh sensed tingling, probably the Elite Guard casting invisible shields, as they stopped before a sewer intersection. A voice came from the left.

"I sense Guardians. Six of them, on our right."

"Take the captives ahead," another man replied.

Linh shivered. There was only *five* Elite Guard. Could they sense Mocco too?

White mist formed before Lenaris and Mocco. Linh stepped beside Fiona instinctively and formed a misty shield wall before them. Fiona gripped its edge and extended it overhead. Linh gripped the shield roof tightly, peering through its faint mist.

The Elite Guard light soared across the water to the left wall, leaving everyone in shadow. Many footsteps echoed down the sewer from Linh's left, and she waited, her body rigid with tension, fearing a hoard of sorcerers was approaching. But no one came.

The footsteps continued. Prisoners? Why so many?

All five Elite Guard stared ahead, waiting for the sorcerers to make the first move. Troy felt sweat trickle down his back.

"Are you waiting for the innocents to move to safety?" a voice called loudly. "I presume you *can* hear me?"

"Why do you not attack?" Captain Rilmar asked.

"You take us for deranged sorcerers who kill without reason?" came the reply. "The centuries have not changed you."

"No," came Captain Rilmar's reply. "We approach rogue sorcerers with caution. Arrest is preferable to killing. That is our code."

"You have a code? This is new."

Linh tensed, as fire flashed on her left, and men ran into view on the far side of the water. Flames dissipated as the sorcerers looked around bemusedly. Dome shields moved with them. More men stepped into view, eyeing their shields suspiciously, except the second from the end on the far right, who watched the Elite Guard critically.

"*You* shielded them?" Troy asked.

"To give them the chance to surrender," Captain Rilmar replied softly, "which they will not take. Get out of here and out of the sewers!"

The Elite Guard were outnumbered by as many as three to one. Linh backed up, careful not to stand on Troy, who was also retreating. Lightning flashed behind a sorcerer's shield. It flashed again. The shield converted to lightning, which shot through the air. Linh ducked instinctively. Mocco pulled Lenaris aside. A male Elite Guard and Michael were thrown into the air.

"*Mic!*" Troy yelled.

Linh hardly dared to breathe and forced herself to turn. Michael lay on his back behind her. His eyes were closed, but his helmet should have protected his head. Did that mean he was … Michael's bronze cuirass rose slightly beneath his chin, then fell again. Linh heaved a sigh of relief. Then she tensed. The male Elite Guard lay on his side, perfectly still, his yellow cloak burnt. She waited for his chest to rise as he breathed, but it didn't. He was dead. And they could have killed Michael too. That sorcerer could kill them all.

Rage burned in Linh. Her faced reddened with it and determination drove her grip on magic. A shield formed before her. It shot forwards, following the trajectory of the lightning. She drove it hard at the sorcerer. It pulsed around him. Then the sorcerer was gone. Dust drifted to the ground he had occupied.

Her knees went weak and she stumbled at the effort and shock of having killed him, and so easily. Fiona steadied her.

"Do *not* shoot shields!" Mocco protested. "You cannot control them!"

She'd had a clear line of fire only because the Elite Guard before her was dead. How close had her shield shot towards Mocco and the other Elite Guard as she hurled it blindly past them?

"*RUN!*" Captain Rilmar commanded.

Linh blinked, not understanding. Dizziness obscured her thoughts.

Half the sorcerers beat against their shields with fists. Several shoved at them, and only four Elite Guard maintained them. Lenaris strung her bow, and Mocco showed no sign of going anywhere. Captain Rilmar wanted them to leave Mocco and Lenaris behind?

There was just one problem. Linh didn't think she could run. It might make her fall flat on her face.

Troy eyed her anxiously.

"I can't run," she said.

"I can't move fast if I carry Mic either," he added.

A bright light flashed before the Elite Guard. The shield above Mocco and Lenaris thickened. Multiple lightning bolts hit the Elite Guard shield continuously. Too many.

Lenaris leant left, her bow nocked and drawn, and loosed three arrows. She ducked as lightning streaked past, making hairs all over Linh's body stand on end. Two sorcerers fell to Lenaris' arrows, wounded. Lines of sorcerous light continued assaulting the Elite Guard shield.

"We can't walk away," Linh said faintly. "Our shields will fail instantly if *that* hits them."

Magic was tingling around her. She straightened. Was this adrenaline, or magic strengthening her? Whatever it was, she felt better. Though her heart drummed against her chest. Surely the Elite Guard's shields couldn't hold against such powerful attacks for long?

She studied the glassy eyed gaze of the dead sorcerer. They could all be like that soon. She shivered. She'd *killed* a sorcerer. And if they were going to get out of here alive, she'd need to kill more. Before everyone's shield magic failed. With a weapon that could cut though magic.

Linh gasped, clutching her sword hilt.

"If the Elite Guard shield fails, we're dead. We need to cut the sorcerers down."

Fiona trembled. Linh would never ask that of her. She could almost see Troy's heart leap into his throat at the idea, despite that a sorcerer had almost killed Michael, and Linh suspected he loved Michael as much as Fiona. Only one of them got better and stronger at magic under pressure. And had apparently lost her grip on reasonable thought.

Lightning struck the Elite Guard shield. All four Guards stood with hands raised as though physically holding it up.

"Shield me," she said.

Fiona's lip trembled, but her misty shield formed around Linh and Troy strengthened it.

A misty layer of shield swirled from Linh's feet up to her legs, wrapping around them. Misty shield moved down before her face and cuirass like a veil, and Mocco nodded grimly. Lenaris gaped and reached out a hand. She didn't want Linh to take the risk. Didn't want to lose another protégé. After all Lenaris had taught her, Linh didn't want Lenaris to lose anyone either. She would just have to live.

Linh seized the adrenaline and magic tingling inside her. She stepped left and leapt over the fallen Elite Guard, praying she wasn't about to join him. She drew her sword, embraced the adrenaline crashing through her veins and ran.

Murky water and blinding attacks of sorcery approached swiftly. Linh launched herself into the air and slashed blindly, right to left through the white light. Her sword resisted, and she shuddered as a man screamed. She collided with someone, and they fell. They hit the ground hard, and she landed on top, dropping the sword. A shocked face stared up at her. Linh used one of Lenaris' moves, elbowing him in the face. The man's head hit the pavement and his eyes closed.

Linh seized her sword and stood hurriedly, magic tingling all around her, sensing eyes on her. A man on her right had blood blossoming across the silk on his chest and clutched at a wound, backing away. He had no armour. Linh had wounded him. Had she cut his stomach open? She shuddered, and he backed out of range.

Something moved at the corner of her left eye. She pivoted and deflected a sword cut.

"Selenia?" the man asked.

"You wish," Linh replied. "She'd go easier on you."

The blade retreated, and she reached out instinctively as magic shifted before her and fire burned. She locked magic before her in place, keeping the heat at bay, then squinted into the glow, beyond which angry eyes stalked her, and too many sorcerers shaped magic striking the Elite Guard shield.

Linh countered two more sword blows. A woman yelled. Linh grinned, as Lenaris leapt the sewer ahead. Apparently Lenaris had decided Linh would live by Lenaris saving her. Linh was in favour of that.

The fire was too hot. Her training with Lenaris kicked in. Linh wielded her blade with both hands, thrusting it into the fire wielder's middle. The fire became smoke as she withdrew her sword, grimacing as blood trickled from the corner of the man's mouth, and he collapsed. His eyes fluttered, then glazed over. Linh had killed him. She'd skewered a man like a kebab.

Someone turned the sound back on. There were footsteps on her right as the wounded sorcerer shuffled away. A man roared in the distance. Mawana charged on Linh's left and tackled the sorcerer at the far end to the ground.

Linh stood paralysed, eyeing the man she had killed, her wild heartbeat thudding in her ears, while the dead man lay silent. He had tried to burn her to death. The bastard deserved it. That didn't stop her stomach's temptation to empty itself.

Bright light dazzled her. Lightning from four sorcerers streaked at the Elite Guard, hitting their shield in multiple places. All four Guard crouched low, as did Mocco behind them. Fiona and Troy were on their knees under a misty shield dome, shielding the unconscious Michael.

But it wasn't shield magic that would save her friends from dying. Linh raised her sword, and barely fended off a blow from a sorcerer she hadn't realised was attacking her. She squinted against bright sorcerous attacks flashing behind her opponent. Lenaris yelled, slashing at two men at once.

Something jolted Linh. Something had changed. Her last magical shield was gone.

The sorcerer's blue eyes blazed with anger, and he attacked fiercely. Linh ducked a savage blow, and nearly fell in the sewer dodging another. She pressed against his blade with magic and stabbed at his throat with all her might, crying out at the strain. He collapsed, gurgling as she withdrew her blade. It was enough, he was dying. But she was so hot, and sweaty and her head was starting to pound. Magic tingled, some of it probably hers. At what point would she pass out?

Only one sorcerer attacked the Elite Guard now. Beyond, Lenaris had probably felled the man lying behind her, and she fought a spectacularly skilled opponent. Mawana wrestled his sorcerer on the end, shields and fire flashing before their faces. But the last sorcerer attacked the Elite Guard and Linh's friends with relentless bolts of lightning, a one-person army.

A bright bolt shot forwards. A female Elite Guard screamed and was blasted off her feet. She landed on her back, her glassy eyes staring at the ceiling. Linh gaped. *No!* Not another one…

Movement drew her gaze from her body. The shield was shrinking before the male Elite Guard. The sorcerer could kill him next. And if the sorcerer turned that magic on her, she was dead. But she couldn't just stand there.

She took a step forward and bumped into something solid. Her sword extended before her, but her knee had hit something.

"Stay back!" the sorcerer ordered, his gaze intent on the Elite Guard, whom his lightning still struck.

Was the *sorcerer* shielding *her*?

"I do not believe in killing children," the man replied. "Even if you have killed two of my companions, not that those didn't deserve it."

"You almost killed my friends!" Linh objected.

"I was too slow to halt the magic when it pierced the Guardians' shield."

"Then stop trying to kill them! You're stronger than they are!" Linh demanded.

Lightning halted, and the man frowned at her, then turned to the Elite Guard, who made no move to attack.

"Then we have beaten them. And it is the people with the cursed swords I should be fighting."

He turned to face Lenaris. Linh lashed out. He stopped, as her magic hit him on the head. He turned to face her, baffled.

"She's my teacher," Linh explained. "I'm alive because of her. I'm *not* letting you hurt her."

"You could cut your way free of my shield to run me through, yet you don't," he said. "You strike me instead. Why?"

Linh shivered. "You're a one-man army. You're fucking scary."

The man frowned. As if he had never considered himself that way. Then he moved, magic tingled and Linh reached out instinctively. She was holding his magic, which gripped her around the waist, lifting her off her feet, over the sewer. She gaped at him.

"I doubt your magic will reach me from over there," he said, as he set her feet gently on the ground.

She sagged, and he frowned, the magic holding her upright. As if he truly didn't want to harm her...

"STAND BACK!" a woman's voice commanded.

Elite Guard ran towards Mawana, who leapt the water. Lenaris felled her distracted opponent and leapt behind Mawana. They landed on Linh's left. The terrifyingly powerful sorcerer and the one Linh had wounded, who stood hunched against the wall on the right, too weak to retreat, faced the Elite Guard. Both fell and didn't stir when they hit the ground.

Linh blinked, falling, as the sorcerer's magic no longer held her up. She braced herself with her hands as she hit the ground and turned to the sorcerers. Both lay still, chests rising and falling gently.

A sparkling dome shield formed around the unconscious sorcerers. Footsteps echoed, as many yellow-cloaked, Elite Guard women approached, probably the twenty the emperor had sent to free the palace women.

It was over, and Linh's friends had survived. But in the end, it was because that sorcerer had stopped attacking them when she pointed out they were losing. She'd survived because he'd chosen not to kill her. Who was he? This man who killed as readily as Vye, but was as determined not to harm a kid as Poran?

She sat, frowning at heat and sharp pains in her chest. Her bronze cuirass was covered in burns. She'd worn it for the victory parade. It might have saved her life. She gasped at the pain.

A yellow-cloaked figure leapt before her. She slumped, feeling sleepy. Her hands tingled intensely, and her chest felt like insects were walking on it as she sat. Then the sleepiness and tingling cleared, and the pain in her chest was gone.

Fiona was in front of her, smiling and crying and hugging her. Linh smiled, hugging her best friend back from the ground. Troy had tears in his eyes.

"Please don't ever risk your life like that again," he said.

Linh kissed him on the cheek. "I promise I won't, unless all our lives depend on it," she replied with a smile.

He smiled sadly and she rested her head on his shoulder as he hugged her. She was exhausted.

"Fiona," she said drowsily. "Do you mind if I use your boyfriend as a pillow for a bit longer?"

Fiona laughed. "I'll need to borrow him to kiss in a moment," she replied. "I couldn't have shielded Michael without him."

Linh looked up then.

Troy smiled sheepishly at Fiona. Unassuming, shy, polite Fiona, who knelt beside Troy and leant in to kiss him. Troy relaxed into her slender arms, reaching to hold her as he kissed her back. Then Fiona looked up and caressed Troy's cheek. He just looked at her, mesmerised.

On the edge of Linh's vision, another female Elite Guard knelt beside Mocco, who sat, drenched in sweat and trembling. The Guard wrapped her cloak around him.

"Sorry," Mocco said to Linh. "My shield started to fail during that burst of fire, and then the Elite Guard shield failed at several points, and I had to let go of yours to reinforce theirs."

"Then you saved us all," Fiona replied. "And…"

Linh turned, wondering why Fiona had cut off. There was nothing shy about the way Lenaris was kissing Mawana, or the way he was kissing her back.

"We're all bloody lucky to be alive," said Troy, shaking his head. "Come on, and he helped Linh stand and they and Fiona walked to where Michael lay.

An Elite Guard examined Michael. Under the Guard's ministrations, Michael blinked, and with Troy's help, he sat up. Linh sighed, relieved to see him conscious again.

"You all right mate?" Troy asked.

Michael frowned, then replied, "Yeah. There's three of you. It's confusing. And my head is killing me."

Troy seized him in a bear hug. Michael smiled and held him back.

"All of you did well," said Captain Rilmar.

Elite Guard women stood on the sewer platform across the water, their captive sorcerers floating upstairs beside them.

"The man who killed Tavorn is the most powerful sorcerer I have ever met," Captain Rilmar continued, meeting Linh's gaze. "In killing him with your flying shield, you may have saved us all. And you distracted a man almost as powerful. We owe our lives to you. We were outnumbered and outmatched."

Her gaze fell to Linh's sword and her mouth twisted, her gaze wrenching to Lenaris and Mawana. It dawned on Linh that she was... afraid.

"Never have I seen such weapons," she said quietly. "May I ask for what purpose you carry them?"

"To use when we go to Azula, to recover Ruarnon's parents, our King and Queen, and my father," Lenaris replied.

"Then you must do everything you can to keep them secret," Rilmar replied earnestly. "Some sorcerers, despite what you might have heard, are peaceable. Many are documented in the Secret Imperial Histories. They report how weapons such as these were forged late in the Sorcery War by sorcerers seeking to kill their rivals. Daring slaves stole them, and they fell into the hands of people who hated and feared magic-wielders. The massacres that resulted are unspeakable, and Narz's reign shall, if it has not already, revive old hatred of magic-wielders. Should *your* weapons fall into *their* hands..."

"So there were good sorcerers," said Fiona. "Did the Guardians spare them?"

"We believe so. The Guardians did not come to destroy all sorcerers. They came to bring peace. That meant destroying sorcerers bent on attaining power, conquest, and cruelty, but letting be all who wanted peace. We serve the emperors, but we are sworn to maintain the peace our ancestors brought long ago, for ordinary folk and peaceable sorcerers alike."

"That's a relief," Linh said softly, her head resting on Fiona's shoulder. "People at home were less sensible about witchcraft."

"I did not think you would share that prejudice when you were willing to fight alongside us," Captain Rilmar replied, "but there is a risk that people will try to imbue it in you and prompt you to kill sorcerers for them."

"Over. My. Dead. Body." Linh declared. "When they were trying to blast us apart or poke holes in me, I was prepared to kill them. But anyone who wants me to murder people is asking for a kick in the head."

And she would hit them in the head, hard, at the idea someone would want her to do what she'd just done to two men, to people who weren't actively trying to kill her and her friends. It was sickening enough when they *were* trying to kill you. She shuddered.

Captain Rilmar turned to eye Lenaris, who watched them, with Mawana.

"I am Tarlahn," Lenaris said simply. "My earliest memories are of witnessing my people's fear that we would be conquered by our enemies when deadly weapons sunk our fleet. I know what it is to live in fear, and I would not wish it on anyone, let alone help generate it."

"I will not kill them unless they try to kill others," Mawana added.

There was a pause, in which Captain Rilmar seemed thoughtful, and then she said, "It may be best if as few know of your ability to wield magic as possible, and certainly for your weapons to remain secret. I will keep your secrets."

"I too," the other two Guard chorused.

"Thank you," said Fiona.

Linh flinched. A figure was floating above the water, a figure wearing a yellow cloak, the Elite Guard woman the sorcerer had killed. The dead male Elite Guard drifted up beside Michael, floating after his fallen companion.

"I'm sorry I could not…." Mocco said softly, from Linh's right. He was on his feet, but Mawana supported him.

"So are we," Captain Rilmar replied gravely. "But your shield is the reason the rest of us are alive. Our shield's failure would have killed the rest of us without you reinforcing it. Thank you."

"Thank you for shielding us," Mocco replied.

Linh blinked. Young, mostly fair-skinned, blonde-haired women followed a female Elite Guard up the stairs across the sewer. The freed Timbalen women shivered and sped up at a loud crash from the direction Mawana had run from.

"I tracked the sorcerers to a warehouse near the harbour," Mawana said. "They were holding most of the women there, and when I told the Elite Guard how many sorcerers were inside, they said they would wait until they had enough numbers to combat the sorcerers before they attacked."

Captain Rilmar nodded. "We will take the young women to Central Square, from which their families will collect them, but we can give you directions to the palace."

She led everyone to a wooden plank over the sewer, where she waited for a stream of young women to pass, then they crossed to the stairs. Linh was still shaky on her feet. Stairs didn't appeal. Lenaris lifted her with a groan and Linh smiled.

"Thanks for helping," Linh said.

"*I* should have thought of it first," Lenaris replied, as she began lifting Linh up the stairs.

Ahead of her, Michael frowned and walked slowly, tapping with his feet before stepping onto the stairs, his vision still affected by his concussion. Troy guided him with one arm. They were a sorry lot, but Linh should be dead, Michael was lucky to be alive, and it was a miracle no one else was injured.

"Do me a favour," Linh said drowsily to Lenaris. "Never go running off after sorcerers again. You too," she added sternly to Mocco.

Mocco smiled shyly and they both promised.

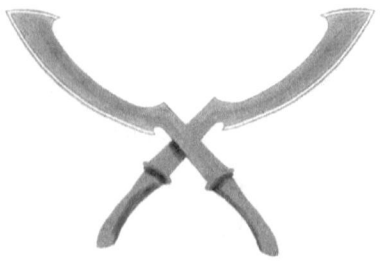

Chapter 28

At the Imperial Palace -Ruarnon

Ruarnon paced the Tarlahn Reception room. It was impossible to sit still. Logic told them their friends were taking so long to return because they had entered the sewers with the Elite Guard.

"What are they *thinking*?" Ruarnon demanded. "They have no idea how many sorcerers are down there! How can they hope to hold them off with shield magic? Or to fight them?"

"I am afraid there is little we can do, Benevolence," Tor replied patiently, his brows furrowed. "No one knows where they are exactly, and they have the protection of the Elite Guard they accompanied, whereas any soldiers we send will not. I would not like to test our soldiers' magical shields against unknown numbers of sorcerers."

"Of course not, because we have more sense than my friends!" Ruarnon retorted.

How was the danger to Ruarnon's soldiers more evident to them than Ruarnon's friends' danger was to themselves? And that very danger prevented Ruarnon from sending soldiers to help. There was nothing they could do. *Nothing*.

"Why would they take such a ridiculous risk?" Ruarnon asked, as their anger faded to exasperation.

"I suspect concern for his cousin sent Mocco after Mawana," Tor replied, "and perhaps Lenaris too. The younger four, I cannot explain. They are all reckless, brave, adventurous and loyal, but they are also more doubtful of their magic."

Ruarnon sighed and stopped halfway across the room. Tor was probably right. Which left their friends in they weren't sure where, in what state or why. And there was nothing they could do to find out.

Ruarnon sank into the red cushioned chair. How much longer were their friends going to take?

Sitting and waiting with nothing to do but wonder and worry and not knowing when it would end was the worst of it. It dawned on Ruarnon that if they stayed in Tarlah, this is what each day would be like, as they wondered what was happening to their friends and family in Azula.

When their parents were abducted, they had helped Omah prepare Tarlah for war, organised Tarlah City against siege, and united the Zaldeaan Realm. One all-consuming challenge after another, but no longer. The Zaldeaans benefited from Tarlahn rule and accepted it. Ruarnon had built relationships with Governors, and they knew that the loss of the governors' brother or cousin had them committed to Peace. The only threat of conflict within the Zaldeaan Realm was the return of the Zaldeaan army, or the next two generations of young men growing old enough to fill out their depleted, almost non-existent army, which couldn't happen any time soon. Zaldeaan pride would tempt revolt before then, but there was a simple solution: abdicate and withdraw the Tarlahn garrisons.

Governor Syenne had already recently restored calm by publicly killing assassins as they attempted to murder Governor Armar. Ruarnon had no doubt she could deal with warmongers, warlords and any who opposed their first female ruler. She could keep the governors in check and would honour and maintain her father's Peace. Ruarnon trusted her, and if the Zaldeaan army ever made it home and Tarlahn labourers and craftsmen returned to Tarlah, there was no reason for her not to be king. There remained only Ruarnon's duties in Tarlah, to rule their subjects and ensure their dynasty did not end, and that Tarlah was not left kingless by Ruarnon risking their life in the west.

But what of their duty to continue their dynasty? They saw the way Mawana and Lenaris looked upon, spoke to and felt about each other. They had never felt that way about anyone. Even Troy in his friendships was more affectionate than Ruarnon could be in any pretence of romance. Ruarnon didn't hug their friends. They weren't interested in holding hands, kissing, let alone having sex. Not with women, men or midluns. If they were honest, they wondered if they could ever look upon anyone the way Lenaris and Mawana had begun to look upon each other.

They had enjoyed not having to think about the possibility of marriage throughout their parents' absence and multiple wars because deep down, they knew it would involve no romantic feeling on their part. It would be a loveless marriage. Worse, the point of the marriage would be to breed Tarlahn heirs. Sex appealed just as little, and in a loveless marriage, even less to Ruarnon. Could they go through with that? Could they do that to someone else? When honestly thinking about it made them sick to their stomach?

It would all be an act of duty, nothing more. And aside from that duty, while Ruarnon's friends risked their lives on Ruarnon's expedition, they would oversee day to day ruling of two kingdoms, tax calculations, trade and disputes between high-ranking individuals. And they wouldn't care about any of it, because almost everyone they loved was in danger in the West.

At best, they would be distracted. At worst …they would resent their position depriving them of their heart's desire. And there was peace. It remained secure during Ruarnon's absence on this eastern voyage for weeks. Which proved other regents could provide it.

There must be another way. There could be a regent; Monin was regent now. But for heir… women who married women, men who married men and midluns in marriages where their partner's body did not complement theirs in reproducing children could adopt children, just as Tor had adopted Drake.

It was more controversial for an heir. Tradition said heirs were chosen by blood. But tradition didn't mention how extensively Advisors like Monin and king's like Ruarnon's father tested heirs. It didn't say what happened to heirs who failed that test. Royal adoption of an heir may have happened before. And it was a possibility now.

Ruarnon shifted in their seat. They were the best of their friends at magic. They had commanded soldiers well against sorcery crafting damars. And Omah had said that as child of the abducted king and queen, Ruarnon would give hope to their subjects during war with the Realm. If Ruarnon could be brave, so could anyone. The same logic held in the west. Ruarnon's leadership there would serve their expedition as well as Omah's had served Tarlah's army during the first stage of the war.

But Tarlah needed a regent and potential successor and heir. Monin was too old. Ruarnon wanted Tor to advise them in the West. But Companion Noma had served them loyally on the first western expedition under trying circumstances and would be home soon. But she and her husband were childless. Companion Noma could stand as regent, and adopt her nephew Drake as heir, successor and coregent. Monin would be more than capable of training, testing and advising both, though Ruarnon suspected that having taken a while to see Ruarnon's value, Monin would prefer Ruarnon came home alive.

Lenaris was an obvious choice for successor. Her strength and intelligence would serve Tarlah well. But her decision to enter the sewers today suggested that, like her father, her greatest strength was her ability to act decisively and take risks in wartime. She would do well in the West and would want to recover her father, but she may struggle as heir and coregent in peacetime Tarlah as much or more than Ruarnon.

Whereas Tor's son Drake was more cautious and level-headed, like his father, better suited for coregency during peace. And Tor was not imprisoned with unknown hope of rescue, like Lenaris' and Ruarnon's fathers. And Drake would have his mother, aunt and uncle to support him. Companion Noma could be the next king, Drake the next heir, and their coregency could begin if Ruarnon died.

Ruarnon *could* go west. Leading their soldiers into danger as Uncle Omah had, fulfilling their duty as heir, kin and regent by recovering their parents, aunt, uncle, cousin *and* they could help Lenaris recover her father. They could help their Australian friends as catalysts and support them in pursuing their way home. Having set their parents aside for nine months, Ruarnon could follow their family, their heart, and restore the rightful king and queen to Tarlah.

They smiled and straightened. But as their decision sank in, worry gnawed. They could only help their friends in the West if their friends made it out of the sewers. They waited anxiously.

"Their Benevolence is through these doors," a voice announced, after a long silence.

Ruarnon rose from their chair, their heart speeding up.

Mawana entered the Tarlahn Reception Room, supporting an exhausted Mocco, and smiled at Ruarnon, Lenaris smiling behind. The four Australians staggered through with her, Troy supporting an exhausted Linh, and they promptly sat on the sofa, Michael looking ill.

"What…" was all Ruarnon could get out.

"They are ok," Mawana replied, as he lowered Mocco into Ruarnon's chair. "Too much shield magic and Michael has had a nasty blow to the head. The healers tended Linh."

They what? Ruarnon turned to Linh and saw burn marks across the front of her cuirass.

"What in the name of Chaos were you thinking?" they demanded of Lenaris, who bit her lip. "Have you any idea how foolish you have been? Any of you?"

Mawana turned, eyeing her too, and Lenaris shifted awkwardly while Mocco gazed at the floor.

"I doubt I need to explain my capabilities to you, Mocco," Mawana said sternly, "but it appears I did not make myself clear; I did not need anyone's help. My tracking abilities allowed me to evade a group of sorcerers after leaving the warehouse. I crept there and back unharmed, whereas you put yourselves in danger, and you led our friends into it."

Lenaris' gaze fell to the floor.

"I am sorry, cousin," said Mocco, "and I am sorry, Ruarnon, for scaring you. I thought I could help. I had no idea how outmatched we were. The Elite Guard were not strong enough, and one of those sorcerers might have killed us all, had Linh not killed him first."

Ruarnon stared at Linh. She was pale, and she swallowed awkwardly. She had probably never hurt anyone before, let alone killed a man. But it sounded like it had been brave and necessary for her to do so. How had it come to that?

"I forgot myself," Mocco said slowly. "I should have left the Elite Guard to do their duty. Linh, Lenaris and Mawana helped the Elite Guard by attacking the sorcerers with their enchanted swords, but we weakened the Elite Guard because they had to shield us as well as themselves. We hampered their ability to do their duty. I should have trusted you to see yourself out."

Mawana's brows furrowed.

"I feared you had finally pit yourself against too much," Mocco added, and Ruarnon saw Mawana's expression soften.

"I am not just angry about you leading our friends into danger," Mawana added, "I am angry about you putting yourself in danger. That is why I told you to stay behind!"

Mocco smiled, but there were tears in his eyes. "You showed the only leadership of any of us this afternoon. But you caught me off-guard, and I failed to follow."

Mawana stepped forwards and embraced his cousin. When they stepped apart, Ruarnon realised Lenaris was glaring at Mawana.

"So *you* can put yourself in danger, insisting *you* will be fine, but *we* are not allowed to endanger ourselves? Do you doubt *our* ability?" she demanded.

Mawana sighed. "I know you can fight," he replied, "and Mocco's shields are formidable. Perhaps the two of you could help the Elite Guard. But you led the others into grave danger when they had far less training and confidence to meet it."

"I told them they did not need to come," Lenaris insisted.

"And if you saw your friends running towards a cliff and showing no sign of stopping, you'd let them keep running?" Troy asked seriously.

"You went *to protect* Lenaris and Mocco?" Tor asked, and Ruarnon turned to their Australian friends.

"They weren't exactly being sensible," Fiona replied. "I doubted how well their magic was going to work while they were worried about Mawana. That's why I thought we needed to be there to reinforce their shields."

"And Linh had the idea of attacking with our swords, and killed two sorcerers and wounded a third, then distracted the most powerful one, which saved everyone," Troy added.

"I don't want to have to do that *ever* again," Linh said forcefully. "Even if that powerful sorcerer thought the two I killed deserved it."

Ruarnon's mouth fell open and words failed them.

"We seriously underestimated you," said Lenaris, eyeing the Australians appraisingly. "I have done all this time. It did not occur to me that you were responsible enough to think of helping *us* or to be as brave as Linh proved today."

Ruarnon realised the problem. They had not been there to lead, and no one had stepped into their shoes. Mocco and Lenaris had focused on worry about Mawana, and their Australian friends worried about them all, and no one had explained themselves. They had chased each other into the jaws of Chaos. They needed Ruarnon's leadership in the West.

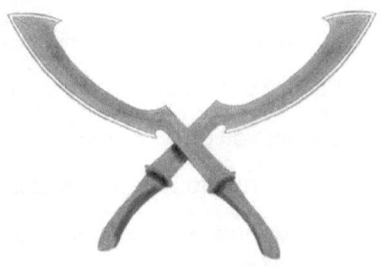

CHAPTER 29

DAXIUS -RUARNON

Ruarnon slept well that night. By the time they, Tor and their companions followed a servant to Yarath's questioning rooms in the morning, they were alert and ready to process whatever they learnt from the captured sorcerers. The servant led them to a cream stone room lit by torches, with a table across its middle, chairs cushioned with Timbalen velvet along one side, and a chair with hand and foot restraints of iron and leather on the other.

Yarath sat in the middle in a silk cushioned chair, his posture perfect and proud but tense. A silver-haired, grim-faced man sat on his right, radiating dislike. As Ruarnon sat left of the questioner and their friends took their seats, a pair of Elite Guard led a prisoner into the room. The prisoner was of medium height, his long blonde hair neatly tied back, his red silk cloak and cream tunic beneath it crumpled, but showing no signs of his involvement in the fighting.

The Elite Guard led him to the chair opposite, and he sat upright, coolly surveying his captors, while the Guard locked his wrists and ankles into iron restraints. He marked Yarath and Ruarnon. But he and frowned as Linh's mouth dropped open and Linh stared. Had Linh fought this man in the sewers?

"We start with the nice conversations," the silver-haired questioner said in a grating voice. "Got anything to say?"

"Why do you need information?" the sorcerer replied.

Ruarnon blinked. The sorcerer understood the questioner, and Ruarnon understood the sorcerer. How?

"Legends say your spy magic will tell you everything," the sorcerer continued. "Unless you have declined in the past few centuries or been degraded by intermarriage with non-magic wielders."

"Who do you think we are?" Yarath demanded.

"What passes for Guardians, in this day and age," the man replied calmly, looking Yarath in the eye. "Legends describing the retreat of the Guardians to these waters are well known. You, sir, we know to be a puppet. A non-magic wielder, king of powerful magic wielders to put his ignorant subjects at ease, while in truth, the Guardians or their descendants rule here."

"Why would they rule an empire?" Tor asked, and the silver-haired man glared at him. "The myths say they came as liberators, not conquerors."

"Because they failed in the West," the sorcerer replied. "The Sorcery War ended, but they left sorcerer-kings in power in the south, because they failed to uproot them. So they tried to fulfil their duties here, with refugees."

"This is His Greatness, Emperor Yarath," said the silver-haired questioner. "Who are you, that you dare speak to him so?"

"I am Daxius III, former King of Tiama, now governor under His Worthiness Narz, Commander of this failed expedition."

"Why would you be *former* king?" Yarath asked. "Did Narz enslave you?"

Daxius glared. "On the contrary, his policies have allowed me to admit to my subjects that I am a sorcerer. They allow me to heal my subjects openly and use magic to accurately investigate and protect them from crime within my kingdom. His Worthiness has a vision I do not, and I was content to abdicate my throne and take up service under him."

"What is this madness?" Yarath asked.

"It is the same talk we heard from sorcerers at Cauldron Island," Ruarnon replied.

"How did Narz know he needed sorcery-wielding damars to fight us?" the questioner demanded.

Daxius smiled. "He *Sees* as much as your Guardian Prophetess, perhaps more."

Ruarnon froze. Narz had the same ability as Red Cloak and Sryah? He could *See*? Had he *Seen* Lylah?

"Is this more mythology?" asked the questioner.

Daxius eyed Ruarnon and their friends, then frowned at the Timbalens.

"You expect me to believe that the Guardians' descendants now forget the spy magic which so devastated my ancestors during the Sorcery War? You *have* degenerated. And if what we met in battle is your entire force, then even though we are defeated, His Worthiness is correct that your Elite Guard can be eradicated."

"ERADICATED!" Yarath bellowed. "YOU CAME HERE TO *KILL US ALL?*"

"We are not like the Guardians. We do not kill women if we can help it, we do not kill children, and we do not kill non-magic wielders. We came only to kill your Guardians in their yellow cloaks, to protect ourselves from them. You should be glad of it, puppet emperor, glad you can be a true emperor after all these years."

"I AM NOT A PUPPET!" Yarath roared, standing and slamming his fist on the table. "THE ELITE GUARD SERVE *ME!* THEY ARE *MY* ARMY, *MY* PEACEKEEPERS, *MY* SUBJECTS! They are descendants of the Guardians, *not* the Guardians themselves!"

"And no more tolerant of sorcerers than their ancestors, I trust," Daxius replied.

"Greatness," said one of the Elite Guard, "may I speak to the prisoner?"

"Yes," Yarath snapped, his face flushed, taking deep breaths as he sat, and Ruarnon realised how truly on edge he was.

"We have only detained those who use their powers to harm others," the Elite Guard said to Daxius. "Sorcerers who do not harm others are watched, especially young ones who do not attend our school while they learn control of their powers. But those who do not break his Greatness' laws are let be."

Daxius frowned. "What trick is this? You do not have the humility to adopt such tactics! Would you feign sympathy with my interests to gain my trust? You would use it to manipulate me into telling things you wish to know?"

"I would inform the ignorant of our creed," the Elite Guard replied, while his companion stared intently at the wall over the emperor's head. "You are misguided, Daxius."

Daxius smiled, his eyes glinting aggressively. "I admit, you are more decent than I thought, using tricks of conscience to have me divulge information. But then, you Guardian rulers have a long history and doubtless have learnt many tricks in your time. You will have to torture me if you wish to learn vital information."

"Shall I ready the irons, the whips or the rack?" the questioner asked the emperor forcefully.

Yarath was seething. He was a proud man who had been frightened by sorcerers, and now he was offended and provoked, so Ruarnon took a risk and answered, "None. Unless you wish to play into his hands."

Yarath blinked at him, and the questioner's features narrowed as he eyed them darkly. Ruarnon took a deep breath and speculated aloud.

"He is testing you. One of your Elite Guard just suggested they are decent and have consciences, which Daxius doubts. If he can easily provoke you into torturing him to serve your interests, he will have his proof that Guardians are as hateful of sorcerers as he believes."

"You are very young to be ruler of Tarlah," said Daxius, eyeing Ruarnon with a penetrating gaze, "yet I am starting to believe it is true. I suppose you would claim these Elite Guard are no threat to sorcerers?"

Ruarnon blinked away their surprise at Daxius knowing who they were, and answered, "The Elite Guard protect the empire and threaten none outside it. But I am surprised sorcerers exist here, for

I know of none in Tarlah. I would have to take the Elite Guard's word about how they treat sorcerers."

Daxius blinked, and Ruarnon realised Daxius was testing them too. He was demonstrating outstanding courage given his circumstances, incredible self-possession and calm, and he was keen to learn what he could of his captors. He seemed to trust his own judgement, which would make it easier to persuade him of the truth of Narz's ruthlessness.

"What did Narz tell you of the Timbalen Empire?" Ruarnon asked.

"That the Guardian's descendants rule it and were powerful enough to attack us without their creature armies. That they hid away here, ashamed of their failure in the West and frightened of the sorcerers who rule there. But the prophetess was monitoring the growth of His Worthiness' power and becoming uneasy. Soon the threat they narrow-mindedly assumed he posed would be so great that their sense of duty would force them to invade us.

"So we brought the battle to the Guardians' empire. We knew they would not suffer their young, weak or elderly to be harmed and would meet us at sea, where their casualties would be minimal. In contrast, our children, wives and anyone suspected of being a sorcerer would be cut down if they brought the battle to our homeland."

So Narz knew Lylah watched him and was concerned about his growing power...

"Your objective was to defeat the Elite Guard here rather than wait for them to invade Azula?" Tor asked.

"That is correct," Daxius replied, "though defeat is inadequate, we had hoped to eliminate them."

One of the Elite Guard shifted, and both men's calm expressions wavered. Yarath was shaking, red in the face. The questioner's eyes blazed with fury.

"Take him out and execute him! NOW!" Yarath ordered the Elite Guard.

Both men blanched.

"Yarath," Ruarnon said, standing and refusing to remain silent, as Yarath lost control, "Send him back to his cell and take time to consider it. There is much he can tell you."

"He is mad!" Yarath yelled. "A mad sorcerer who would kill *all* of my Elite Guard! He admitted it! Kill him!"

Ruarnon took a deep breath, turned to the Elite Guard and said, "Take him back to his cell."

Both Elite Guard blinked, and one said, "Greatness, our Code. Their Benevolence is reminding us to keep to it."

"GET THAT MAN OUT OF MY SIGHT!" Yarath roared, leaping from his chair.

He wrenched the door open and slammed it into the wall as he stormed out. Ruarnon exhaled with relief that he had enough self-control to withdraw. The questioner glared mutinously at Ruarnon and departed. The Elite Guard unbound Daxius and marched him from the room. The former western ruler eyed Ruarnon with interest as he left.

"That was well done, Benevolence," Tor said when the door closed. "Hopefully, His Greatness will realise he is in no fit state for this and put it off until he is calmer."

"And if he doesn't?" Troy asked.

Facing an attack that exposed the previously invincible Elite Guard as vulnerable, hearing that the man behind it was delusional and bent on destroying the Elite Guard, whom he mistook for Guardians, seemed to have unhinged Yarath. At this moment, he was probably as unstable as Narz himself. Ruarnon had to calm him before he made a decision as rash as Narz's.

"I need to speak to Yarath," they said, standing.

"I shall accompany you, Benevolence," Tor replied.

"Wait here," Ruarnon told their friends as they and Tor left the room.

They guessed Yarath would be in his private quarters and asked a passing servant for directions. The woman led them up a staircase of white marble and bowed them down the corridor. Ruarnon found Yarath pacing up and down a richly furnished sitting room overlooking a lake. The empress sat on a couch, her embroidery abandoned as she talked calmly to Yarath, but her features were narrowed with worry.

The couple turned as Ruarnon stepped nervously into the doorway, anticipating Yarath to be furious at them for countermanding his order to execute Daxius. But Yarath's anger had disappeared. Premature lines stood out on his face, and there were dark circles around his eyes. Worry dominated his expression.

"How have you dealt with him?" Yarath asked softly. "When those fiends arrived north of your country on a killing rampage, how did you deal with it?"

Ruarnon sighed and shook their head. "I have always lived in a smaller, weaker kingdom used to facing a more powerful enemy. I am used to the odds being stacked against me, and though the damars were a terrible shock, we had the resources to slay them, and some of your phalanxes as additional support."

Yarath turned and stared out the window. "I kept too many Elite Guard back, at every stage. That is how the ships came so close to Timbalen Island. Despite the terror they evoke, I underestimated sorcery-wielding damars. And when I realised their power, I was reluctant to send all my Elite Guard against them.

"There are only four hundred Elite Guard Ruarnon. My commanders estimated the damarian numbers at a thousand, with at least fifty sorcerers in addition. Narz knew our numbers. This fleet was calculated to destroy us. The only reason we won the sea battle was that they sent most of their sorcerers to shore, and your suggestion to use power bows against shield magic.

"But the shore battle...." Yarath paced the room. "My commanders were convinced that if they put most Elite Guard on the beach and left reserves along the wall to attack from above, they could win swiftly. But the enemy landed in force, shielded, and they almost encircled us before I put enough Elite Guard onto the field. Twelve Guard died of exhaustion trying to destroy damarian shields. Seven ships were lost before that. *Seven*!

"My commanders and I were too horrified by damars wielding sorcery to think logically, too slow to respond, and we failed to refine our tactics. I have never seen commanders at each other's throats with such fear and anger before, disputing orders, producing wild suggestions. Sending in regular soldiers was a suggestion we should have thought of, yet it was a Guard, new to his position who suggested it."

Ruarnon sighed. Yarath had won, but the invasion had demoralised him.

"I downplayed the importance of your tactics," he added, meeting Ruarnon's gaze. "My commanders knew we could try charging magical shields, but having already lost more Elite Guard than in every previous conflict and knowing that a charge by ordinary soldiers would be effective, we chose that option instead.

"And then you came. Your soldiers proved that charging shields was highly effective, and you gave my commanders the confidence to order the Elite Guard to try it. The battle that looked set to drag on until it cost me many more Elite Guard was finished in a morning."

"Narz is the kind of enemy who leaves you stunned on your first encounter," Ruarnon replied, "and shocked and struggling to understand him at every other encounter. It has been over eight months since I first heard his name and fought his underlings, so I have had time to accept."

The emperor exhaled deeply and slumped into a couch. "What do I do now?" he asked, his tone utterly lost.

Ruarnon stood mutely, unsure what to say.

"You continue questioning sorcerers," the empress replied, "or better yet, you get others to do so, so we have the intelligence to understand our enemies, at which point you will be able to decide what to do about them."

"Thank you, dear," Yarath said gently. "Ruarnon, I should like you to continue questioning the sorcerers. I can only assume having done it before allows you to be calm enough to take in the madness they come out with and make sense of it, and I ask you to do so here."

"May I ask that your questioner leaves the questions to me?" Ruarnon asked, and Yarath eyed them critically and nodded.

"Thank you. I shall report to you on everything they say, but also on what I deduce."

Yarath nodded, thanking them, and Ruarnon excused themself, motioning Tor to accompany them. They returned to the questioning room.

They weren't sure if Yarath's rage abating was a good thing or not, when it had given way to worry, fear and doubt. The man was terribly shaken, and Ruarnon hoped he would take the needed time to pull himself together before he decided how to respond to Narz's invasion.

Ruarnon entered the questioning room to find another sorcerer in the chair. Two Elite Guard stood on either side of it, and the sorcerer eyed their friends with a puzzled expression. Ruarnon's Australian friends fidgeted, nervous and uncomfortable, while Lenaris, Mawana and Mocco waited calmly.

This sorcerer was older, his face care lined, and fear flashed in his eyes, as Ruarnon entered. The man wore only a linen shirt and linen pants, a commoner, and a chance to see how what they had been told tallied with Daxius' claims.

"Why did you come here?" Ruarnon asked.

The man licked his lips. "I'm a sorcerer, aren't I? I've no reason to love Guardians. And someone had to lead the young ones. There's too many young ones in His Worthiness' service, too many dreamers."

"Is that how you would describe most of your companions?" Ruarnon asked.

"Many, perhaps not most," the man replied.

"If these 'dreamers' came to defeat a threat to Narz's vision of sorcerers practising magic openly," said Tor, "why did others come?"

The man frowned. "Most people are too scared to use their powers openly. Some will heal for His Worthiness, even enforce the law for him, but confronting Guardians? Few have the nerve. I've never been so frightened in my life, but the young ones needed a leader. The others...

"I'm guessing you were born to status son, but many who aren't dream of it or want more than they have. And many wouldn't say no to gold. He pays well; King Narz does. Half what came didn't care much for his vision. Mercenaries serve only one master, gold, and their vision is lots of it. Others wanted power."

"What sort of power?" Ruarnon asked.

"Being captains in the greatest army on earth appealed to a few. And His Worthiness' power is growing, so new governorships are becoming available, and all number of advisory positions, all well-paying, come with a good house. There's many won't say no to that, and involvement in this expedition improves credentials for those positions."

"They're mercenaries," Linh explained. "In our world, in ancient times, there were a lot of professional soldiers who didn't fight for their king and country, but anyone who paid them, even against their countrymen. As sorcerers come into the open, sorcerer-mercenaries are starting to exist."

A paid force of sorcerers trained in combat... the idea sent shivers down Ruarnon's spine.

Ruarnon questioned many sorcerers over the next few days, building on the information they would report to Yarath, then it was time for personal questions. They had Daxius brought in first and drew a deep calming breath before they began.

"Do you know the name Selenia?" they asked.

Suspicion flashed in Daxius' eyes. "Of course I know it."

"You had orders concerning her? What were they?"

"To locate her and bring her back to His Worthiness."

"Are you aware that she is a sixteen-year-old girl?"

"Her whole family are a grave threat. A powerful enchantment safely restrains the others, but Selenia is at liberty, and she is the key that will unlock the annihilation of my kind by Guardians."

He seemed ignorant that he was unclear of the exact nature of threat Selenia posed.

"How did you intend to locate and capture her?" Ruarnon asked.

"She was touched by the enchantment which holds her parents. I could have detected a trace of it on her, but she was not among the nobles we abducted on Bareek Island. Before I could infiltrate the palace to locate her, a devastating new tactic on the shore hastened our defeat. So we seized women in the temple and as many young women as we could from the capital, hoping to take Selenia by chance."

"And if you didn't have her then?"

Daxius' eyes widened. "You *know* where she is. She is not near Timbalen Island."

"She has never been here," Ruarnon replied. "What were you going to do with the women if you did not have Selenia?" they pressed.

"Offer their safe return in exchange for Selenia. If they refused, I know sleep magic so powerful that it makes people look dead. I would have returned the hostages appearing dead to different parts of the city until Selenia was brought forward."

"And how would you ensure their safety in the meantime, when some of your numbers are motivated only by greed and lust for power?" Ruarnon asked.

"Some are criminals, and they and those after power care for one thing above all else, themselves. They merely needed to know which body parts they would lose for which offences to keep them in line," Daxius replied firmly.

Ruarnon's eyes widened. Daxius seemed as captivated by Narz's vision of magic being used for the good of humanity as Poran, but he wasn't as naïve by half.

"What are you thinking?" Daxius asked.

"I am wondering how Narz deceived someone as intelligent as you. Dargus and Poran were more naïve."

Daxius' mouth opened. He knew Poran.

"You were his king," Ruarnon remembered.

"He was a good man," Daxius replied earnestly. "What did you do to him?"

"I told him the truth and set him free to warn other sorcerers against becoming tools in savage attacks on people who mean Narz no harm. Did you know that Poran helped transport damars that attacked the women and children on the Zaldeaan coast while their men fought us in Tarlah?"

Daxius frowned. "He did not. Narz put his expedition under the leadership of a man I was suspicious of. Lord Vye's orders were to display the damars when he issued His Worthiness' declaration of war. He was to unleash them only against soldiers assembled to fight in pitched battle. But my spies tell me he sent Dargus, Poran and any sorcerer of good reputation home early, then unleashed many damars. Which is true, is not it?"

His gaze was distant and conflicted, but he looked up to meet Ruarnon's gaze when Ruarnon replied. Ruarnon nodded, feeling growing respect for the man.

"Luvaras preserve us. His Worthiness has *Seen* enough of the Zaldeaans to know of their bloodthirsty appetite for conquest, their proud history of slaughter. But that does not justify exposing Zaldeaan women and children to the invasions their men carry out on other kingdoms. It makes Vye as low as they. And far more dangerous because he defied His Worthiness. And the fact only my spies reported this means he has bought the silence of sorcerers who witnessed his actions."

"Why did Narz invade the Zaldeaan Realm?" Ruarnon asked.

"He knew the prophetess had watched Zaldeaan bloodshed for centuries with despair. And that Guardians would send only conventional soldiers to fight Zaldeaans, rather than magic crafters against non-magic crafters. When his Worthiness rose to power, the prophetess gained the chance to dispatch the Zaldeaan army by bewitching it to fight Narz's conventional soldiers. She could have destroyed the Zaldeaans and countered Narz in one stroke. But we lured the Zaldeaans to their coast and abducted them first."

Narz believed the Zaldeaan army would be used against him because Lylah had power and reason to send it? But if Lylah, Flariah and Sryah could control creature armies, and sorcerers could control damars... could human armies be controlled the same way?

"What proof did you have of the Guardians intending to invade the West?"

"The Galvations sent a ship east, seeking Guardian aid. His Worthiness searched the seas for weeks for it and any sign of Guardians. First, he found rumour of Elite Guard, then he *Saw* the Zaldeaans and prophetess, the creature armies, and at last the Guardians themselves, training in offensive magic and rallying their army. So we planned our eastern invasions in haste."

"He wasn't searching for Selenia?"

"His Worthiness sent someone to her home city of Tira to check on the enchantment binding her family and realised she had escaped. That is why *we* were searching for her."

Ruarnon exhaled deeply. Fear of Guardians responding to an actual Galvation call for aid had turned Narz's gaze east... He had probably searched for Elite Guard around Tarlah, *Seen* Lylah, and learnt of the conquests that united the Zaldeaan Realm and the Wars. He assumed pitting the Zaldeaans against a sorcerer-king was the most ethical way Lylah could bring peace to Ruarnon's continent and wage war against Narz's conventional army.

"There were two letters sent to a Zaldeaan lord," said Tor, "the first suggesting the abduction of the Tarlahn King and Queen to spark war during Peace, the second suggesting the abduction of our Regent. What do you know of them?"

"Nothing. The Zaldeaans abducted the Tarlahns. Lord Vye merely had his people gathering intelligence take the Tarlahns off Zaldeaan hands and shipped them to Azula."

"Narz signed those letters, and that was the first time we heard his name," Ruarnon added. "Even the Zaldeaans did not know who Narz was."

Daxius' brows furrowed at the table. "Then Vye lied. He must have sent the letters himself. Did he do anything else in the Tarlahn-Zaldeaan war that may have overstepped his orders?"

"He murdered twenty-three Zaldeaan soldiers to convince the Zaldeaan army that he could perform magic and cow them into following him," Ruarnon replied.

Daxius paled. "My spies mentioned a Zaldeaan ship being set on fire for reasons they could not explain. They failed to mention sorcery, but is that how the fire started?"

"It is."

Daxius shook his head. "I should have acted more on my instincts. I feared his potential for cruelty, but I underestimated it, and His Worthiness was too distracted to see it. The Zaldeaans, they are your subjects now?"

Ruarnon nodded.

"Then your subjects have suffered at Vye's hands. Please warn His Worthiness. There is only one kind of sorcerer in the east who would treat the lives of non-magic wielders with such contempt, the God-Kings of the Far South and their high-ranking relatives.

"The God-Kings claim their powers are evidence of their divinity and that all sorcery power comes from royal blood. They will view His Worthiness' vision as the deepest of insults because it involves sorcerers using their magic to heal magic non-crafters and protect them from crime. Yet the God-Kings view non-magic crafters as slaves.

"Vye must be a low-ranking sorcerer, from a kingdom ruled by a God-King, and the only thing that will have attracted him to His Worthiness' service will be rank and power. He will leave a trail of abuse and death everywhere he walks in which His Worthiness does not have a clear view of the bodies. His Worthiness needs to execute him for murder before he harms anyone else. I implore you, as someone whose own subjects have suffered at Vye's hands, send word of everything we have discussed about Vye to His Worthiness."

Ruarnon had struggled to believe Poran's claims that Vye was wicked and everything bad that happened in the Zaldeaan Realm was his fault. But Daxius clearly agreed with him and Ruarnon was more inclined to trust Daxius' judgement.

"I shall send word to the Zaldeaans to pass on to Narz."

"Then take this ring. It contains my seal and will tell His Worthiness that I am the source of the news. He will trust it."

Ruarnon accepted the gold ring from Daxius' right hand, and the act of trust on Daxius' part prompted them to ask something that had nagged at them in recent weeks.

"Daxius, if Narz questioned my parents about the Elite Guard, and they have already told him everything they can, why are they still prisoners?"

Daxius sighed. "I have tried to raise the matter with him and Companion Pamoran's release. But he will not hear me. He is irrationally evasive of the subject. I do not know why."

"Are they well?" Ruarnon asked.

Daxius smiled. "Of course! We have no reason to harm them. I spoke with them on several occasions."

"What of Companion Pamoran?" Lenaris asked. "Of my father?"

Daxius face fell. "His is imprisoned on Mt Ice. The soldiers suspected he could wield magic and were reluctant to imprison him near His Worthiness. His accommodation will not be so pleasant, but he lives."

"What of my Aunt Merlah?" Ruarnon asked.

Daxius frowned. "I do not know that name. I am not aware of anymore Tarlahns imprisoned in Azula, just those three."

Ruarnon slumped. Their aunt, uncle and cousin should have reached Narz's custody before Daxius set sail for the Timbalen Empire. Daxius knowing nothing of them suggested they were imprisoned with the Zaldeaan army and may be far harder to free.

"Can I ask you something?" said Michael and Daxius turned to him. "If you don't believe the sorcerers in the south of your continent are Gods, and you accept that they have a magic crafting army, then why are you so convinced the Elite Guard are Guardians? If sorcerers can pose as Gods, why can't they pose as emperor's servants?"

Daxius eyed him in wonder. "I was going to ask why they would. But all of us who follow His Worthiness are but servants in the end, and he wishes to serve his people. It is possible. But why would the Elite Guard possess armies of creatures enchanted during the Sorcery War? How else did they obtain them?"

He turned to the two Elite Guard on either side of him, who frowned.

"They didn't," Ruarnon replied. "I suspect they know nothing about them, just as I knew nothing of the creature army living on Cauldron Island not two days from my capital city. I have been to both islands with creature armies, and I saw only one person guarding each army, and they may be *actual* Guardians, but the Elite Guard are not."

"But Elite Guard claim Guardian descent!" Daxius protested.

"No," Ruarnon replied. "The emperor claims their Guardian descent."

Daxius turned to the men on either side of him. "What do you believe is the source of your origins?"

"The source of power is of no relevance," the man on the left replied. "It is how it is used that matters. We have our code."

Daxius' mouth tightened, but Ruarnon could see the worry in his eyes. "By that logic," Daxius replied, "we were no threat to you in our homeland."

"You were not," replied the other Elite Guard.

"And this is truly what you, Guard believe?" Daxius asked, eyeing them both. "This is your creed?"

"It is," the other replied.

"And if you caught parents teaching their children sorcery, what would you do?"

"Offer them a place at our school," the first Elite Guard replied. "The safest way to have children using their powers is under our supervision and by our creed, which we teach them."

Daxius' eyes became distant. "You integrated them. Whomever you once were, you controlled sorcerers by integrating, training and taking them on as yourselves. Once your reputation as Guardians was established, it was safe for you to raise young sorcerers, and you could give them a future. But why was your army mobilising eight months ago?"

"Perhaps Narz witnessed the Selection Festival," an Elite Guard replied, "an annual event at which all Elite Guard gather and compete in magical competitions, which historically determined candidates for available commands within our ranks."

"What of the ship the Galvations sent?"

"The East Islanders discovered a shipwreck in the reefs some leagues south of their islands, before the Selection Festival," the second Elite Guard replied. "They could not identify its origin and found no survivors. It may be your Galvation ship."

"You would have me believe that *every* eastern expedition His Worthiness sent was mistaken?" Daxius asked, his features tightening and face draining of colour.

"No one has claimed with any confidence to have met Guardians this far east for centuries," the first Elite Guard replied. "Even in the empire, most people do not pretend to know what became of them after the Sorcery War."

"But in the sewers… I killed one of them, a young woman. You are telling me she was a sorcerer, a protector of her people, like His Worthiness' Keepers of the Peace?"

"Indeed."

"How did this happen? The evidence Narz *Saw* was compelling…."

"My friends believe it was compelling to him because he views the world through a lens of extreme fear and expects everyone to oppose him as a sorcerer-king," Ruarnon replied.

"Of course he does. That is true of many in the West."

"Then his mistake was to assume that the east is also hateful of sorcerers. History since the Sorcery War here apparently involved the Elite Guard integrating sorcerers in the empire. All sorcerers on my continent live in the North Lands, and their Zaldeaan neighbours pretend they don't craft magic. Most non-magic crafters believe sorcerers to be a thing of myth, and real sorcerers live happily in their reclusive communities."

Daxius stared into the distance. What he believed warred with all he had been told, but Ruarnon suspected he knew the truth. He was just struggling to accept it. If only Ruarnon could persuade Yarath to let them take Daxius on their Recovery Expedition. That would neutralise Vye, who was responsible for the murder of at least twenty-three Zaldeaans, if not the deaths of every innocent the damars had killed in the Zaldeaan Realm.

Daxius was probably everyone's best hope at making Narz see reason and calling off his war against the East. It seemed Narz had trusted him with everything except the true nature of the threat Selenia posed and he was of high rank. But Yarath was too afraid of Daxius. He would never release him.

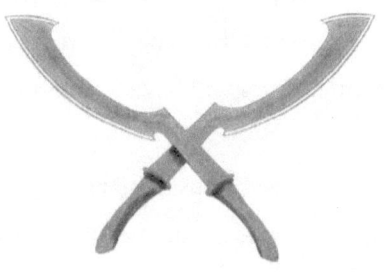

Chapter 30

The Future -Ruarnon

N arz has weakened the two greatest armies in this part of the world," Yarath said to Ruarnon, his face haggard as he sat heavily on his yellow silk cushioned chair in the Tarlahn Reception Room. "He is expanding his kingdom and crushing all possible resistance. Driven by fear, he will expect us to be vengeful, and his pre-emptive strike shows he will not wait for proof we are coming. His ambition, fear, weapons, and madness threaten us so long as he lives. To ensure the safety of my people, Narz must die."

Ruarnon shivered. Yarath was thinking precisely as Narz did, though after being invaded by a delusional sorcerer-king, Ruarnon supposed he had cause to feel that way.

"We have destroyed his sorcery-wielding damars here, and his damarian armies were wiped out in their eastern incursions. He will be frantically trying to breed more, and if you intend to free the Zaldeaan army from his forced service, that will weaken him further. We will invade Azula, now, while Narz is weak.

"My commanders are already planning, as are my Elite Guard captains. We will help you free the Zaldeaans and your parents if we can. But I suggest you return home, Ruarnon, and ready your expedition. The formal treaty will have to wait until the war is over."

Ruarnon's fists clenched. Was there no way to deter him?

"What if your invasion is as successful as Narz's?" Ruarnon asked.

"We will gather intelligence first and stay offshore. We will not strike until we have identified his weaknesses and know where to direct our killing blow."

Ruarnon stared across the room, unseeing. Narz's invasion of imaginary enemies in the empire had frightened Yarath sufficiently to turn him into a real enemy. And the problem with Yarath's logic was that he was right; even if Narz realised every eastern invasion had been a mistake, he would expect the Timbalens to retaliate. Narz would be preparing to meet the Timbalens in battle.

Ruarnon tried to dissuade Yarath all afternoon, but it was impossible. In the end, they only managed to persuade the emperor to take Elite Guard advice and send the captured sorcerers to imprisonment in the North Lands when the western invasion began.

Ruarnon took a reprieve in their guest chambers and finished a letter to Selenia, which described a colourful city of graceful beauty and Narz's sorcerers' attempts to abduct her. They argued it was essential for her to learn her role in Narz's war, now that the

Timbalen army was preparing to invade Narz and expressed the hope that they could see her before they set sail for Azula.

They gave the letter to a servant, then walked through grand corridors of white marble, feeling like a greater opportunity to make peace than unifying the Zaldeaan Realm had slipped between their fingers.

As they walked, Timbalen messengers would be leaving the palace, delivering orders to the city's weaponsmiths and armourers to ensure the Timbalen army was equipped. More messengers would be taking ship to summon levied soldiers from across the empire. Every Elite Guard would be preparing to travel, and soon, the largest army in history would mobilise and prepare to sail west.

Ruarnon strode into the Tarlahn Lounge, where their friends and Companion Tor sat on the edges of red silk cushioned seats. Their faces fell at Ruarnon's expression.

"Yarath has reasoned without me. He is going to invade Azula. He will help free the Zaldeaans to weaken Narz and to free my parents and Pamoran if he can. And with the Elite Guard intending to bring the Second Sorcery War west, my mind will unravel if I stay in Tarlah. I will lead the Recovery Expedition myself and restrain the Timbalens, Galvations, and sorcerers wherever I can, because I fear Yarath's declaration of war will place far more lives at stake than King Kuyra's.

"I will name Companion Noma regent in Tarlah and Advisor Monin regent in the Zaldeaan Realm. If I die in the West, Companion Noma will take the crown, and Drake will be her heir. I will have these conditions set out in an agreement signed by the Royal Council, myself, Drake and the Generals. Anyone who does not wish to sign it will be banished here. I will not allow the chance of disagreement over the succession.

"I will also hold a Council of the War Leaders and tell the Governors that if we should be so fortunate as to succeed in recovering the Zaldeaan army, I will abdicate the Zaldeaan throne, leaving the crown with the High Priestess, and make it known that I intend for Syenne to be king. I will insist on the Governors and the Royal Council signing documents for that. And I will, I am glad to say, be there to help you free your father Lenaris, and to help you four get home and play my part as a catalyst for peace in the West."

Troy fell backwards into a chair, with relief, Ruarnon assumed. Linh and Michael's postures relaxed, and Fiona smiled. Mawana smiled approvingly, Mocco nodded, looking apprehensive, and Lenaris studied Ruarnon curiously, her mouth open in surprise, as Ruarnon expected. Tor's expression was grave, as he replied, "I do not think there was another honourable decision to be made. May I accompany your Benevolence?"

Ruarnon smiled, despite everything. "I hoped you would. That is why I did not name you successor."

"Monin is going to have a fit," Tor added.

Ruarnon nodded. "I will listen to his objections, but they will not move me. My head will be of little service to Tarlah or the Realm when my heart lies in the west and my mind is fixated on it."

Tor bowed his head in acknowledgement. "That is very wise, Benevolence. I anticipated having to advise you of that myself."

"I will spend our return journey to Tarlah thinking of reasons why the Council of Elders should send me," said Mocco.

"But not why they must send me with you?" Mawana asked.

"You will not let them stop you either way," Mocco replied, the corners of his curling in the hint of a smile. "But I have hopes of becoming an Elder one day."

Mawana laughed.

"I will be breaking more traditions and customs," said Ruarnon.

Their decision to abandon their duty to stay safe and to potentially delegate kingship of Tarlah was a far cry from what their father and uncle had taught them. They hoped to have the chance to explain to their parents and that Urmilian and Corina would understand.

"Your succession may be by adoption under any circumstances," said Lenaris. "I did not know how to tell you that, but I could see it."

Ruarnon smiled at the extent to which she saw and understood them. It was a shame they hadn't had that conversation, especially when she had invited them to confide in her. But the idea had been too painful, with everyone else committed to sailing west and Ruarnon to remain in Tarlah on their own.

"Traditions come from history," Linh asserted, "and nothing in the history of Tarlah has produced traditions that relate to your situation Ruarnon. Appointing a conditional ruler and heir is setting a precedent, so that if another Tarlahn ruler finds themself in a situation like yours, they can look to your example to deal with it."

"I am not sure Companion is the best position for you Linh," said Tor. "In some ways, you appear to be preparing to become Advisor."

Linh beamed with pride and Tor smiled back at her.

"Even in this, you think I am leading my people?" Ruarnon asked Linh, and she nodded.

"Listen to Linh; she knows everything," Troy instructed with the same confidence and seriousness.

Linh's mouth opened, and she pushed him, assuming he was making fun of her. Troy smiled, and Ruarnon suspected he sincerely meant what he said.

"You lot sure you can handle this?" Michael asked their older friends, nodding sideways at Linh and Troy. "We're about to spend three months at sea together."

"I think we will manage," Ruarnon replied. "We can always banish you four to the boats and tow you along behind if we need to," they added solemnly, to four surprised faces and their elder friends and Tor's smile.

"You are sure about everything?" Lenaris asked Ruarnon seriously.

"I have known what I wanted all along. It just took me a long time to realise I could choose it and how to make it happen."

Ruarnon smiled, feeling oddly, despite all the dangers yet to be faced, and obstacles yet to be overcome, at peace with themself and their circumstances. Weight fell off their shoulders, knowing they were about to uphold only certain duties, instead of juggling every duty at once.

They breathed more easily knowing they were about to follow their heart, support their four Australian friends and seek their family and Lenaris' father in the west, in the company of most people they held dear. They would need that company, and their role as catalysts for peace would be crucial, when Emperor

Yarath's army set out to meet Narz, his damars and sorcerers and the Second Sorcery War began in the west.

Acknowledgements

The final stages of this book's editing suffered a seven month delay due to me having long covid. So firstly, I'd like to thank everyone who checked in and listened patiently, and everyone who made me feel heard and my illness validated when the first two doctors tried to gaslight me into thinking I had depression. Special thanks to colleagues who were patient and supportive of me at work. And thanks to new my doctor for listening, diagnosing me correctly and his continued support with managing chronic illness.

Secondly, thanks to my beta readers. There were pacing and some character development issues when Adam and Kel and first got their hands on Secrets of the Sorcery War. Adam's feedback helped me keep an eye on the mystery of Narz's motives and Kel helped me cut down the cast of thousands I am want to write in early drafts. Meanwhile, Reggie's feedback helped with technical edits and Erin's assured me that my plot and characters had matured sufficiently to be released into the world.

Thanks to book one readers for coming back, especially if you left a review! If your review contained some constructive feedback, I have tried to bare those points in mind while editing this book, while giving you things you enjoyed about book 1. I hope I succeeded in both! Which brings me to…

PLEASE LEAVE A REVIEW!

A few sentences of your overall impressions of Secrets of the Sorcery War can indicate to other readers whether or not it's likely their cup of tea. So I'd appreciate you spreading the word by telling fantasy lovers in your life about it and or leaving a review on; Goodreads/ BookBub/ StoryGraph/ and or a bookstore. (Trilogy links via my books page and QR code)

About the Author

Elise Carlson's love of adventure began with a childhood diet of Narnia and teenage years spent playing Final Fantasy. Fascinated with the ancient world, Elise majored in Archaeology and History at University. Then it was time to travel (Europe, Egypt and Turkey).

Their need to earn a living and a desire to work alongside enthusiastic and imaginative counterparts –children— resulted in a teaching career. They taught in Australia, moved to England for exploration of castles, ruins and stately homes and then New Zealand to explore volcanic areas, mountains and to visit Hobbiton. They are now living, teaching and writing in their native Australia.

To stay in touch with Elise and get *Rebellion is Due,* about a turbulent night in Tarlah in Ruarnon's father's youth, sign up Elise's newsletter.

Far from being permitted to enter another world on a whim, Linh, Troy and their friends stand at the heart of a struggle. Narz is more complex than anyone guessed, and what ties Ruarnon, Linh, Troy and their friends to Narz could stop a sorcery war in its tracks.

Sythe Series

3,000 years later, Sythe (founded at the end of Ruarnon Trilogy) has become a global peace keeping, law enforcement, monster containing, search and rescue and healing providing organisation. Sythe Series is told in first person by a teenage tough from the wrong side of town, Rarkin, who seeks qualifications at Sythe School and Monster Containment employment to escape his abusive father.

But it's a dangerous time to work for Sythe. In the centuries following a Nuclear War that destroyed a continent, and drove modern Umarinaris to abandon modern tech and retreat into city-states, one other organisation remained global in its reach; organised crime. And Organised Crime is entering a bold new era, where it moves against Sythe directly, leaving Rarkin and Sythe's newest students and employees most vulnerable of all.

Selfless and brave, with a strong sense of right and wrong and a thrill for adventure and recklessness, Rarkin must overcome personal trauma, compounded, but ultimately assisted by his autism, to make friends at Sythe, trust them and let them in. The days are coming when his own and his team's lives will depend upon it.

You'll find the latest Sythe Series information on my books page.